THE CHANCE

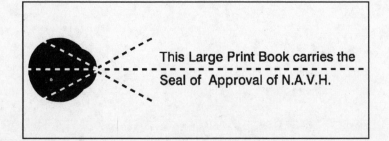

This Large Print Book carries the
Seal of Approval of N.A.V.H.

THE CHANCE

ROBYN CARR

WHEELER PUBLISHING
A part of Gale, Cengage Learning

GALE
CENGAGE Learning·

Farmington Hills, Mich · San Francisco · New York · Waterville, Maine
Meriden, Conn · Mason, Ohio · Chicago

GALE
CENGAGE Learning®

LIBRARY OF CONGRESS CATALOGING-IN-PUBLICATION DATA

Carr, Robyn.
    The chance / by Robyn Carr. -- Large Print edition.
        pages cm. -- (A Thunder Point Novel) (Wheeler Publishing Large Print Hardcover)
    ISBN 978-1-4104-6678-5 (hardcover) -- ISBN 1-4104-6678-7 (hardcover)
    1. Oregon--Fiction. 2. Large type books. I. Title.
PS3553.A76334C43 2014
813'.54--dc23   2013049533

Published in 2014 by arrangement with Harlequin Books S.A.

Printed in the United States of America
1 2 3 4 5 6 7 18 17 16 15 14

This story is lovingly dedicated to
the caregivers of the world.

ONE

When Laine Carrington arrived in Thunder Point, she went directly to the hill above the beach and sat in the parking lot beside Cooper's bar. She didn't go inside — she would do that later. She just wanted to see if the view from this perch matched the pictures she'd been sent. She let out her breath, not even realizing she'd been holding it. The vista before her was even better. *What am I doing here?* she asked herself again. She'd been asking herself over three thousand miles of driving.

The view was stunning. The beach was wide and long. The huge, black haystack rocks were a powerful contrast against the gray-blue water. The mouth of the bay lay between two promontories, the Pacific stretching endlessly beyond, crashing against the giant rocks, but the water in the bay was calm.

She shivered in the cold and pulled her

jacket tighter. It was late January and the damp cold caused her right shoulder to ache all the way to her elbow. She'd had surgery on that shoulder three months ago. A bullet was removed and damage repaired. Maybe it was the bullet that brought her to Thunder Point. Laine had been wounded on the job, then pulled from FBI field service and put on a desk while recovering. She wasn't given any active cases but she had a computer — she was limited to what amounted to research and clerical work for other agents. When she realized they were going to keep her on that desk for a long time, light duty, assisting rather than leading investigations, she requested a one-year leave of absence to focus on rehab.

Rehab was an excuse. She didn't need a year. She was close to seventy-five-percent total recovery of the shoulder and in another six months she'd be a hundred percent. But even though she was cleared for duty by the shrink, she wanted time to rethink her career path. And she was allergic to that full-time desk.

Plus, she'd had a miserable holiday visit with her father in Boston. She left angry, went back to her Virginia town house, got in touch with a Realtor in Thunder Point, where she knew a couple of people, and from emailed photos she had chosen a house to rent. A house with a view of the bay. Because Thunder Point, Oregon, was just about as far from Boston as she could get.

Her car was in the parking lot of the bar and she leaned against the hood for a long time, staring at the sea. It was overcast and cold, and there was no one on the water. It was glum, actually. But she liked cloudy or stormy days. Her mother used to call them soup days. Although her mother had been a career woman, she had loved to cook and bake and it was particularly on days like this that she'd come home from her office or the hospital early, arms filled with grocery bags, and spend a few hours in the kitchen. It relaxed her. She loved filling her family with comfort food — thick soups and stews, hearty casseroles, pastas in rich sauces and sweet, soft breads.

Laine sighed. She would never get over losing her mother. It had been five years and she still reached for the phone. Then she'd remember. She's gone.

It was time to get to town to meet the Realtor. She got in her car, drove out of the parking lot and took the road that crossed the beach and led to the town. There was some construction on the hill — it looked

9

like a few houses were being built on this beachfront hillside. Like Cooper's bar, they would have the best views in the town.

She drove to the main street and parked in front of the clinic. When she got out of her car she locked it out of habit. She looked up and down the street lined with lampposts still boasting a bit of Christmas garland. Well, it was only January, she thought with a private chuckle.

Laine walked into the clinic and there, sitting behind the counter at her desk, was Devon McAllister. She rose with a wide smile on her face.

"You're here," Devon said in a near whisper. She came around the counter and embraced Laine. "There was a part of me afraid you wouldn't come. That something would happen, that the FBI would have work for you . . ."

"Can we please not say a lot about that?"

"About what? The commune? The raid? The FBI?"

Laine couldn't help herself, she brushed the hair back from Devon's pretty face as if she were a little sister. Laine had taken Devon under her wing in the commune. "About all of it," she said. "When people find out I work for the FBI they either ask me a ton of weird questions or *they* get strange, like they're worried I'm going to do a background check on them or something. At least until I settle in a little bit, let's downplay all that stuff."

"What will you say? Because these people want to know everything about everyone. They're nice about it, but they will ask."

"I'll just say I worked on a federal task force, but most of my work was just at a desk, compiling data, research, that sort of thing. Not at all a lie. And I'm on leave because of shoulder surgery."

"Okay," Devon said, laughing softly. "They really don't need to know your task force was counterterrorism until you stumbled on an illegal pot farm in the middle of a cult and that you had shoulder surgery because you were shot in the line of duty." Then she grinned.

Laine groaned. "Please, I really don't want to sound that interesting."

"Well, the only people who know certain details were there that night and they were briefed pretty thoroughly. Rawley, Cooper and Spencer will be very happy to see you," Devon said. "And of course Mac knows — he's the law around here, can't get anything by him. I told Scott, my boss, but I can keep him quiet. He's pretty easy to control."

"Is that so?" Laine asked with a smile.

"Oh, yes," she said. "In Dr. Grant's case it has more to do with me being happy so I can keep track of all the paperwork in this clinic. He dreads things like insurance filing, especially Medicaid and Medicare. He does it when he has to and frankly, it takes him five times as long as it takes me. He's not even very good at keeping lab work and patient files up to date."

"You're so different from the person I knew on the farm."

"Actually, I was different in the commune from the person I really am," Devon said. "This is more me. I was always a good student, a hard worker. But you are the curiosity. How did a sophisticated city girl like you manage to fit into the family like you did?"

Laine smiled, secretly proud. "Specialized training, research, good role-playing."

"I can see that working for a couple of days, but it was over six months!" Devon reminded her.

She knew. Only too well. "Very good research and role-playing," she said. Not to mention the fact that lives were at stake and rested on her success or failure. Laine had done a lot of undercover work over the years but her time with The Fellowship had been the longest deep-cover assignment in her career. She had requested it, thinking it would be a brief fact-finding assignment. She thought she could probably fit in, get to the bottom of what was happening there, but what was going on was quite different than what the FBI suspected. They had been looking for evidence of sovereign citizenry, tax evasion, fraud, human trafficking and possible domestic terrorism. What she found, once she was inside, was a giant pot farm fronted by a fake cult.

Laine could have left then, escaped, turned her information over to the task force and let them figure out how to proceed, how to best serve a warrant and get inside to make arrests without creating a small war. But there were women and children behind the fence that surrounded The Fellowship and the men in charge would fight back — they were armed to the teeth. So she stayed, getting as many of them out safely as she could before law enforcement breached the compound. It had been a dangerous and complex operation and in the end, she'd been shot by the cult leader, the boss. Jacob.

"Are you ready to have a little quiet now?" Devon asked.

"You have no idea," Laine said. But she'd never actually had quiet before. The thought of whole days without plans stretching out in front of her was intimidating.

"I saw it," Devon said. "The house you rented."

"You did?"

"Ray Anne, the Realtor I suggested to you, told me which house it was and I peeked in some windows. It's beautiful. So beautiful."

"I've only seen pictures," Laine replied. "I understand I was very lucky — that there's hardly ever rental property available around here."

"At least not real pretty rental property. This is a vacation home that for some reason the family isn't going to be using for a while so they're renting it."

"Do you know them? The people who own it?"

Devon shook her head. "But I haven't been here that long. I don't know everyone, that's for sure."

Laine looked at her watch. "I better go meet Ray Anne. Want to come? See the inside from the inside?"

She grinned and nodded. "Let me check with Scott, then I'll follow you so I can come right back."

"Maybe I better follow you," Laine said. "I haven't even looked in the windows yet."

14

Devon led the way to Laine's rental. They drove down the main street, past what seemed to amount to the entire commercial district of Thunder Point, took a left and entered a residential neighborhood. A woman who appeared altogether too dressed up exited her BMW in front of a very small house that sat in the middle of about a dozen nondescript houses. The foliage and pines surrounding the little house were deep green even though it was the dead of winter. Virginia or Boston at this time of year would be covered with snow and the trees bare.

Laine was a little shocked at how ordinary and dumpy the little house looked; she had never seen a picture of the front exposure. It seemed very small. There was an ordinary white door with a diamond-shaped window in it and one front window. If this were her house she'd paint the door dark green and add identically colored shutters to that window.

Laine parked, got out and stretched a hand toward the Realtor. "Ms. Dysart?" she asked.

"Call me Ray Anne. So nice to finally meet you, Laine." She dangled house keys.

"I think you're going to love this. Please, do the honors."

With Ray Anne close on her tail and Devon following, Laine stepped into the small house and entered a whole new world. Right inside the front door was a spacious foyer and the house opened up before her. To her left, an open staircase and small powder room, to her right, a small and unfurnished room with louvered double doors, perfect for Laine to use as an office. Straight ahead was a great room with a large picture window. To the left of the great room was a big open kitchen with a dining area in front of a matching window. Dividing the two windows were French doors that Ray Anne immediately opened, revealing a very large deck and a view of the bay that just about knocked Laine out. She inhaled deeply, appreciatively. She walked outside to the railing and looked down — the deck sat atop a rocky hill.

"You can't get to the beach from here," Ray Anne said from behind her. "There really isn't much beach — only a little when the tide's out. You'll have to go down the street and back through town to the marina. This is considered oceanfront. The only beachfront in Thunder Point is over there, where Cooper is building. Most of us thought there would never be any building there, but Cooper has a plan for maybe as many as twenty single-family residences. The rest of us po' folk have to get to the beach either from his bar or the marina. This is the north promontory. Straight across there, that's the south promontory. The previous owner, the guy who left it to Cooper in his will, had always wanted it to be a nature preserve, safe for the wildlife. Much as I'd like him to cut it up and let me sell lots for him, you have to admit it's beautiful."

"Beautiful," Laine said in a breath. A few trees growing right out of the rocks and hillside below her deck reached up so that their branches brushed the railing. They needed trimming so they wouldn't obstruct her view.

"It's so wet and cold right now I didn't uncover the grill or deck furniture. I thought I'd leave that to you. You might not want to sit outside in this weather."

Laine looked around for the first time. It looked like she had a table and four chairs, a chaise and a rather large grill under the weatherproof drapes. Laine turned and went inside again, taking note of the great room, divided from the kitchen by a break-fast bar. The pictures had done the interior more credit than it deserved. There was a maroon sofa, two uncomfortable-looking rattan chairs, a nice fireplace and zero homey touches. The breakfast nook held a beat-up but large table with eight cane-back chairs. There was a short hall that led to a laundry room, pantry and interior garage door.

"Bedroom?" she asked.

"Right this way," Ray Anne said, leading her back toward the front door and up the stairs. Laine and Devon followed along. At the top of the stairs was a set of double doors that stood open to expose a rather small but comfortable-looking master bedroom. Not a suite, but a bedroom. One queen-size bed, one bureau, one bedside table and a fireplace. But it had a triple-wide set of sliding glass doors and a small deck again with the most stunning view. Laine was drawn to it. Her eyes nearly rolled back in her head at a vision of sitting against big pillows, looking out the window at the clouds, only the fireplace lighting the room.

Falling asleep with the light of the fireplace in the room held a special appeal. Since the shooting, she'd left a light on at night. She never told anyone.

"When the weather gets exciting, watching the lightning over the bay is like a fireworks show," Ray Anne said. "Around here, it's all about the view. There are a lot of views in this town. Some have the view in front, some in back, some up the hill, some closer to the water, sometimes from big houses and sometimes from little ones." Ray Anne stepped to one side. "Bath," she said, indicating a very functional master bath, dressing area and closet. There was a glassed-in shower, large spa-style tub and wide closet with built-in drawers and shelves.

Laine merely glanced, then her eyes were drawn back to that view again. Devon was oohing and aahing over the size of the master bath and closet space.

"There are two bedrooms down the hall with a jack-and-jill bathroom dividing them. The owner has queen-size beds in each. Storage is limited. They're small bedrooms but the sofa downstairs pulls out — the house can sleep at least eight. The owners wanted a place for their children and grand-children to visit. Linen closet across the hall from the master. Downstairs front closet under the stairs. You have a two-car garage," Ray Anne said as she continued the tour.

And only a few rather tacky prints on the walls, no little touches of home, no plants, of course, and the lamps had been around a long time, Laine thought.

"I had a cleaning crew come through — the carpet is shampooed, bathrooms and kitchen scoured, clean sheets on the beds, some towels on hand. The carpet is fairly new. I don't know what your plans are for the house, but it will accommodate a large group."

Laine looked at her in some surprise. "My plan is to live in it."

"Oh! Wonderful! Are you planning to work around here?"

She shrugged. "I'll probably do a little computer work. I'm actually on leave from a government job but I can do some work from here — you know, clerical stuff. I had a pretty serious shoulder surgery and with all my vacation and good benefits and —"

"I hope it wasn't rotator cuff," Ray Anne said, moving her own shoulder up and down. "That's the worst! I had that surgery a few years ago and it's hell, that's all I can say. It's fine now but I thought it would take forever!"

Devon met Laine's eyes, but didn't comment. She just stood in the master bedroom and looked out at the rock-studded bay.

Laine was thinking about other things, like what the place would feel like with a nicer sofa, with a throw on it for winter nights in front of the fire. And how about some accent tables, designer lighting, paintings on the walls, books on her own bookshelves? Her own sheets and towels and some of her favorite cookware and dishes? And her mother's small kitchen breakfront, her treasure.

She turned to Ray Anne. "Did you ask the owners if they mind that I store their furnishings and use my own? Of course I'll cover the cost of packing, moving and storing their things."

"They said that's fine as long as their things aren't damaged." Ray Anne shrugged. "I can't imagine how they'd ever know if anything was damaged. This stuff is adequate but old. In fact, as long as you pay your deposit and rent on time and put the place back the way you found it when your lease is up, there are hardly any restrictions in your lease. You should read it over. You can paint as long as you either stick to the colors or return it to the original." She wrinkled her nose. "Which appears to be renter's white. No knocking out walls or redesigning the property." Then she lowered her voice as if to tell a secret. "If you paint some walls, which I would do before nightfall, try not to make them too bold so you're

21

able to return them to their original color when you move out."

But Laine could only think of one thing. "Let's go take a look at that kitchen, see what the owners left for me to use until my stuff comes. The moving truck is on the way — should be here in a day or two."

"Okay," Ray Anne said, "but there are plenty of places in town where you can get a bite to eat until you get settled."

Laine was already on her way to the kitchen and when she got there, she started opening cupboard doors. She found plates, a few pots, a frying pan, utensils, some kitchen linens, just the bare essentials, designed for a vacation rental. But that was all right. She closed the last cupboard door, turned and smiled at Ray Anne and Devon. "I'm good," she said. "If you could just give me directions to the nearest grocery, I'm going to light the fire and make soup. It looks like a soup day to me."

Eric Gentry sat at the counter in the diner having a late breakfast. Next to him was Cooper from the beach bar, doing the same. Then the sheriff's deputy walked in. Mac pulled off his hat and took the seat beside Eric. Mac's wife, Gina, brought him a cup of coffee. Then she leaned over the counter and collected a kiss.

"I certainly didn't get that kind of first-class treatment," Cooper said with a smile. "And I ordered a whole meal."

"Yeah, buddy, the day I hear about you getting treatment like that is the day you start walking with a limp."

Eric chuckled, but he'd never make such a remark. He and Gina had history. And he liked walking straight.

"Mac," Gina chided with a laugh in her voice.

"What are you doing here, anyway?" Mac asked Cooper. "Get sick of Rawley's cooking out at the bar?"

"Rawley doesn't cook," Cooper said. "Sometimes he warms things, but that's just sometimes."

"Sarah says he's a good cook," Gina pointed out.

"Oh, he cooks for Sarah," Cooper said of his wife. "When she wanders into the kitchen he asks her right away what she'd like. Now that she's packin', Rawley takes real good care of her."

"Packin'?" Eric asked.

"Pregnant," three people answered in unison.

"I see," he said, sitting back and wiping his mouth on the napkin.

"Business must be good," Mac said to Eric. "I saw a dually pulling a trailer through town, an old Plymouth on the trailer."

"A 1970 Superbird," Eric told him. "It's in for a rebuilt engine, new bench seat and a refurbished dash. I think we're going to have to refresh that roof, too. It's the original vinyl and not going to be easy."

"Bench seat? Not buckets?"

Eric shook his head. "Not in the Superbird. I guess if you drove one of those you got girls and if you got girls, you wanted them sitting right next to you."

"Where'd it come from?" Mac asked.

"Southern California."

"Someone would bring an old car up from Southern California?"

Eric sipped his coffee. "It's a two-hundred-thousand-dollar classic. The owner would bring it across six states for the right work. I've done a lot of work for him. He owns twenty cars. I think it's most of his estate. He likes to do a lot of the restoration work himself and he does a great job. He doesn't have the equipment for replacing an engine block and the car is his baby."

"His baby?" Gina asked.

"He kisses it before he goes to bed every night. He probably treats the car better than he treats his wife."

"Boys and their toys," Gina said.

"You're putting us on the map," Mac said. "Imagine — that car is worth more than this diner."

Eric noticed a couple of young women walking across the street from the clinic. One he knew to be Devon, the doctor's office manager — he'd met her a couple of months ago and had seen her around. The other one he didn't recognize. She was wearing a ball cap low over her forehead and fitted yoga pants, a jacket and running shoes. Her blond hair was strung through the back of her cap, noticeable when she turned to laugh at something Devon said.

When they walked into the diner Gina beamed a happy grin and said, "Hey!"

"What's this?" Devon asked. "Grumpy old men's club?"

"I beg your pardon," Cooper replied. "I'm not old."

"He's older than me," Mac said.

Eric said nothing. His eyes were busy with the new girl and when something like that happened it tended to tie up his tongue.

"Laine, you know Cooper and Mac, but have you met Eric? Eric owns the service station and body shop at the end of the street. Eric, this is my friend, Laine Carrington. She's new in town."

Eric found himself on his feet. "Nice to meet you."

"And you," she replied. "Please, sit. We're just going to grab a cup of coffee." She looked at Gina. "You due for a break?"

"I am," she said. "I'll bring the coffee."

As Devon and Laine headed toward the back of the diner to a booth, Eric followed them with his eyes. Then he guiltily returned his eyes to his coffee cup, grateful to note that Cooper and Mac were discussing how much money was too much to spend on a car. A two-hundred-thousand-dollar Super-bird didn't even enter the conversation.

Eric had a couple of classics, cars he'd restored himself. He'd salvaged them and had planned to restore and sell them, then he got attached. It happened. There were dealers and then there were collectors. Then there were guys like him who were looking to make a few bucks and turned into collectors.

He talked with his friends for a while longer, forcefully keeping his eyes from wandering to that back booth, until finally Mac stood and left the waitress a tip, making the men laugh. Cooper left a ten on the counter for his seven-dollar breakfast.

But Eric walked to the back booth. "Gina, I'm going to need some change. You're

26

good, but not that good."

"I'd argue with that, but it will be quicker to get your change." She snatched the twenty out of his hand and headed for the register.

"Nice meeting you, Laine. If you ever need any dents popped or rough edges smoothed out, I'm your guy," he said. When he saw Laine and Devon looking at him with wide eyes, he winced. But the women laughed.

"I'll keep that in mind," she said.

Two

Even though Laine needed help with the heavy lifting and some of the picture-hanging in her new home, it didn't take any time at all to begin to feel settled. She had learned long ago how to be extremely focused. In less than a week all her furniture was in place right down to throws over couches and pictures on the walls, thanks to a lot of help from Devon and her fiancé, Spencer. The owner's furnishings were now in storage, packed up and taken away on the same truck that brought hers. She had picked out a couple of walls she wanted to paint and purchased the supplies. Despite the challenge painting with her right arm presented, she was determined to get it done. She could handle most of the trim if it was shoulder level or lower, but reaching the roller above her head would be a job for her left arm. She was getting really good with that left arm! She'd try using her right arm, though — it was great therapy. She was very dedicated to her exercises.

This place was going to be different — she was going to make this home. Her town house in Virginia was where she *stayed.* Although she had her own things — furniture and accessories — in all the years she was there she had only rented the place. She traveled, went undercover, visited her brother and his family on weekends and holidays. Her town house had been temporary for years and she was away as much as she was there. But this — the house with the view — she was going to make it hers. It was going to be her refuge for the year. She had earned it.

It was Saturday afternoon and the sun was shining for a change. There was one person in Thunder Point she knew and hadn't yet seen. Someone she really *owed.* And it looked like a perfect day for a jog through town and across the beach.

As she ran, her mind wandered back to that last assignment. She had gotten almost all of the women and children out of the commune compound through a break in the fence, but her success had been completely foiled when Jacob figured her out. He beat her and confined her, tying her to a chair in his house. She was further foiled when

Jacob somehow located and abducted Devon's three-year-old daughter, Mercy, bringing her back to the camp. Later, when it was all over, the FBI learned he had simply done a computer search for Devon's address.

At the time, Laine had been his prisoner. So had Mercy. It had been Jacob's plan to escape with his daughter and whatever money and documents he could gather together. And then he planned to burn the place to the ground, leaving any others, like Laine, behind. He torched the warehouse holding the marijuana plants knowing the fire could spread into a full-on wildfire that would threaten the whole valley — something he no doubt hoped would occupy law enforcement long enough for his escape.

Laine had managed to free herself and grab Mercy, but in the process she'd been shot in the shoulder. By the time help arrived in the form of Rawley, Spencer, Cooper and Devon, she was nearly unconscious from blood loss — her brachial artery had been nicked.

Of course Laine had known Devon and Mercy from her time in the camp but she had no idea who these men who saved her might be. She found out later — it was Rawley Goode, a Vietnam vet in his sixties, who put together a rescue plan in mere minutes. Laine got the details after she was conscious and recovered enough to take it all in.

She jogged across the beach. By the time she got to Cooper's, she was panting pretty hard. She found the proprietor sitting on the deck in the sun, though he wore a jacket. He had his laptop open and was studying something closely.

"Hey, there," she said. "How's the house coming?"

He looked up and smiled at her. "About time you checked out my place. House is coming along ahead of schedule, thank God. Sarah's had about enough of living in one room."

"When's the baby due?" she asked.

"July. We should be in the house by June at the latest."

"That's awesome, Cooper."

"How about your place?" he asked.

"It's looking good. My stuff came right behind me and the movers took the owner's furniture to the storage facility. I'm pretty settled already. Just a matter of putting a few more things away."

"I heard you have a good view."

"Oh, yes. A big deck and a big kitchen and a couple of fireplaces. If I'm not happy every day, I can't blame the real estate. Hey, any chance Rawley is around?"

"Last time I noticed he was carrying in supplies. He should be in the kitchen."

"Thanks. I'll see you on the way out."

She went through the bar and into the kitchen. Rawley was crouched, rearranging some things in a cupboard. "Hey, stranger," she said.

He stood and turned toward her. He wore worn jeans, boots, a heavy shirt over a T-shirt and a red cap. She knew he was in his early sixties but because he was skinny and his face was deeply lined, he looked a little older. She caught the light in his pale blue eyes as he recognized her. Only one corner of his mouth lifted. He nodded toward her right arm. "How's the wing?" he asked.

"Coming along," she said, automatically rotating her shoulder. "I'm in good shape now."

"What are you doing here?" he asked. "Don't you have spy work to do?"

She smiled, looked down, shook her head. "I'm on leave," she said. "I need more time before I —" She cleared her throat. "I'm not a spy. I . . ." He smiled at her and put his thumb in the front pocket of his jeans, leaning on his left leg. "Well, not exactly. I'm an investigator. And I think we should downplay that role a little bit."

"Whatever you want, chickadee," he said. "Good work," he added.

"You saved my life."

"Nah. Not really. I got in that camp to find Mercy. I think it was Spencer saved your life, jogging down some back road, carrying you with his fist shoved against your shoulder on account a' the bleeding. Yeah, he's the one I'd say saved you. I'm just an old vet. But I got attached to that little girl and I wasn't about to let some lunatic take her away from her mother."

"Some old vet," she repeated. "A Green Beret with two Purple Hearts, a Bronze Star and a Silver Star. . . ."

"Window dressing," he said with a shrug. "It's the by-product of staying alive."

"You're one of the most decorated men I know."

"It was a bad time, back then, but we all did our best," he said. "And there's a rumor you got yourself a little window dressing, too."

She gave a nod. "I've been notified. I was recommended for an award. You know these things take time."

He grinned at her. "Notified of what kind of award, exactly?"

"FBI commendation. It's very big in my

crowd. But that's another thing I'll try to keep to myself. I'd appreciate it if you'd do that, too."

"No problem, chickadee. I was never one for struttin' so I get it."

"I wanted to say thank you," she said. "I know you weren't alone, but I read all the transcripts and everyone agrees, you put a plan together to get Mercy out, along with anyone else stuck in that camp. Will you come to my house for dinner? So I can thank you with food? I love to cook."

"Might could," he said. "Cloudy and wet weather this time of year, Cooper can manage. But I ain't much company. . . ."

"How about if I invite Devon, Spencer and Mercy. I've been meaning to anyway. They helped a lot with the whole move."

"Sounds okay." He reached in his pocket and pulled out a cell phone and showed it to her. "Got one of these now. Cooper couldn't stand it if he didn't know where I was every second. Now he calls this. And I usually don't answer. But it's got games and books and a flashlight. Not a bad contraption. Want the number?"

What a kick he was. And he was so full of it — he was *not* the old bumpkin he portrayed himself to be. He bordered on genius, but he battled PTSD and had for years so

34

he'd never really developed his intellect as much as was possible for him. He told her his number and she merely nodded.

"You don't wanna write that down somewhere?" he asked.

"I got it," she said. "I'll give you a call. And listen . . . Rawley, there are no words. If you hadn't done it, gotten inside, run the rescue like you did . . ."

"Some things just work out to be kismet, chickadee," he said, showing her a wide grin. "Right place, right time, luck."

"Skill," she added. "Courage."

He looked down, maybe uncomfortably. "Courage. Kind of funny what you're left with when there ain't no way out. I just put one foot in front of the other, that's all. Glad it worked out. You gonna be able to paddle a kayak with that busted-up wing?"

"By spring. I'll call you in the next day or two."

"Sounds good. You ain't one of them vegetarians or anything, are you?"

She laughed. "No. I like hearty, meaty meals."

"That's a blessin'. I hate leavin' the table hungry." Then he grinned at her again.

She couldn't help herself. She hugged him. She laid her head against his shoulder and wrapped her arms affectionately around him. He might look like a skinny old man but there were solid muscles under her cheek, her arms. She just stood like that for a moment and then she felt him wrap one long, strong arm around her back while the other hand stroked the top of her head a little bit. Then she let go of him.

"I'd say you were the brave one," he said. "You could'a bled out from that bullet."

"I'm getting a medal," she said. "The by-product of staying alive."

He smiled. It was melancholy.

"You lost a few along the way, didn't you, Rawley?" she asked.

He lifted a thin, graying eyebrow. "A few. Didn't you?"

She just nodded, but she wasn't willing to think about or discuss the details. Ten years in the FBI, a lot of it undercover, they'd lost a couple of men. And then suddenly she knew what he was getting at — he'd rather have the men than the medals.

She slapped his arm gently. "Thanks," she aid. It came out very softly. "I'll call you about dinner. And you won't go away hungry."

"Good enough."

She left him then and as she walked through the bar she was thinking that old soldiers go away quietly. It was apparent to her that Rawley had used his time in the Army well, but it had also used him up. True heroes never talked about their acts of heroism. He was one in a million.

I've used my time in the FBI well, she thought.

When she got back to the deck, Cooper had the laptop closed and his feet up on the rail. "I take it you found him?"

"I did, thanks."

He pushed a bottle of water across the table toward her. "Are you running back to town, too?"

She took the water and unscrewed the top, taking a drink. "Just across the beach. Then, even though I have 'house' things to do, I'm going to take advantage of this sunny day and sit out on my deck. It's too cold, but the sun feels good."

"Want some advice? Get yourself one of those little fire pits to put out on the deck. It only gives off a little heat, but it's cozy."

"Good idea," she said.

"I'm putting a fireplace on my deck," Cooper said. "A half shade out there, too — the sunset is not only stunning, it's blinding. And a half cover. This place is wet, but the view doesn't let you ignore it — rain or shine, you like being right in front of it. Truth is, I'm building a deck that happens to have a house attached to it."

She laughed at him. "How long have you known Rawley?"

"Just a year and change. He kind of came with the property. Ben found him and brought him here. Ben was my friend and left me the property. Rawley had been with Ben a few years."

"Nice to have someone working for you who knows the business."

Cooper laughed. "Don't kid yourself that he works for me. He pretty much does as he pleases, checks in as little as possible and if he tells me to do something, I usually do." He winked at her. "Chickadee."

"Is it like having your father around?"

"My father's not nearly as ornery, but in that age range," Cooper said. "Rawley is an interesting guy. Real solitary. Real quiet. But he can develop some deep attachments — like to Devon and Mercy. They're family now. And since Devon doesn't have any family, that's good. For that matter, Spencer doesn't have family, either."

"But you have family?"

"Tons. All in or near Albuquerque. Parents, sisters, brothers-in-law, their kids. Plus, I have a son — Austin. Spencer and I share a son." Her expression must have been shocked because he smiled and said,

"Spencer married my ex-fiancée and she passed away last year. How about you?"

"I lost my mother a few years ago, but my father and brother live in Boston. I'm very close to my brother — he's married and has two little girls I adore, even though in my line of work I haven't seen enough of them."

"And you're not on the East Coast?"

"I needed a change," she said. "There's something about this place. . . . In the time I lived on the farm, although under adverse conditions, I got a little attached and wanted to see a little more of the state. And there was the matter of getting to know the people who put everything on the line to get me out of that camp. Plus, my brother is a busy, busy man. And now that I have the time, I'll probably visit him. Long flight, but so what? I talk to my brother at least a couple of times a week. I guess we're all used to me living away from the family, so to speak. And hey — you're not in the mountains of New Mexico."

"That's not the surprise. I left home when I joined the Army as a kid and haven't lived there since. The real surprise is that I live here! I was a rolling stone until I came to Thunder Point. Now I'm a land baron."

Laine stood on her deck, hands on hips,

looking around, when the phone rang. Her cell phone was sitting on the kitchen counter and she went for it. No need for a landline in this house, she only had her cell. When she saw that it was her brother, her face lit up. "Pax!" she said. "How's it going?"

"I missed two calls from you," he said. "Sorry about that. Busy week. Lots of surgery."

"No big deal. We have an understanding — first thing after work comes the wife and kids, then me. I'm very patient."

"What's it like out there?"

"Heat wave," she said with a laugh. "It's fifty degrees and sunny. I was just looking around the deck to find a good spot for a little portable fire pit so I can bundle up and sit out here at night. What's Mother Nature doing out there?" she asked.

"You don't watch the news, I guess."

In fact she had been obsessed with news of Boston from the weather and current events to the crime. That was where her family was and she thought of them all constantly. But she said, "Not if I can help it."

"We're bracing for a nor'easter. Looking at two feet tonight. Roads and airport will probably shut down and everyone will stay home and watch old movies until the electricity goes out."

"Except you."

"I'm on call tomorrow night. Tonight I'm watching snow fall and listening to the wind howl."

"How are Missy and Sissy and Miss Perfect?" she asked.

He let go with a bark of laughter and said, "One of these days I'm going to slip up and call my wife Miss Perfect and when that happens, I'm selling you out. I swear it. Everyone here is fine. Missy is having her first school concert in six weeks and is practicing the cello day and night — it's almost as big as she is and sounds like mating season at an elk ranch around here. And Sissy is gearing up for a spring dance recital, which for six-year-old girls should be enchanting. Thank God she didn't choose a musical instrument or I'd start sleeping at the hospital."

His eight-year-old daughter was Melissa, who they called Missy. His six-year-old daughter was Catherine, who they called Sissy for "sister." And his wife, Genevieve, she had secretly named Miss Perfect because she was the ultimate wife and mother. She *never* complained at all. It was unnatural. Here she was, stuck with a couple of kids, tons of responsibility, a mostly

41

absent husband, and yet she took it on with a contented smile. What the hell was that? Laine wondered. Had she no limits?

But Genevieve had two sisters and they were all thicker than thieves. She was a dear and good mother, a faithful wife, a dedicated friend, a beloved daughter and a little too domestic and nurturing for Laine's blood. And she had taken away Laine's best friend, her twin brother. She was perfectly wonderful to Laine, but Laine had never warmed to her. They weren't girlfriends. But then not only did Laine have very few girlfriends, but it was also impossible for anyone to be closer to her than Pax.

"And Senior?"

"The same. You haven't heard from him, huh?"

"No. Frankly I'm not surprised. I told him not to call me until he's ready to apologize for being such an ass and has something positive to say to me, so I imagine hell will freeze over before I see his name on the caller ID."

"You take him too seriously," Pax said. "Learn to not hear him. Nod, say nothing, do as you please."

"I can't," she said. "You get away with that. He's not as critical of your choices. . . ."

42

"Yes, he is. But I don't care. He's not driving my bus. And if you're honest, you have to admit, no one but you has been driving your bus for a long, long time. Like since you were seven."

"He aggravates me so," she said. "He thinks if he opens his mouth it must be gospel and we should all thank him for taking the time and trouble to move his tongue against his teeth."

"Don't get worked up all over again," Pax counseled. "It's over. You moved. I just wish you weren't so damn far away. Get your computer set up and use Skype with the girls — they miss you."

"He doesn't treat you like he does me," Laine said, unable to let it go yet. "He's very proud of you!"

"He thinks I took his advice and became a doctor. I didn't. I'm doing exactly what I want to do. And he's still telling me how to work even though he doesn't know shit about pediatric surgery. I try to tell him as little as possible, but I also never take him seriously. Now tell me what's new and exciting in your little town."

"I painted a wall," she said with a weary sigh. "Mostly with my left arm. And I'm going to paint another wall, but I think that's it. I had to have a friend hang the pictures

43

— this arm isn't strong yet, especially when reaching over my head. I've read three books since I talked to you last Tuesday, today was the first day it was decent enough for a good run, but I swear to God the cold makes the screws in my shoulder throb. . . ."

"You know it's not the screws. . . ."

"Feels like it."

Laine's parents were both doctors. Her grandfathers on both sides were doctors. She had two cousins who were doctors. Successful men and women, all. Laine wasn't the first Carrington or Wescott to choose another profession, but Dr. Paxton Carrington Sr. was appalled when she changed her major from premed to criminal justice. "Believe me, you don't want to live in a blue-collar world," he had said. *Blue-collar world?* It was almost impossible to get into the FBI without an advanced degree.

Laine's mother had said, "You must find work you feel passionate about. The most important thing in life is finding what gets you up in the morning, what you would do for free, the thing that makes your heart beat. I'm not a doctor because my father was a doctor. And I'm damn sure not a doctor because my husband is one. And I could care less what my children choose to do. Well, if you choose to be homeless drug ad-

44

dicts, I might have an issue. . . ."

"But aren't you more proud of Pax? A premed honor student?" Laine had asked.

"I look at what's ahead for you, Laine, and I find it all so exciting, I wish I could live in your skin for just one day!"

"But Dad hates what I'm doing!"

"Does he? He probably thinks he knows what's best for you, but I'm here to tell you — you're the only person who can make this choice. And it doesn't matter what anyone else wants."

"But admit it, Dad is more proud of Pax!" she had insisted.

"I'm not sure about that. What I know for a fact is that Pax is acting on script. He's doing exactly what your father expected him to do and it's easier, more comfortable. You, my darling Laine, are a challenge for him."

All through college, all through her postgrad program, all through her early years at the FBI, her mother couldn't wait for her to call, fill her in on all the edgy, interesting stuff she'd worked on or even just knew about.

Senior had said, "What's that girl thinking? She's wasting her life on the underworld! The dregs of society!"

When Laine told her father, over Christmas, that she'd been recommended for a commendation from the FBI for saving lives in the line of duty he had said, "As if a medal is going to validate you. Doctors save lives every day."

And she'd left Boston in an angry huff, vowing she was through with him.

Laine missed her mother so. . . .

Eric was grateful every day that he had asked Gina McCain if she'd be comfortable with him living in the small town of Thunder Point because he was in the diner where she worked almost daily. Half the time her husband was also there. Eric and Gina went way back. High school for her, though he had been a dropout. Their relationship had been brief but to both of them, very memorable.

Eric bought the local service station in October, had spent two months expanding and updating, and for all that time right up to the present he'd been living in the local motel — the Coastline Inn. It wasn't much, but it was clean and cheap. There was free coffee in the early morning but no restaurant. Only the diner and McDonald's served breakfast, unless he felt like going all the way across the beach to Cooper's place. Since he had no time to look for a house or the energy to fix up both a business and a residence, he bought himself a small dormitory-sized refrigerator and a toaster and settled into the motel. He'd walk down to the motel office early in the morning, grab a large coffee and a newspaper, then head to the station. At lunchtime he'd head to the deli or diner for more satisfying food. He wasn't much for fast food, something he was stuck with more than he liked. Many busy nights he and his employees made do on burgers or pizza.

He walked into the diner and saw the new girl in town sitting at the counter in front of Gina. She appeared to be finished with breakfast; she looked at him and smiled.

"Hey, Mr. Scratch-and-Dent, just the man I wanted to see!" she said.

"Well now, I don't get that kind of welcome everywhere I go," he said.

"I heard you have a great reputation for cosmetic work but I was wondering, how are you under the hood?"

He raised his eyebrows. It was a great double entendre. He sat down and a cup of coffee instantly appeared. "I was a mechanic before I was a body man," he said, smiling a small smile.

Laine laughed at his wordplay. "I have a little work that needs to be done," she said. "Can I make an appointment?"

"You don't need an appointment. Is the car drivable?"

"Yep. But I just drove it across the country from Virginia and it needs an oil change and everything checked." She shrugged. "I'm sure she's very tired. Maybe sore."

He grinned at that. Only a collector of classics could appreciate an owner who had given her car a gender and possibly a name. "Do you live in the neighborhood?"

She laughed. "Look around, Eric. Everyone lives in the neighborhood."

So, she remembered his name. Or, maybe Gina had told her. "Right. Then just bring it by when you won't need it for a few hours and I'll get right to it." To Gina he said, "Can you ask Stu to mess up three eggs with some green chilies and cheddar?"

"You got it. Side of beans?"

"Pass. Toast, please. And are there any home fries back there that Stu hasn't burned yet?"

"Tell you what, because it's you, I'll flip 'em over on the grill a couple of times. God knows if he gets his hands on 'em, they'll be charred."

"You are a queen," he said.

When Gina took Laine's empty plate and turned to leave, Laine asked Eric, "You're here every day?"

He shook his head. "Almost, though. If not for Gina, I'd live on coffee and Pop-Tarts."

"Is that so?"

"I'm new in town, too. I bought the service station and there was so much to do there, opening it under a new banner after a remodel, I've been staying in the Coastline, which makes the Motel 6 look like a five-star luxury resort. One of these days I have to get serious about a house or apartment. It's so easy, though. And I like walking to work."

"A car man who likes to walk . . ."

"I have plenty of other places to drive. Even though we're operating at full speed, I'm still busy upgrading the station. The previous owner didn't do any body work, and that takes space. I have a pretty large classic-car clientele." He took a sip of coffee. "What do you do, Laine?"

"Shoulder exercises," she said. "I had shoulder surgery about three months ago and it's a lot better, but I'm not there yet. I decided to take a leave from work and try a new landscape."

"So you don't work at all?"

"I'm set up to do computer work, but I'm avoiding it. I just did research — you know, boring stuff. Data, statistics, background checks, tax records, that kind of stuff . . ."

"For a big company?" he asked.

"Yeah, the biggest company. The Feds." Then she grinned at him.

"That sounds really . . . boring."

She laughed. "I know. I'm sadly good at it. But if anyone from my old department calls me and asks for a hand, they have to clock me in, pay me in comp time. I did a little math — I think I can turn a few months of rehab and vacation into a year off with a view just by doing a little off-site work from home."

"I dated a woman a while ago who created and managed websites and she hardly ever left the computer. . . ."

"I'm not that girl, I can tell you that. I have no trouble walking away from the computer. And leaving the headquarters meant no more traveling or supervising anyone. I really didn't love supervising or training computer techies and researchers. I might come up with a new idea for earning a living during the next year."

With an elbow on the counter, Eric leaned his head into his hand. "How are you with a wrench?"

"Better than you think."

Gina brought his breakfast.

"I'll let you eat," Laine said. "I'll bring my

car over one day this week."

"Great," he said. And he watched her walk out the door.

When he turned back, Gina was staring at him. "Did you ask her out?"

"Of course not."

"Why not?" she asked. "You obviously want to."

He picked up his fork. "You don't know that," he said, then shoveled eggs into his mouth.

"Those pretty green eyes of yours lit up when you saw her sitting at the counter."

He swallowed. "I can still appreciate a good-looking woman," he said. "But I'm very busy these days."

"You should make time for a more interesting social life than catching meals at the diner."

"Well, I'm not completely comfortable talking to you about that possibility since you and I were . . . you know what we were. Involved."

She laughed and her eyes twinkled. "We were involved for about two weeks and I hope you don't take this too hard, but I'm completely over you. I was over you at least fifteen years ago."

He ate more eggs. "It was more than two weeks."

"Not much more."

"And I'm over you, too."

"Good to know. So . . . how about Laine?"

"Bugger off," he said.

"She seems to be a nice, stable, attractive —"

The door to the diner opened and Gina's husband came in for his morning coffee break. He was all uniformed up, gun and all, and although Eric was roughly as tall as Mac, law enforcement uniforms always seemed to take about four inches off his height. Mac leaned over the counter to collect a wifely kiss. Then his coffee appeared.

"Good, you're here," Eric said. "Your wife is getting into my personal life. She's giving me dating advice."

"You're dating?" Mac asked.

"No, which is why I shouldn't have to listen to dating advice."

Mac raised one eyebrow and peered at Eric. Then he lifted his cup. He was a man of few words.

"You should see his eyes when he runs into Laine. Bip, bop, whiz! And smile? Oh, she makes him smile," Gina said.

"Bugger off," Eric said again. And Gina laughed while Mac chuckled into his coffee cup.

"You should be on the lookout for the

right woman. You've never been married or even engaged, you work all the time. You could use a little stability. And the right woman tends to level a man out. Mellow him. Right, Mac?"

"Whatever you say, baby," he said, bringing his cup to his lips.

"I'll take that under advisement," Eric said, scooping up his home fries. "And thanks for keeping these potatoes out of the kiln."

"My pleasure," she said. "Business good?"

"Excellent. Now that the station offers more services, we have more business. Norm was winding down, getting ready to sell, looking at retirement, so business was moving out of town. We're spooling up, adding services, bringing business back. It turns out it wasn't such a big gamble."

"Great," Gina said. "But you're still living in a motel, not dating. We have to take care of that. You need a decent place to live and a woman."

Eric drank the last of his coffee, stood, put a twenty on the counter and said, "Extra big tip, Gina, with thanks for the excellent advice." Although she was laughing as he left the diner, he was thinking, *I'm going to have to learn to like fast food. She's killing me! She's nosier than a sister!*

But he also thought, *I could really use some leveling. Some mellowing.*

THREE

Laine brought her midsize SUV to Eric on Tuesday, the day after they talked. It was a new model and in excellent condition. If he subtracted the cross-country miles from the odometer, she'd only put a few thousand miles on it in a year. Ordinarily he'd have Norm or Manny service the vehicle, but he did it. He found nothing wrong with the car, so he washed and detailed it. Himself.

Eric had four employees. Norm, who had sold him the station, was trying to avoid going on cruises and Elderhostel trips with his wife, so he kept working. No doubt he told the missus it was absolutely necessary to help out during this ownership transition, but he was more honest with Eric — he wanted to unload the station and put the money in the bank but he wasn't quite ready to indulge in retirement activities that sounded like sheer torture to him. Nor could he fathom spending day after day with his wife.

Manny had come with Eric from Eugene after Eric sold his body shop there. Manny was a good friend from way back and had a wife and a passel of kids. Howie had worked part-time for Norm, was about the same age, didn't do much — if any — mechanical repairs and the two of them gossiped, drank a lot of coffee and pumped a lot of gas. From the look of the place when Eric took over, neither one of them ever pushed a broom or applied a rag to windows or other surfaces. Both of them might quit before too long because if there was one thing Eric hated it was a dirty shop. Classic car collectors especially liked the garage to look like an operating room. He pushed both of those old boys hard.

And then there was Justin Russell, a lanky, moody seventeen-year-old, who was either troubled or very shy and reminded Eric of himself at that age. Eric suspected he'd hired Justin out of some desire to groom him. It was almost like some sort of psychological experiment, as though by straightening Justin out he could make up for his own delinquent youth. So far that wasn't happening. But Eric was, if anything, stubborn.

Justin worked hard, had good hands under the hood and remarkable instincts for a kid who hadn't tinkered with engines much.

Eric went into the bathroom, scrubbed his hands, swiped water over his face for good measure, rinsed his mouth and gave the mirror over the sink a shot of glass cleaner. He wiped out the sink with the paper towel he'd used to dry his hands. Then he appraised himself in the mirror. He had taken off his coveralls and was wearing a mechanic's uniform — dark blue pants, light blue shirt, *Lucky's* sewn onto the shirt. His name was embroidered on the pocket. He'd opted for the new business name since he'd been feeling pretty lucky. There was a part of him that wished he were dressed as a civilian, but this was who he was — a mechanic, a body man. His uniform was clean — he always donned a jumpsuit over his clothes when he got into or under a car engine. His hands were clean, even under the nails.

And then he found Manny and said, "I'm going to deliver a car. I won't be gone long."

"Yeah, boss."

He drove the few short blocks to Laine's house. He turned off the car. He had her cell phone number and called it from the driveway. "Is this a convenient time to drop off your car?" he asked.

"You don't have to drop it off," she said.

"I'll come and get it in an hour or so."

"Ah, I'm in your driveway," he said. "If I can just leave the key fob somewhere, we can settle up when it's convenient." She didn't say anything and he waited. "Laine?" he asked. And then he watched as the front door opened and she walked outside, an astonished look on her face. She was dressed the same way as when he'd seen her other times in the diner — yoga pants, heavy short-sleeved sweatshirt over a long-sleeved T-shirt, tennis shoes, blond hair pulled back into a ponytail. She looked like a young girl. A very pretty young girl.

Eric got out of the car and handed over the key fob. He pulled out a receipt from the inside pocket of his jacket. "We serviced the brakes, changed the oil, gave it a lube, rotated the tires and I checked over everything. You're in very good shape, no surprises. I'd recommend service checks regularly, which depends on how much driving you do. Your car is well cared for."

"You should've just called me," she said. "I would have come for it."

"No problem. I was happy to bring it over."

"But I was going to use plastic to pay for it."

He pulled his iPhone out of his pocket.

"You can do that now if you want to or you can come by the shop another time." He popped an attachment for scanning onto his phone. "Whatever works for you."

"I didn't expect you to get to it today," she said, obviously still surprised.

"We weren't busy. But there's no rush on —"

"No, I can pay you now. Come inside, Eric."

"I don't mind waiting. . . ."

"For Pete's sake, come inside!" And she turned to precede him into the house.

Eric stood there for a second. He hadn't meant to disrupt her day, just wanted to make an effort, show he was both a businessman with great customer service and . . . well . . . a gentleman. He followed her a bit slowly. She'd left the door standing open and he entered. It was just a few steps past the foyer staircase into the great room.

"Wow," he said.

There was a fire ablaze in the hearth, cozy furniture complete with pictures and hangings on the walls, throws on the chair and sectional sofa, a panoramic view of the bay out of the back windows, flowers on the table and wonderful smells coming from the kitchen. Something was simmering on the stove and Laine used an oven mitt to pull something out of the oven.

"Wow?" she asked.

"It's so . . . *domestic,*" he said. He ran a hand through his hair, looking around. It was earth tones with splashes of lavender and blue here and there. And there was some red but just some, not much. Welcoming. Warm.

"It's a home," she said with a laugh.

"I know, but aren't you single?"

"I am."

"I'm sorry. I've only seen you out for a run and you said you do computer research. The only girlfriend I've had in the past few years was that web designer. I don't think she knew where the kitchen was. And she was allergic to housework. But she loved her computers."

Laine took off the oven mitts and grabbed her purse. "If I'm going to live here, it's going to be comfortable. And I like to cook. Not all the time, but it relaxes me. I'm having company for dinner tonight, but I also do this for myself. What happened to the girlfriend?"

"She dumped me for a computer programmer. I bet they live in squalor and are either thin from starvation or getting fat on take-out."

He saw a framed picture of Laine with a man — a very good-looking man. They appeared so happy. Then there was a second picture on the sofa table, a picture of two little girls. For a second he felt almost sick. She couldn't have lost her family! That would be too cruel.

She found her credit card and presented it. "My nieces," she said. "You don't seem to be too traumatized. About the computer girl."

She didn't explain the man, but that was all right. He swiped the card and presented the screen for her to sign. "We probably weren't right for each other anyway. The biggest thing we had in common was that we worked a lot."

"Well, what drew you together? Ever ask yourself that?" She scrawled her name across the small screen.

"A friend. You know — one of those friends who can't stand to see a single man on the loose and has to do something to hook 'em up. Don't friends do that to you?"

"No," she said. "Apparently none of my friends were ever concerned."

"Never married?" he asked.

She just shook her head. "I haven't dated that much. I travel a lot in my job."

"But you do computer work. How do you

travel for that?"

"No one likes sending people to training, seminars, leadership workshops or temporary duty to other divisions like the government does. To me, the computer is a tool. I'm no more fascinated by it than that. When I'm not working overtime or on the road, I have other interests. I've always liked to cook. It reminds me of my mother, who loved to cook."

"Wow."

"You're getting turned on." She put her card back in her purse. "You just met a woman who likes to cook and live in clean environs and you're actually getting turned on."

"No, I swear . . ."

"Yes, you are! I think you'd marry me right now if I'd promise to love, honor, vacuum and cook."

"Seriously, no . . ."

"It's because you live in a motel. And probably because none of your friends are trying to fix you up," she said. "You're looking for a domestic."

"Hey, I am not. I'm a good cook, too. Very good. In fact, I'll be happy to cook for you. . . ." He stopped and rubbed a hand around the back of his neck, embarrassed. "I'd have to borrow your kitchen, however."

She laughed.

"I've been renovating and updating the station. From early in the morning to late at night . . ."

"You're welcome to join us tonight, if you like. It's just my friend Devon, her fiancé, her three-year-old and her friend, Rawley."

"Thanks, that's very nice, but I don't want to intrude." He put the phone back in his pocket. "I'll probably run into you at the diner or something. Let me know if the car is unsatisfactory in any way."

"Can I give you a lift back to the station?"

"Nah, I like the walk. Have a nice evening."

He walked outside, into the brisk, moist air. He took a deep breath.

Not only had finding a woman been the last thing on his mind, but he also thought it made perfect sense to avoid such attachments in a little town like this, a town where he needed to make a living, needed to be respected by his friends and customers. He really couldn't risk things like romantic drama. Plus, the only female who really had his attention was Ashley, his seventeen-year-old daughter. And he was making a real effort not to dominate her time — she was a high school senior and had better things to do. Besides, he needed little more than work, peace of mind, a little time with Ashley and an opportunity to watch her complete her growth into a fine young woman.

But then he noticed Laine. And damned if all those resolutions started to grow weak.

Laine had a very nice dinner with her friends. Spencer brought his son, Austin, a polite and funny ten-year-old. She got the biggest kick out of Rawley, who did very little talking, but was constantly finding things to point out to Mercy. He asked if she wanted her doll to sit at the table with them, prompted her to scrape up red sauce onto her garlic toast, asked if she had drawn any pictures of him lately and wanted to know what movies she'd been watching on her hand-me-down portable DVD player. To the adults, he didn't have that much to say unless he was asked a direct question.

Two days later she ran into Eric in the diner. True, she thought she might and timed the end of her run specifically for that purpose. And of course he asked about her little dinner party and if her car was running all right. Two days after that she saw him walking into the deli and she decided it was time to get a pint of Carrie's fabulous crab salad. He asked how her car was running. Two days after that she saw him in the diner again and he asked her what she'd been cooking lately and . . . *how the car was running.*

She could tell he liked her. When he saw her, he brightened. His face opened up a little and she got a good view of that wide, white smile. He kind of leaned toward her to talk. He was starting to really piss her off! She was going to have to make the first move.

It had been ten days and five random meetings since he'd delivered her car. Then she ran into him again. She was going home from the diner, he was headed there. There was the usual small talk — weather, car, cooking — and she said, "This is getting really old, Eric. Why don't you ask me out? Am I that unappealing?"

His eyes got round and his mouth fell open. "Huh?"

"Very eloquent, but for God's sake, my car is running just fine, I don't cook big meals every day but when it's cloudy, dark and wet, I like soups, stews and casseroles, and I can tell you like me. I can't tell how much you like me, but I'm sure I'll get a fix on that in no time. So — we're both new in town and we only have a few friends. You probably have more than I do, being in business and all, but since we get along, like

65

each other, aren't dating anyone else, why don't we go out? We'll just go eat something. Maybe we can talk about anything other than my car, like our hobbies or something."

The look on his face was priceless. He was clearly stunned. "Sure," he finally said.

"Friday night. And I'm not cooking for you. That hungry, desperate look you get in your eyes when you come face-to-face with my domesticity is alarming. I'm not looking for a man to take care of. Or one to take care of me, for that matter. But I wouldn't mind getting out of the house for more than a run. And I haven't been out on a date in so long . . . Well, you wouldn't believe how long. I've been working. Then I've been . . . I'll explain another time. So, Friday night?"

"Yes," he said immediately. "Friday night." Then he grinned hugely. "You asked me out on a date. *You* asked *me.*"

"I got very tired of waiting," she said with a bit of superior impatience.

"I've never been asked out on a date before."

She looked him up and down. Six-two, one-eighty and built, copper hair, the most enviable green eyes she'd ever seen, a little shadow of beard. Really gorgeous. Those eyes. God those eyes. "You big liar," she said.

He shook his head and gave a shrug. "Not since the Sadie Hawkins dance in eighth grade."

"But people fixed you up all the time," she reminded him.

"That's when you go to the same birthday party or wedding reception. That's not a date. And if I liked the woman, I asked."

She frowned in doubt. "Are you wearing contacts?"

He shook his head again, but he was still grinning like a fool. "A gift from my mother. So, do you like seafood?"

"I'm from Boston," she informed him.

"I'll find something. I'll pick you up at six. Is seven too late for dinner? Because I have to —"

"Shouldn't I pick you up? Find the restaurant?" she asked.

"Nah, you did the hard part, the asking. I'll do the rest. And by the way, I'm glad you asked. Thanks."

"Were you ever going to?"

"I think so, yes. I was being cautious. Not for my sake. For yours."

"Hmm. You'll tell me more about that at dinner."

"Fair enough. And you can tell me about the exciting world of research."

She shook her head. "I really want you

awake on this, our first date."

Laine was very good at not overthinking things; she rarely found herself dwelling. On the Friday of her date, she dismissed it from her mind and focused on other things — a computer search for the right new rug for in front of the fireplace in her bedroom. She read a few chapters from a book she'd been into, put in a call to Pax and did a load of laundry. She was highly trained and knew how to place focus exactly where she wanted it. She had proven herself disciplined long ago — it was especially important in deep cover.

She could manage not to think about the fact that she hadn't been on a date in a year and a half. How the devil had it been that long?

She also added a layer of blue polish to her toenails. It was funny the things one missed during a deep-cover assignment. The first two she'd been on had been relatively short — two weeks in a clinic that was suspected of drug trafficking and then four weeks working in a trucker's dispatch office trying to ferret out the human trafficking connection. But it was over six months in The Fellowship and what she'd really come to grieve was toenail polish, perfume and bath gel. Not to mention hair products. Just because Laine was an FBI agent and an expert markswoman didn't mean she was a thug or a tomboy. No, sir. She was actually a girlie girl. Yes, she could throw a big guy over the hood of a car and cuff him. And yes, she'd been in some fights — not by choice, but hell, sometimes duty called. She was strong, tough, fearless and feminine.

Finally it was nearly time and she showered, blew out her hair and donned a pair of nice wool slacks, boots, sweater, jacket and long silk scarf. The boots had thin, high heels — Eric was a solid six-two. She could use a little lift.

Her first surprise when she answered the door was how well he cleaned up. She nearly laughed at herself. Had she expected him to arrive in his mechanic's uniform and sensible lace-up boots? He wore dark jeans, a nice sweater, suede jacket and black cowboy boots. And his name wasn't sewn anywhere on his outfit.

"Ready?" he asked.

"Ready," she said, turning to lock the door and flinging her white fringed scarf over her shoulder. He stood aside to let her proceed and she suddenly stopped because there in the driveway was the shiniest, cranberry-red, restored car. "Wow."

"I guess you can appreciate an old car."

"Nineteen-seventy Chevy El Camino. Car or truck? That's the question."

"You know your cars," he said, coming around her to open the passenger door. "You into cars?"

"Not in a big way, but this is beautiful." But she did know her cars. She could identify just about any vehicle make and model on sight. That was part of police work. She could also remember license plates without the need to write down the numbers — not exactly a common thing among law enforcement officers, but she had a skilled memory. Beyond skilled, really.

A beautiful restored classic was all about aesthetics and Laine had a sudden and respectful appreciation for what Eric could do. When he joined her in the front seat she was caressing the dash. "Did you do this?"

"I did," he said, turning the key and bringing the engine to life. "A friend saw her at a farm, a nonworking farm, along with four other old, wrecked cars. The property owner was ancient and didn't give a hoot about those junkers, so I went there and made him a quick deal, handed him some cash and hauled them back to Oregon to work on. This one, I got attached to. I upgraded it, obviously — it's not all original."

"So you buy and restore old cars?"

"Sometimes. I have a steady clientele that comes to me for body work and I'm always on the lookout for deals, steals and old abandoned classics, not to mention original parts. Just body work . . ."

"This isn't just body work," she said, running a hand along the smooth dash. "This is art."

That made him smile. "That's my business."

"I thought your business was mechanics, maintenance. And gas."

"That's part of it. We mean to take care of the town if we can. But body work and restoration is my first love. We're finishing up a new paint bay in the shop. I left a lot of our specialty tools behind and this is a little like starting from scratch, but building a business makes sense. And it's already working."

"Wait a minute — left behind?"

"Oh," he said with a laugh. "Okay, here's how it went. I bought a failing business a little over ten years ago in Eugene. Over the past decade, with the help of some great mechanics and body men, we made it good and developed a loyal clientele and then some moneybags comes along and wants it bad enough to keep upping his offer until I started looking around for another place to work. Norm's station had been for sale for years. It's not much of a garage, really, but it sits on a real nice piece of land with plenty of room to expand. Norm never paid much attention to the space he had — all he wanted to do was pump gas, fix small stuff like brakes. He let a lot of junk collect on his lot rather than putting the space to use. I bought it, cleared it, poured a big slab and we're expanding, literally one wall at a time. Plumbing and wiring takes more time than anything and in three months, we have a body shop and full-service garage up and running, not to mention new pumps. I'm hoping a couple more former employees from Eugene decide to join me here. We work well together. And I like the ocean." He glanced at her, eyes twinkling. "Nice little town."

"Nice little town," she echoed.

"You're the mystery," he said.

"Me? Nah. I'm just someone who finagled an off-site telecommuting job because I had shoulder surgery. We can call it rehab plus leave of absence plus vacation, but it really boils down to — I can't travel or manage temporary duty assignments, so I get to work from home when I can. And home can be anywhere, right?"

"Yet you drove three thousand miles to get 'home'?"

"I can trust you to keep your mouth shut about that, right?"

He shrugged. "Who am I gonna tell?"

"Good," she said.

"No, Laine. I mean, *who* am I gonna tell?" Then he peered at her with those haunting green eyes.

"The IRS? Because those sons of bitches are mean as snakes."

He laughed. "Who's your boss?"

"President Obama. And there could be a supervisor or two between me and Mr. President." Then she gave him her teasing smile.

He laughed. "Why Thunder Point?"

She sighed. "The short answer is, I have a friend here. Devon is a friend of mine and once she moved here she just couldn't shut up about this little town. I went online — my specialty, remember — and got a Realtor to send me a bunch of pictures. The longer answer — I put together a plan to take an extended leave from the government job, time to rehab, to think about whether I want to continue to live in the D.C. area, to work that much, that hard. To think about whether my heart's still in it . . . It's complicated. The pressure is terrible some-

73

times. I'm good at what I do, but seriously, what's too much? I mean, do you have pressure?"

"Yes," he said instantly. "But only the kind I like. And that wasn't any brilliance on my part. I chose this — I like the kind of pressure I have. I serve some pretty high-dollar masters and their half-million-dollar classics. I can't make too many mistakes. But then, I don't make too many mistakes. Not at that, anyway."

I don't make many mistakes, either, Laine thought. *I'm the best at what I do. Yet I can't keep doing it.*

FOUR

Eric had been optimistic regarding his date with Laine, but he had not really expected it to go as well as it did. First off, she asked a million questions about the restoration of the El Camino, right down to the vinyl truck-bed cover and dash instruments, where he found parts and how he pulled it all together. He wasn't an idiot, he knew she was appealing directly to his male pride. But he could also tell she was genuinely interested, not just trying to pump him up. By the time they got to the restaurant in Bandon, he had already passed the point of no return. He was no longer just attracted to her, he really liked her.

"I hope this is okay," he said, pulling into the parking lot of a small restaurant. "It's not fancy but Cooper says the food is great and it's not loud."

"Perfect," she said, unfastening her seat belt and reaching for the door handle.

He grabbed her wrist. "Wait," he said. "Let me be a gentleman. At least for tonight. I'm trying to make a good impression."

"Well, knock yourself out," she said, waiting as he came around and opened her door.

When they were inside, he rejected the first table the waitress showed them. "How about that one?" he asked, pointing to a table in the corner rather than in the middle of the room. Then he leaned close and said to the waitress, "First date."

"Gotcha," she replied, smiling approvingly.

When they were seated, Laine said, "Either you're very experienced with first dates or you're actually suave."

"How old are you?" he asked. "You look young, very young, but when you open your mouth there's a whole lot of experience there."

"Thirty-three," she said. "Looking young was a problem when I was fifteen. When I was twenty-one, too. But at thirty-three I don't mind that much and I think when I'm fifty I'll be grateful. And you are . . . ?"

"Thirty-six. For one more month."

She ordered a glass of Cabernet, he ordered a beer and they looked at menus. Once they had decided and ordered, he said, "Now it's your turn, Laine. I want to hear about being a researcher."

"Aw, no you don't. But let's get this out of the way. I work for a government agency on a task force that involves a lot of different government agencies. Like I told you before, I do a lot of background checks, all over the place, none of which I'm allowed to talk about. I have a security clearance. Ninety percent of the time it's not interesting and when it is interesting I *really* can't talk about it. I don't mean to be dismissive and I'm certainly not being coy, but that's not what I'd like to talk about, if you can live with that. . . ."

"Secret clearance, huh?" he said. "I bet you're connected to spooky stuff."

She shrugged. "I used to think so. But seriously, since that's not what I'm doing right now . . ."

"All right, tell me what you're interested in besides cooking."

It was unmistakable, how her eyes lit up. "Lots of things. I love horses, though I haven't had one since college. I rode as a kid — English saddle and dressage competition. I also took karate and competed. First my mom had me in gymnastics, which I remember as great fun, but then I grew into karate, which I still love. I love parasailing and rock climbing — all things I can't do

77

right now because of a weak arm, but my shoulder is healed and getting stronger all the time, so one of these days . . . The family had a sailboat, so I know how to sail. By the time the weather warms up, I'll be ready to strengthen the shoulder with a kayak paddle on a bay that's usually still and calm. I really love being outdoors."

"You did all those things as a kid?"

She gave a nod. "What did you do?"

He laughed. "Laine, I think we had very different childhoods. My dad was a postal carrier and my mom was a housewife. I played Little League and sandlot soccer — teams and uniforms were pretty expensive. I suspect you had lots of advantages."

"My parents were both surgeons. My mother passed away a few years ago and my dad is approaching seventy but he has an active practice and still operates. Not the way he used to — just sometimes. He's winding down, his partners doing the bulk of the cases, but he's still involved. Orthopedics."

"You were a lucky kid," he said, smiling at her.

Their salads arrived and they talked while they dug in. She told him she had no idea she was a lucky kid and spent far too much time focusing on things that didn't satisfy her and he admitted that in his neighborhood, he'd had no idea he was poor, until much later, when he could see the difference between the haves and the have-nots.

"And you come from Thunder Point?" she asked.

He shook his head. "We moved there when I was in high school. My folks only lived there a few years, then moved closer to my older sister and her family."

"And you're definitely not poor now," she said.

"I get by. I have some money saved. Not a fortune. I'm pretty tight, when you get down to it."

"A by-product of growing up not having enough?"

He chewed a mouthful of salad. "More likely a by-product of worrying that I don't deserve what I have. I didn't even graduate from high school. I got my GED later."

"At least you got it!"

By the time their entrées came, they were talking about the differences in their lives to this point in time — she admitted to a successful college experience, while he claimed a few college courses. He told her it was his brother-in-law who helped him buy the first auto body shop in Eugene, but he managed to pay him back and buy him out. Eric was enjoying the conversation, even though he was the poor cousin to her privileged little girl. That didn't bother him — his parents were good people, just not rich people. He was well aware that their differences ran far deeper, but he wasn't going to get into that tonight. He wanted to get to know her first; wanted her to get to know him for the person he was now, not the person he had been in years past. Besides, she was playing some cards very close to her own chest — like the top secret jazz she couldn't talk about. Surely her good friend Devon had been privy to what Laine actually did for a living. And he was willing to bet it wasn't "research."

But no matter what was missing, what was there for Eric was plenty. He was further across the line — he *really* liked her. She was fun and smart and sexy. It sounded like she had a complicated life that she took in stride, which spelled maturity — he appreciated that. There was a certain young wisdom about her when she said things like, "I think it's too bad when our parents don't live up to our expectations when it's even more likely we didn't live up to theirs."

Plus . . . he liked the way she lifted the fork, licked her lips, brushed back her hair. She had a small dimple on the right side of her mouth, very deep blue eyes, one slightly crooked front tooth that gave her smile an impish quality. She was so articulate; he had had to work hard to become articulate when he began to draw a sophisticated clientele. He hadn't come from a well-educated background and as a kid he hung with low-lifes. She said she didn't have a million friends, just a few good ones. "I can relate to that," he said. "Me, too."

"I'm not very social, when you get down to it," she said. "I'd much rather have a small dinner with a couple of friends than go to a party. I don't think I've been to a party in . . . years. A couple of wedding receptions or retirement parties, but those are almost mandatory events."

"Would you like to be more social?" he asked her.

She shook her head. Then she shrugged and said, "I like what I like. I love fixing dinner for friends. I have a twin brother — another doctor, which makes my father very happy. Pax is his name and he's the most remarkable man I know — Harvard bred, he's finishing up a fellowship in pediatric surgery at Brigham and Women's and he actually has a personality. He's kind and brilliant." Then she laughed and said, "I guess you can tell, we're very close. I'm not close to my sister-in-law, but we both love Pax, so we get along well enough."

He laughed at that. "I have to admit, my brother-in-law and I are closer than I am to my sister. My sister has been trying to fix me for at least twenty years, my brother-in-law thinks I'm cool."

They shared a rich chocolate cheesecake for dessert and Eric asked for a cup of coffee while she finished her second glass of wine. "What about that beer?" she asked. "Wasn't it okay? You didn't even drink half of it."

"It was fine, but I'm not much of a drinker, and I'm driving. I should probably worry more about my coffee consumption."

On the way home he asked her, "When you were a kid, did you do any middle-class stuff, like . . . you know . . . Brownies? T-ball? Explorers Club?"

"Nah, my parents had us in accelerated academic programs. We had tutors from the beginning. My father pushed really hard. I didn't even know about those other things. I was playing chess by eight, Pax was an elementary school leader in science club. My dad had a plan and my mom pretty much went along with it. The only reason I was in karate is because Pax was." She turned toward him and grinned. "But I took to it better than he did. I can kick the stuffing out of him."

"Spoken like a true sister."

Eric pulled into her driveway. He turned to look at her and damn, she was so pretty. This was just about a peak experience for him. "Good first date," he said, oh so eloquently.

"Excellent first date."

"Don't move," he told her. "Let me be a gentleman."

He led her toward the door and when they got there she stopped and turned, looking up at him expectantly. "Well?"

He wasn't an idiot. He knew what she was waiting for. "Don't you want to get to know me better before we have that good-night kiss?" he asked, giving her a chance to make a break for it.

"Look, I haven't been out on a real date in over a year and before that it was a series of really bad dates with guys I'd never date a second time and this was an excellent date. Didn't I just say that? And damn it, I want to cap it off with a —"

It rapidly crossed his mind that she must have been a supervisor, at least. He slid his arm around her waist and lifted her up to his lips. She was small but not that light; he could feel the muscles that hadn't been so obvious. This was a strong woman. He found her mouth with his and planted one on her and then, almost instantly, he fell in love with that mouth. With one hand supporting her at the small of her back and the other plunged into her soft hair at the back of her head, he urged her lips open. He was cautious with his invasive tongue but she wasn't. She welcomed him, pulled him in, joined him in tongue-play. Her arms circled his neck and held on tight and he moved over her mouth hungrily, drinking in her taste. She was just perfect. It was almost scary how perfect she was. He lapped at her mouth, devoured her, started breathing hard in spite of his intention to be cool. He was *not* cool. He was over the edge.

He slowly broke away, but didn't put her on her feet. He loved having her up against him. "Tell the truth. The president works for you. . . ."

That made her laugh. "Want to come in?" she asked in a breathy whisper.

He shook his head. "If I come in, I won't leave till morning."

"That's negotiable. . . ."

"Let's get to know each other a little better."

"Wow. I didn't think men said no."

"I like you," he said. "A lot. I don't want

84

you to have any regrets. I want you to be sure."

"And you? You want to be sure?" she asked.

Oh, man, he was too sure. But there was a lot about him she didn't know. And the front stoop was not the place to go through the details. "At least one more date, honey," he said. "I think we're both ready, but let's take it a little slower. . . ."

"You think I'm a slut?"

He laughed at her. "I think you're a goddess!"

"Correct answer," she said, wiggling in his arms until he set her on her feet. "Good date, good first kiss, let's see if you can live up to the rest of it."

"Oh, the pressure," he said, chuckling. He leaned down and kissed her nose. "Thank you, Laine. I had a good time."

"Do you think you'll ask me out again or are you just going to ask how my car is running for the next week?"

He loved her sass. Loved it. She was so bold; not a coy bone in her body. "Sunday night?"

"Something going on tomorrow night?"

He shook his head. "I'm pretty busy tomorrow during the day, that's all."

"Can I cook us dinner?" she asked.

And he knew. He knew. He was going to have to lay it all on her — everything he held in his past. It might just freak her out. And if it didn't freak her out, he'd be staying till Sunday morning. This was a beautiful, terrifying impasse.

"Sure," he said. "What time?"

"Six?"

"I'll be here."

After her date, Laine washed her face, brushed her teeth, put on her favorite pajamas, lit the fire in her bedroom and snuggled into bed. Ordinarily she would close her eyes, take a few deep, slow breaths and worry that sleep might elude her or that she'd wake with a start because some deep, subconscious fear chased her in the dark of night.

Before the shooting she had been so highly disciplined she could grab sleep whenever it was available. After the shooting, she had suffered bouts of sleeplessness. Sometimes she thought she heard a gunshot and jolted awake, panting. When the FBI shrink had asked how she'd been sleeping she said, "Groggily, because of pain meds, I suppose. But I sleep. I've always been good at sleeping." She could tell the shrink wasn't fooled. Agents probably told her that all the time.

But tonight she welcomed a little sleeplessness.

She watched the fire and thought about that man, that handsome, delightful man. And thought about sex. Everything Eric had said and done on their first date indicated a man who was confident and thoughtful enough to be good in bed. She couldn't remember when she'd had sex last.

Oh, yes, she could — she'd just rather not. It was an agent she'd worked a case with in New York; when the case was wrapped, they'd gone out for drinks, back to his hotel and *splat*. Very disappointing sex. What was his name? Oh, right, Paul Remmings — DEA. Very nice guy, very sharp and quick, with *quick* being the operative word. Hmm.

She knew one of the problems in law enforcement was being drawn to like creatures, probably because that's where she spent most of her time. And when it came to civilians, she couldn't let herself be transparent with them, which didn't lend itself to intimacy. If she were completely honest with herself, that was one of the reasons for this hiatus — she needed to expand her boundaries, check out the real world, far away from the FBI.

And bingo, what had the real world offered up? Oh, my, oh, my, oh, Eric. Both tempting and, based on what he said, tempted.

Then she thought about cooking. It would have to showcase the best part of herself. Seafood chowder or bouillabaisse. Maybe crab legs. Or fresh catch . . . but she was partial to soups and stews, especially on cold nights. She considered a lot of options from chili to chicken soup.

When she did finally fall asleep, she woke to a dark dawn, drizzle and frigid temperatures and it made her smile. This was custom-made for her second date — there would be a fire and a hot, comforting meal. She made a list that included gourmet coffee for him and a nice bottle of Sauvignon Blanc for her. She would make her own cheesecake — something cool on the palate after a heavy meal.

She got her shopping out of the way first, settling on one of her passions — chicken and dumplings. No one had made dumplings like her mother and Laine had all her mother's skills . . . and recipes. She'd start with crab-stuffed tomato halves and crispy Parmesan bread sticks. She got a start on her chopping and mixing and then, despite the cold drizzle, she went for a run to burn off a little of that hyper, anticipatory energy.

On her way back to her house, she paced

in front of the diner for a while until she was breathing more evenly. Then she went inside and jumped up on a counter stool in front of Gina.

"Hey," Gina said. "Great day for a run?" she asked, grinning.

"It is, actually. Can you bring me something hot and wonderful?"

"I have a secret stash of instant hot chocolate," she said, pulling an envelope out of her apron pocket. "I can shoot a little whipped cream on top."

"Oh, yeah, I want that," Laine said. Then she looked around. "No crowd today?"

"Saturday lunch in the rain doesn't usually draw a crowd, which is fine by me." Gina poured hot water into a cup, added the mix, stirred and put it in front of Laine before bringing out the can of whipped cream. "You must be a dedicated runner to be out in this slop."

"I like the slop," she said. She took a sip and said, "Ahhhh."

"That makes one of you," Gina said. "I get tired of the rain and fog and live for the sunny days."

"I had a date last night," Laine said softly. She smiled and knew her eyes glittered. "A good date. A nice date. And I'm having an encore tonight. I had to burn off some energy. I really don't want to peak too soon. That's always a prelude to disappointment. . . ."

Gina looked stunned. "With . . . ?"

"Eric. The gas man."

"Oh! Wow!"

Laine looked outside and saw him walk out of the deli and hold the door for someone. "And speak of the devil," she said. And then she watched in wonder as a pretty young woman came out. Eric let the door close, spoke to the young woman briefly, then they hugged. She thought her throat might close. "Oh," she said quietly. Eric walked away. The woman crossed the street to the diner and Laine saw that she was just a girl, really. "God, she's so young. What's going . . . ? He is *much* too old for her!"

Gina laughed softly. "They're not dating, Laine. He's her father."

Laine's head snapped back into forward position and looked at Gina in shock. "But . . ."

The girl came in and walked right behind the counter. "Hi, Mom. Eric gave me an Amazon gift card." Then she looked at Laine. "Hi," she said, and Laine could see the resemblance — red hair, green eyes, but that smile belonged to someone else. Gina.

"Ashley, this is Laine. Laine, meet my

daughter, Ashley."

"Nice to meet you," Ashley said. "I'll go change and be right out to relieve you."

Laine was speechless. She didn't even know what question to form first and she felt the color drain from her face. *Great game face, Laine,* she chided herself.

"High-school romance," Gina said. "Eric didn't know about Ashley until about a year ago. I was very young and raised Ashley alone, with my mother's help. The deli is my mother's business — Ashley works there part-time, whenever Mom needs her help. And she's here a few afternoons and evenings a week."

"He didn't mention . . ."

"I guess you can't know everything about each other after one date," Gina said with a shrug.

"Having a daughter would seem real high on the list," Laine said. And then she felt the color come back to her face with a vengeance and she thought, *What the hell? I'm an experienced undercover investigator! I don't go pale, don't flush, don't allow personal emotions to dominate my behavior or responses.* But she said, "You and Eric?"

"Getting along better than I expected we would. I located him and met with him to get some medical history from his side of

91

the family, a purely practical thing. It was Ashley's decision to meet him and at first it made me very nervous, very paranoid, but it's worked out well for both of them, I think. He's changed a lot in seventeen years. But then, so have I."

But for Laine, there was a red flag. Having children, having a child, being a parent — even a recent or part-time parent — would seem to be one of the most obvious things to mention, maybe right after what you did for a living. How had they spent almost four hours together without that subject coming up? Concealment? Because hiding information was one of the first signs something was wrong.

Is that so, Agent Carrington? she chided herself. But wait, wasn't her situation a matter of public safety? National security? Almost?

But she said to Gina, "It seems to have worked out, then."

"Don't let this get under your skin, Laine. I'm a very happy woman. Mac seems to respect Eric. And Mac isn't easy. I'm sure when you bring this up to Eric, he'll give you the whole story. He's a very nice guy. Now."

"He wasn't then?"

"I don't know, that's a tough one. He was

nice to me, but he was such a typical nineteen-year-old — shiftless, irresponsible, egocentric. And I was a completely typical teenage girl — love was more important than common sense. It's a terrible trap — but I do believe we've outgrown those tendencies. Look, we all have baggage. Don't we?"

"Sure," she said. However, Laine believed she could keep the heaviest of her baggage to herself for a long time. And it wasn't all about her work with the FBI. "But you know what? The best way to take care of this is to take care of this." She stood up. "What do I owe you for the cocoa?"

"On the house. Don't draw blood. I forgave him a long time ago and I think he's forgiven me for keeping Ashley to myself."

"I won't hurt him," she said with a weak smile. Then she got out of the diner before she thought about it any further.

She jogged down the block, hood up and covering her head, and went straight for the station. There were a couple of cars at the pumps being taken care of by a teenager. Inside the garage, she could see someone under the hood of a car. He had long legs she recognized, although now he was wearing a coverall of some kind.

"Eric?"

He peeked out. First he smiled, then he frowned in concern. "Laine, you're all wet. . . ."

She stepped toward him. "I just met Ashley in the diner. You didn't mention her."

He grabbed a rag and wiped his hands. "I meant to, but we were talking about other things." He grinned at her. "Obviously I can't keep her a secret. The hair, the eyes — she's either a clone or mine. Isn't she beautiful?"

Laine nodded but felt numb.

"She's beautiful inside, too. Just an awesome kid. Gina and her mother really worked their magic raising her."

"It makes me wonder, though, what other important things you might be waiting to tell me. Because I like the really major stuff up front. I don't want to get involved and then find out there are issues like having a family that wasn't even mentioned."

Eric frowned as if in thought. He was quiet for a moment. Then he took a deep breath and spoke. "There's no privacy for talking here, Laine. Go home, get dried off. I'll wash my hands and come over. I'll tell you the circumstances, you'll ask me anything on your mind. We'll get it all on the table. Before tonight."

"Before tonight?" she asked, already disappointed.

"I don't want you to waste your time. I like you. I want you to like me. But I'm not perfect by a stretch. So let's do it." He lifted one of those copper brows. "How's that sound?"

It sounded like bad news was coming. But it had to be done.

"Don't make me wait too long," she said. Then she turned and jogged out of the garage and down the hill to her house.

Laine threw on a warm, dry sweat suit and put her chicken on to stew with a halved onion and the end of the celery stalks in the water. It was one o'clock. She put the ingredients for the Parmesan breadsticks on the counter — that would be her next project. She was determined to make her chicken and dumplings whether her encore date happened or not.

And then there was a knock at the door.

She opened it and there he stood in that blue jacket and pants. She took a breath. "I don't mean to be like this — so suspicious of everything. Certainly a beautiful, sweet girl like Ashley is nothing to be —"

He came inside, took her elbow in a firm grip and said, "Come on, Laine. Let's talk." He directed her to the sofa. They sat there, facing each other. "Ashley's one of the best things that ever happened to me. She's letting me help her look at colleges. I shouldn't even have that privilege — not only am I not educated, but Gina and Mac have been her parents, not me. I didn't know about Ashley. Well, I wondered . . ."

"Huh?" she asked.

"I dropped out of high school at sixteen. I thought I had the world by the balls because I was making nine dollars an hour changing oil and tuning up engines. And girls — I had girls. And boy," he said with a rueful laugh, "I thought I had all the moves, too. I thought I was so slick — God's gift. And I was just a stupid horny kid. And Gina — she was the prettiest girl. All of fifteen, but I had no brain and it didn't even register that she was too young. We dated, if you can call it that — it was a few fast-food meals and movies and a lot of making out. And then she said she thought she might be pregnant and I ran like my pants were on fire. I was nineteen and she was fifteen — I almost heard the cell door slam behind me. I headed out of town and didn't look back. I found work in Idaho — more mechanics. And I found my kind of buds — the kind that worked by day and drank and partied and did some recreational drugs at night.

We spent our money partying and I thought I had life figured out until I saw the flashing lights in the rearview mirror. My new buddies stopped for a case of beer and I was driving while they bought the beer because I was nineteen and they were twenty-one."

Her eyes narrowed. She had not expected this, but she was a trained interrogator and nothing much surprised her.

"Yep. They held up the store. Took the case of beer and eighty dollars — they were such high rollers. There was a silent alarm and my buddies . . . ? They didn't even really have a gun, thank God, or we might've all been killed. One of them stuck his finger out in a sweatshirt pocket and said, 'Hand over the cash!' We were tried separately but I had the worst public defender, toughest judge and the longest sentence. I did five years."

She was quiet for a long moment. "Crap," she said before she could stop herself. She fell against the couch back and closed her eyes. She put her hand against her forehead.

"Five," he repeated. "I don't drink much because for five years I didn't drink at all and while I was on parole, no drugs and no alcohol was the price of freedom. Believe me, a case of beer is never going to be that important again. I have no intention of going back to the useless imbecile I was. I cleaned up my act, learned some lessons, moved on to a better life. That's it, Laine. I'm an ex-con. Gina, Mac, Ashley and for all I know the whole town is aware of it. I'm not trying to hide anything but I don't advertise it. I was going to tell you tonight — I'm not trying to pull anything."

She opened her eyes and looked at him. "Do we have *anything* in common?"

He shook his head. "I'm also afraid of heights," he said. "I won't be parasailing or rock climbing with you. I can't even watch movies that have people fighting on the rooftops and ledges of buildings. And I'm in passable good shape but I never took karate. I never took lessons of any kind. You can probably kick my ass, too."

"You don't know the half of it," she muttered. "What a mess."

"Well, I'm sorry," he said. "But this is all I have. I'm a mechanic who was a delinquent and had a baby I didn't even know about. I thought about Gina and wondered, but I didn't think she'd appreciate a letter from prison asking about her condition, so I kept my curiosity to myself. That's it — that's all I've got." He stood up.

"Eric, I'm an FBI agent."

He sat back down. "Jesus."

"Yeah. Not on the job at the moment but that doesn't change my status. I guess you've figured out — I'm not talking about that around town. I don't need people looking at me funny. I'm a Fed. A fibbie. I hurt my shoulder by getting in the way of a bullet. I *can* kick your ass. We don't fool around about that stuff. . . ."

"You can't weigh one-twenty soaking wet!"

"And I know every dirty trick," she told him. "I can kill you with my bare hands."

He shuddered.

"Okay, not with my bare hands, but if I had a corkscrew or hat pin, you could be history. My brother thinks I'm cool. My father thinks I'm 'blue-collar.' "

Eric laughed in spite of himself. "He's jealous."

"Probably not. I've never quite measured up to his expectations."

"Well, after getting arrested, going to prison and being forever an ex-con, my parents have been pretty disappointed in me, as you can imagine. We get along better these days, but they're older than dirt and lack the energy to stay mad at me. And then there's Ashley. My mother and sister had no idea I could actually produce something that pure, that brilliant, that beautiful." He shrugged. "But then, neither did I. I give all the credit to Gina. If I'd had half a brain back then, I'd have let her straighten me out. . . ."

"Do you still love her?" she asked.

He ran a hand through his thick, dark hair. "I never loved her, Laine. I was attracted to her and knew she was an awesome person, but back then I lacked the capacity for real love. She was so lucky I ran. I would've dragged her down."

He stood again. "So, look — I'm sorry. I'm really sorry, I mean it. I wanted us to get to know each other a little bit. I was going to tell you tonight. I would never try to trick someone into a relationship with me. It's all public record. I have no control over that."

"And you're trying to start a business in Thunder Point," she reminded him.

He shrugged. "If I'm lucky, my new customers won't know I'm an ex-con until they've gotten to know me for the guy I am now."

"I'm stewing the chicken," she said.

"I'm sorry for the inconvenience. I should've told you last night. But damn, I just couldn't. I was having such a good time. I wanted you to like me, I did."

She stood up. She put her hands on her

hips. "Go home and shower after work and come back. I'm making my mother's dumplings. They melt in your mouth. I bought special coffee for you and special wine for me. . . ."

"Laine, maybe we're better off just letting it go right —"

"I'm not supposed to get involved with persons of ill repute, so you better have turned a corner. Because damn it, I'm stewing the chicken. And it's a wet, cold night."

"You sure?"

"Are you?" she countered.

He grinned. "As long as you promise all hat pins and corkscrews are out of reach."

"Six," she said. "I'll drop the dumplings after you get here. They're fragile. We don't screw with dumplings. Don't be late."

FIVE

Eric felt the impulse to run away, something he hadn't felt in many years. He wasn't even sure how many years. This time it was for an entirely different reason — for once he wasn't afraid of being trapped, he was afraid Laine wouldn't give him a chance. He was afraid she'd come to her senses. That fear was torturously coupled with his overwhelming desire for her, and his willingness to take any risk to make it happen. It was undeniable. He wanted her. It was so new and hot, he didn't even recognize the emotions.

His last girlfriend, Cara, had not inspired these feelings in him, not at all. He'd been fond of her. More than fond, really — she was adorable. Cute and funny. When they were together, which hadn't been too often even when they lived together, they enjoyed each other. They had good sex and he'd been tremendously grateful for that. And when she'd told him they were over, he had barely grieved. It felt a lot like saying good-bye to a friend at the train station. Like, "Good luck, be safe, stay in touch if you can, take care of yourself, I'll be thinking of you." Even then he knew that the thought of her wouldn't keep him awake at night. She was a sweet girl. He'd been lucky to have two nice years with her. He was all too aware Cara had never created a fierce hunger in him. They were like roommates with privileges, excellent privileges. Eric had thought that's what it was supposed to be like.

But now, he *ached* for Laine.

All through the afternoon he did what he did best — buried himself in an engine and just let his mind argue with itself. He could do the noble thing and let this relationship end before it began because it was destined to be a disaster. Well, that was if Laine wanted him as much as he wanted her. She was the law, he was the reformed criminal. She came from an educated, mucky-muck Boston family. He came from a lower-middle-class background in which only his brother-in-law had attended college. She wanted to soar from great heights, he liked his feet firmly planted on the ground. And yet he was drawn to her like a moth to a flame.

Eric's instincts told him it was a dangerous prospect to want someone with the kind of hunger he felt for Laine. It couldn't work. He tried like bloody hell to turn back, to call her and say, "Look, let's not be stupid here, we are not going to last through the weekend and we both know it. Let's cut our losses."

Instead, he asked Manny to keep the station open for Saturday evening, asked Norm to open Sunday morning, asked Justin to work with Norm.

"My mom usually needs me Sunday mornings. I have to take her to church," Justin said.

Eric grinned. "You? Church?"

"My mother, church. Didn't you hear me?"

"Jeez, I just got very excited," Eric said. "Any chance you pick up pointers while you're taking your mother to church?"

"Yeah. I don't pick my nose in public anymore."

Eric frowned. "Progress," he said. "Norm can probably handle things in the morning. I won't be too late."

Well, look at me, he thought to himself. *Trying to talk myself into running for my life before two perfectly innocent people get hurt, but instead I get people to cover for me in the morning like I'm already invited to spend the night. If she's half as smart as I think she is, she'll nip this idea in the bud.*

He went to his motel to shower, shave and change clothes. At exactly six, he knocked on Laine's door. She opened the door and just looked at him for a long moment. She looked at him like she hadn't been expecting him. Then she pulled him inside, kicked the door closed and jumped into his arms. He lifted her off the floor and went after her mouth. Everything he thought about all day long was gone. He leaned back against the closed door and held her against him; he loved that strong, muscled, supple little body in his arms. Had they said hello? They hadn't even said hello. . . .

He held her tight, his hand running over her butt, his lips urging hers open, his tongue penetrating . . . He was getting ideas, which preceded getting hard by about three seconds. Her breathing was already rapid and somewhat labored and he was dizzy. He leaned his head back, breaking the lip-lock for a second. "Whoa," he whispered.

"Double whoa," she said. "You smell good."

"You smell even better," he said.

"I lit the fire upstairs."

"I love a woman with a plan," he said, kissing her again. Long and wet and deep and luxurious. She was delicious. She was willing. She was *his.*

"I didn't have a plan," she said. "I didn't know I was going to do that. I'm not sorry. Let's just go upstairs. Huh, Eric?"

"What about those fragile dumplings . . . ?"

"Screw the dumplings — they'll be fine. After we're fine . . ."

He slid an arm under her knees and carried her up the stairs. "We're crazy, you know," he pointed out to her. "No way this works. . . ."

"This is going to work just fine," she said, unbuttoning the top button of his shirt. Then the second. Then she had to stop because he was wearing a heavy sweater over his shirt.

"I should've known you were a woman who had no trouble asking for what you want."

"If you have other ideas, you better speak up," she said.

He stopped in the middle of the staircase. Holding her with one arm, one foot on the next rising step, he rested her bottom on his

raised thigh. "All I can say is thank you."
Then he took her lips again. "I've been
thinking about your mouth all day."

"Just my mouth?" she said, smiling against
his lips.

"If I let myself think about anything else,
I might've had an injury. How fast can you
get naked?"

"Faster than you, I bet."

He raced up those stairs like lightning.

He put her on her bed and she was up on
her knees, shoving his jacket off his shoulders, lifting his sweater by the hem, over his
head. He took care of the shirt he wore,
disregarding buttons and pulling it over his
head. Then he pulled off her sweater and
she flopped back on the bed, kicking off her
pants.

There he stood in his jeans and boots,
looking down at her. "Ho, boy," he said.
"You're gorgeous. And you're very fast."

"Come on, Eric. I showed you mine. Show
me yours."

He sat on the bed and worked off his
boots first. "Patience."

"I don't have that," she informed him.

He pulled a couple of foil packages out of
his pocket, tossed them on the bedside
table, then slid down the jeans. He put a
knee on the bed and let her have a look.

"Holy guacamole," she said. Then she opened her arms and he filled them.

He rolled with her so they were on their sides, locked together with their lips while he slowly caressed her breasts and back and belly. When his fingers moved lower, she grabbed his wrist. "Eric, suit up. The second you touch me, I'm gone. I'll be way ahead of you."

He grinned at her and gave her lower lip a gentle nip. "The first time, anyway. I can catch up, no worries."

Eric wasn't always great at following orders; he didn't get the condom right away, as she instructed. He'd spent all day trying not to think about this and the last few minutes praying he wouldn't be too fast. That became a nonissue right away. He slid a slow, easy finger into her, his thumb brushing against her clitoris, and she went off like a firecracker, clenching and throbbing and drenching him in liquid heat. "God," he said. "Beautiful. Beautiful." And then he kept her going for a long, long time until she collapsed beside him, flat on her back, spent. He kissed her cheek. "Can you do that again?"

"I don't know," she whispered weakly.

"If you give me two things, I can die a happy man."

"Name 'em," she said, her eyes still closed.

"Let me have a little taste, then do that when I'm inside. Let me watch your eyes while I'm there. Blow my mind. Kill me. I'm on a hair trigger."

Her eyes opened a slit, but they sparkled. Her lips curved in a smile. She opened her legs for him.

He slid down her body, stopping to make sure her peaked nipples got the attention they deserved, then he went farther. He kissed the inside of her thighs, but quickly. He was anxious. He was ravenous. He was ready to explode. He gave her a few licks with a gentle tongue, then a little rougher, thoroughly enjoying her moaning and wiggling against him.

He went back to her mouth. "More later," he promised. "Laine, you're the sweetest thing I've ever had on my tongue and I want you so bad, I think I might pass out. Tell me what you want. You can have anything you want. You own me right now."

"Just get inside me, Eric. Before I climb on you and just take the choice away from you."

He didn't make her wait — he slid in slowly, luxuriated for a moment, then began to move. He grabbed her hands in one of his, stretched them over her head and moved faster, then harder, then deeper and harder. She bit his shoulder, groaned, and let him have it, throwing another climax at him. So fierce, so tight, so powerful, he let it all go with a loud moan. She was unstoppable; she was hot as lava. He came until his brain was empty and she was a limp pile of moist flesh beneath him.

"My God," she said.

"Yeah," he concurred in a weak breath.

He held his weight off her until he could catch his breath, then with his arms gently cradling her, he rolled them onto their sides again. He kept his mouth on hers, just pressing his lips and tongue against her lips and tongue, holding her against him for as long as he could — he didn't want to leave her body. He thought it was very probably the best sexual experience of his life. He certainly couldn't remember anything to compare it to. He wanted to say something emotional, intimate. Something memorable. But all he could come up with was "Are you okay?"

"No," she said. "All my bones melted."

He chuckled. "A-plus?"

"Don't get full of yourself. And don't stop trying. God, Eric. Have you always been a sex god?"

He raised up on one elbow and looked

down at her. He shook his head. "I think I can honestly say, you bring out the best in me."

"Whew. In a few minutes, I'll think about those dumplings. . . ."

"Screw the dumplings. I can just live on you."

"You'll get very thin," she said with a smile.

"I'll be fine. I think we need to do that again. Right away. Before we forget how that works. Damn, baby, we were very good. I think we found what we have in common."

They made love again, then showered together and that was just another opportunity to enjoy each other's bodies. Then they were going to dress to go downstairs to eat but were sidetracked by the bed. By the time they got to the kitchen they were weak with hunger and drunk on sex. Eric had never made love so much in one evening in his life.

They didn't get to the dumplings until 11:00 p.m. Laine told him she thought they were probably her best ever, but the taste and texture barely registered with Eric. The only thing he could taste was Laine and he didn't want to forget it for a second.

They sat on the floor in the great room, in

front of the fire, trays on their laps, knees almost touching. While they ate, they talked. "This is a completely inappropriate question," Laine said, "but will you tell me about all your lovers?"

"No," he said with a laugh. "There haven't been very many. I told you, my last girlfriend was a cute little computer nerd and we lived together for almost two years. She was special in a hundred ways, but we both knew we were temporary from the start and she dumped me last summer for someone more her type."

"How do you know when you're temporary?" she asked.

"You tell me, Laine. You're not married or engaged or serious — and I can't believe every man in America doesn't want you for his very own. And you're here while on leave — you'll go back to the Bureau. You won't work out of Thunder Point, I know that. I just refuse to think about it right now. Want to tell me about your men?"

She just shook her head. "My professional life didn't leave a lot of room for that. I was in a few relationships, short-term, with guys whose lives were just like mine, which meant high pressure, bad hours, temporary assignments, traveling a lot. But your life is different — one business, one address, not so much uncertainty."

"I found my love mostly in cars," he said with a shrug. "I'm not a ladies' man. I like women, but I was busy. Busy trying to rebuild myself. Ten years is a long time to be out of circulation."

"You said five years. . . ."

"Five in jail, five on parole. Ten years under a microscope. I didn't test the rules, not even a little bit. And I was nervous about forming attachments."

"But when you were young, before jail . . ."

"I was a fuck-around idiot. There's nothing more to tell about that."

"There's a daughter."

His eyes actually got a little dreamy. She couldn't help but smile as he talked. "I got so lucky there. And after hearing those scary words one time — 'I think I might be pregnant' — I was very careful. I'm sure she's the only one, and what a miracle. Wait till you get to know her better. I can't believe I was a part of creating her. You won't believe how great she is."

"Well, Gina's pretty great, so . . ."

"I must have a guardian angel after all," he said. "What are we going to do after we finish dinner?"

"What do you want to do?"

"I want to go back to bed. I want to sleep with you tonight, but that's your call. I can put on my boots and jacket and head home. I'm just saying, I'm yours tonight."

"Then you wash, I'll dry, then we'll snuggle in."

"I like that idea."

When they were back in bed, they whispered to each other, telling little bits of their lives. It was true, they seemed to have little in common, and yet Laine hadn't felt this compatible with another human being in her adult life.

At three in the morning, Laine woke and reached for him and his side of the bed was empty. "Eric?"

He sat down on the edge of the bed. "Shhh. Go back to sleep. I didn't want to wake you — I was going to leave a note. My phone went. I have to go tow someone. . . ."

"I didn't hear the phone," she said.

"It was on vibrate and I heard it bouncing around the nightstand. The number on the side of the truck, the number the cops have, it's my cell number. I got a text, wanna see?"

She liked that he wasn't private about it, hiding his text messages. She shook her head. "What's up?"

"Big mess on Freemont Bridge near Bandon. The cops threw out stop sticks to disable a car they were chasing and ended up blowing out tires on three civilian cars that weren't being pursued. My job is going to be easier than theirs. They're going to have some very annoying paperwork. I texted that I was on my way."

"Did their man get away?" she asked.

"I have no idea. I can come back. It's up to you."

"How long will you be?"

"That depends on how many tow trucks respond. It could be a few hours."

"You should call me. It's the only way I'll know you can't stop thinking of me." Then she smiled just as she closed her eyes sleepily.

He kissed her forehead. "I have a feeling you're going to be under my skin for a very long time," he said.

Eric jogged to his station, where he covered his decent clothes with a work coverall and changed out his boots into lace-up, steel-toed work boots. Because he wasn't sure of the terrain around the bridge, he opted for his flatbed side puller with the nine-thousand-pound hydraulic winch. If he found a car off the road or down an incline, he could get it on the truck. If all he needed to do was tow, he could manage that easily.

Lots of flashing lights along the bridge greeted him. He shone his overhead beams on the scene and got out to investigate. There were two state police cruisers along with a couple of local cop cars from a town south of the bridge. And because this was pretty close to his territory, Mac McCain was there. Eric saw two cars with flats along the side of the bridge and then, predictably, down the hill on the near side of the bridge, a large SUV flipped on its side. The driver must have lost control when the tires were spiked by the stop sticks.

He approached Mac first. "Injuries?"

Mac shook his head. "Guy and his wife in the SUV are a little shook up and she has a couple of bruises, but they exited the vehicle without incident. They're over there, moaning and groaning about the car."

"And the bad guy?"

"Who knows?" Mac said. "The Keystone Kops over there thought they had him. I think he pulled off the road into some trees or something and when they came peeling down to the bridge, he turned around and headed in the other direction. Stolen car. We'll probably find it abandoned before very long." He grinned. "All these state troopers and sheriff's department crew look like they're feeling pretty smug, don't they?

That's relief you see — so glad *they* didn't fuck this up. Can you get that SUV? We have another wrecker coming."

"I got it. Where do you want that SUV to go?"

"That's between you and the owner. We're not impounding anything."

"Well, let's see what they want."

Eric made his way over to a couple standing by the side of the road. He touched the brim of his hat. "Folks? Rough night, I see. I'm here to get your car up that hill. I haven't looked at it yet, but it's probably going to need four new tires and since it took a slide, I'd recommend an axel and frame check. It needs to get up on the lift and the undercarriage should be checked to make sure it's safe. And someone should look at the body for damage. I can handle all of that in Thunder Point. Where are you folks headed?"

The man sucked noisily on a mint. "Home from a visit in Sacramento. We're almost home. Eugene."

Eric nodded. "I had a business in Eugene for years," he said. "Well, I can't take the car all the way to Eugene for you, but there are good shops in Bandon, North Bend, Coquille or Thunder Point. There's a motel in Thunder Point — not fancy, but clean and nice. And I can take care of the car tomorrow. I can send someone for the right tires, take a look at your undercarriage, brakes and other essentials. I can even do the body work, but you might want to get closer to home for that, once the car is drivable. If so, I can get you some pictures for your damages report." Then he ducked slightly to see the woman's face. She was looking down but lifted her face briefly. "You want someone to look at that, ma'am?"

She just shook her head. "I'm okay."

"Is the police department going to pony up for the repairs?" the man asked, an obvious edge to his voice.

"You'll have to work that out with them. Why don't I get this car up the hill while you talk to that man over there," he said. He indicated to Mac and pulled some gloves out of his pocket. Then he lifted the brim of his hat to look at the man. "Let's just get you back on the road."

"You're kind of cheerful for the middle of the night," the man said sourly. "Big commission here?" he suggested.

Eric smiled. He was cheerful all right and it had nothing to do with the money he'd make on this tow. "I'm on call to local and county police. As a matter of fact, they woke me up from a very good dream. Now if you'll talk over where you want me to take your vehicle and move to the other side of the road, I'll get to work. By the time you decide where you're spending the rest of the night, I'll have her loaded on the rig."

He positioned and braced the wrecker at the side of the road. Using a large flashlight, he moved cautiously down the hill. It wasn't too rocky; he wedged a boulder out of the way. Examining the car, he found some surprising things. Only one tire was flat and though it was dark, it didn't appear to be a puncture. There were plenty of scratches and dents, with a small amount of fuel leaking on the ground and dripping into the creek. The chances were excellent that the tank had been nearly empty, but Eric had an industrial-strength fire extinguisher handy on the chance of a spark. The car was lying on the driver's side, so he pointed the flashlight inside the passenger's open door and looked inside.

He didn't think this vehicle was going to cost the cops any money.

He laid out his chains and cable, then he walked over to Mac. "Listen, it's none of my business, but . . ."

Mac smiled. "What are all these folks doing out here between two and four a.m. on a back road? Curious, I agree. That young lady over there works the night shift in a nursing home and was feeling sick, so she left work early. The gentleman over there — fisherman. He wants to be on his boat by four. The couple with the SUV and back full of luggage are heading home from a visit. Seems kind of late."

"Lots of breath mints at work there," Eric said. "No punctured tires, wife or girlfriend with a nasty bruise . . ."

"She said she hit it on the steering wheel."

Eric shook his head. "The driver's seat's way back. She's not even five and a half feet. There's paint on the guardrail, over there."

"He said she was avoiding the stop sticks and went off the road."

Eric shook his head. "I think if you could see and avoid stop sticks, the police would find a better option for disabling a runaway car. But this isn't my business. You'll figure it out. . . ."

"But you think you know what happened?"

Eric looked upward and put his hands in his pockets. "The bruise on the woman's face bothers me a lot. Looks like she got coldcocked."

"Maybe she had to put the seat back to get out of the vehicle?"

Eric gave that thought little time. "Anything's possible, I guess, except the car's on the driver's side and it would be hard to reach the controls, but the passenger's seat is forward," he said. His gut told him the man was driving, at least a little drunk, got into it with the woman and during a fight that got physical, saw cars stopped right ahead, right in front of him, and swerved, going off the road. He hadn't made it to the stop sticks. "Why don't I just load that car while you think about it."

He had a feeling he'd be taking it to an impound lot.

Six

Eric sent Laine a text at 6:30 a.m. to say he was back at the service station. And that he couldn't stop thinking about her. He didn't call because he didn't want to wake her and didn't ask if he could come over, even though the thought of curling around her warm body was enough to get him excited. Instead, he changed his clothes and prepared to work at least through the morning. He could call her later, maybe set up something for the evening. But waiting was hard. He wanted to get back into that soft bed. Now.

While he was still alone at the station, when no one could observe his silent struggle, he tried having a conversation with himself about exactly what kind of relationship he thought this might be, where it could go, what he should do with it.

Then he told himself to shut up. Who the hell cared? Everything he felt when he thought of her was good. God, they fit together perfectly. They had all the same moves. Only a stupid fool would look that gift horse in the mouth.

Besides, he had work to do. The police had impounded the SUV with one blown tire but Eric inherited the small truck the early morning fisherman was driving. The deputy gave the fisherman a lift to North Bend and Eric had to find four new tires. He couldn't wait to hear what happened to the couple with the SUV. Though he believed he knew.

To his surprise, Justin showed up at seven. "What are you doing here?" Eric asked.

The kid kept his head down, which was typical Justin fashion. "My mom didn't feel so good so she decided to skip church. I called Norm and told him I could handle the morning."

"What's up with your mom?" he asked.

"Just a bug," Justin said. "No biggie. My brothers are home if she needs anything."

This wasn't the first time Justin's mom had needed him because she wasn't feeling well. "Seems like she's sick a lot," Eric said.

"She's a little sickly, yeah, but she's tough."

"Is your dad around to help?" Eric asked.

Justin gave a short huff of laughter and

averted his eyes. "They've been divorced since I was twelve. He doesn't come around."

Eric hadn't known that. It hadn't occurred to him to ask. "That puts a lot of responsibility on you and your brothers."

"We're up to it," Justin said, moving away to get one of the work suits off a peg to put on over his blue shirt and pants. Eric was a real stickler about clean work clothes and Justin's were always perfect — clean and pressed. His mother was consistent about that much. That was a good sign.

"Your mom work?" Eric asked.

Justin shook his head. "You turn on the pumps?"

"Yep," he said. "If you can manage, I should find some tires for this truck. I'm going to put it up on the lift then drive to Bandon."

Justin frowned. "What happened?"

Eric explained about the stop sticks and for the first time since he'd hired Justin, the kid almost laughed his ass off. He thought it was hilarious that the police screwed up and Eric began to wonder if Justin had a problem with cops. It wouldn't surprise him; he was a surly kid. But he took the bonding moment to laugh with him.

"Will they get fired? The cops?" Justin asked.

"Nah. But their department will have to pay for the repairs. And I imagine they'll have great drama about it. Could be some punishments involved. So, you ever see him? Your dad?"

Justin sobered and glared at Eric. "He left us. Why would I want to see him?"

"Gotcha," Eric said. "Listen, I don't have a lot of practice at this, but if there's ever anything you need that you'd, ah, ordinarily ask a father for, you can always try me. I'm a helpful guy."

"That's okay," he said.

"I have a seventeen-year-old daughter," he reminded Justin.

"Right. I'm good." And then he turned away to get busy cleaning up around the pumps and in the garage.

"Well, that was awkward," Eric said quietly to himself.

Justin had worked for him for a couple of months and he was dependable, but ornery. Eric had suspected there were problems at home but he had no idea what kind. A single mother was a hint; they were probably under a lot of pressure. But it seemed like at least once a week his mother was sick. Maybe she was a drunk, Eric thought.

Maybe she was chronically depressed. Whatever it was, it wasn't doing positive things for Justin's attitude.

Justin was a high school senior and one of the drawbacks to hiring high school students was having their buddies turning the station into a hangout, so Eric had warned Justin not to let that happen. Justin had said, "Don't worry about that, man." It was a nonissue. When high schoolers came by to get gas, they barely passed words with Justin. Maybe the kid was just real unpopular.

Eric thought he'd ask Mac. Mac knew everyone. Then he told himself that might piss off Justin. But Justin was already pissed off. Was it his business? The kid was seventeen and on the brink of adulthood. But that was right about the age Eric had decided he knew more than anyone else, dropped out of school, got a girl pregnant, threw in with a bad crowd and eventually ended up in prison. And he thought he might have looked and acted a lot like Justin.

He had no experience with this. So he drove to Bandon to get tires. He put them on, balanced them, checked the undercarriage, looked for damage, then he called Mac.

Eric drove the truck to the North Bend marina and Mac was waiting there in the parking lot to give him a lift home. He left the invoice in the glove box and left the key with a guy named Sammy at the gas pump on the pier.

"You were right about the SUV," Mac said. "I should get you signed up for the police academy."

"The background check might not go so well," Eric said.

"It wasn't even his wife. His wife thought he was on a business trip — he sells something. I think he said paint. Or maybe it was manure . . ."

"How can you get paint and manure mixed up?" Eric asked.

"It wasn't my case. Not really. But I tipped off the state police. Well, I passed them off to my uncle-in-law, Joe, who took over. So, they were at some hideaway down the coast, got into a fight, headed back up the coast, still fighting. Not only did he hit her in the face, she broke right there and said she had bruises on her arms from him grabbing her and shaking her and shit. He passed a Breathalyzer, but barely. But the woman had had enough and sold him out. He went to jail on battery charges. I'd love to be a fly on the wall when he calls his wife for bail. . . ." Then Mac laughed. Evilly.

It was midafternoon by the time Eric got back to the station. Manny was there, prepping a car for a paint job. An old car with salt damage from the ocean. Not a classic, but give it a few years. He had discussed the painting service and the only way they could make money, be competitive, was to use cheap paint, but Eric wouldn't have a car he painted chip and peel two years out so he used good paint and made less money. His name was on it, after all.

Manny had one of his sons with him — twelve-year-old Robbie. He had four sons and two daughters ranging in age from sixteen to four. When he worked weekends he almost always had at least one kid with him. Manny had the most respectful, well-behaved kids Eric had ever known.

He talked with Manny for about ten minutes, told him about the tow, asked if his wife would bring him dinner. And Manny said, "If you're going to get calls for tows, especially from the sheriff, you gotta get yourself a night man. Go get a nap, boss. See you tomorrow."

Eric didn't schedule himself to work nights, but he was there most of the time anyway. This weekend was a real anomaly — a date Friday night, a bigger date Saturday night, a lot of hopefulness for Sunday night. He walked down the hill the few short blocks to Laine's house and knocked on her front door. She opened it and smiled at him. "Why don't I go catch a nap and call you later. Maybe I can take you out for something to eat tonight?" he said.

She reached for his hand and pulled him inside. "You must be so tired," she said.

His arms went around her automatically. "Someone kept me up most of the night."

She pushed him away. "You said it was the sheriff's deputy." She laughed. "Come on," she said, pulling on his hand. "Come in here. It's a lazy Sunday."

"For you, maybe."

"Lazy Sundays really don't feel the same when you don't work all week."

The fire was lit and she pushed him down on the couch in front of it. "I don't know if I'll be good company, Laine. I'm shot. But I could —"

"Lay back on those pillows," she said. "This is the best couch in the world. When I was buying a couch I had very high standards — I lived alone and needed something that would *embrace* me. Do you want something to drink? A hot chocolate? A Coke? How about tea? Milk?"

He leaned back and the soft cushions

seemed to wrap around him. "Wow."

"That's what I'm saying — perfect, right?" She sat down at the other end and lifted his feet one at a time, unlacing and removing his boots. "No shoes or boots allowed on my baby. Tell me about the tow and the cops. Tell me everything. From the beginning."

He shook his head. "I was born in the house my father built. . . ."

She gave him a whack. "Starting with the text."

"I think Mac was throwing me a bone. They needed three wreckers, had massive tire damage and they were midway between Thunder Point and Bandon. My daughter's stepdad is lending a hand, I bet." He yawned. "But it was interesting because I was the guy with the side puller who could get an SUV up the hill and it turned out they weren't a victim of the stop sticks, but were having a domestic in the car. We won't get the exact details but she was bruised and upset, he was a little bit drunk and they didn't hit the spikes. I bet he slugged her and swerved onto the shoulder, lost control and flipped the car. Why would a guy do that?" he asked, still bewildered. He yawned again. "The other two were innocent victims of stop sticks — one was a nurse's aide and

130

there was a fisherman. I got the SUV up for 'em, but then I took the fisherman's truck in for tires and a check."

"And the couple?"

She was rubbing his feet. His toes curled inside his white socks. He smiled. "You're like a fantasy woman, you know."

"Yes, I know. And the couple?"

"I think they're in trouble. Mac had their vehicle impounded. And he hopes the guy has to call his wife for a ride home from jail."

"They weren't married?" she asked. "He was slugging his mistress?"

"Or maybe not even a mistress. Maybe not a whole lot more than a date."

"What an idiot. Didn't he realize she didn't have that much to lose? I mean, if she wasn't the wife, if she wasn't invested, if he abused her or misled her, she'd flip on him in a second. *She* wasn't going to jail. Stupid ass. Talk about job security — most bad guys are just too dumb for words."

Eric smiled. Spoken like a true cop. And he yawned. She'd done a very good job on this couch purchase. And he heard her talking about dividing couples to question them about what really happened. . . . He loved the sound of her voice, so he closed his eyes for just a second.

When he opened his eyes, the house was dark except for the fireplace and one light across the room. There, in the big chair close to the fireplace, she was curled up, reading a book. One standing lamp, positioned behind the chair, was shining down on her golden hair and the book. Sometimes she bit on a nail as she read; sometimes she frowned a little bit, then turned the page. He wondered what time it was, but didn't want to look at his watch. He didn't move because moving would alert her and watching would come to an end. But what time was it when he dropped by? Two? Three? He had closed his eyes for a second and it had been hours.

His stomach growled and she looked up. She smiled at him. He smiled back and realized she'd covered him with a throw from the couch.

Laine unfolded herself from the chair and went to him, crawling right onto him, looking down into his eyes. "Well, Mr. Gas Man, you have a little nap?"

He chuckled. "Please tell me that's in reference to my service station uniform. . . ."

"Well, you do snore. But it's kind of adorable."

"Only if I'm on my back. You did very well on couch selection."

"Oh, I know. I told you — it has to hug you. Feeling better? Besides being hungry?"

"I forgot to eat. I got busy. Did I fall asleep while you were talking? Because that's very rude and besides, I love to listen to you talk."

"You missed a discourse on interrogation 101. It was fascinating."

"I bet it was," he said, smoothing her hair back over her ear. "What time is it?"

"Six-thirty."

"I should get a shower. . . ."

"Upstairs?" she asked.

He shook his head. "Where I have a change of clothes. If you invite me to come back, I will."

"Will you bring a pizza?"

"If that's really what you have to have. Otherwise, I'll bring something that's not fast food."

"What?" she asked.

"Be surprised. I won't disappoint you."

"I do like pizza," she said. "But I also like some of your surprises, though so far they haven't had anything to do with food."

"You're coming on to me again," he said. She nodded and smiled. "I like it. Let me up — I want to make it a fast shower."

"You walked here, didn't you?"

133

"It's only a few blocks, but I'll drive back here."

"Take my car," she said. "And bring your morning work clothes because I already know, you work every day and you're on call every night."

"What if I want to sleep in my own bed?" he asked, but he smiled teasingly.

"Last I heard, you didn't have your own bed. You have a room with a bed in it."

"Hey, I also have a small refrigerator and a toaster. It's very comfort — Okay, I almost said comfortable, which it barely is. And compared to your bed, which includes that nice, warm, soft body — no contest." Then his expression grew serious. "Laine, you don't have to let me stay the night every time we're together. I know you've lived alone, slept alone. You won't injure my male pride if you tell me to go home."

"Ditto. If you want to leave, I'm not taking hostages." Then she grinned at him. "I like it, though. Not something I've done much of. You must be a nice sleeper. . . . Or something . . ."

"I snore when I'm on my back. . . ."

"I know."

Eric called Cliffhanger's at the marina before he got into the shower and ordered takeout. He stopped in on his way back to Laine's and saw four people he knew while he picked up his clam chowder and Crab Louie for two. Mac, Gina, Cooper and Sarah all sat in the bar area and after saying hello, they exchanged glances in a very all-knowing and superior fashion. They said nothing besides hello; he admitted to nothing. And yet, he didn't doubt for a second that even with neither himself nor Laine saying a word, everyone who didn't know about them soon would.

While he'd been gone, Laine had fed the fire, put on music and set a table. There were place mats, cloth napkins and even a candle. And she was pleased with what he chose for them. The clam chowder came in a takeout carton, but included were Cliff's sourdough bread bowls, which she loved. "One of these days I'm going to make this — bread bowls. But maybe for my steak soup or chili. I love bread bowls!"

"Steak soup?" he asked hopefully.

"You're getting that look again," she teased. "I'll make it for you on the next really good soup day."

"I love soup days," he said. In fact, he loved it all — her couch, her soup, her sweet body, her passion, the sound of her voice, the blue of her eyes . . .

She dished everything up, tossing the disposable containers in the trash in the garage, hiding them from view. And while they ate, she talked about food, about how she had lived for those days her mother came home from work early and spent a few hours in the kitchen, preparing her favorite meals. Laine loved to sit on one of the stools at the kitchen counter and watch her mother prepare food. That's when they had their best talks about cooking, school, friends, plans, boys . . . Anything from karate to horses to colleges. It was never planned. In fact, there were times her mother had canceled evening plans because her meal was more important, just as there were times everyone else in the family was busy — but that didn't deter her. She made the meal, robust enough to feed as many as showed up, even if she had to eat it alone and refrigerate the rest. She loved the aromas and the science of it. The work and the flavors relaxed her.

"She was a plastic surgeon," Laine told him. "She did wonderful work and was completely dedicated. By the time I was twelve and she was fifty, she had cut back on her hours somewhat. She didn't want to miss our adolescence. She loved her work, but she said that there was lots of time to work. She wanted to see our plays and games and meets and competitions. She wanted to be around when we were struggling with our choices, like colleges and professions. And thank God, because Senior had a one-track mind. We were both supposed to be doctors. Period."

"But that's not the way you went," Eric said.

She shook her head. "And then to further upset him, I didn't choose a career as an attorney after a degree in criminal justice. I wanted to catch crooks. He's very disappointed in me. My whole life he always said, 'Good job, Pax,' and 'Laine, not like that — like this!' "

"He's a fool," Eric said.

"But you're a crook!" she said, clearly baiting him. "And look — I caught you."

"Nah, I never wanted to take from people or hurt anyone. I was just a self-indulgent idiot. It's a lot harder to recover from being an idiot than from being a crook. I deserved what I got, but I was just stupid. Not evil. Have you been around some evil?"

"Some. A lot more idiots . . ."

"Hopefully I've learned. I take it your mother was encouraging."

"She was. She loved the idea of what I was doing. It scared her, but she loved it.

And she loved Pax's decision to go to medical school just as much. She had very few vetoes in her. She was so supportive, but more important, she was interested. She was fascinated."

"And you lost her. . . ."

Her chin dropped. She put down her fork. She nodded solemnly. "Pancreatic cancer, the devil. She had very few symptoms — some heartburn, an occasional pain. She didn't pay too much attention since her life was hectic and stressed, and don't kid yourself, standing in an operating room isn't easy work. Then she passed out at work, had a battery of tests. . . . She told herself they were ruling out the gallbladder, but the diagnosis was advanced cancer with metastasis to other organs and bones. We were right up against the end. Of course, we tried everything, but she slipped away from us very quickly. And, as is often the case, the treatment appeared worse than the disease and she stopped. She said 'enough!' "

Laine gave a huff of sad laughter and said, "Right up to the very last weeks she wanted me to tell her FBI stories. She loved them."

"So you told her?" he said, smiling.

"She's my mother!" she said. "I told her anything she wanted. Not just my experiences, but cases I was peripherally involved in, just the drama and chaos and hilarity of it all. Very entertaining stuff." She picked up her fork and smiled again.

"Maybe someday you'll tell me stories."

She put a bite of Crab Louie into her mouth. "When I get your security clearance."

A few hours later, Laine was gasping, panting, sighing in Eric's arms. "Oh, God," she said in a weak breath. "Have you always been this good at sex?"

He kissed her forehead, her nose, her chin. "I think maybe I've been underappreciated. Or it's you and you just think it's me. That's more likely."

"I can't even describe what you . . ."

When she didn't finish he said, "You make me feel that, too. Be careful, Laine. You could be stuck with me longer than you want."

"Just do it again," she said.

"It's late."

"I let you nap. It's only sleep. . . ."

"Oh, man," he whispered. "Oh, man . . ."

Eric tried to keep his mind focused on his work and his hands busy, but his thoughts strayed to Laine at all hours of the day. He felt like a fifteen-year-old boy who'd just discovered girls. He had to work at keeping dopey song lyrics from passing his lips. And it wasn't easy, which only reminded him how totally uncool he was.

Neither were his hours easy. Until he began seeing Laine, he hadn't minded making sure that the service station opened early and stayed open late, tow truck on call 24/7. Now he had to do two important things — hire one more person immediately and adjust the schedule to make sure he had three nights off a week. Justin, greedy for hours, was more than happy to work until 11:00 p.m., but Eric wasn't about to leave a minor in charge alone so late. It was a safe town and there was always a deputy somewhere nearby, but it was too much responsibility. He usually got one of the old boys — Norm or Howie — to stay with Justin when he worked late. Eric didn't mind manning the pumps himself but if someone else did that he could concentrate on mechanics or body work.

On the nights Eric worked late he snuck like a prowler into Laine's house. They'd been together every night since that first night.

"I feel creepy doing this," he told her. "Like a man who can't get enough of his woman. I should leave you alone some nights."

"I like that you can't get enough," she said. "I'm perfectly capable of tossing you out if I don't want you here. Remember, I'm a black belt."

"I'd never make you throw me out. All you have to do is tell me to go home."

However hard it was to keep from constantly thinking about her or sneaking to her in the dark of night, he was determined to do two important things — keep his business growing and spend time with Ashley. This was her last year of high school and he'd barely found her.

It was Eric's night for closing the station so he had a late lunch at the diner. He wanted to be there when the place was quiet and Ashley arrived after school to work her shift. When he ordered his sandwich he told Gina he was hoping to catch their daughter to find out what was new in her life. He was just finishing his food when Ashley came in. Just the sight of her filled him with pride. And gratitude to Gina for all the sacrifices she'd made to bring her up right. It didn't hurt a bit to see she smiled just as broadly at him.

"Let me change clothes. Then I'll sit a few

minutes until the after-school crowd descends."

"Just what I was hoping," he said.

She took his empty plate with her when she went back through the kitchen on her way to the bathroom to change. Just minutes later she brought herself a soda and slid in across from him. "How're things?" she asked.

"Good. But that's my question for you. Have you given any more thought to U of Oregon? We could drive up to see it, talk to someone there."

She grinned. "I'm set for now. Besides, I've seen the campus. I've gone to see some games — you're right, it's a great place. But I'm good."

"Still planning on community college?"

"It's a good decision. I'm not ready to commit to a four-year program yet. I want to dip in, work part-time, live at home for now. I have to give some more thought to what I want to study."

"As long as it doesn't have anything to do with the cost of tuition because I said I can help with that. I want you to feel like you can stretch if you want to."

"I'm stretching," she said. "You aren't trying to get me out of town, are you?"

"Absolutely not! Eugene isn't that far!"

"But now you have a girlfriend."

He was shocked. He shouldn't have been. He'd known from the first date this would be all over town.

"Eric," she said, laughing at him. "You have a girlfriend. A nice girlfriend."

"I'm in denial," he said.

"Why? Aren't you ready for a girlfriend? Too soon after being dumped by the computer geek?"

"No," he said. "To my embarrassment, that wasn't serious. It should've been, since we lived together, but really . . ." He cleared his throat.

"I'm sorry I never met her," she said with a laugh. "Then maybe I'd understand why you were never brokenhearted."

"Cara's a great girl. You would've liked her," he said. "But she wanted someone entirely different and I understood. It was time to move on. That's why we never got serious, I guess. And now . . ."

"Now you're hooked up with the mystery woman," Ashley said.

"Huh?"

Ashley just laughed again. "Gimme a break, Eric. Computer researcher? For some agency? Good friends with a woman who was in a cult for years before she escaped with her daughter? I should say barely escaped. And later both of them had to be rescued?"

He could feel his eyes grow about as large as hubcaps.

"Whoa," Ashley said. "You bought all that research stuff?"

He thought she did investigative research for the FBI and he was keeping a tight lid on that, per her instructions. He knew she probably went out on search warrants from time to time or something. What was this cult and rescue stuff? "I don't like to pry," he said evasively. "And apparently I don't get much gossip."

"Probably because you're always under the hood of a car. Haven't you wondered about her?"

He just shook his head. "Do you?"

"Well, yeah! Not that she isn't well-liked. Everyone likes her a lot because she's very cool. And she's tight with Cooper and Spencer and Rawley, who just happen to be the three guys who staged a big rescue to get Devon's three-year-old out of that cult after she was kidnapped. Come on, Eric," she said with a laugh. "Your girlfriend is some kind of secret operative. She can probably build a car out of her cell phone or something."

He swallowed with a gulp. "Kidnapped?

Operative?" He gave his head a shake. "Jesus. So what are people saying?"

"You mean guessing?"

He just nodded stupidly.

"Well, like she's undercover. Or in the witness protection program. Or she was a cult member who's going to testify against the ones who got away. Or that she's on the run, hiding from bad guys. Or maybe she's a computer researcher, but that's so boring. And she just doesn't seem boring. Have you checked to see if she has a Wonder Woman outfit in her glove box? Because I bet she is — Wonder Woman. Or something."

"No shit," he said before he could stop himself. He looked up and colored a little. After all, this was his daughter!

But she didn't seem embarrassed. "Not boring, huh?"

"She's amazing," he admitted. "But I bet she doesn't know the town is talking about her."

"It's because she stands out. Not in a bad way. Laine seems totally cool." Then she got a little serious. "I'm glad you like someone, Eric. I don't think you've liked many women since you got out of prison."

He looked down. He could say those words pretty easily but it still filled him with shame when Ashley said them. After all, he'd never been there for her. He gave her a biological father she should probably be ashamed of. He wished, for her sake, he'd learned about her after becoming a Rhodes scholar or something. "Not many."

"And apparently no one special," she said.

He met her eyes. Green on green. She was so intuitive. So smart and empathetic.

"I'm very accomplished in the skill of identifying and avoiding potential problems. Now, that is."

"So you found yourself a woman who could shake up your world?" She didn't wait for him to answer. "Awesome. I have to get to work. Listen, I'm set with school. I've been planning very well and I looked at all the internet links you sent me and I appreciate it a lot. And your offer is very nice. I might take you up on some help — I hear the cost of books is just deadly. For right now, I'm all set." She winked at him and flashed him a smile. "And I'm glad you have a cool girlfriend."

"Thanks," he said.

She laughed a little more. "You're so cute."

"I don't want to be cute," he said.

SEVEN

Eric was restless and troubled through the rest of the afternoon. He needed to talk to Laine, to understand a few things about her, like what it really meant for her to be an FBI agent. It wasn't like he never watched TV, but he just assumed she didn't punch the clock and go to work like the NCIS team did. It was one thing for the rest of the town to speculate and he was fine with not knowing all the finer details, but still . . . they were lovers. And Eric was surprised to realize he was a little old-fashioned. He thought lovers should be straight with each other. He'd been straight with her. She should tell him what her job really meant.

Justin had come in at 4:00 p.m. and at five Eric asked, "Will you be all right here for an hour or so if I step out?"

"Sure," he said.

"If you have any problems or questions, my cell is on."

"Relax, man. I'm just pumping gas."

"Pay attention, Justin. If anyone gives you any trouble . . ."

Justin straightened, insulted. "I can handle it for an hour, man."

Even though it was misty and the sun was lowering, dropping the temperature even more, Eric walked to Laine's house. He hoped the cold, damp air would clear his mind. He was worried about how she'd respond to his questions. After all, she'd implied this business of hers was classified, that she couldn't talk about it. Did that mean even if the town was speculating? When she answered the door she had a paintbrush in her hand.

"What are you doing here?"

"I came to ask you something. What are you painting?"

"The backsplash behind the stove. I thought you worked tonight." She stepped back so he could come in.

"I have to go right back. I just want to talk to you about something."

"Shoot," she invited, heading for the kitchen to put down her brush.

Eric stood on the other side of the breakfast bar until she came back around. Then he threw it out there. "Are you in the witness protection program?"

"Huh?" she asked with a sharp laugh. "No!"

"Okay, were you in a cult?"

"Eric, what's going on?" she asked much too calmly.

"People are curious about you. Talking. Trying to guess what you're about. I didn't hear FBI agent, but I heard operative. Spy kind of stuff. They're making connections. Between you, a kidnapping, a rescue, a cult. What the hell, Laine?"

"Eric, I told you. I'm an agent. I'm a field agent. I don't talk about my cases."

"No kidding! What does that mean — you're an agent? Other people know things — apparently some people around here are in on it. And I've been having scary pictures in my head all afternoon."

"What kind of pictures?" she asked, hands on her hips.

"Pictures of you facing off with bad people, vulnerable, in danger. Somehow when you told me you worked for the FBI all that stuff didn't pop into my head. I thought you filed stuff or looked up stuff. But scary pictures are there now. What are you?"

"Crap," she said, running a hand through her hair. "All right, this is need-to-know, okay? The case isn't closed, though our

149

primary suspect is dead. But there are still loose ends to wrap up. So, I was on an assignment, which is how I met Devon. I was undercover. Only the third time I've done a deep-cover assignment, which means 'live the role.' And it stretched out way longer than we expected. It was a mess."

"In a cult?"

She nodded. "It was a commune, really. A farm. A kind of loose religious order without much religion. Or order, for that matter."

"How'd you end up there?"

"I asked for it. I looked the part — our suspect liked young blue-eyed blondes. I look younger than I am. I thought I could do it if we created the right backstory. And as it turned out . . ."

"Whoa," he said. "You *asked* for it?"

She gave a nod. "I had to give the pitch of a lifetime to get it. Our bad guy was recruiting young women to make a part of his 'family.' He found them when they were down on their luck, rescued them, then held them against their will. We knew he was working on his antigovernment manifesto, spewed a lot of violent-sounding, antiestablishment rhetoric —"

"Since when is antiestablishment rhetoric against the law?"

"When it's accompanied by threats, human trafficking and the purchase of large quantities of fertilizer — the kind used to make bombs. Since they were running an organic farm, we were concerned about the commercial fertilizer. We already knew he had defrauded charities, didn't pay taxes, wouldn't acknowledge law enforcement and kept his commune surrounded by a locked fence guarded by a few armed men. He was suspected of plotting domestic terrorism and I was part of a counterterrorism task force. Some of his clan had gotten away and tipped the police. He hadn't been real violent, according to the reports, but the potential was escalating. He was escalating." She shrugged. "We had to get ahead of it. Before he blew something up."

Eric wiped a hand down his face. "I think I better sit down," he said.

"Take it easy, it was expertly planned. And it wasn't what we thought at all. It was a pot farm concealed behind a fake cult. Oh, he was crazy," she said, following him to the couch. "He believed all his own B.S. about how he could run his own world, populate it, conceal it and keep it separate from the rest of society. He thought he was creating a peaceful sovereign nation, which of course takes piles of money. Drug money. And it was peaceful, right up to the point when

151

someone disagreed with him — then it was less peaceful. It was when he said the world was going to go up in flames but his *family* would be safe — someone had to take a closer look." She stood in front of Eric while he sat. Then she sat down beside him. "He was the king of his little empire and his fertilizer wasn't for bombs, it was for marijuana. And he had a few men to guard it and move it. Armed men."

"So you found out? And left?"

"No, Eric. There were women and children there. It took me a long time to get the lay of the land, communicate with my team, start evacuating the captives. I didn't seem to be in immediate danger. And if I had to run, I knew a couple of exit routes."

"He prevented them from leaving? How?"

"Intimidation, brainwashing, convincing the women they couldn't legally remove their children. *His* children. He threatened them, told them if they took his children from him, he wouldn't rest till he found them. Plus he had his guys, the ones who helped with the heavy chores around the farm. The marijuana grow wasn't revealed to his female clan, so we hadn't gotten the word on that until I found it. I think only a couple of them were aware of it. I had to sneak around after dark and peek in open doors and slats in the walls of the barn — it wasn't easy to find. It was across the river where none of the women went, where Jacob's house was and the men lived. Till then, we had only heard about his collection of women and children and his determination to keep them inside the fence."

"What about him? Jacob? What did he expect from you?"

"Well, that's a little complicated. He thought he was healing me. We built a story about me being a victim of sexual abuse so he would probably understand why I wasn't willing to be involved with a man. And it worked, thank God. But I had to endure a lot of preaching and his attempts at seduction. Whew. Those were hours that passed like days. I cried a lot, acted vulnerable and grateful, begged, bought time. Some of the other women helped shield me, helped me avoid him."

"What if it hadn't worked?" he asked. "You could have been in serious danger."

"We planned it for a year. The FBI had watched for longer than that, interviewing people who were closely acquainted with him and his commune. We even tried to get a man inside, but that didn't work. We just didn't have a model for the kind of man he wanted to work with. But we understood the women he targeted."

"It was risky," he said. "Very risky."

"There's always risk. Thus the training and planning."

"He could have assaulted you. Raped you."

"He was a megalomaniac, but predictable. We didn't go in there without profiling him — we knew him pretty well. We interviewed a couple of women who left his commune. The women inside talked to each other — they were like a bunch of sister wives. He hadn't raped anyone as far as anyone knew. But, I knew that going in without a wire or weapon could be dangerous, especially if he found me out. I wasn't going to let him rape me."

"But he could have."

"If he'd had help," she said with a shrug. "Eric, if the whole thing had turned, if he'd used his big armed men to hold me down he could have, but we knew he worked alone with the women. He thought they all loved and adored him. And he was just one man."

"You're a spook!" he said.

She gave a twist of the mouth that said, *oh, well*. And shrugged.

"But why, Laine? Why do you do that stuff? I have to understand."

"Because it needs to be done! And I'm

good at it! If we hadn't investigated, gone inside, gotten people out, there would still be eight to ten women and as many children in there and he planned to fight to keep his property and his farm and as a last resort, burn the place to the ground and run, leaving the women and children inside!"

"And why didn't you leave when you found out what you needed to find out?"

"Because I was *in*!" She took a breath. "Getting inside wasn't easy."

"Are you undercover now? Here?"

She gritted her teeth. "I'm on leave. Why are you so upset?"

"I don't know. I don't know," he said, shaking his head. "I knew you worked for the FBI. I didn't think you were that . . . that . . . Thinking of you doing something that dangerous, I guess it just . . ." He put a hand on her shoulder and ran it down her arm. "When I hold you, you seem small against me. You're soft and pliant and I feel protective and it's hard for me to imagine . . ."

"Eric, I'm soft in your arms because I want to be. Not because I'm helpless. Because I like feeling that way with you. Now get a grip. I'm a professional."

"It's a big thing for me, getting a picture

of you in my head taking on some terrorist. Alone."

"Yeah? Well, the DEA was a little pissy, too."

"Huh?"

She gave a shrug and a little snort. "We're all a little possessive with cases. Once I found the pot, we could've called in DEA but it was our case and we worked it to the end. DEA wasn't happy about that. Federal agencies are territorial. Everyone wants jurisdiction. In the end a DEA interdiction unit picked up two of our four escaped guys, so they got a piece of it."

"I'm going to need a dictionary. . . ."

"Interdiction unit. They interrupt the trafficking of drugs, humans, weapons, cash — all fuel for more crimes."

"Can you show me?"

"Show you *what*?"

"How you were trained to defend yourself? Just for my peace of mind? Because I don't want to have thoughts in my head of anything bad happening to you. And because you'll go back to that life and I — Just show me, okay?"

"Eric, nothing bad is going to happen to me. Not here, for God's sake. I'm on *leave*. . . ."

"You won't be on leave forever. I don't

know what I thought you did in the FBI but it wasn't going undercover against terrorists."

"If it's too much for you, what I do for a living, you can opt out. I told you, I'm not holding you hostage."

He shook his head. "Too late for that," he said. "I'm in. So, can you show me something?"

She took a deep breath. "All right, listen. I learned some defensive moves for competition when I was a kid in karate, which is the same as a fair fight and there's a referee present. But what I learned in training is how to do whatever it takes. If you're my brother or my boyfriend and you just want to test me, it's hard to pull off. If you're a bad guy and you get the jump on me, I'm going to kick you in the balls and rip your ears off and gouge your eyes out. Do you hear me? Do you? Because it's better if you just take my word for it."

He grabbed her wrists. Tightly. "Just get out of this for me."

She deftly twisted her hands toward his thumbs and pinned his thumbs back, making him yelp. "Jesus."

"A preschooler could have done that."

"Try not to totally emasculate me," he said, rubbing his thumbs and wrists.

"I'm going to need a dictionary," she said, grinning.

"Okay, I'm six-two and one-eighty. If I somehow got the slip on you, got you down, covered your little body with mine . . ."

"Wanna go for it, champ?" she asked, lifting a brow.

"You're a little cocky," he said.

She lay down on the floor. "Take your time," she said.

He studied her position. He really didn't want to get kicked in the nuts. On the other hand, he wanted assurance that she was capable. Safe. That she could, as she insisted, take care of herself.

He approached her from the side. Slowly. He covered her small body with his much larger body.

"Well?" she said. "What's your plan? You going to suffocate me? Rape me? Beat me?"

He laced his fingers through hers, hoping to avoid that uncomfortable preschool move. He stretched her arms out, pinning them.

"Very good, Eric. How are you going to get my pants down?"

He thought about this for a second, then grasped both of her hands in one of his and lifted himself just slightly. He thought he'd snake one hand down between their bodies just to illustrate that he could, but it never got beyond a thought. She freed her hands, socked him in the jaw and from nowhere her legs came up from beneath them, wrapped around his torso and, with amazing strength, she flipped him off her. He landed with an *oomph,* flat on his back. Then, as fast as greased lightning, she crawled right over his body and kneeled on his arms, pinning him. He could probably get out of this hold, but until he did, her hands were free. And he had grown so attached to his eyeballs.

"Whoa," he said, breathless.

"Do you have any idea how tired I get of proving myself to the boys?" she asked. And she was not smiling.

"In the FBI?"

"No. They know I can take care of myself. We have defensive training courses all the time. Sadly, I haven't learned how to stop a bullet, but I'm relatively smart and competent in other areas."

Relatively, my ass, he thought.

"Remember, I have a twin brother and he's big, six feet. Pax now knows size isn't the key factor so we've reached a mutual peace. And I have a father who thinks I've lowered my standards to do what I do. I didn't. It's hard to do what I do."

He nodded. "If I had to, I could fight you," he said.

"Don't," she advised. "Stay out of fights. And please, can we be done with this conversation?"

"How'd it turn out? Your assignment?"

"I got them out," she said. "Only one wouldn't leave and it was a sad, tragic decision for her. I'm very unhappy about that — I wanted them all out. And Jacob got himself shot in a standoff with police. But the other women and children are all safe."

"You got them out," he said. He smiled at her. "Damn."

"Don't tell the town what you know."

"I won't," he promised. "I think they're figuring it out, though. And someone else might tell." He sighed. "I have to go back to work. Can I come over tonight?"

"Can you behave?"

"I totally had this coming," he admitted. "You only look five-foot-four. You're really very big and scary." He smiled up at her. "I'm losing the feeling in my hands."

She slid her knees off his arms. His arms went around her and rolled with her until he was on top, but he didn't let all his weight fall on her. It was obvious by the way her hands rested lightly on his shoulders that she acquiesced.

"Feel better?" she asked.

He nodded. "Were you scared?"

"A couple of times I was terrified, but not so much for myself. I was afraid of not getting them out. I worried about one or more of the kids getting hurt, especially the littlest ones. Scared me to death."

"That's when you got shot, isn't it?"

"Yep. I never saw him with a gun before. The men who worked for him, yes, and they never threatened anyone with guns. Their guns were for their movement of drugs, not to use against the women. That night he picked it right up off his desk and fired." She moved her shoulder. "I'm good now."

"You must be proud of yourself. I'm proud of you. Scared of you," he said, smiling, "but proud."

"It's funny about that. I never quite get there — proud. Even though it was ultimately successful, it was too close. And I lost one. I lost one — that eats at me. I keep going over in my mind how I could have played it smarter, done better. Then I tell myself there's no point, but I slip back into that old loop — if I'd just done this and not that . . ."

"I can relate. So can everyone. It's hard to get to the point of accepting the past as is and remind yourself that everything going

161

forward now counts."

"And are we going forward?" she asked, her fingertips running through the dark auburn hair over his ears.

"I want to," Eric said. "If I can get up, that is."

"Pain?"

"I don't think you broke anything," he said, smiling at her.

He hoisted himself up and immediately grabbed the small of his back. Then he grinned into her shocked face and held out a hand to help her to her feet. "I lock up at around eleven. I'll grab a shower and come over after."

"I have a shower," she said. "I'll be up."

Laine texted her brother. If you're still awake, can you talk?

An hour later, 9:00 p.m. her time, her cell rang. It was midnight in Boston.

"Are you in trouble?" was his first question.

"Get serious. Why would I text you if I was in trouble? I'd call the police."

"This kind of text — I don't get this from you. Where are you?"

"I'm home! How come you're up?"

"I had surgery and I'm hanging close to this kid for another couple of hours, so if I hang up on you . . ."

"I have a question for you. How did you know you were in love with Genevieve?"

He laughed. "She told me I was."

"Seriously."

"Are you high?" he asked. "I've been married for nine years!"

"*Still* married, you should say. So — how? Why?"

"Laine, you don't even like her that much! What's up with this?"

"Don't be ridiculous — I love her. We're not close. We have nothing in common. We're not alike, but I . . ."

"All right, let me take another angle. You don't care why I love my wife. You're a wonderful sister, a spectacular aunt, a good and faithful friend, but I think if you had your way, you'd find me a different wife."

"Have I been that bad?" she asked, suddenly ashamed of her behavior toward her sister-in-law. She'd never been cruel but no one knew better than Laine how to create emotional distance. Besides, Genevieve didn't need her. She had her own sisters. But still, Laine had kept her at arm's length.

"You haven't exactly bonded with Genevieve," Pax said. "Now why the question?"

"Because," she said softly. "I think I have a man."

163

"Congratulations," Pax said. "It's not your first man."

A long moment of silence stretched out between them. Finally she said, "He just about is."

Pax cleared his throat. "Okay. Well, here's how it happened. I was a med student. She was involved in some fund-raiser for sick kids . . . she was volunteering or something. I saw her and I tripped. Literally, I fell right into a kitchen cart and sent about twenty dinner trays sailing down the hall."

Laine laughed. Genevieve was very pretty, she'd give her that.

"The minute I was done helping to clean up and the attending resident was done yelling at me, I talked to her. She was holding a small child who'd had brain surgery and although she talked to me a little bit, she wouldn't take her attention off that child. But I did get her phone number. I had absolutely no time to date anyone but I wanted to go out with her so bad I couldn't sleep at night. And I'm all for sleeping when there's time to sleep. It was killing me — she was killing me. I had to suffer through about ten phone calls and then I had to give her references before she'd date me."

"References?" Laine said with a laugh.

"Yes, references — she wasn't about to go

out with some clumsy stranger without knowing she'd be completely safe. I think you were in the middle of finishing up your master's or interviewing with the FBI or maybe even in the academy because you were useless to me."

"Wow," she said. "I never gave her enough credit."

"She has a passion for children," he said almost reverently. "Especially children in need. She wouldn't let me distract her from that. I didn't know I'd be a surgeon at that time. I wasn't even sure I'd be a pediatrician. That was my goal but Dad was pushing me toward neurosurgery. All that was peripheral — I asked Genevieve to marry me six weeks after our first date. There was just something about the way she hugged me."

Laine laughed out loud.

"Seriously," he insisted. "She's the most nurturing woman. She has compassion to spare — she's the most supportive woman I know. There's not a malicious cell in her body. And look at what she's gotten herself into! A surgeon in a difficult fellowship after both med school and a grueling residency, two kids, a million responsibilities, and yet she's never too busy or distracted to give me her full attention, to cheer me on. . . ."

"Oh, my God," Laine said suddenly. "Oh, my God, Pax! You married our mother!"

Laughter answered her. "You're just getting that?"

"Then why haven't we been closer?" Laine asked.

"Twenty reasons, and not entirely your fault, so relax. I don't blame you and it doesn't matter. First of all, when we got married, you still had Mom. Mom was your best friend. . . ."

"You were always my best friend. . . ."

"Not after marrying Genevieve. You had Mom, though. And Genevieve had her own mother and sisters — she's very close to her family. And you're right, you're nothing alike. You're scrappy and she's made avoiding conflict a science. She has no trouble telling me what she wants, however. She's so like Mom — she knows how to smooth things over, make things work, show ways that everyone can be right. . . ."

"Wow, how did I miss that?" Laine asked.

"Who cares how? She's a good woman. I knew that right away. Pretty soon I realized she was like Mom and I appreciated her even more. She's kind," Pax said. "Wise. She makes me a better father. She tells me when the girls need something so I never fall short with them. I'm telling you, she's the most giving, nurturing person I know. And trustworthy. I trust her as much as I trust you. She admires you so much, you have no idea. . . ."

Laine swallowed back some sentimental tears. She coughed. "So. You knew right away."

"Right away. Now tell me, who is this unworthy bastard you think you love?"

"A guy from town. I met him in the first couple of days I was here. He's very handsome. And funny. And also kind. Thoughtful. But he's just a mechanic. I mean, he has his own service station and body shop, but he's basically a wrench. Very smart for a wrench. He must do a lot of reading or something — I'll look deeper at that. And I don't *love* him. I just like him. But a lot."

"Well, has he done anything really special?" Pax asked.

There were so many ways to answer that. He restored classic cars — he was an artist. He built and sold one successful business and was building a second here in Thunder Point. He just found out he had a child and was stepping up, trying to help her with college. How many men would do that? But what did she say? "He's paid his debt to society."

EIGHT

After a morning jog, Laine stopped into the deputy's office rather than the diner. Mac was on the phone so she paced by the front door while she waited, hands on her hips, taking slow breaths to even out her ragged breathing. When he finally hung up, he shot her a smile. "Well, hello. I was going to call you this afternoon."

"Why?" she asked.

"You first," he said. "What can I do for you?"

"Hmm. Personal business between a couple of cops," she said. "I've been sort of dating Eric Gentry. . . ."

Mac's grin was large. "How does one 'sort of date' these days?" he asked.

"I doubt that's changed much over the centuries. So, I know about his history with law enforcement and the judicial system. I was wondering if you'd looked any further. Any deeper."

"The facts of the case and the trial are public record," Mac said.

"I read all that. Thus the question — did you look any further? Earlier issues and associations of his? Problems with the law since? You know . . . did you run him?"

Mac leaned forward. "If he's not a suspect and if there's not probable cause, that would be wrong. A private detective could do that without getting in trouble, but our procedure . . ."

"And yet, he's your stepdaughter's biological father," she said, raising one brow.

"I wouldn't let him near Gina or Ashley if I had any doubts about his character," Mac said. "I'm willing to bet you have good instincts about him or you probably wouldn't 'sort of' date him."

"I also have good instincts about my instincts — that is to say, when emotionally involved, I could miss some signals."

"Then let me give you some peace of mind here. I didn't want to like the guy. Really, he did my wife wrong when they were just kids. Her life was harder because of him. And Ashley, as a little girl growing up without a father, had her struggles. The emerging facts are, he was a stupid, reckless ass and made some very large mistakes, for which he's made amends. And the man he's become seems to be beyond reproach. Plus, I'm not emotionally involved, my instincts are good and I like him. He does anything to hurt them and I'll kill him, but I like him."

Laine smiled lazily. "Don't worry, I'm not going to rat you out to the sheriff. I just had to ask."

"I would've asked," he admitted.

"He was screwed, you know."

"How's that?"

"Come on, you read the reports and transcripts. He had inadequate counsel. He was the driver of a car carrying 'armed felons' who weren't armed and he had no idea anyone had done anything wrong. They were twenty-one — they stopped for beer and Eric was nineteen so he didn't go in, even the store owner verified that. He assumed they bought the beer. He wasn't speeding, wasn't trying to make a fast getaway when the officer made them. He pulled over for the flashing lights. He was unaware of any crime."

"That doesn't get a pass," Mac said.

"The other two got off. One got probation, one got a year, Eric got five to eight and did five and he was the least guilty. Does he know he was screwed?"

"I think he's smart enough to know it

didn't go his way. But he can also figure out that it no longer matters. However unfair that five years might've been, some good came of it. He turned his life around, made something of himself. What's he gonna do about it now, huh? Sue the public defender?"

"He could be bitter," she pointed out.

"Well, you're close to him," Mac said. "Let me know if you find bitterness. He seems pretty well adjusted."

"Man," she said with a laugh. "You're a regular ex-con cheerleader. This guy give you money or something?"

Mac leaned forward. "He's what I wish could happen to everyone who stumbles. Look, his crime that night might not have been too dangerous, given there was no real weapon involved, but Eric will tell you himself — he was a badass. He drank and doped and took stupid chances, lucky he didn't kill himself or anyone else on the road. And he's what I wish every young man who does time could be — rehabilitated. I don't have to tell you — it doesn't usually happen that way. The rate of recidivism is enormous. But Eric got a better life out of it. That's how it looks. If you're worried, date someone else."

"I like him, too," she said.

Mac was quiet for a long moment. "Let me know if you need anything. Help or anything."

"I'll be fine." She turned to go. "Thanks," she said over her shoulder.

"Laine," he said, causing her to turn. "I ran him. He's clean."

"I knew you ran him! You'd *have* to!"

"I hope we can keep this between us."

"Absolutely! If I suspected you hadn't, I was going to find a way. I knew he was okay. I knew it."

"I was going to call you today. About something else."

"What?"

"You said something about working while you're here. Is that FBI work?"

She gave a shrug. "I can do computer research or field investigation for them if they ask. They haven't asked yet, but I've only been here a month or so."

"Douglas County Sheriff knows you're here, of course —"

"I made sure the county knows where I am in case they need further interviews or testimony. Just follow-up."

"Interested in some consulting work?" he asked.

"Depends. Do you know what it is? Because I'm resting. I'm not infiltrating any cults or communes, if you don't mind."

"I don't know what he wants, exactly. He's probably going to call you. He mentioned to my boss — who mentioned to me — that if they were looking for someone with federal investigative experience, you were still in the area. And you know how to work with the local cops."

"We all know how," she said, a little irritated by the inference that the fibbies took over. Even though they had earned that reputation very honestly.

He chuckled. "Just so you know — I think he'll call you."

"Side jobs like that while I'm on leave have to be cleared through my division, not his."

"I'm sure you can work out details like that. I thought maybe a part-time job could come in handy. Just in case you could use a couple of bucks."

"Thanks," she said. "I'll let you know what I hear."

As it happened, Laine didn't need money. She had money. She'd always had money. And her mother, Janice, had made sure that upon her death Laine and Pax would have what she referred to as a parting gift. Of course her father, Paxton Sr., was loaded and unless he decided to punish her for disobedience, she'd eventually have a big load of his money dumped on her. Of course, Senior was also young and healthy — seventy, sturdy, strong, robust. Very stubborn. He'd live to be a hundred. And she wouldn't be surprised if the division of assets favored Pax.

But Laine had always been very careful not to live rich once she left home. She was also cautious about how she parceled out information about her youth and her parents — it wasn't typical for an agent to come from wealth. In fact, it was the rare law enforcement officer or agent whose family was stinkin' rich. It came out, of course. She'd been razzed a little bit about being born with a silver spoon in her mouth, as though that meant she wasn't clear on how the other half lived, or as if that had anything to do with her ability to do the job well. There had been one agent who called her Duchess. She pretty much wanted to kill him. That guy wasn't just jealous of the money he thought she had, he was also jealous of her brain. But she was promoted ahead of him and was better respected, so he could go to hell. She lived conservatively; had a modest town house, drove an Acura. An upgraded Acura, but still . . .

Here in Thunder Point, they didn't know.

Eric sort of knew. He knew how she'd grown up and easily surmised her childhood was more advantageous than his. But like everything with Eric, he seemed to take it in stride. In fact, his whole existence was that way — just nice and easy. It was as if he knew everyone had baggage and his wasn't any heavier than what anyone, rich or poor, carried. Maybe that was his trick — if he didn't make something a big deal, then it wasn't. It was as if he was in some Zen place with life and the world.

In fact, the biggest baggage he'd displayed so far was his concern over Laine finding herself in dangerous situations. After throwing him, she hadn't heard about it again.

So, Laine didn't need to earn any money. But there was something she realized she needed after a little more than a month in Thunder Point. She needed something to do. She'd always worked or gone to school or both. Always. And now not only did she have time off, but she also had a man in her life, a man who put in very long hours. If she didn't find productive ways to fill her days she'd find herself building every second around the reappearance of her man. And she was not that kind of woman.

Just the suggestion of work lit a fire under

her. It was time to get moving again — the shoulder was no longer an excuse. She searched out karate dojos and found that while there were many, she'd probably have to drive to North Bend for the one that appealed to her the most.

A few days later she went to the Douglas County Sheriff's Department and found they had a few cases of interstate flight that had gone cold, mostly domestic situations, custodial interference, et cetera. The FBI had bigger fish to fry and would be of little assistance there, but the sheriff wanted to pursue them. Dedicated but boring work, yet something she could do with a minimum of aggravation.

Getting cleared to consult for the sheriff through her boss started something of a firestorm, however. Her division chief said if she was willing to spend some hours, they had a crunch of background checks in the area they could use help on. So within a week she had a full roster of investigative jobs. And they weren't all at the computer. She would be needed in the field. Since she hadn't been firearm-qualified in a long time, she had to get that done. The sheriff's department was happy to assist.

Out of the blue her phone rang and caller ID identified Senior. Still angry with him, she flipped him to voice mail. His message was "Where are you? When will you be home?" She was baffled at the nonchalance and lack of any attempt to apologize. She didn't respond, of course. Two hours later, Senior called again. Every couple of hours he called, but didn't leave another message.

She called her brother. "What's up with Senior? He's been calling but only left one message, asking where I was and when I'd be home. Like he's pretending we're not estranged. Have you talked to him?"

"Yesterday," Pax said. "He didn't mention you. Are you two ready for a truce?"

"I don't know about that. Maybe too much has happened between us. To me all a truce means is that I'm willing to accept his negative attitude toward me and what I do. I can't change him. I'm happier just being estranged. But will you please do something for me? Will you call him and ask him why he's calling me? What does he want? Because you can actually talk to him."

"If that's what you want. But that doesn't sound like you're through with him."

"Please?" she asked.

An hour later Pax called her back. "He said he doesn't know what you're talking about. He hasn't called you. He asked me to check on you and make sure you're all right."

"What? Why wouldn't I be all right? I'm not calling him!"

"Okay," Pax said. "I'll tell him."

"What else did he say?" Laine asked suspiciously.

"He said he didn't . . ." Pax paused. "He asked me if you had our mother's phone and I said of course not. Doesn't he have it? Did we throw it out?"

"I thought Senior put it in a drawer or something. We stopped service when she . . ."

"Then . . . listen, I don't know how to say this, Laine. He wondered if you were finally flipping out. He suggested PTSD from all your insane undercover work. His words, not mine."

She growled into the phone. "Thanks! I'll be texting you from my new number in the next day or two!"

Eric was ready to leave the station before Norm arrived to watch over the evening shift. Norm had called to say he was running a little late but would be there by seven. Ordinarily that wouldn't make any difference. Up until now, there were only two things that mattered a whole lot in

Eric's life — Ashley and the station.

But now there was Laine. And something had been bothering her the past day or two. When he tried calling her cell the call wouldn't go through.

"Just go," Justin said. "You're going to Laine's, right? Two blocks away? If I have a problem in the next hour, I'll call you. But I won't."

"I guess it would be okay," Eric said.

"You worry too much, man," he said. "What's going to happen? Armed bandits? Or maybe you're afraid I'll steal from you?"

Eric frowned. "You'd do that exactly once," he said. "Actually, I thought something might come up for you, that your mom or brothers might need you for some reason. If that happens, call me. I can be here in five minutes."

Justin actually laughed. "That so? Five minutes? Then your love life is pretty sad. Maybe you need a few pointers?"

"Oh, really? Do we need to talk about that?" Eric asked, really hoping the answer was no.

"I'm not talking," Justin said. "Just trust me — you can't even compete!"

"Check," Eric said. "The topic of our next weekly meeting."

"We don't have weekly meetings!"

But Eric had accidentally fathered a child, something for which he was grateful now, but that didn't speak to the fact that it shouldn't have happened. "We do now, Casanova. Call me if you need me."

"Y'know, if you pay attention you'll see I can manage nights and weekends just fine. And I could use the hours anyway. In fact, I'm up for learning some more mechanics. Doesn't that get a little bump in pay?"

"We'll talk about it at our next weekly meeting."

Eric stopped off in the washroom to scrub up a little bit. It was a habit. He didn't go out before making sure there was no grease under his nails. He also washed his face. He used to brush his teeth, but now there was a spare toothbrush in Laine's bathroom. In fact, a couple of changes of clothes had somehow drifted over to her house. And he had a key for those late nights.

The French doors were closed against the late February chill, but he could see she was out on the deck, reclining on the chaise, wrapped in a quilt, her fire pit lit against the descending darkness. He moved out onto the deck cautiously. For all he knew, she was armed! As he moved toward her he could see her earbuds in her ears. She was gazing out over the fire toward the bay. He casually stood in front of her.

"Eric!" She pulled out the earbuds. "I'm sorry! I forgot it was your early night!"

He smiled at her. "That's okay, you've been preoccupied with something. You look comfortable. And warm."

"I didn't cook anything," she said apologetically.

He moved closer and pushed her feet up so he could sit on the end of the chaise. "You're not looking for a man to take care of, remember? I'll make sure we eat. What's taking up my space in your brain?"

"Huh?"

"Usually when you know I'm coming you lay a nice trap for me." He grinned at her. "The past couple of days something has been off. You know you aren't stuck with me. If you need alone time, all you have to do is —"

"Stop," she said. "You're the best part of my day. Every day. It's not you."

"Wanna talk about it?"

"I don't know what to say," she said with a shrug. "I told you, I'm at odds with my father. I always have been, but it's worse since my mom died. A couple of days ago he called my cell phone every couple of hours for a whole day and only left one message — asking me where I was and when

181

was I coming home. That's it. No apology, no asking me to call him, just that one odd message. So I called Pax, asked him to check with Senior, find out why he was calling me. He said he had never called, said I had PTSD from all my 'ridiculous undercover work.' "

"I'm sorry, baby. He's a fool. Even if he doesn't approve, it's still your choice. You're all grown up." He reached out and ran his fingers through her hair over her ear. "He should know better than to put you down like that. Doesn't he know it will only build a barrier between you?"

"He should know by now. We had a big blowout at Christmas. What is it about Christmas? Can't blame it on booze. We're pretty conservative with liquor, even on holidays. But he started in on how I was wasting my life on scumbags when if I really wanted to make a difference in the world there were better ways. We argued. I mean, we fought. I lashed out at him for his regular if not constant criticism of me and what I do. I was so angry. He was just as angry. It was awful. We weren't content to just argue over the crime of the moment — we both reached way back in time, remembering every disappointment. My sister-in-law took my nieces into another room!"

"Honey . . ."

"I told him I was through listening to his negative, critical remarks, that I was done and he shouldn't bother to get in touch with me unless he could apologize and change. And then I left Boston in a huff, furious. We haven't spoken since. When I saw his name on the caller ID I wondered if our two months of not speaking at all had finally . . ."

"I guess it caught up with you," he said.

"I just got home a couple of hours ago. I went to the phone store — I changed my number. I have a long contact list to go through, a lot of colleagues and supervisors to email. Tomorrow is soon enough. But it was the last straw, Eric. When he suggested my work had made me delusional . . ."

He just kept running that hair over her left ear. She looked into her lap, looked at the phone. "Getting a new number is pretty dramatic," he said.

"I probably should have done this five years ago. We had a big argument about my work as an agent not long after my mother died. He thought that since she died and she was my biggest supporter, it was time for me to quit the FBI and find something he referred to as 'more respectable' to do for a living. What is it with him? He doesn't have to be proud of me but how can he be so hard on me? I can't really be that inadequate. I get the job done. I don't get any complaints from the FBI."

"Did he ever suggest he could take you? Ask you to break free of his hold? Because that could have been interesting. . . ."

A little puff of laughter escaped her. "He's seventy. A very tough, strong seventy, but I wouldn't throw him. Things are bad enough between us."

Eric got up and went behind her. "Scoot," he said, pushing her forward a little bit. "Let me back here." He stepped over the back of the chaise so that he was behind her, his long legs on either side of the chaise. He pulled her back against him. Once she was settled there, he put his hands in her hair, his fingertips gently massaging her scalp.

"Ohhhh . . . Whatever that is you're doing, it's okay to keep doing it. . . ."

"When I get worried about my parents or frustrated with them, it gives me a headache. And I'm not a headache kind of guy."

"Do they get you upset regularly?"

"Hmm. Very regularly. My mom is a very negative person anyway and she really has an excuse in me."

"So what do you do?" she asked.

"I apologize for getting in so much trouble as a kid, for embarrassing the whole family, promise I'm doing better now, all the same stuff. Over and over. And I try to be patient."

"And who rubs your head?" she asked.

He laughed softly. "I take aspirin."

"What do you think I should do?" she asked.

"Well, my first reaction would be to remember your dad might be too old to change his habits. Maybe he's just one of those negative people."

"I just couldn't ever impress him. Period. He's always been that kind of guy who knows it all, though. He knows what's best for everyone, what's right for the whole world. He's arrogant. Omnipotent."

"How about your brother?"

"It doesn't seem like he picks at Pax as much, but then Pax studied medicine, which was what Senior had in mind for both of us. And also, Pax just ignores him. He never argues with him, just lets him rant on. It's true, if he doesn't get an argument, he runs out of steam pretty quickly."

"Have you thought about doing that? Just let him have his say, however unfair or unkind it is, and put up with it? Because he's your father and you're stuck with him?"

She leaned back against him. "My mother used to say I was as stubborn as he is. And that I have a real problem with needing to be right. I don't want to be like him, needing to be right all the time. It's awful. You're not like that."

He leaned forward and kissed her neck. "Laine, you have to remember, I'm the cause of my parents' unhappiness. I didn't just shoplift a candy bar and take it back to the store. I was convicted of armed robbery."

She turned to look over her shoulder at him. "But you didn't have a weapon and you didn't rob anyone!"

"I was there. That was enough."

"You know you got screwed, right?"

"Whatever you say. . . ."

"I looked at the record and the transcripts. You had an inadequate defense and a hanging judge. . . ."

"You looked," he said with a shallow laugh. "How does that not surprise me."

"Occupational hazard. . . ."

"It's okay. I have no secrets."

"Not that I could find. . . ."

"I'm sure you don't care, but I didn't run a background check on you."

She chuckled. "I'd love to see you try." She glanced over her shoulder. "What should I do about my dad?"

"I don't know, Laine. It must hurt so

much. Instinct says, he's your dad. Do your best to get along, you won't have him forever. And you can fix your own boundaries."

"Which I have. I moved to the other coast and changed my number."

"Pretty serious boundaries," he said. "That explains why my call to you didn't go through a couple of hours ago."

"Sorry. I was caught up in what I'd done. I can usually make very dramatic moves without getting emotional, but this time . . . Well, I've been threatening to just disengage from Senior since our relationship is at least fifty percent misery. But I kept hoping. . . ."

"Understandable," Eric went on. "If I were your best friend and you were dating a guy who treated you like he owned you, I'd tell you to break away. Fast. Because you just don't treat a person you love like that. It's not good. It won't work. For either of you."

"I think you *are* my best friend," she said. "And I don't think my father has ever loved me. If he loved me, wouldn't he be nicer to me?"

"Pax is your best friend," he reminded her.

"He's my twin. It's a whole different thing. But you? You're a friend. And you're wonderful with scalp massage."

He chuckled. "As for your dad, who knows what makes him tick. If you've told him how he makes you feel and nothing changes, maybe he just doesn't get it."

"Will you move in with me?" she asked.

He stopped massaging.

"I scared you, didn't I?"

He put his hands on her shoulders. "Turn around for me, Laine." She moved around so she was facing him and crossed her legs. "You've never lived with anyone, have you?"

She shook her head. "Have you lived with a lot of people?"

"Just Cara. Look, I know what I told you about that, that it had run its course and we knew it. But I didn't go into it thinking it had an expiration date on it. I thought our relationship would get stronger. I knew there would be adjustments to sharing space, but I thought once we figured it out, it would be easy. It wasn't easy. And it didn't get stronger."

"You don't think we'd get stronger?"

"For what's left of your leave from the FBI? Before you go back to the East Coast and get back to doing work you can't talk about?"

"Oh. You want to see some long-term potential before you even share a closet? Even though we sleep together every night and you have a key and your own tooth-brush?"

"I don't know if this will make any sense, Laine, but here goes. . . . If you told me right now that you're done here, that you're leaving next week to go back to that life you left behind, that would really bite. I'm not done with you, not by a long shot. It would be hard, but it wouldn't be a shock. I could still grab my toothbrush, the spare jeans, extra jacket, garage uniform, leave my key on the kitchen counter and go back to my place. Not much of a place, but I can live with it. But the idea of living with you for a year, getting deeper and deeper into you and then suddenly — bam — there's noth-ing. That just feels bigger than what I'm up to. I can't explain it any better."

"You're scared," she said.

He gave a nod. "Scared."

"Were you scared with Cara?"

He shook his head. "Not at all. Not scared, not worried, not much in love. Comfortable and relaxed with her, sure. We worked well together. But I never once thought, if she leaves me I'll crash."

That actually made her smile. "You're in love with me."

"Is that what it is? I wouldn't know. All I know is I haven't been in this place before.

It's brand-new. It's terrifying. Why couldn't I feel this way about someone simpler? Easier to understand? Someone I have something in common with?"

"I guess I'm a big risk. I like that. I'd like to take the chance. You'll do what you think is best, but I'd love to live with you. I've never done it before, but I think I could do it with you. Or you can keep that hotel room. But gee, I hope you don't stop spending the night. . . ."

"I probably couldn't if I tried."

"I'm so happy about that!"

"So here's the deal. You know that judge you called the hanging judge? He was the best judge there ever was. I'll never forget what he said when he sentenced me. He said, 'Son, you probably feel completely ruined and lost, but you're really the luckiest man I know. You're stripped down to nothing. You've got nothing but another chance. It's going to go one of two ways. You're either going to sink even lower, find ways to make your life harder and meaner. Or you're going to use this time to turn it around, build the kind of life you can be proud of. It's all on you. Let's see what you've got.' " He ran a knuckle along her cheek. "I remember the day he sentenced me — May 19. I send him a thank-you note every year on that day."

She tilted her head, wondering what this had to do with her. With them.

"I need you," he said. "The way I see it, we have months ahead to find out if what we have is really special or if it's just temporary. Nobody ever won a race by standing at the starting line. Let's see what we've got."

She smiled at him. "Let's see."

NINE

Eric didn't pack all his things and move in with Laine. He kept his motel room but slowly, so slowly, transferred personal items to her house. His laundered work clothes, hanging so politely in the dry cleaning bags, went directly to Laine's closet rather than back to the motel and he carried a small duffel back and forth, dropping off clothes. He caught her moving some of his things around between drawers and refolding them. She held up an article of clothing — plaid flannel pants. "What are these?" she asked.

"Pajamas," he said.

"Hmm. What an absurd idea."

He laughed at her and thought to himself, if a man is going to move in with a woman as sexy and tempting as Laine Carrington, it's damn lucky she likes sex. More than that, she fell into cohabitation seamlessly. His days were long and he was up early, yet she would slip into the shower with him and shave his face. "You'd think a mechanic would be more scruffy and less meticulous," she said.

"Would you like me scruffier?" he asked.

"I'd like you to sleep a little later, but I understand you can't."

And yet he'd never felt more rested.

Domesticity appealed to him. He realized that maybe he had moved in with Cara searching for something along these lines. Living with Laine was entirely different — there was a routine, for one thing. Intimacy, for another; intimacy that wasn't limited to sex. Sometimes they cooked together; sometimes it was his turn or she'd cooked earlier in the day. Sometimes they went out or if they'd each had long days, he brought something home. On those evenings when he didn't have to be at the garage, when they read or watched TV, she slowly moved into his space until she was cuddled up to him, soft in his arms, her hair tickling his chin. She brought home another chaise for the deck and on rare sunny days, they walked across the beach to Cooper's. She rubbed his feet and he massaged her shoulders after a karate session at the dojo she'd joined. They found a division of chores that came naturally. He usually did the dishes, they shared the laundry and he pushed the vacuum around because her arm was still weak and sometimes sore. They were always cleaning the bathroom or kitchen — they were equally fussy about those rooms. The one place she wanted autonomy was when she got a rainy-day cooking urge. If he got in her way, she shooed him out of the kitchen. She could be so focused. She allowed him to sit on a bar stool across from her work area. And though he watched her closely, she didn't seem to even notice he was there. All these simple acts brought him amazing comfort.

While he was slow to make that transition from his motel to her house, one day he overheard her say something that stroked his male pride very nicely. At the diner Gina asked Laine, "And when your leave is over and you have to go back to work?"

"I can't even think about it."

Things were good, so good.

Eric didn't necessarily want to put less energy into the service station, but he had been in touch with a couple of his best employees from Eugene to see if there was any interest in relocating to Thunder Point. So far he'd had no success. And then, in the middle of March when the buds were just forming on the plants and trees, when the sun came out more often than it hid, when he'd been a kept man for just a month, a truck pulled up to the station and parked outside the garage doors.

Eric wiped his hands on a rag and went outside to see what the customer needed, but as the man stepped out of the cab, Eric's face split in a huge grin when he recognized Al Michel. He walked toward him and grabbed his hand in a firm grip. "Al," he said. They pulled together, shoulder to shoulder. "What are you doing here?"

Al shrugged. "Just thought I'd check out your new setup," he said. Then he looked around, sizing up the front of the station. "Lucky's, is it?"

"You have no idea." Eric laughed. "Looking for work?"

"I could do some, yeah. Unless you're full up."

"I'm not. In fact, I'm looking for help but the last time I called Eugene, no one knew where you'd gone."

Al shook his head. "The new owner, he has some policies that didn't sit well with me. He brought in some of his own people, lowered some wages — And he's not interested in hiring any gypsies."

"Lowered pay? He wasn't supposed to do that," Eric said, frowning.

"Seems like he forgot what he promised you. You might wanna give Rafael a call, ask him how he's getting along. That man's got a flock of kids and you know kids," he said, rubbing a hand along the back of his neck. "They're so damn stubborn about eating. And they grow out of their shoes all the damn time."

"Last time I talked to him, he was worried about the cost of a move. And his wife's family is in Eugene. I'll check in again and see if anything has changed for him. When can you start here?"

"I travel real light. I'll go find myself a room somewhere and get right to it." He nodded at Eric. "Guess you're gonna make me wear one of those fancy uniforms."

"I'll take care of that for you. And I've got a place for you to stay."

"Ah, appreciate it, Eric, but I'm not real big on roommates. . . ."

Eric shook his head. "No roommates. I've been slowly moving out of my room at the Coastline Inn. I holed up there when I got to town and didn't bother looking for anything permanent because I was busy working on updating the station and pouring a slab for a body shop. Keeping this place open seven days a week at the same time — I never had time to think about moving. I bought a little refrigerator and toaster. The motel has coffee in the morning and there are plenty of places to eat around town. I still have a few things to take out of that room — it's a good weekly rate. Use it as long as you want."

"Where are you hanging your hat these days?"

"I moved in with a woman," he said.

Al whistled. "You move fast."

Eric chuckled. "No, I don't. I've been with her since January and I've been taking one shirt at a time to her house, giving her plenty of time to realize she's lost her mind. But she's crazy, I guess. I can clear the rest of my stuff out of that room in ten minutes and leave you the little appliances."

"Can't wait to meet this mentally challenged woman," Al said with a big smile.

"I'll give her a call . . . ask her what her plans are for dinner. If she's busy, I'll take you to the restaurant at the marina." Eric couldn't stop grinning. "Damn, I'm glad to see you, Al. I'm not real well fixed here. Got two old boys who pumped gas here before I bought the place, Manny came with me and there's Justin — seventeen and full of attitude."

Al smirked. "Sounds like hats and horns all day long."

Eric was thinking, *No way you can make me not love my life right now.* "I'll take you over to the motel. Let you settle in. If you have too much stuff, there's storage space in the garage."

"I never carry more than I can lift, Eric."

Eric cocked his head. "You ever put down any roots? Even for a little while?"

"What constitutes roots? I had a few years here, a few there. I wasn't too impressed with roots. Any of our old customers head this way with the classics?"

"A few. I haven't been looking for them or advertising yet. I've been busy just running the station and the wrench end of things. I guess it's about time for me to get on that. Let me get Manny. He's going to want to say hello. Then I'll take you over to the Coastline Inn."

Eric walked into Laine's house at five-thirty, early for him. He was met with delicious smells and the sound of faint music coming from upstairs. In the kitchen he found a pot simmering. He lifted the lid and just inhaled greedily — his favorite meal, steak soup. Then he climbed the stairs.

Laine was humming to the music; she had her iPod attached to the speakers in the bathroom. There was also the sound of water sloshing around. Eric sat on the bed and took off his boots, smiling to himself. Then on a whim, he took off his shirt and pants.

The soaker tub was large enough for two, but he didn't want to presume too much so he wrapped a towel around his naked body and made a little noise in the bedroom.

"Eric?"

"It's me," he said. He moved into the bathroom.

"You're early," she said.

"And so happy to be early." He dropped the towel and stepped into the tub with her. "Come on, make some room here."

She pulled up her knees for him. "Why are you early?"

"Why are you making steak soup? The sun is shining. You never make big soups or stews when the sun is shining."

"I had an overwhelming day. Nothing I can't handle, but Jesus, does everyone have skeletons in their closets? I was looking for one of my deadbeat dads for the sheriff's department. He was supposed to have left the state and I found him right in North Bend. Working in a garage that, unless I don't know anything, is a chop shop!" She sighed. "Now it's going over to auto theft. The police thought they were just dealing with unpaid child support and alimony but when they lock this guy up, he's never going to pay a dime to his family. I wanted to slug him."

"Did you arrest him?" Eric asked.

"No, I told him he'd won the lottery and asked for his address so I can send him the check. He's so stupid, he doesn't have a clue I figured out what was going on in that garage. Why'd it have to be a garage? *You* have a garage!"

"Not that kind of garage. How'd you find him?"

"It was too easy. He has a shiny new credit card and he likes to pay his cell phone bill with it. And a few other things like sexy lingerie, clubs, booze. No car insurance, rent or doctor's bills, but his cell phone bill goes to an address for some woman's apartment. His last known address was in California and he's used a bunch of different names, but he always pays the cell phone bill. He's very attached to his phone. And of course the imbecile is on Facebook." She shook her head. "He probably has some very valuable pictures on his phone. I'll bet he does Facebook from the phone. And he has to use his real name so all his buds and girls know it's him. The dumb-ass."

Eric frowned. "Wait a minute here. You

found him from a cell phone number? And Facebook? How'd you do that?"

"I sent him an email," she said with a shrug. "Asked him if he was the John Doe who entered a lottery contest in California three years ago at that last known address and promised to send a representative to his place of employment with the paperwork so he could collect."

"Paperwork?"

"I created a form. Easy."

"And he bought that? That you were from the lottery?"

"He didn't ask for ID."

"And what if he'd figured you out? What if he realized he was being tricked?" Eric asked.

"That would have been totally awkward. . . ."

"Or dangerous?"

"Nah. I wasn't confrontational. I would've gone away quietly."

"How did you know? About the chop shop?"

"I could smell it. They weren't open for business. No sign, no opened garage doors, nothing — yet they were full of late model vehicles in varying states of dismantling. Not a big chop shop — a nice small one. So I interviewed him a little — that lottery prize was going to come in handy. I mentioned to him I knew pay on a mechanic's salary could be tight especially with a family, et cetera. Did he want the prize money deposited or mailed to him by special courier? And the idiot asked if he could get the prize in cash because car thieves live on cash. But don't worry, Eric. I was vigilant. Cautious. And armed."

He was quiet. Then he smiled and touched that little dimple in her cheek. "I'm so glad I'm not running from the law. . . ."

"I just wanted a deadbeat dad. I didn't want all that felony drama. This is supposed to be part-time!"

"Scary . . ."

She didn't respond. Then she said, "Are you in the mood for steak soup? You love steak soup."

"I have a new employee. A former employee, actually. He's worked for me on and off since I got into this business. He showed up out of the blue, which he usually does, but today it was just when I was really needing someone like him. His name is Al Michel — damn fine mechanic. I told him I'd see if you have plans and if you're busy — like with steak soup or something else — I can take him to Cliffhanger's for dinner. Oh, and I gave him my motel room."

She grinned at that. "So. You're finally ready to commit?"

"I've committed to bringing the last of my clothes. Come here," he said. "Come closer. I want to feel your naked slippery body up against me."

"I'm not having sex in the tub." She laughed. "I was relaxing. I'm okay with you asking Al over for dinner."

"Are you sure?"

"You have to go get one more bread bowl from Cliff — I stopped and got two. And you can't let him stay too late."

"I'll get the bread bowl. I'll get rid of him early. But you'll like him. He's one of those easy, laid-back wrenches. He'll be good to have around the garage. He's an uncomplicated guy — kind of sticks to himself, but he's not unfriendly at all. You'll see. Just a good old Midwestern farm boy."

Al wasn't old or young, Laine realized immediately. He looked to be in his fifties with a toned body and full head of brown hair threaded with gray. He was very pleasant, had an easy smile, a sense of humor, made eye contact and yet didn't have a lot to say. He came from a small farm town — Boone, Iowa — but left there as a young man. Growing up, they called him Mick, short for Michel. He'd been married once, when he was a very young man, and he must not have been very good at it because his young wife invited him to depart. He'd been single since. He had worked in many different areas — construction, mechanics, the occasional factory, drove a semitruck and did farm work as a fallback. He lived cheap and traveled when he could. He had one sister who was busy saving the human race, one third-world country at a time. She worked for a Christian charity and moved around the world. She was single, as he was, and there was no more family in Iowa, but he still went back there about once a year, just to check in with his hometown.

Then he left to go back to the hotel, thanking her for the great soup. Eric walked him to his truck, then came back to Laine.

"He said to thank you again," Eric said. "And he asked if you were a cop."

That sent up red flags. "Ohhh, he might be hiding something if he caught on to my questions. I'm sorry, I tried not to do that, it's just so automatic!"

"I told him you were a psychologist." Eric laughed. "And he's not hiding anything."

"How do you know?"

"He was one of my first employees in Eugene and my parole office had to approve every one. Al is exactly what he appears to be — a good old farm boy who travels, takes jobs when he needs to, moves around."

"Women?"

"I've seen him with a woman or two," Eric said. "That's all I know. That's all I want to know. Seriously."

"You really like him," she said.

"He's always looking out for me. He was working for me when I found out about Ashley — he thought that was very cool, that I was getting a second chance. I didn't know he'd been married once. Men don't ask those kind of questions, in case you haven't figured that out. I asked him all the places he'd worked and lived and he got a very big kick out of it since I was an ex-con kid and he's fifteen or twenty years older and hasn't been in any trouble. That I know of."

"Isn't it strange? The way he just ambles around, picking up jobs here and there?"

"No," Eric said. "Not in a business like mine. It's good work. Requires skill. And if he was a problem around the shop, I wouldn't welcome him back. All right?"

"I hope you keep an eye on things," she advised.

He pulled her against him. "Laine, it's my store. I keep an eye on everything, everyone.

Even you."

"Hmm," she said, stiffening. "Well, that's good, I guess."

"What's good comes next. Let's see how fast I can do the dishes and get you into bed."

"Okay, I'll help with the dishes."

"You're on the insatiable side," he said.

"That's true, yet another thing I didn't know about myself. Coming home to you is still the best part of my day even if you only *barely* took your last personal item out of your backup motel room."

Al Michel's life wasn't as uncomplicated as he let on, though he worked hard at making it appear so. He'd had troubles just like anyone else. Like Eric, who had that old wild-youth thing to live with. It didn't take him long to get the lay of the land. And, as he got to know some of the folks in town, it was as he expected — there were other folks who looked as though they were holding life together real well, when in fact they had their own issues. That Cooper, very nice guy, found out he had a son by an old girlfriend just a year or so ago. Gina and Mac, they'd gone through a lot before getting to a place where they could combine families and enjoy a peaceful existence —

as peaceful as a house full of teenagers would allow. The young town doctor — he'd lost his wife with the birth of his second child. And Devon? Pretty, young Devon — she'd gotten herself involved in some cult. Of course as a rule folks didn't tell a newcomer like Al their life stories — they told *other* people's stories. Whether it was at the pump, in the diner, out at the beach bar, it didn't matter. All he had to do was answer the question "Who have you met so far?" and the next tale had something to do with one of his new acquaintances.

There was a cute little real estate agent who liked to have a glass of wine at Cliff-hanger's bar. Apparently she didn't have much of a story except that her clothes were too sexy and she was a flirt, two qualities that Al found completely desirable. Her name was Ray Anne and she made him laugh so two Friday nights in a row he financed her wine. Then while he was at work, he heard the little *ping* that an-nounced a customer at the pump and he looked out the window to see her BMW. "I've got this one," he told Justin.

"She must sure do a lot of driving. Isn't that her fourth time here this week?"

"Might be," Al said. "I'm not keeping track. Are you?"

Justin laughed and shook his head. "Yeah," he said. "And so are you."

He was, in fact. He enjoyed Ray Anne's company and looked forward to every encounter.

In no time at all he could tell he was well-liked in town. Probably because he was a real friendly sort. He'd look over the menu at the diner and ask Gina, "What's good today?" And she'd tell him exactly what to order. He was never unhappy and always left a generous tip. The same applied at the deli and again at Cooper's place on the beach. All his change went into a big jar that he would soon begin taking to the local bank every month to have added to his new account. It was so simple and tidy.

He found there was much about Thunder Point to suit him. That ordinary little motel room worked just fine. He tended to like boarding houses. He only had to be concerned about himself and one room yet there was a sense of family, even if it was usually a haphazardly thrown together and odd family, but no attachment required. Boarding houses were almost a thing of the past and pretty hard to find. He thought the demise of the boarding house was a great loss to society.

This town, with its clinic, diner, beach

bar, deli and garage, it was like a big boarding house. He got used to seeing the same
people over and over and before very long
they were not just cordial, but connected,
making him feel like a new friend. And that
was really all Al was looking for.

Al had known Manny for a long time.
Manny had been with Eric for a good eight
years and helped to manage a lot of the
business. He was good under the hood and
with restoration and body repair — he could
really do it all. Al was good at engines and
priceless at keeping things spotless. And
Manny liked paperwork, which Al hated.

He'd been in Thunder Point and back in
Eric's shop for a few weeks when Eric said,
"I'm putting Justin with you. He wants to
learn a few things about engine repair and I
figured when things are running a little slow
at night, maybe you can show him a thing
or two."

"If that's what you want," Al said.

"Try to soften him up a little, will you?
He's prickly as a cactus. I don't know if it's
because he's seventeen or if he has other
problems. I'd like the kid to have a chance."

"What makes you think he doesn't have a
chance?" Al asked.

Eric shook his head. "He reminds me of
me. Except Justin hasn't figured out cool

yet. I had too much cool for my own good. This kid, he just doesn't add up."

"I'll pay attention," Al said. "I'll ask him if he wants me to show him a few things." But, he thought, most of us probably don't add up.

TEN

April brought yet more sunshine to Thunder Point and Laine felt her life was more stable than it had been in too long.

She was enjoying working as a consultant for the sheriff's department, researching their investigations to advise on driving their prosecution to the federal level. She was also doing the odd job for the Bureau. The sheriff's department work was more satisfying than consulting for the Bureau, but it occurred to her that she could make a painless career doing background checks for schools, industry, law enforcement, et cetera. The problem for Laine was that she kept tripping over infractions. Serious and felonious breaches. A routine check for admission to the police department turned up a felon who failed to disclose his long and rather colorful record; a teacher application to a public school showed a history of sex crimes in another state. She was like a bloodhound — she could smell it. Her instincts had become razor-sharp. She knew she was useful in this new capacity and that worked for her for now.

She was also getting back in shape. The dojo she had joined was an excellent workout facility and she had a private instructor and well-known acupuncturist — her shoulder and elbow hardly bothered her these days. The town of Thunder Point was her new playground; she had friends and fun — two things that had never registered high on her list of priorities. And she had Eric, the kind of wonderful, smart, passionate man she never expected to have in her life.

But she hadn't seen Pax or his family since Christmas. Missy was getting ready for her spring concert. Sissy was practicing for a dance recital. She had the time and the money to get home to check in with them, feel the hugs of the little girls and experience that odd connection with Pax that only twins had. They'd often talked about it, the way they knew when they needed each other, and speculated on how logical it was for identical twins and how illogical for fraternal, who were mere siblings. And yet . . .

"What about Senior?" Pax asked.

"I'd rather skip that, if you don't mind.

Unless he insists on being present for the concert or something."

"I'll mention to Genevieve that you're still avoiding him. I'll ask her not to call him. The truth is, I haven't seen much of him lately. I talk to him every week, just long enough for each of us to say we're fine and nothing is new. And our schedules are . . . You know how they are. I think it's very unlikely he'd make a surprise visit while you're here. In fact, if I were an investigator, I'd suspect him of laying low since that row at Christmas. He offended everyone, not just you."

"I drew a line in the sand," she said. "We don't communicate again until he apologizes and stops ridiculing me. He went too far."

"He did," Pax agreed. "And if by some wildly unlikely coincidence he shows up over here or we run into him, we're all going to be grown-ups and no blowups. Right?"

"Right," she agreed. "I never meant for this to hurt you. I can live with whatever you want. If you want us to have a little family party, a reunion, I can go with that. But I'm not giving him my new phone number."

"You weren't wrong. He was out of line. But listen, all I want is to be a good brother, a good husband, a decent father to my girls. And I know you don't think Genevieve is quite good enough for me, but she is my wingman."

In spite of herself, Laine actually sucked in a breath. He was so devoted to Genevieve. But *she* was supposed to be his wingman!

"My other wingman," he said patiently. "I rely on my wife to not only support this fellowship, this career choice that keeps me awake at night and gone on weekends and birthdays, but I'm counting on her to let me know when my girls need their father. And she's made it clear — if I start to show signs of being the kind of father Senior is, with unreasonable expectations of our girls, I'm in serious trouble."

"I give her a lot of credit for that," Laine said. Laine had always felt their mother was too patient with Senior, excusing his impossible-to-please attitude toward Laine. Janice had occasionally said, "Shut up, Paxton!" But not often enough.

"I'll be there Wednesday," she said. "I'm only staying two days. Please let me have a sleepover with the girls. I'll be unbearably nice to Genevieve."

"You'll stay with us, as usual," he said. "No tattoos for the girls."

Then she broke it to Eric. "I miss them so much," she said. "I'm okay being away from them when I'm deep in some case, but when I was working four or five days a week I just couldn't stand it if I couldn't be with them on my days off. If it wasn't such short notice, I'd ask you to come along. Next time, I promise."

"What about your dad?" he asked. "You going to talk to him? Make up with him?"

She turned away from him.

He turned her back. "Level with me. What would your mother think of this situation?"

"My mother always said we were too much alike, equally stubborn and pigheaded — two people who had to be right. And when I lost my mother, I lost the buffer between us. I told you that when I was visiting Pax over the holidays, my father was even more cruel than I can remember. God," she said, looking down. "It embarrasses me to even tell you this. . . ."

"You can tell me anything," he said.

"I told him I'd been recommended for a service award, for saving lives." Tears gathered in her eyes. "He said I'd lost my mind and deserved an award for being the biggest idiot. That only a fool would take the risks I took routinely and if I wanted to save lives, there were more logical, safer and profitable ways." She took a breath. "My arm was still in a sling, I was feeling pretty weak and vulnerable and not too sure of myself. Then he said if I expected him to celebrate the fact that I'd stopped a bullet I was dreaming. Didn't I know doctors saved lives every day without putting themselves in mortal danger? And I lost it. I told him he was a self-centered bastard and I was finished with his criticism and his disrespectful treatment. He said I was the disrespectful one and he was bloody tired of my bragging and wearing my close calls like a badge of honor. There was a lot of arguing that evolved into yelling. It was horrible."

There was a long moment of silence before Eric said, "Wow."

"It disrupted the whole family. Pax was furious with him and worried about me. The girls were upset and scared. Genevieve was stunned. But for me, there was just no more going on. I was recovering from an injury that nearly cost me my life and he accused me of showing off! I haven't spoken to him since. He's a popular doctor, pretty well-liked as doctors go even if he can be a narcissistic dick sometimes. . . . But the way he talks to me? It's terrible. And it hurts. It just . . . hurts."

Eric was speechless. Finally he asked,

"And your mother?"

"A goddess. One of the kindest, most generous women I've ever known. She was completely supportive. She hated that he wasn't and most of the time she could shut him up before he said something really awful. She always said that Pax had more of her temperament, a much gentler nature, and I had more of my father's. She said my father could have made a good operative — he's fearless and stubborn and there's no one more determined."

"And she put up with that from your father?"

"They loved each other. He didn't give her any shit and she could put him in his place with one word. But then she died and he was on the loose. There was no one to keep him in line."

"He must not know how much this hurts you," Eric said.

"Oh, I think he knows," she said. "And he thinks his opinions are more important than my feelings. So I'm done. Unless he can change his attitude, I don't need him in my life. The problem is — I'm thirty-three, I've been putting up with this my whole life, and it can still break my heart."

Eric pulled her into his arms and held her. "I'm sorry, baby. I wish I knew of a solution. . . ."

"This is the solution," she said. "I have to let it go. Let him go. And carry on. I miss my mother every day."

"Oh, she's not all that far away," he said, brushing her hair away from her face. "I've had your dumplings, remember."

She smiled back at him. "Boy, have you ever."

Laine remembered when her mother had said, *"Do what makes your heart beat."* She said that right until she died. But she had also said, *"You don't need approval and you don't need an excuse or explanation for living your own life. Remember that."*

Oh, she remembered. But it was easy for her mother, who had the approval of her parents and her husband and her children. Easy for Pax, who had done as he was expected to do. Laine was the only one who had really defied custom, gone her own way, quite successfully, and yet was considered by her father to be a failure.

She had Eric's support and even though they were still new, that meant so much to her. She was so anxious to have Pax get to know him. In fact, Eric and Pax were a lot alike, when she thought about it.

She flew to San Francisco and took the

red-eye into Boston. She had given Pax the flight details and said she would be waiting at his house when the girls came home from school and when he was done at the hospital. But when she deplaned at 8:30 a.m. there were two little blonde bombshells standing on the curb near the taxi line, jumping up and down, yelling at her. "Auntie Lainie! Auntie Lainie!"

It took her a moment to catch her breath. She put her hand to her chest and gasped in sheer, tear-gathering delight. She opened her arms to them and they rushed her, nearly knocking her over. "My babes, my angels! Are you angels? You promised you would be angels!"

They giggled and said, one at a time, "You said to be devils!" and "We were very bad, like you said!"

"Oh, thank goodness! I'm proud of you!"

"And we have blue polish for our toes," Missy said.

"And I have silver," Sissy said.

"But you have school!"

There was a fit of fake coughing. "We're very sick!" Sissy said.

"I can see that, poor devils!"

Laine stood up and looked into the kind blue eyes of the sister-in-law she made work so hard for her affection. "I told Pax I'd grab a cab."

"We can't have that," Genevieve said.

"I can't believe you kept them home from school. You never do that!"

"You only have two days," she said. "We don't want to waste a second of it. The girls are so thrilled. You guys really have to use Skype more often."

"How did you know to wait by the cab line?" Laine asked.

Genevieve just laughed. "You? Check a bag? For a couple of days? Laine, you'd take carry-on to Europe!"

Well, true enough, she thought. "Breakfast?" Laine asked.

"Whatever you want. Did you sleep on the plane?"

"I can sleep anywhere," she lied. It used to be true.

"I wish I could," Genevieve said. "Let's get breakfast, then you can play."

Play? It wasn't exactly play as it completely wore Laine out, but it was fun. They started off with rehearsing — Missy on her cello and Sissy wearing her tutu and dancing around the family room. Before long Missy and Laine wore makeshift tutus and were learning dance steps from Sissy. Then it was time to do art in the kitchen — clay and paints. Then lunch, then makeovers —

fingers and toes, mani-pedis. Baths and hair curling. Then off to a dress rehearsal for Sissy's dance recital at four; Laine couldn't miss it as she would miss the actual performance a week later. Then home for pizza and the elementary school strings concert at seven. Of course Genevieve's two sisters and her parents were also there. Pax showed up at the last minute, wearing scrubs, of course. He had barely escaped the hospital and was on his way back the second it was over.

"How do you stand it?" Laine asked Genevieve.

"The concert? Or the doctor's hours?"

"Well, since you mentioned it — either one."

"I've learned not to hear too much of the music. It reminds me a lot of slaughter day at the farm. As for the hours, I think about what baby or little kid he might be operating on — that gets me past the jealousy. I complain, though. I don't want to, I don't mean to, but I complain."

"You probably get lonely."

"Lonely for adult company, even though the girls fill up the days and nights. We try to schedule time together," she whispered. "But the doctor he works for is such a nasty dick and I think he enjoys messing up our little bit of family time!"

Laine chuckled behind her hand and whispered back, "I've never heard you use that word before."

"Pax has never worked for such a dick before. Really, he's impossible. He owns my husband. And he doesn't deserve him."

After the concert came ice cream, after ice cream it was pajamas and then it was back rubs with lotion. The girls would sleep in the guest room's big king-size bed with Laine. It had been such a big day, they were both asleep in minutes.

Laine stumbled into the family room, where she heard the TV volume turned low. Her sister-in-law sat on the sofa, her feet propped up on an ottoman, a bottle of wine open and breathing on a tray that also held two glasses.

"Oh, my goodness," Laine said happily. "How did you know I wouldn't be passed out in the bed between two little blondes?"

"I think it was when you tried to order Cabernet ice cream at Baskin-Robbins," she said, lifting the bottle. "Plus, you're on West Coast time — you should be rockin' until midnight, at least. But, I was prepared to drink alone if necessary. I got a text from Pax that he should be home in an hour, which usually means three. But I like to wait up if I can."

Laine slumped in the corner of the sectional beside Genevieve. "I think that ice-cream guy was a little rude to me. He couldn't take a joke."

"You were joking?" Genevieve poured two glasses, handed one to Laine and toasted her. "Welcome home," she said.

Laine took a sip and then was stilled for a moment. "This *has* been my home. This house more than the house I grew up in, at least since my mom died."

"I told you when we got engaged — our home is always your home. It always will be. I know giving him up to me was hard for you."

Laine shrugged. "Don't make me out to be too possessive. I knew I'd have to give him up to a wife eventually. I just didn't realize he'd decide to get married when he was twelve."

Genevieve laughed at her. "We were pretty young. I could have waited a couple of years, but Pax —"

"Fell hard," Laine interjected. "Hard and fast."

"He's always like that — when he decides he wants something, he's single-minded. A lot like his twin. How's the arm, Lainie?"

She flexed and straightened it as if on

demand. "Better. I haven't been able to do a push-up yet, but I've been working out in a dojo and getting some acupuncture. I think if the girls didn't wreck me today, I'm in pretty good shape."

"You look wonderful," Genevieve said. "Something in the water out there on the coast?"

"Yeah." She laughed. "Fish. The sun just made its debut a couple of weeks ago. Did Pax tell you? I'm doing a little part-time investigative work for the sheriff's department. And the Bureau has sent me a little work — nothing big, but enough to keep me busy so I'm not sitting around, just waiting for something to happen. As it turns out, I'm not really crazy about time off."

"You never have been, but then you've never been shot before. And even though you and Senior have always had your issues, I don't think I've ever seen you as angry as you were at Christmas."

"I hope I apologized for that. I shouldn't have put you and the girls through that hideous shouting match."

"You apologized two or three times and each time I told you I didn't blame you for being angry. He crossed the line, suggesting a commendation for saving lives wasn't impressive or important. Sometimes I just don't know what's the matter with that man."

"Aside from being an arrogant ass, not too much. . . ."

"I encourage Pax to ignore him, but let me tell you something — he won't talk to my daughters that way or he'll answer to me."

"But you had to take them out of the room because I was yelling and Senior was giving it right back to me."

"I took them out of the room to explain that tempers were lost and that their grandfather behaved very badly to you. We're very proud of you. We're *all* very proud of you. Sometimes a little worried, but proud. That six months undercover somewhere that turned out to be Oregon, that was scary. The FBI is so good about checking in, letting Pax know that you were all right, but until it was over we had no idea what you might be doing or where you might be doing it. I just hope I can be as brave as your mother was — I hope I can encourage my daughters to do what makes them happy." She took a sip of wine. "Judging from the past week, I don't think it will be either music or dance."

Laine laughed. "That does seem kind of obvious."

"But you knew at an early age. That's so lucky, isn't it? We all live for your visits, Laine. You have to know that."

"You've always done that, made me feel welcome when I'm sure I disrupt everything. I know I'm not easy," she added reluctantly.

"You're a cop. An agent," Genevieve said with a shrug. "A twin. I knew what I was getting into."

Laine cocked her head and studied Genevieve. "Have you changed?"

Genevieve shook her head and just laughed.

"Are you pregnant or something?"

"Are you kidding me? I'm done with that — two is enough for us. Two of our own and the thousands Pax treats and I volunteer for."

Laine burrowed back in the elbow of the plush sectional and gently swirled her wine. "Something's different about you," she said. "I'm trying to figure out what it is. . . ."

Genevieve laughed again. "Auntie Lainie, it's not me. It's you."

"Me? I'm the same! Nothing different about me."

"Except the radiance. The shine. The calm. You've always been very cool on the outside, but it doesn't usually feel like it goes too deep."

"Well, like I said, I've never taken an extended leave before. And I might have a better appreciation for living. I have to keep that in perspective. . . ."

Genevieve was shaking her head. "You're in love."

Laine was shocked. "Bull pucky," she said. "I have a guy, that's all. Not my first guy, either. Though I haven't had many good ones."

"You're in love. Tell me about him. Everything. The secret things."

Laine sat straighter. "Okay, you're totally different. You never swore, you never called people dicks, you never asked me about guys or secret stuff. What's going on here?"

Genevieve took a breath. "We never spend time alone together. You just didn't see me," she said. "It's all right, I completely understand it. If some interloper came into my life and said she was taking my place as my sister's new best friend, I wouldn't be impressed or real accepting. I wouldn't like that person a lot."

"Did I treat you like that? Like you were an interloper?"

"Oh, of course not," Genevieve said, lifting the wine bottle and tipping it over Laine's glass. "You'd never do anything to hurt Pax — he's your best friend. No, you've always been very respectful. Cordial. Tolerant."

Laine gasped.

Genevieve smiled. "Wallpaper," she said. "I was wallpaper — something in the background. You could see the color but not the pattern. Sometimes I felt more like a mother-in-law than a sister-in-law, but I knew you'd come around. And see? You came around. You finally have more than one best friend!"

"What the hell . . ."

"Pax had you *and* me. Not you *or* me. I had my sisters. But you — you had Pax. Only Pax — and you were so bonded to him. Closer than just brother and sister — like the other half of each other."

"My mother," she said. "There was always my mother. . . ."

"Not the same," Genevieve said, shaking her head. "You've always shared your mother, since before birth. And now you're in love. Oh, you can deny it if you want to, but you're so gone it's awesome. I want to know what happened!"

Laine thought for a moment and then she said, "There was this guy in town and I kept running into him. I knew he liked me — eyes, body language, he was obvious. I'm a trained interrogator, you know. But he was holding off. So I asked him out. And then I might've fallen for him a little bit. Even though we have nothing in common. Nothing. Well, except maybe the way we are together."

"Tell me how you are together," Genevieve asked, looking a little wild-eyed.

Laine frowned. "Only if you promise *never* to tell me how you and Pax are together. . . ."

Genevieve giggled and pulled the throw from the back of the sectional and covered their legs. "Promise," she said.

"Are you sure it's me?" Laine asked. "Because I think this is a new side of you!"

"It's you," she insisted. "Now hurry up and tell me the good stuff before Pax gets home and distracts us."

"Okay. All right. Well, he's got the most amazing green eyes I've ever seen. And he's strong because he works on cars, but not athletic — not into the same stuff I'm into. And he's very interested in my self-defense maneuvers, challenging me all the time, because he's just a guy, like Pax. . . . So I've had to throw him a couple of times. Which I think he secretly likes. And then there's a whole bunch of other background stuff that makes us even more opposite. . . ."

"But how does he make you *feel*?"

"Like the only woman in the world."

"Oh." Genevieve sighed. "I know that feeling!"

Pax walked into the house at midnight. He found his wife and sister snuggled under a throw on the couch, a couple of wineglasses on a tray on the floor. He bent over and picked up the wine bottle and tilted it. They'd almost killed it.

This was something he thought he'd never see — his sister cozied up to his wife, asleep. They didn't actually dislike each other, but they'd never really taken to each other. Until tonight?

He noticed Genevieve looking at him through barely opened eyes. She was smiling. It was a sly, secret smile. He had known for a long time that his wife admired Laine and wanted to be closer. But Laine was a pill.

Apparently while he worked late at the hospital, some sort of magic had happened between his two most beloved women.

ELEVEN

Al got a big kick out of Eric. He always had. That Eric — he was at once serious and easygoing, a rare and welcome combination. That's why when he was looking for work, looking for a change, he'd often find himself back at Eric's garage. This time, this new town suited him fine.

While Eric's girlfriend was back East visiting family she was texting Eric pictures of herself and her nieces making faces, painting their toenails blue, eating pizza or ice cream, dressed up in tutus — all of them, including Laine. Eric showed Al every one. Then she returned to Thunder Point and Eric seemed to go missing. He left the station early and gave Al the keys to the tow trucks.

Al was growing fond of the little town. He now had several acquaintances, folks he saw almost daily. He liked the diner for breakfast and got to know Gina and the owner, Stu.

Mac, the deputy, was a regular presence all over town. Now and then he saw Hank Cooper and he spent a little time at the beach if he wasn't at work, just to sit out on the deck at Cooper's to check out the morning or watch the sunset. And there was Cliffhanger's at the marina for a fancier meal. He figured out right off the bat that Ray Anne was a regular both there and at the diner so he began to watch for her, which wasn't hard — now that she knew Al's work hours Eric had confirmed that she seemed to need a lot more gas than she had in the past. She was a consummate flirt and Al never got tired of attention from a pretty woman. He could guess she was as old as he was, possibly held together with duct tape and bailing wire just under those tight clothes, but she sure looked good for a woman of a few years. He liked looking at the girls, but he couldn't quite get interested in women who could be younger than his daughter, if he had one. Ray Anne had a mature sense of humor and it was clear she'd been around the block. This was good for him, since he'd probably been around a few more blocks than she had.

"What does a man like you do on days off?" she asked him when they were sitting in the diner one day.

"You're looking at it," he said. "Nothing too exciting. Sometimes, if I have a project, like a salvaged car to work on, Eric welcomes me to use his shop. Then he expects first bid on a restored vehicle. And he's got a kid working for him — Justin Russell. He has me training him."

"How's that working out?"

He shrugged and said, "It's going okay. He's seventeen."

In fact, it was working out great. Al was getting attached to the kid. There was a time — a very long time ago — when he was a young man that he'd expected to inherit his father's farm in Iowa, settle down and have a bunch of kids. While his father had been pretty harsh, Al was a patient man. Even though he had only a sister, he and his young wife thought a big farm family would suit them. Then the marriage didn't work and that idea limped into an uneasy death. But that was a long time ago and it didn't mean he had stopped appreciating the humor and challenge of kids even though he obviously wasn't meant to have any.

The more responsibility Al gave Justin, the more Justin warmed up to him. Al not only showed Justin how to service the cars and trucks, but also had him filling out the paperwork for invoices. "This brake job is four hundred, one fifty is parts, the rest labor," he'd informed the teenager. "Then figure the tax and I'll show you how to run the credit card because no one has cash anymore. We do a few of these together and you'll be president of the company."

"What company?" Justin asked with a laugh.

"Okay, you'll never be president, but you'll be irreplaceable. You're brilliant. You hungry?"

Justin laughed at him and began on the paperwork for the invoice.

"I'm going to get us a pizza," Al said.

"I can help with that, too," the kid said.

In the few weeks Al had been there he watched as Lucky's became a little bit of a hangout, too. Laine was there regularly, whether she'd been out for a run or on her way home from one of her consulting jobs. She often checked in, asking Eric what they should do for dinner. When Mac filled up the sheriff's department SUV, he managed to stay awhile because the crew at Lucky's made good company. Such was the case with many residents. And, of course, there were Ray Anne's visits, seldom for a full tank and never in a big hurry. If Al was aware she was at the pump, he took the job. He wiped off his hands, excused the rest of

234

the garage team and spent a little quality time on Ray Anne's little BMW. He knew he did a lot of grinning while she was there.

Eric said, "You ever wonder how she walks in those shoes?"

Al had lifted a brow and said, "Walking is way overrated."

On one of her passes through the station she said, "I guess I'll see you tomorrow night at Cliff's, since it's your night off."

"I guess so," he answered.

"You know, one of these nights you'll have to stay for dinner. . . ."

"I've had dinner there a time or two," he said, grinning. "But I'm thinking it's about time for something Italian."

"Sure," she said, clearly disappointed.

"You can probably recommend a good place."

"Of course," she said. "I'm a full-service Realtor."

"I thought you could. Let's see — I'll get to Cliff's around five. Maybe five-thirty. That's about when you get there, right? You think of some good Italian place and I'll take you out. How's that?"

The disappointment on her face melted instantly into a look of pure pleasure. "That would be perfect. I know all the best restaurants in Coos County."

"I'm not surprised."

Al found himself looking forward to a dinner out with Ray Anne more than he'd looked forward to a date in a long while, and it was entirely successful, starting with their hysterical laughter when he folded himself up in her BMW. "I don't know if this is gonna work," he said.

"I can't get in that truck!" she said, laughing. "It's as far off the ground as I am tall! And I'm in a tight skirt and heels!"

"And those heels do you proud, too. You don't weigh much. I could pick you up and throw you in," he suggested.

"Aw, you don't think I weigh much? Not only do I love you for that, I can eat more Italian tonight than I'd planned to. Now just put your chin on your knees like a good boy and let me worry about getting you there!"

"Drive carefully," he said. "If you hit a berm or pylon, I'll have to have my knees removed from the back of my head."

She took him to a hole-in-the-wall restaurant decorated with plastic vines and grapes and he told her he'd forgotten his reading glasses and asked her to order for them both. She did an expert job and they laughed all through dinner. He wanted to know all about what it was like growing up in Coos County and she wanted to know what it was like just moving from job to job with no real commitments.

"It's not exactly like that," he said. "I've worked for a few of the same people, like Eric, who are willing to hire me even though I don't seem to be looking for a career. In a dozen years I've worked for Eric several different times, then I'd hear from someone who needs help or wants me back for a contract they can't fulfill without extra help. I don't like the north in the winter, I don't like the south in the summer. I'm not saving up for a European vacation or big house, that's just how I roll. I like Eric. I don't work for people who don't prove to me they're honest and straightforward and Eric is."

"So you'll move on and probably come back in six months or a year?" she asked.

He tilted his head, wrinkled his brow and said, "That just seems to be the way of it. Maybe I like too many things. I like driving a truck, like mechanics, and since I was raised on a farm, that still has appeal. I go back to Iowa just about every year even though there's hardly anyone there I know anymore. Sometimes I hang around, help out old neighbors."

"What happened to the family farm?" she asked.

"We gave it up. Sold it. There's just my sister and me. She gave her half to charity and I put my half into a few bonds and a new truck. It wasn't that much land. It seemed like way too much farm when I was working it, but once it was for sale it turned out to be a little dinky farm."

"Do you miss it?" she asked.

"I do," he admitted. "But I didn't want to be a farmer all alone and with no other siblings and my parents gone, it didn't hold much appeal. Plus, it didn't take me long to see I could do without those really bad Midwestern winters. . . ."

Ray Anne, he learned, loved what she did and where she did it. Loved it with a passion. Thunder Point was an easy place to live, she knew everyone, and her work took her all over Coos County and beyond. She loved being with people all day, as many days a week as she could stand it. She had a few really good friends in town, made a decent if modest living, mostly by managing rental property in the area, and life was as she liked it — maybe not cosmopolitan but satisfying. "If I could've talked Cooper out of that beachfront property, the commission would've been incredible, but the greedy bastard wouldn't let it go. I love him, but that was on the selfish side."

When they finally left the restaurant after a long dinner, Ray Anne drove them back to Cliff's, Al's chin on his knees. His truck sat in the parking lot, looking pretty lonely. It was late and the restaurant was near closing.

She turned toward him. "If you're interested, you could follow me home to my house for a nightcap or cup of coffee."

Al frowned a little bit. He gently touched her shoulder. "Listen, that's nice. I have to mention a couple of things. You already know — I'm not likely to be here long-term. If I'm here a year, that's real long-term for me."

"I know," she said, smiling. "If I date you a month, you're really something. I didn't ask you if you wanted to make an investment. I asked you if you wanted a drink."

"The other thing . . . I was married. It was a while ago. Over thirty years. I wasn't good at it. I haven't been tempted since."

And she laughed.

"I know you don't think that's funny," he said.

"I do, as a matter of fact. I've been married three times. I'm a very slow learner. Apparently I'm not good at it, either. And

239

I'm not looking for a family, for God's sake."

"What are you looking for?" he asked. "Because I like you, but I don't want to end up in a bad situation. You know — where we're angry at each other because of someone's failed expectations. I like my job, the town, you, and I hate drama. I'd like things easy. Do you know what I mean?"

"Can we start with a drink?" she asked. "I like you, too. I think I'm past romantic expectations. Or illusions."

"How old are you?" he asked.

She shrugged. "Forty-two," she said. "Or fifty-two. Or sixty-one. I can never remember. How important is that?"

He grinned. "Show me the way, Ms. Ray Anne."

He pried himself out of that little car, found his way into his truck with some relief in his joints. He followed her to a little house up the hill. It was a comfortable, small house, maybe a little overdecorated — lots of mirrors and candles and other girlie things. He had a Scotch. It turned out there was no duct tape or bailing wire involved in her figure — Ray Anne was nicely put together.

He left in the morning. With a smile on his face.

■ ■ ■ ■

When Laine stopped by the diner on her way home one sunny afternoon, Ashley was behind the counter. She said, "Mom said to send you out to Cooper's if you dropped by today."

"What's up?" she asked.

"I think it's an impromptu hen party. In the sun for a change, instead of in a back booth."

"Sounds like a good plan," she said. "I'm walking and leaving my car right where it is."

"I'll make sure my new stepfather doesn't tow it, how's that?"

"You are a generous woman," Laine said with a laugh.

By the time she got just past the marina she could hear the laughter of women floating down the beach. It put a little spring in her step. How long had it really been since she'd had the kind of women friends who could laugh like idiots over every other comment? She'd had women friends, of course, even though law enforcement was still dominated by men. But friends like these — from various walks of life, from waitress to Coast Guard pilot recently retired? Not even in college! If Eric was the greatest benefit from this hiatus from the FBI, the women here were a close second.

She could see them up there, commanding the deck. They had pulled a couple of tables together, divided by generation. At one small, round table sat Lou McCain and her best friends Carrie James, Gina's mother and the deli owner, and Ray Anne Dysart, Realtor extraordinaire. At the table next to them were Gina, then Sarah, Cooper's very pregnant wife, and Devon.

"Laine! Hurry! You have to hear this!" Gina shouted.

Laine took the steps two at a time.

"Maybe she already knows," Ray Anne said.

"Know what?"

"She's seeing Al, from the station," Lou announced.

"I didn't say 'seeing,' " Ray Anne corrected. "I said we'd been out to dinner a couple of times. We happened to show up for happy hour at Cliff's more than once, decided to have dinner."

"At Cliffhanger's?" Laine asked.

"Well, no. We just went to Bandon — not too far. We had Italian once. And once we went out for Chinese. And ended up getting takeout . . ." She fluttered her lashes.

Everyone howled.

"How's he like that pole-dancing routine?" Lou asked, laughing.

"As a matter of fact, I took pole-dancing lessons to keep my legs in shape and he said he liked what I did to a pair of high heels. So there! He's very polite. Not like you, Louise."

"He is polite," Laine acknowledged. "Very nice man."

"Handsome man," Sarah said. "He's been out here a couple of times and he pumped my gas last week. He has very good teeth."

"Yes, he does," Ray Anne said. "I'm not even sure how old he is."

"Yes, but does he know how old you are?" Carrie asked.

"Pfffttt. I don't even know how old I am."

"We do," Carrie and Lou said in unison, making everyone laugh again.

Laine reached over and gave Sarah's hand a pat. "How are you feeling?"

"All right," she said. "I'm not sure where I'm going to put two more months of little girl."

"A girl, then?" she asked.

Sarah smiled a little sentimentally. "Exactly what I ordered. We have Landon — he's graduating in June. And Cooper has Austin. A girl should fit in just right. I asked

Cooper to give me a girl and he got right on it." Then she grinned.

"Is the house going to be done in time?" Laine asked.

Cooper appeared in the doorway. "The way she's riding the contractors, they're afraid for their lives. They'll make it. Something to drink, Laine?" he asked.

"Whatever the big girls are drinking, I'll have one."

He ran a hand over Sarah's shoulder. "Honey?"

"Water?" she asked, looking up at him sweetly.

He leaned down and kissed her forehead and all the women said, *"Awwww"* at the same time.

Sarah looked over her shoulder, following Cooper's departure back into the bar. Then she leaned close to the women to share. "Have you heard of those pregnant women who just crave sex all the time?" she asked in a lowered tone. They all leaned forward expectantly. "I'm not one of them," she said.

And they came apart in laughter yet again.

"How about the baby daddy?" Lou asked.

"He hasn't changed," Sarah said. "You think he'd be intimidated by this big mound, but no."

"We have to talk about the shower," Gina

said. "We haven't had a really good party since their wedding."

"What kind of shower?" Sarah asked.

They all looked at her very strangely. Cooper chose that moment to bring her a water and Laine a glass of wine. "Baby, Sarah," he said. "Baby shower. You're pregnant."

"I mean, just for girls? Or for men, too."

"Aw, please," Cooper said, pathetically. "For girls. Please."

"But sweetheart, I want you to be involved, to be able to play all the baby games!" she said.

"Oh, God," he said, turning away. "Can't you just shoot me?" he was heard to mutter inside the bar.

When he was gone the women were laughing again. "You have no idea the strain Cooper is under," Sarah said. "He's trying to do everything he can to make me happy, to help me, and a couples shower might put him over the edge. Right now he'd give anything to trade places with me. For one pass on a baby shower, he'd be willing to carry her *and* push her out."

An hour later Laine and Devon were walking back across the beach together. Lou was dropping off Gina at home, Carrie was hanging around the beach a little while to talk to Rawley about his deli orders for the rest of the week, Ray Anne was off in her fancy little car to get a little work done.

"Do you have to go back to work?" Laine asked her.

"Scott's holding down the fort. I'll at least check appointments, messages and ask him if anything's going on before I head out for the day. Spencer is coaching track and field till the end of term so he won't be done early and I have kids to pick up in an hour. How about you? Done for the day?"

"Except to check the computer to see if I have any emails. Not urgent. A night like tonight deserves something on the grill. I think I'll run by the station and see what Eric is in the mood for."

"Tell him I said hi."

They parted in the street. Laine took her car from the front of the diner while Devon went into the clinic. She drove the short distance to the garage, but parked in front of the big doors and not at the pump. She went inside to find that Eric was leaning into an engine and the long legs sticking out from under the car must have belonged to Al. Eric ducked out from under the hood and looked at her. He grabbed a rag from the back pocket of his coverall. His eyes sparkled and he smiled as he wiped his hands.

She had found him in January, moved him in with her in February. It was the middle of April and he still looked at her as if she were brand-new. It hadn't been that long, really, but still . . . There was something about that look, that twinkle, that smile that promised he would see her that way forever.

She had not known she could have this kind of life.

The next day Eric had errands in Bandon — he was in search of some new tires for a customer and a haircut for himself. He stopped at a small market on the edge of town — his assignment from Laine had been baby blond potatoes, Vidalia onions, two large carrots, frozen peas, sour cream and Dijon mustard. He had no idea what this would become, something that was going to combine with chicken, but his mouth watered just the same. She was so right about him — it turned him on to see her cook. What a throwback to an earlier time he was. Also on his list was a box of tampons. He figured that was some kind of test, like a husband test. He laughed at himself. He should bring home a boat and rod and reel instead, like the old joke — guy goes into a store for tampons and comes home with a bunch of sporting equipment because the salesman convinced him, *Well, you might as well go fishing.* . . .

He didn't even have the first item in the basket when he saw Justin. He was alone, pushing a cart away from Eric.

It was probably the sight of Justin's shaggy haircut that caused Eric to run a hand around the back of his neck. He'd just gotten himself a nice trim and suddenly he knew quite a few things. Justin wasn't getting a haircut in a barber shop, he wasn't in school, he was shopping for food for the family. Was he the man of the house, with his father gone and his mother unemployed?

Eric followed him a little, pretending to look at certain items, glancing out of his peripheral vision to see where the kid was headed. It didn't take him long before he was checking out. He used some kind of credit card. This didn't take a brilliant investigator — the cashier didn't smile, Justin looked down, the total was reached, Justin bagged his own groceries and took back the card and the receipt. It had to be a voucher for food, the new form of food stamps. But what was he doing way over here? There was a grocery store in Thunder Point.

Justin left the store and Eric finally got around to getting the rest of the items on his list. He was back at the garage just after lunch. It wasn't unusual for Al to be there already, though he was early. During the morning and early afternoon Eric could leave the station in Manny's capable hands with either Norm or Howie or both to help him, while the afternoon and evening were his with Al, sometimes Justin and one of the old boys.

Eric put his vegetables in the refrigerator they kept in the garage. He went to talk to Al.

"So, what can you tell me about Justin?"

"Kid's doing great," Al said. "He's keeping up with his regular work, learning new things, writing up invoices and even helping with ordering parts. He's a whiz on the computer. He likes it, his mood is civilized, he's good with customers. He's happy twenty-five percent of the time, which for a seventeen-year-old boy is very positive." Al grinned. "He has a lot of family responsibility — two younger brothers and a mother who isn't well too much of the time. I noticed that's typical around here. . . . Not sick mothers, but kids with a lot of family responsibility — they help on family fishing boats, they help farm or deliver produce, they take on part-time jobs to help out, to pay for extras, like their own underwear. It's like where I grew up in Boone. We thought it was normal." And Al smiled his friendly smile.

"You have any idea what's wrong with his mother?"

"No idea," Al said. "Sounds like she's got some kind of chronic thing — Justin said she has regular bouts and the doctor looks after her, but she needs the kids to help with chores. With all he's got on his plate, he's holding up real fine."

"My part-time job was my undoing," Eric said. "It went too well. I dropped out of school because I thought I was making the big bucks. Justin wasn't in school today. I saw him in a grocery store over in Bandon. I don't like the idea he's skipping school. That could lead to him skipping too much school . . ."

"Want me to talk to him?" Al asked.

"Nah, let me. He likes you better — keep it that way. Stay on his good side. Let me be the bad guy, see if I can figure out what's going on with him. Then you can pick him up, dust him off, talk sense to him." He took a breath. "Al, it's not good for him to quit learning so early. . . ."

"He's learning," Al said with a frown.

"He's growing in this job. He's got good instincts, good hands."

"I'd like him to have better odds than I did."

"You landed on top, man," Al said. "Twice!"

"I was lucky. If you don't have luck along with determination, it can get bleak."

When Justin came in, Eric tried to talk to him, but it was a waste of time, except to make Justin pretty mad. "My mom's doing great, but she needs our help. She's in a wheelchair and if you know anything about people in a wheelchair, they're pretty easy targets for falls, for things like pneumonia, that kind of thing. And she takes medicine, so someone needs to be close by in case she needs help with something. She can't be cooking and shit like that. She can't drive anymore. So, that enough information or does my job require copies of medical records?"

"I just want to know if there's any way I can help," Eric said in frustration.

"Yeah. Gimme hours. She doesn't work, doesn't get support from my dad, and we're stretched pretty tight. If you're not gonna give me hours, stay outta my personal life. Do I ask you about your personal life?"

Eric shrugged. "Sometimes," he said.

"And it doesn't really piss me off as much as this pisses you off."

"Tell you what," Justin said. "If I need anything, I'll let you know. For right now all I need is hours. I'll take whatever hours you can give me. After three in the afternoon, at least after two, and all day and all night Saturday and Sunday. That's what I need."

"You skipped school today," Eric said. "I saw you at a grocery store near Bandon."

"That's right, dude. I had to take my mother to the doctor. I stopped to get a couple of things. She was still in the car, waiting." But when he said that, he flushed. "We get along fine. Leave it alone."

And so Eric said to Al, "I can't crack that one. He's all yours."

Later that same day when Eric had gone home, Justin said to Al, "Any chance you can tell me how to replace break shoes?"

"Tell you?" Al repeated. "What good is telling you going to do?"

"The breaks on the van are slow and sometimes they cry. I'm going to have to do something."

"You're the only one who drives the van, right?"

"Yeah — the boys are too young and my mom can't drive anymore. But I drive everyone everywhere."

"At seven, when the place slows down, go get the van and bring it to the garage. We're gonna do brakes. We'll call it on-the-job training."

"I need to do it myself," Justin said. "We're on a tight budget. I can get parts cheaper somewhere else. . . ."

Al put a hand on his shoulder. "Kid, we're gonna do it here. We're gonna do it on the house. Now go home and get the van. Tell the boys you could be a little late tonight. We're gonna service that vehicle, check everything, change the oil, give it a lube, go down the checklist, make sure you have first-rate transportation. . . ."

"I can't," he said. "I can't do that. If Eric finds out and thinks I'm taking freebies from the station . . ."

"If you asked Eric he would be glad to help. You asked me and I'm glad to help. We're not going to cover it up — I'm going to tell Eric we worked on your van. We're going to document it. I'm going to train you and Lucky's will be glad to eat the cost of parts because Eric is good to his employees. I work on my truck right here, Manny takes care of his vehicles here."

"You sure he won't get mad? Because I need this job, man."

"I'm sure," Al said. "Go get the van. If it's not busy tonight, we'll be done by eleven. Otherwise, we'll work till the van is perfect. Safe and dependable. How does that sound?"

Justin's lips got a little pink around the edges. His eyes might've gotten a little glassy. But all he said was, "That'd be real good, Al. You ever need a favor, all you have to do is ask."

"Hey, friends take care of each other. Friends can count on each other."

TWELVE

Laine asked Eric if he could take an afternoon off to go somewhere with her and of course he arranged it. He'd do anything she asked and she knew it. She drove him a little over an hour away to a river in Douglas County, down a lonely, tree-lined road. He kept asking where they were going and she told him to be patient.

She finally pulled up to a closed gate. A county sheriff's car was parked outside the gate and Laine jumped out, flashed her badge, chatted with him for a moment. They laughed together over something, then she got back in the car while the deputy opened the gate.

Eric was catching on — there was yellow crime-scene tape on the fencing. And an armed officer. "Is this place being guarded?" he asked her.

"Not exactly," she said. "It's under routine surveillance. We still have two suspects at large, although I'm sure they're nowhere near here. Police do regular inventory of the contents of the buildings on the property to be sure nothing is missing or disturbed. Everything that amounts to evidence has been taken out of here and we don't expect our suspects to return, but one never knows."

"So, this is the place," he said. "This is where it all happened."

She took a deep breath. She nodded. "The commune. The place. This is the second time I've been back. The first was not long after my injury and surgery. Agents brought me back to walk through the property, go over the events and give them a tour. It wasn't easy — I couldn't document things while I was here. I did pass information through the fence behind the chicken coop, but that was infrequent. It really smelled back there — Jacob's 'soldiers' didn't like to go back there to check the security of the place and the brush and trees grew up against the fence so it was a very unlikely place for anyone to break in . . . or out. When I came back with agents I was still taking some pain medication so I did my best, but I didn't really register what I was seeing or remembering. Want to see the place?"

"Want to show me?" he asked.

"I wanted to see it again. I wanted to look at it with some objectivity. The women and children lived over there, in the big house. There were only six women when I got here but the place was built for twenty, plus children. When the women began to thin out, there was more space."

"At first glance, it looks like such a safe place," he said.

"I know. The entire estate is beautiful. On this side of the river there were livestock, massive organic gardens, chicken coops, the house and barn, corral, playground. The animals have been removed for their welfare. There's a bridge across the river — on the other side were the men's bunkhouse, Jacob's house and two warehouses that Jacob said held supplies, equipment and some of his experimental organic plants. They were warehouses dedicated to marijuana plants."

"A big federal crime," he said.

"We thought it was a big federal case before I saw the pot," she said. "He was bringing these poor, destitute women here, from out of state in some cases. We were afraid he was going to wage war on the establishment. It's possible that was his end-game, but at the time he was getting rich illegally and holding captive women and children." She looked around. "If people had had the freedom to come and go as they pleased and if he didn't have an impressive drug farm on the property, this could have been an amazing little commune. Of course, it would've been very poor. And there was the little matter of being led by an ego-driven lunatic, but merely being crazy is not against the law."

"What will happen to this place?" Eric asked.

"Auction, I suppose. Come and see," she said, leading him to the house.

It was a beautiful structure undamaged by the fire, a large Victorian style with huge rooms and a wraparound porch. Inside it was not only abandoned and deserted, but also dirty and cluttered. Detectives had plowed through every drawer and cupboard, but of course, nothing was put back. It was plundered in search of evidence.

The kitchen was enormous with a long, family-style table that could seat at least twenty. "The family ate here. The women, children, Jacob and often the men who watched over the place."

"Did you cook for the family?"

She shook her head. "I had chores and sometimes I had chores in the kitchen, but they didn't know I could cook. Or that I liked to cook."

"Why not? That's important to you."

"Oh, lots of reasons. My backstory — I was poor, down on my luck. I wouldn't have had the means. And . . . I wouldn't bring my mother into this. It was subtle, but it was perverse." She walked through the kitchen and out the back door. She started down the porch steps, then stopped and sat down. "The women who lived here were all afraid of the same thing — that they had no options, no choices. They let Jacob have his way because that made him happy and while he was happy, they had safety and plenty to eat. They had children and nowhere to go. They were afraid if they left, if they ran away, they wouldn't survive. Since they'd been in shelters or living on the streets before he found them, it wasn't too hard for him to convince them that's all they were worth."

Eric sat down beside her and took her hand.

"You can't imagine how much I wanted to start working to convince them they'd been manipulated, tricked. Brainwashed. But I couldn't. I had to be one of them so we could get to the bottom of what was going on here. And of course, get them out before Jacob and his little militia used them as shields. I had to take my time, sneak them out slowly so it would seem they ran away, so they wouldn't give me or anyone inside away. It was hard to go slowly."

"I'm surprised you wanted to see it again," he said. "Why did you bring me?"

"You asked me about it. I wanted you to see it." She pointed to the structure across the river, half burned down, half just charred. One of the warehouses was just a lump of black ash, the other was still standing. "That's Jacob's house, half-standing. The bunkhouse is gone — it was next to the burned warehouse. The house is where I was shot. Then I got Mercy, Devon's little girl, and we hid in the river while Jacob drove away. He went straight down the river then took some hidden back road I didn't know about. And not long after he escaped, Rawley found us. It was Rawley, Cooper, Spencer and Devon. Spencer carried me down the road to the police blockade, where I got medical attention. But none of those men knew me or were in it to rescue me. Devon was coming after her child and they wouldn't let her come out here without them."

"You must have been terrified," he said.

"Before I passed out, yeah. Before we were

260

rescued I heard a shot in the house — the woman I had to leave behind. She was the only one I couldn't get out and I don't think I'll ever get over that. Right after that shot was fired and Jacob was gone, I passed out. I woke up in the ambulance for a minute, just long enough for them to knock me out again. Then long enough in the E.R. to hear the doctor explain I was going to surgery. The news that I would have died had I not been rescued is still kind of hazy to me. Surreal. Or, out of reality, maybe. I never had any of those near-death visions or anything. What I had was pain in my shoulder and neck. White-hot, blinding pain. And before that was resolved, I was on a plane back to Virginia, where the self-proclaimed best orthopedic surgeon in Boston was waiting for me so he could look at my medical records and treatment options."

"Your father," Eric said. "Was he awful?"

She shook her head. "He restrained himself. I think he could tell by one look at my expression, which was not tolerant, I wasn't putting up with anything from him."

"But he was there," Eric said.

"He was. And he stayed for days . . . days without giving me any shit about my job — a record for Senior. My shoulder fixed up pretty quick but my elbow was killing me until a few weeks ago. I mean, what's that about? I didn't get shot in the elbow!"

He laughed at her. She was the strongest, bravest woman he'd ever met.

"I must have fallen on it, that's what the surgeon said."

"I'm surprised you didn't stay on the East coast."

"Well, that's the other thing I wanted to tell you. I thought I was running away from Senior and at the same time, getting a think break from the office. But I was really coming back for this. I just didn't realize it."

"This?"

"I needed closure. I had to see this place disarmed. I wanted to know it was really over. Behind me."

He took a deep breath. "Do you have some closure now?" he asked hesitantly.

"There are things you should know. If you're not beside me, I like a dim light on at night or I can't fall asleep. I have dreams — sometimes I hear a gunshot. I refuse to tell anyone from work that this is hard for me because they want to be accepting, but they would judge me as 'affected.' I'm not. I'm just a person recovering from a violent crime. I'm not the strongest person alive. I'm strong, but not infallible. And I needed to do this with you, Eric. I want you to know the truth about me — that I get scared like anyone would, that I'm vulnerable sometimes, and that you're the only person I trust enough to be completely honest with. I always told Pax I was fine — I wouldn't let the agents I worked with know how messed up I felt, sometimes still feel. I could never tell Senior. To survive something like this," she said, waving a hand at their surroundings, "only to be called an idiot — it was the last straw. But I want you to know the truth."

"What happens when you have closure?" he asked.

"I don't know. I was kind of hoping for a mysterious calm. I do get the sense that one small edge that gnawed at me is defused. It's like when the doctor is coming at you with a syringe with a big fat needle in it — and the needle is gone and it's just a syringe. Harmless. And right this minute, I don't feel scared, but that's not just about this compound being disarmed. It's about seeing it with you."

"You never let on that anything about it bothered you. You're the most controlled person I know."

She laughed softly. "I've just about got that perfected, huh? I can look that way when I have to. It's just a look."

"You thinking about going back to work or something?" he wanted to know.

She shook her head. "I like this consulting work. I'm happy doing that. Poor bastards — if there's anything sketchy to be found, I'm going to find it. Force of habit, I guess. And a really good nose."

"You're not heading home? To Virginia?"

She shook her head again. "You ready to be rid of me?"

He gave a short laugh. "I keep waiting for the other shoe to drop. You keep me wondering, keep me surprised. You asked me for a date, you asked me for that first kiss, you wanted me to spend the first night, you wanted me to share closet space. One of these days you're going to be ready for something more. Or maybe something different. Or ready to be finished with this, with us. I'm getting sore muscles from bracing myself."

"I like my life," she said. "I've gained five pounds, have you noticed that? As much as I run and work out, I still gained five pounds. Most of it on the ass, by the way. I think it's from having so much time to cook and eat. But I think it also might be from just being wound down a few notches. I'm so relaxed."

"You don't miss the adrenaline?" he asked.

"I get an adrenaline rush when it's time for you to come home from the station. . . ."

He leaned closer and kissed her cheek. "I like that."

"I'm getting that commendation from the FBI," she said. "The one Senior said he refused to celebrate. I wanted to come here one more time, look at where it happened, close the door. I thought by now I might be itching to get back to it, on to the next case. Hopefully the biggest case yet. But instead I have the feeling I've gone as far as I need to go in the Bureau. I might be ready to move on to the next chapter in my life. It's so funny that it would be in Oregon. In a little dinky town in Oregon, close to where I could have lost my life."

"Can we leave?" he asked.

"Why? Does it give you the creeps? Thinking about it?"

He shook his head. "You like your life now. That includes me. That makes me want to be alone with you, make out with you for a while. But not here where that other life was. I want to be alone with you. No ghosts. No edge. No needle."

She smiled at him. "You asking me to step away from that job I had? The one that gives you scary pictures in your head?"

"I think I convinced myself that if that's

what it took to keep you happy, I could shut off my brain. I know you can do anything. Anything. No matter how difficult or scary."

She laughed. "My mother used to say that *capable* was my middle name. She said I would do what I set my mind to, no matter how hard it was, and impossible tasks would just take me a little longer."

"Yeah, that's you. The idea that you're ready to try a new kind of adrenaline, a new kind of restless, I could live with that. And about the five pounds? I hadn't noticed, but I like it."

"You love me," she said, grinning at him.

"I'm not making out with you here, in front of the cop, in the shadow of a place where you risked everything. Come with me now. Let me drive us home. Let me find an abandoned farm road and pull over and show you. Anyone can say it. I want to show it."

"Will you go back to D.C. with me when I get my commendation?"

"If you want me to, I will. I'm proud of you. No, it's bigger than that. I admire what you can do, what you're willing to do. You amaze me. I have a feeling you always will."

She stood up and pulled on his hand. "You have a way with words. I'm just a glutton for praise. Take me out of here."

Laine was making a blackberry pie when her cell phone rang. She wiped off her hands, looked at it, saw it was her brother and answered cheerily. "Hey, Pax."

"Got a minute?" he asked. His voice sounded grave.

"Sure. What's up? How is everyone?"

"We're all good — headed for the last weeks of school before summer." And he ran through a litany of what was happening with each female in his world.

"And how's Senior?" she asked.

"Not completely sure," Pax said. "There's some kind of drama with him that I really don't get. I heard through the grapevine that a couple of weeks ago, he left the O.R. after a patient had been anesthetized and didn't come back. He didn't come back all day. He didn't answer his cell phone for hours. When he finally did answer a call from the head nurse in O.R., he said he'd had the phone turned off — he was playing golf."

"Playing golf?" she asked. "Wait a minute . . ."

"You heard this right. He put a patient under for a knee replacement, excused himself, walked out of the O.R. and apparently, out of the hospital. The O.R. staff went looking for him and couldn't find him. Ultimately, they woke the patient and said they were worried that something had happened to the surgeon, maybe he was suddenly ill or something. Since the surgery is elective, they discharged the patient and rescheduled him with Senior's partner for a week later."

"This can't be right. There must be something else."

Pax took a breath. "I'd talked to him a few times the past couple of weeks. Briefly, but we talked. He never mentioned this. Not once. I called his office and they said he was out and asked if I'd tried to reach him on his cell. I called him again, but this time I told him what I'd heard and he got angry — said it was a schedule conflict, that he wasn't supposed to be there in the first place and had turned the case over to the resident, who was more than capable. He said he didn't know why the resident didn't finish the case. He blamed the resident."

"Wow," Laine said. "You think he got pissed about something and stormed out?"

"He must have got into it with someone. But that's not like him, not really. I can name a dozen surgeons who pop off, swear at their O.R. staff, throw things . . . Senior actually has a good reputation in the O.R. Generally speaking, people like to work with him. When he's at his worst he's critical or snide. He rarely loses his temper. . . ."

"Just with me," she said.

"That's an old problem, you and Senior," Pax said. "That's one of those things between the two of you and I've never understood. Let me be clear — I don't understand his point of view. . . ."

"God, do you think it finally happened? That it's my fault and I put him completely over the edge?"

"You can't take that on. No, I don't think that. This is completely out of character. But he said someone filed a complaint and he's not seeing patients for a couple of weeks. Totally weird."

"What the hell . . . Is he going to get sued or something?"

"Don't think so. The office seems to be running interference. Apparently he's been a little unreliable the past year or so, but he's seventy. He cut back on his patient load and surgery after Mom died. He's been talking about retirement."

"God, if he retires, you'll be stuck with him in your business all the time. Unless he gets a woman. Pax, could he have a woman?

A girlfriend? He never did that before. He was pretty flaky after Mom died but . . ."

"No one mentioned a woman," Pax said. "He blew me off. He said it was no big deal, that it was a scheduling mistake, that he wouldn't have left the O.R. unless he was either finished or someone else was taking over the case."

"Maybe he has some health issue he doesn't want to talk about," Laine said. "Maybe he's on medication and it's making him loopy — like blood pressure medicine. Or Viagra?"

Pax laughed in spite of himself.

"Okay. Okay. Talk to the housekeeper, Mrs. Mulligrew — she's been around almost as long as we have. She probably knows more about him than we ever did. Trust me, the cleaning lady knows all — ask her to check in the medicine cabinet. Is he close to his nurse? It's a fairly new nurse, right? Pax? Can I do anything?"

"No, that's not why I called you. I only mentioned it to keep you up to speed. I'll look into it, but I wanted to know how you are. I had a few minutes to talk and . . . I'll talk to Mrs. Mulligrew, that's good advice."

"But you don't have time for this," she said. "You barely have time to talk to your own wife and kids."

"Well, you're on the outs with Senior, which doesn't lend itself to open communication, even if you weren't in Oregon. I'll handle it."

"I didn't mean to abandon you," she said.

"I don't see it that way. I miss you, but you did the right thing. There are boundaries and I wouldn't put up with that kind of constant criticism from anyone."

"So you don't want me to serve up my new number and talk to him?"

"No, you can just tell me how you are."

"Well, I'm getting more interesting, as a matter of fact," she said. "I knew I wanted a change of scenery and I had a lot of logical reasons for trying out Oregon for a while, but none of them made a lot of sense to me until a couple of days ago. I went back to the commune, to the scene of the crime. I suddenly realized that was something I had to do — not only to completely understand what happened, but to close the door on it. I didn't even realize how heavy that baggage was."

"How could you not?" he asked.

She laughed. "I'm disciplined. And I never take time off. Real time. I have vacations here and there, but I haven't had any real space from the Bureau in years. I've been thinking about something, but you have to

271

promise me you won't mention it to Senior."

"You know I'm good with your se-crets. . . ."

"I've been thinking ten years is enough. I think I've given the Bureau just about all I have to give them." Complete silence answered her. "Pax?"

"Sorry, I think the call was dropped. I thought I heard you say you were done."

"Funny," she said.

"You'll miss the excitement eventually. You've been eating stress three meals a day for over a decade."

"I think I'm full," she said with a laugh.

"I think it's him," Pax said.

"You're being ridiculous. Would you stop your fellowship because you're crazy about Genevieve?"

"That's not what I mean. I didn't mean you'd give up the Bureau because you're into him. I think being with him has made you look at your life differently. It's okay, Auntie Lainie. Life is very big, you know. And only one thing is required."

"Oh, really? And what's that?"

"That when you're done with it, you don't have regrets about your choices."

"Don't we all have regrets about some of our choices?"

"Not the really important ones."

She was quiet for a long time. Finally she said, "Don't make me think too hard. Let me be happy."

"Absolutely. And in case you need permission, I'll encourage you to stay happy."

THIRTEEN

The busiest time of day at Lucky's was from three to six when school let out and folks were getting home from work. That's when they'd gas up for the next day or bring in a problem they had with the engine. That's when Eric had the most hands on duty. After six things slowed way down. His employees who were not scheduled to work after six could start leaving then, including himself.

Justin came in at three. As usual, he got right to work. At three-twenty Eric answered the phone. "Lucky's full service, Eric speaking."

The young voice, clearly rattled, said, "Can I talk to Justin. It's Danny, his brother."

Eric called Justin to the phone and overheard Justin's part of the conversation. "Did you try to sit her up? Call Doc Grant's cell phone and 911. I'm on my way." He hung up and saw Eric's stunned expression. "I gotta go. My mom." And he took off at a dead run.

Justin might be in shock, Eric thought. He watched the kid run out of the station and down the street. He ran like he had only seconds; it was a total sprint. Before the sight of him racing down the street faded, Al was standing in front of him, questions in his eyes.

"He got a call," Eric said. "Something about his mom."

And then as though Eric caught the same virus, he bolted for his Jeep, wrangling keys out of his pocket as he jogged. Behind him he heard Al shout, "Howie, pump gas! Shut it down if necessary. We got an emergency." And then he was at the passenger door to the Jeep, opening it up and jumping inside even as Eric was backing out.

"What's going on?" Al asked.

"No idea," Eric said, making a T-turn to head after Justin. And man, could that kid run, even wearing his station coveralls and steel-toed boots, he was like the damn wind. When the Jeep came up behind him and Eric gave the horn a blast, Justin didn't even slow down.

"Pull alongside," Al commanded, lowering his window.

Justin had already run through town, past the diner and sheriff's office, three more blocks and up the hill.

"Justin!" Al yelled, leaning out the window. "Get in! We'll drive you!"

But the kid didn't even slow down. He just kept running, pumping his arms, panting, his floppy hair slicked back with wind and sweat. Uphill, and still flying.

Al pulled back inside. "Just follow him," he told Eric.

"What the hell is he doing?"

"We'll find out soon enough. We either let him wear out or I get out and chase him and tackle him and I'm not doing that. Follow him."

So, driving about five miles an hour, Eric followed behind Justin for a few more blocks, then the kid cut across some lawns to get to a very small house in the middle of the block. Justin's van was in the driveway but another newer car was parked in front. Justin crashed through the front door.

"I guess we're here," Al said.

Eric parked his Jeep and the two men walked up the driveway to the front door, which still stood open, and what they could see inside was shocking. The small living room was dominated by a hospital bed and Dr. Grant was sitting on the edge of the bed. There was a wheelchair, oxygen tank, other hospital paraphernalia. Dr. Grant had his stethoscope in his ears and was listening to the woman's heart. Oxygen was being administered and the woman's eyes were closed. Justin leaned over her from the other side of the bed, panting. He tenderly touched her forehead while two younger boys stood off to the side, worry etched into their features.

Dr. Grant took his stethoscope out of his ears and looked at Justin. "I'm afraid this is the end of the line, Justin."

Oh, shit, she's dead! Eric thought.

Then the doctor continued. "I called for an ambulance. She has to go to the hospital. She's breathing better now, but she needs close medical supervision."

Justin swallowed and said, "Then she comes home, right?"

"Come on, Justin. You gave it your best shot. Your mother needs a full nursing-care facility. We can try to get her a bed. This is end stage. Her quality of life will be improved in a care facility. And so will yours."

Justin gave a short, bitter laugh. "Not for too fucking long!" he barked.

"I give you my word, I'll do everything I can to help DHS find you boys a place together. I know right now you think it's the end of the world, but this can work out. You can't take on any more."

"Six months, that's all I need! Six months and I'm eighteen and —"

"Just being eighteen doesn't guarantee you'll get parental custody of the boys."

"There isn't any other family," Justin said. "It has to be me!"

"We've talked about this. I'm going to step outside and wait for the ambulance while you talk to your brothers. You have to stay calm now, son. Don't get your mom upset with a lot of emotion. Remember what I told you — you'll have a little time. This isn't going to happen overnight."

Scott Grant draped the stethoscope around his neck, picked up his bag and stepped past Eric and Al and outside. Eric and Al followed him.

"What the hell?" Eric said.

"Justin's mother is sick," Scott said. "She has MS. She's had it for a long time and she's not going to get better. She's been virtually bedridden for over a year now."

"And Justin takes care of her?" Eric asked.

"He takes care of her days and the younger boys keep an eye on her when Justin works, but there's also home health care. There's a visiting nurse who looks in on them regularly and I check on her all the time. Justin wants to do the right thing for the family but I think the strain of what this is doing to her sons is also showing on her."

"He takes care of her days," Eric said. It was not a question.

Scott nodded.

"He dropped out of school. I should've known."

"He just wants to keep the family together, but I think his decision to do that was as hard on Sally as anything. I found him a laptop and we got the GED information downloaded, if he ever has time to concentrate. He wanted to make it to eighteen, gainfully employed, so he could take on the house and his brothers. So they could be together."

Eric frowned and shook his head. "How's he going to manage all that on a service station attendant's salary?"

"The family gets help from the Department of Human Services. Food stamps, health care and supplemental income, that sort of thing. It's not a lot but it keeps body and soul together. But DHS is going to want to take over, get those younger boys placed in foster care. I can stall for a while — Justin and his brothers have been running that house for a long time, they're capable. If I don't place Sally in a facility right away, and in fact I might not be able to — it's all about available space — DHS will have to be patient. But they've been ready to pounce for a long time now."

"Are you telling me that three young boys are able to stay on their own with an invalid in the house, but they can't stay alone without all that responsibility and stress?" Al asked Scott.

"The invalid mother is not only over twenty-one with a sound mind and their biological parent, there is also a doctor and home health-care nurse on the scene regularly."

"What about Justin?" Eric asked.

Scott shrugged. "They might give him six months of foster care, but at eighteen, that program closes for him."

"Why didn't he tell me?" Eric asked. "I asked him if his mother was sick and he said she was tough. I saw him buying groceries in Bandon and he said he'd taken a day off from school to take her to the doctor. He said she was in a wheelchair and I thought maybe an accident or . . . Why didn't he tell me the situation?"

"For the same reason he uses his food stamps in Bandon, Eric. He doesn't want anyone's pity. He doesn't even shop for food in town. He's a proud, strong, devoted young man."

Al was scowling. "Where's their father?"

Scott shook his head. "I have no idea. Maybe Justin knows, but he's pretty bitter about his dad leaving them when his mother was sick. I haven't had any luck getting that information out of him. And I couldn't tell you if finding the father would be good for the family or only make things worse."

They chatted for a while longer and finally a county ambulance pulled up to the house followed by Mac in the sheriff's department SUV.

"No lights or siren," Eric observed.

"It's medical transport not an emergency. If you call 911 you get the fire department's rescue squad."

"I heard Justin tell his brother to call 911."

"He called me first — I got here fast. He didn't need rescue. Sally was having trouble breathing but didn't need resuscitation."

Just as he said that a couple of ambulance EMTs with a gurney passed them on the way to the front door. "Hey, Doc," one of them said.

"Hey," he returned. "I'll follow you to the hospital, get Sally admitted. She's stable at the moment but she needs the oxygen. She's recovering from pneumonia — a complication of her MS. She shouldn't need an IV until we get her to the hospital."

"Thanks. We'll see you over there."

Mac joined them. They all kind of stood around, saying nothing, until the EMTs emerged from the house with a woman still wearing the oxygen cannulas, sitting upright on the gurney.

Eric looked at Mac. "She's not doing very well. She's being taken to the hospital."

"So I heard," Mac said.

When Al and Eric got back to the station, everything was fine. Howie was under control, pumping gas like mad. And Al said, "Listen, I know it's your night to bug out early while Justin and I manage things, but I need a couple of hours."

"For?" Eric asked.

"None of your business, but I'm not going to rob an armored car or anything that would reflect badly on you."

"You're going back there," Eric said.

"I think someone should and I think it shouldn't be you."

"Why not? Seriously, I've been looking out for the kid since I hired him and —"

"And he thinks we have a common enemy — the boss. Let me go."

"I'm not the enemy!"

"I know that, but he's got a bomb inside

him. Come on, try to remember how little sense the world made when you were his age — try to remember how many innocent people you thought were plotting against you. He's a mess. He didn't ask for the mess, either."

Eric thought about that for ten seconds. "Yeah. Go. Take all the time you need. We got this. And if you see a chance, tell him I'll do anything I can to help."

"Sure I will," he said. Al grinned. "You and Howie got the station. Have fun."

Al took off before Eric could think of something more to ask or say. He went back to the Coastline, where he'd left his truck, and drove first to the pizza place, ordered two big ones, then returned to Justin's house. The door was now closed. In fact the place looked sealed up, but the van was still in the drive. He knocked.

Justin opened the door with a snarl on his face. Oh, man, this was one tough customer.

"What do you want?" Justin asked.

Al shrugged. *Okay,* he thought, *I'm balancing two large pizza boxes on one hand. . . .* "Well, I invited a few friends over to your place for pizza, I hope you don't mind." Justin started to close the door and Al put his foot in the way. "I want to talk to you."

That sneer didn't go away. "I *have* food,

you know."

"But do you have this kind of food? Because I never met a young man in my life who didn't like pizza. Jesus, can I come in? You're being such a pain in my ass!"

"Then just go away."

Al pushed his way inside. The younger boys were sitting at the table, where there were three glasses of some kind of liquid, no ice. It looked like a meeting had been taking place. He put the pizza boxes on the table. "One is pepperoni and sausage and some other stuff and the other one is just lots of cheese because I wasn't sure what would float here. Maybe someone could get me a drink or something? Whatever that is you're drinking?"

"It's Kool-Aid," Justin said. "We were just talking. Then we might head over to the hospital. But I'll call Eric, tell him I can't work. . . ."

"Justin, he's not expecting you to come back to the station tonight. I think he's pretty clear you've had some crazy stuff going on." He opened the top box. "Kool-Aid is great."

Justin sighed. "Al, this here is Danny. He's fourteen. And this is Kevin. Twelve. Guys, this is Al Michel. The guy I told you about. I work with him."

They each said, "Hi." Very quietly.

Al nodded at them, then opened the two pizza boxes. "Dig in."

"Thank you," two quiet voices said.

And a glass of Kool-Aid was placed before Al by Justin. "Sit down, son," Al said. "I'm not dangerous. And I'm not going to injure your pride, which is about the size of the Pacific Ocean."

Justin sat down, but no one reached for pizza. Finally Al did, pulling a piece out of the pie and lifting it to his mouth. "First, we eat," he said. "Then we talk." No one moved. "Come on, boys."

"I'm not that hungry," Justin said. And once he said that, his younger brothers nearly sat on their hands.

"I'd appreciate it if you'd try to choke down a piece, just to be polite. Justin, take a piece of pizza so your brothers don't feel so uncomfortable."

Still, it took him a long moment. Then when he finally lifted a piece and took a bite, his brothers followed suit. And within ten minutes one of the pizzas was nearly gone. Al hid his smile. Not hungry? That would make sense after their mother was taken to the hospital. But it wasn't the truth; they were growing boys.

He watched them with appreciation.

Good-looking crowd, all of whom could use a decent haircut. Brown hair, brown eyes, straight teeth. Danny was getting a peachy, fuzzy stubble. Kevin wore glasses. Justin was thin, but then he was also tall. Maybe he'd recently shot up a few inches, growing into those big feet.

Danny sat back first, hands on his stomach. Kevin was next, but he pushed in one more piece first. There were only three pieces left when these boys without much appetite were full. "Get cleaned up while I talk to Justin," Al said. "Then I'll take you over to the hospital to see your mother, make sure she's settled in all right."

Danny and Kevin got up from the table but Justin said, "You have to go back to work."

"Don't worry about it. Eric's fine. And we're not going to rush this. Tell me something, Justin — where's your dad?"

He shrugged and shook his head. "We don't know. We don't care."

"When was the last time you talked to him?"

"You thinking we can just call him up and he's going to make this right? Listen, he left because he couldn't stand sickness. It changed his life too much, he said."

He couldn't have said that, Al thought.

"And when was that?"

"Over five years ago."

"He left you here?"

Justin shook his head. "We moved here. My mother needed a flat house with handicap stuff. We've been here almost three years."

"I thought you were from around here. . . ."

"Elmore, way smaller than this, if you can wrap your brain around that. We were in a two-story. That wasn't working."

"Okay, back in Elmore, were there friends? Family — even distant family? Neighbors you've known awhile? Anyone we could reach out to now?"

"Look," Justin said impatiently. "When people get sick, people are nice, all right? But they don't want to have to be nice and help out forever. It gets old. My mom needs a *lot*. I mean a *lot*! Twenty-four-seven. And two teenage boys . . . they need stuff, too. They don't need as much and I can take care of what they need, but no one's gonna take 'em on. And they need me and I'm not gonna be around because no foster family takes a legal adult in, gives him free room and board. Are you getting this?"

"Settle down," Al said. "Everyone gets it — your situation sucks. But your mom needs more help than three teenage boys can supply. And you boys need a life, too. So — you're not that much trouble? Know what that tells me? This is your father's responsibility. He doesn't even have to do anything — just be the responsible party. Pay the rent, maybe. We just have to track him down. . . ."

"He doesn't want to be tracked down! I don't want him around, but do you think my mom was gonna let that go? She had me look around, see if I could find him. I couldn't, all right? What I need is to get to eighteen before my mom gives up. Then I can take over. We'll be fine."

Al held his tongue. It was on his mind to say *That ship has sailed.* If he understood Dr. Grant, no one in this family had any quality of life — not the poor woman who was hanging on when every day of her life from now on was going to be beyond difficult, not the three boys who had spent the last half-dozen years struggling to take care of her and themselves. "Maybe, if we don't panic, a solution will come to mind," he said. "For right now, let's go see your mom, make sure she's in good hands. I'll drive you. Bring you home."

"I can take us over. . . ."

"Let me do this, Justin. Concentrate on

your family. I won't interfere or crowd into the hospital room with you. I'll just be the driver."

"You're supposed to go back to —"

"I'll call Eric. He said I should take as much time as I want. He also said he'd be glad to help if he can. I know you hate to ask for help, but try to remember it was offered."

Justin told Al about his mother's disease and he was amazingly articulate. She might live a few more years, might not. She'd been diagnosed a long time ago, when Justin was still little. Sometimes she fell and couldn't get herself up and he'd come home from school and find she'd been lying on the floor for hours. Or their dad would come home and find her in some trouble and it would get him all crazy because he couldn't stay home from work. But Justin and his brothers had a routine now — Justin was there for her days and when his brothers came home, he went to work. A nurse came at least four days a week to help her with bathing and such and when the nurse was there, Justin could go out, just for a break or for errands.

Al waited in the hospital parking lot while the three boys went upstairs to check on their mother. He was curious about what was happening with her, but the boys needed some space right now. Eric wasn't the only one who saw himself in Justin. So did Al. In fact, Al hadn't been that much older than Justin when his life had come apart and everything had changed.

He'd grown up on the farm, had a girl-friend through high school — she was also a farm kid. Her name was Carol and that's when he was called Mick, short for Michel. They got married at nineteen and lived on his family farm — that was their destiny. They were going to be a farm family and have a slew of kids. Carol could handle all the business and Al could manage the farm. He'd been doing it since he was a kid. Carol got pregnant and had a baby boy — Ethan. And when Ethan was only three months old, he didn't wake up. Classic crib death — no explanation and no reason to expect it to happen again.

But Al and Carol were completely devastated. Ripped apart. Al felt like he didn't take a deep breath for a year. His mother was shattered, his father was in so much pain he barely spoke. Carol's family, which was larger, was in agony as well and they embraced Carol as best they could. She had a lot of support from them through the worst of it.

But Al checked out. He ran.

He was so far from being able to cope, he just made an excuse to get away from the scene of the worst tragedy of his young life. He took a job driving a big rig, a semi, and managed to be gone at least four days a week. He didn't have any trouble explaining it was a good job, hard to get, and the money would come in handy. While he was gone, Carol had her family to prop her up and she could express her grief to them. Al just wanted to be alone, to lick his wounds, to take an emotional journey to get back to where he was functional. He'd never again be a young man with hope.

Carol asked him to stop, to come home and work the farm alongside his father, but he was helpless. When he looked into her pretty eyes he felt like he'd failed her in every possible way imaginable. First of all, she'd carried him all through high school, helping him with his school work, tests, everything. She was the only reason he had graduated. Al could barely read. It was another dozen years before he heard the word *dyslexia* and realized he must be dyslexic, something no one even talked about when he was ten or fifteen years old. Second, she was the only way he could have a farming business. He could manage math in his head pretty well and he had the instincts of a great farmer, but he was hell with reports, articles, printed information, forms. He had spent a lifetime memorizing. You only had to tell him something once; he couldn't afford to forget anything because he couldn't look it up. Third, all she ever wanted was a family and he'd given her one only to watch as that precious child had died. Then he watched her collapse as she buried their son. She had been so fragile and he wasn't strong enough to hold her up. He felt so overwhelmed, he didn't know what to do.

After a couple of years his agony settled into a dull ache that left him numb and uncommunicative but feeling as though he could breathe again. He said to Carol, "Good news. I'm quitting the trucking company and coming home to work the farm."

And she said, "That's great, Mick. But you're too late to come home to me."

She did the only thing she could do — she cut her losses. She said, "I'll always love you but I can't depend on you. When everything falls apart and goes to hell, I'll be alone and you'll be somewhere else. If you want to suffer alone, I can't change that about you. But I can't do that."

He argued that for a while — she wasn't alone. She had a big family — parents, grandparents, aunts, uncles, siblings.

But her husband, the father of her child, had run out on her.

Carol had done the right thing, he eventually realized. She remarried, had a couple of kids who were healthy and strong and went to college. They were in touch regularly; Carol's husband tolerated that and was even friendly because good old Mick was no threat. He'd learned to make a good life for himself, solitary though he was. He made sure he was easygoing, generous, a good friend when a friend was needed. But he didn't get attached because damn, when that went south it hurt like hell. There'd been a woman or two along the way who would've liked to settle down, make a family, but he wasn't up to it. He'd lost his nerve way back.

He wasn't sure anyone realized he was handicapped, that he couldn't really read much, if at all. He thought maybe the people who were closest to him over the years thought he just wasn't too bright, which didn't really upset him.

He spent a lot of time saying things like, "Can you read this? I forgot my glasses."

Or, "Why don't you order the two best things on the menu and we'll share." And now that he was fifty-six it was easy: "Do you think that print could be any smaller?"

There was help out there. He knew that. The problem was that even knowing you have a condition that prevented you from reading, sometimes from learning, it didn't keep you from feeling like an idiot.

Here he stood. In a hospital parking lot at dusk. Three young boys upstairs visiting a mother who was on borrowed time. Even if she didn't pass away, she was pretty much done raising her sons — they were on their own. They had no one but each other.

Al had wanted sons. If things were different, he could help out here. He liked Eric's station, liked the town, liked Ray Anne, liked the boys — but who would elect him as a foster parent? He couldn't help with homework, couldn't even read their book reports. Hell, he'd probably struggle with reading report cards!

There was a bench outside the hospital's front door. He sat down and got out his cell phone. He called his ex-wife. She sounded happy to get a call from him. "Mick! How are you?"

"Fine. Good. How are you?"

"All is good," she said. "Tony is better.

His kidney function is improved and his doctor is happy. Bless that man, he hates not being able to work right now, but that's just a man thing. I'm working and everyone in the family is healthy. Where are you?"

"Oregon," he said. "Eric sold his business in Eugene and opened up a new one on the coast. It's a small town, small station, very friendly. How are your kids?"

"Fine. Lindsey's getting married. Mick, what's wrong?"

"Nothing. Why?"

"There's something in your voice. I haven't talked to you in months. Are you all right?"

"I'm fine, fine. Well, I'm waiting out in front of a hospital right now. One of the young kids I work with, his mother has MS and is real sick. The ambulance took her to the hospital and I brought the kid and his younger brothers to see her. Seems like they're pretty much on their own. I'm just waiting here to take them home. Nothing I can do about this, but it's too bad. You know?"

"I know," she said. "You always were tender-hearted."

Except with you, he wanted to say. He just wasn't there for her. He regretted that but you can only regret the agonies of youth for so long. He just hadn't been emotionally equipped to do any better. "I'll lend a hand if I can, but I don't think I'm going to be here much longer."

"When will we see you next?" she asked.

"Summer," he said. She knew exactly when he'd be in Boone, but she didn't say that and she never made him say it. "I don't go that way in winter, you know that. But I'll see you in the summer. Is there anything you need in the meantime?"

She answered him with a small laugh. "I have everything I need. What about you?"

"Isn't something important coming up? Birthday or anniversary or something?" He knew exactly what was coming up — her fifty-sixth birthday in May, sometimes it fell on Mother's Day. It had when she was pregnant with Ethan. He bought her a fancy rocking chair and she made such a fuss over it.

"Another birthday," she said.

"That's right. Well. Listen, those boys will be coming out in a minute so I'd better get off the phone. I'll . . . ah . . . give you a call before I head that way so maybe we can get together for a cup of coffee. Or something like that . . ."

"That would be nice, Mick. Now you be careful out there on the road. Be careful on your way back home."

"You take care, too. Hope Tony keeps feeling better."

Tony wasn't exactly sick, but he had some kind of kidney problem that Carol described as not too serious. He was sixty and not as lucky with his health as Al was — he'd been forced to stop farming for the time being at least. Probably those god-awful winters . . .

Al would see Carol like he did every year. On July twelfth. Ethan's birthday.

FOURTEEN

Al got the boys back home after 9:00 p.m., considerably later than he expected. By that time Eric told him to quit for the day, get himself a cold beer or something. There was a spring storm rolling in over the bay and if there was lightning, he might be shutting the pumps down anyway.

Al had a couple of beers in that little refrigerator in his motel room, but the night called for something different. He was still in his uniform but hadn't had time to get dirty at work yet. It was getting late when he knocked on Ray Anne's front door. She opened it without asking who was there. She had a rag of some kind tied around her hair, a green, gooey mask on her face, cotton balls between her toes and was wearing cutoff sweatpants and a baggy T-shirt. "Whoa," he said, taking a step back.

She put a hand on her hip. "I see. You thought I was naturally beautiful. . . ."

He lifted his brows. "Well, hell, you sure come out looking real good."

"Did we have plans?"

He rubbed his jaw. "Nah. I just had one of those days and was looking for a beer. I can find one somewhere else. I'm obviously interrupting something very important. . . ."

"You scared to come in?"

"I wouldn't say so, no." He peered at her closely, squinting. "Does that do anything?"

"It makes my pores small and my wrinkles smaller. You can come in. It's ripe. I can take it off now."

"Not on my account," he said, smothering a laugh.

"Get yourself a beer. I'll be right back." And she turned and left him standing in the open doorway.

He got himself a beer from her refrigerator and sat on the couch. A few minutes later she returned to the living room in different clothes, her blond hair fluffed up, eyebrows drawn on and a little lipstick. There was still a little green stuff stuck at her temples. "Wow. What a transformation," he said.

She went to the kitchen; he heard a cork pop. While she was in there, she said, "I can only assume you now plan to marry me." She came back with her wine. "Now that we've been intimate."

"Ray Anne, we were intimate before."

She laughed. "That was sex," she explained. "Seeing me in the throes of pre-construction — that's intimate."

He touched his temple. "You got a little . . ." Her hand went there immediately, scraping it away. "Who knew you had to go to so much trouble?"

"You'll appreciate me more now, I bet." She sipped her wine.

"I apologize. I should've called. It was just a shot in the dark."

"Literally," she said. "Now what has you knocking on doors at ten at night? Don't you work late tonight?"

He started to tell her about the Russell boys but found he didn't want to go into too much detail. It brought his own conflicted feelings out when he thought about how intensely screwed up their little lives were. He just gave her the bare facts — Mrs. Russell went to the hospital, Al drove the boys to see her, make sure she was all right, by the time he took them home it was late and Eric had the station covered. The pumps might be shutting down on account of lightning anyway. . . .

"I heard some rumbling out there," Ray Anne said. "When you live around here you soon learn the best thing is the sunset over the bay. The second best are the storms. The lightning over the bay." She closed her eyes and smiled. "It's spectacular."

"We could drive down to the marina in the truck. Grab your wine," he suggested.

"We don't have to go that far," she said. "I have a deck on top of the garage. There's a view from there. I can't see the whole bay but I can see the sky over the bay and one of the haystack rocks in the water. Wanna go up?"

His eyes lit up. "I wanna go up," he said.

She grinned at him. "Let me grab this," she said, pulling the throw off the sofa and tossing it over a shoulder. "It's still cold out there at night. Come with me. This way."

She led him through the kitchen, out the door and into the garage. "Grab a beanbag," she said. "I'll get one, too." Then out the back door into the yard where there was a narrow staircase to the roof. "I'll hold your beer while you toss these beanbags up there."

"Have you ever thought about a couple of lawn chairs?"

"Oh, you're new in town." She laughed. "They'd blow off."

It only took a minute to get situated up there. Just as they were getting comfortable reclining against the beanbags, lightning over the mouth of the bay started flashing. The wind picked up a little bit and Ray Anne snuggled under the throw and against him. She held her wine, he held his beer and his arm pulled her closer.

"I *love* this," he said. "I wonder if I can get on top at the Coastline. . . ."

She laughed at him.

He leaned toward her, nuzzling her neck. "How many lovers have you brought up here?"

She chuckled. "Too many to count."

"Really? Take a stab at it. How many?"

She sighed. "I haven't been in this house that long. Just a few years. And I was convinced to buy it when I found out I could put this deck up here. It's kind of a special place. It's kind of a secret place."

"How many?" he persisted.

"Okay, none. All right? It's all mine."

"Have you ever slept up here?"

"Not really. I've fallen asleep up here a couple of times, just watching the sky."

"When the weather gets warm we're going to make love up here," he said. "Then we're going to sleep for a while and make love again. This is a great secret to have."

"I haven't said I'd do that with you," she informed him.

"You'll have to because you said you were going to make me marry you. For, you know, seeing what you do to your face to be beautiful. It's incredible. Horrific, really."

"I'm never getting married again," Ray Anne said.

"Okay," he chuckled, kissing her ear. "We'll just have sex on the roof and sleep under the stars. This is great up here. You're brilliant."

"If you ever tell anyone about my preconstruction face I'll sue you."

"Ray Anne, do you think you're not pretty? You're beautiful. And I've seen you in the early morning without any makeup."

"No, you haven't."

"What are you talking about? Of course I have."

She shook her head. "When you stay over, I don't remove my makeup before bed and when I slip in the bathroom to freshen up, I freshen up — repair the damage, renew the lip gloss, fluff the hair. When I'm alone for the night, I put green stuff on my face and then I lather up in moisturizer, fighting back time. I color my hair. . . ."

"Are you gray?" he asked. He didn't have that much gray for a man his age.

"Mrs. Santa Claus."

"Seriously?" he asked with a laugh.

"That goes no further. . . ."

He brushed her hair off her forehead. "You know, you don't have to go to all that trouble for me — the fluffing, repairing, glossing. You can grease up if you want to."

"You said you like the way I look. . . ."

"I do," he said. "You look damn good. It makes me look good, taking you out to a restaurant. Hell, it makes me look good buying you a soda at the station! But when we're alone, if you want to put on all your lotions, I can go along with that. In fact, I bet all that lotion comes in handy." He leaned over and kissed her. "You're a pretty little thing, Ray Anne. But you know what I like best? The way you flirt with me, come on to me, tease me a little bit. And I like your personality — you're smart. Funny. A little dirty . . ."

"Dirty?"

He laughed at her. "I mean that in a good way. You don't have too many inhibitions when we're alone. I like that. But you know what I like best? I like that you can put me in a better frame of mind. I can be worried or unhappy and the minute I'm in your company, I feel better."

"You don't seem like a guy who ever gets unhappy or stressed," she said.

He pulled her a little closer. "Ah, hell,

honey. Under all this perfection, I'm just a regular guy."

With the storm building and lightning flashing over the ocean Eric sent Howie home at nine and closed the station a little early. He went home to shower off the day and when he emerged from the bathroom, towel wrapped around his waist, he found Laine sitting on the bed beside a tray. He grinned and rubbed a small towel over his hair. "What's that?"

"It's too late for a big meal, but I know you didn't eat. . . ."

On the tray was a small artichoke dip and crackers, some sliced meat and cheese, a bunch of grapes, a round of brie. His stomach growled. "I'll be right with you." He ditched the towel in favor of sweats and came back to the bed. He noticed she had an open bottle of wine and two glasses on the bedside table, but there was also a tall glass with ice and a Coke. His choice.

"Pour me a little of that wine, will you?"

"Walking on the wild side tonight?" she asked. She poured a small amount into a glass and handed it to him.

"Not very wild — I have the tow business tonight. This looks awesome." He ran a cracker through the dip and chased it with a sip of red wine.

"My food preparation really lights your fire. I think in an earlier life you liked to drag your woolly mammoth home to the cave for your woman to butcher and roast."

"And then she tanned the hide and made me pants." He chewed a couple of grapes. "What have you been doing tonight?"

"Mostly watching the show," she said, pointing her wine toward the sliding glass doors. "It's the first really good one since I moved here."

"Well, it gets better and more frequent through summer," he told her. "We're going to spend a lot of time on the deck."

"And in bed," she said, taking a grape and sip of wine.

"Storms or not," he said.

They leaned back against the pillows and headboard of the bed, tray between them, and watched the fury over the bay. Sometimes, when the lightning was close, the noise was so deafening they both jumped in surprise. When the lightning struck one of the big rocks in the bay, they shouted in excitement as if they were kids at a fireworks display.

And then the rain began in earnest and Laine moved the tray, put her wineglass on the bedside table and curled up against him.

The lightning became flashes behind clouds while the wind blew the rain against the windows.

"If you had told me five years ago that one day I'd have this kind of life, I never would have believed it," Eric said.

"You mean 'stable'?" she asked.

"Once I got prison out of the way, stability became my middle name. It was a priority. I didn't make too many fast moves — I liked the no-drama zone a lot. But I was sometimes overworked and pretty often bored. No, I didn't know I'd be working on my second business, that I'd be a father to a wonderful girl, that I'd be laying in bed with the most incredible woman I've ever met. . . ."

"Well, does it come as any surprise that I didn't see you in my astrological charts, either? I thought I'd spend half my life investigating, establishing probable cause, and the other half undercover or in court. And then there's the paperwork . . ."

"Is this life getting too dull for you?"

She shook her head. "This is the best I've felt since my mom passed away. I wish I'd had my aura read or something — I bet it was spikey and black and nervous before." She turned her head and looked up at him. "I bet it's all soft pink and lavender now. I was all about controlling the stress before. I think you sucked the stress right out of me."

"Me?" he asked.

"You and a couple of other things. Some healthy distance from Senior helped. A second look at the commune, disarmed. And I don't know what's different about this place but the people are . . . They're nice. They let me in. I didn't realize how few women I had in my life. Well, I realized it, but I didn't know I could do anything about it. I didn't know what kind of friendship I was missing."

"Were there just men in your life?"

"Not what you think. I worked with mostly men and the women I had grown close to were more mentors than girlfriends. I don't have to prove myself to these people, to these women, and it's different. I can tell you something that might scare you to death."

"I've learned to be very brave where you're concerned. . . ."

"I'm going to resign from the FBI this week. I like my new life. I like being here, being with you. I've gotten a little lazy. . . ."

"That last assignment took a lot out of you," he said. "Another few months like this and you could be ready for your edgy life again."

"What if I'm not?" she asked.

"And what if I'm not enough?" he asked her.

"Eric, you're not under any pressure, please believe that. My expectations of you are the same as they've been from the start — just having you in my life is enough."

He slid an arm around her and pulled her on top of him. She was stretched out over the length of him. He pulled her mouth onto his while thunder rumbled over them. He kissed her deeply. When he let her go he said, "Don't tease me. You know you're all I want."

When the rain was driving inland over the bay, Hank Cooper grabbed his rain slicker and flashlight and went outside through the back door of the bar. He crossed the parking lot and shone the light on the path that would soon be a stone sidewalk. He braced a foot on the raised floor of the structure that would be his house and pulled himself up and inside. He pointed the flashlight toward the large open room in the front of the house. Sarah sat on a stack of two paint cans, looking out the glassless window at the storm. Her growing middle seemed to be precariously balanced over her thighs.

"I wish you wouldn't prowl around over

here in the dark," he said.

"I wanted to check out the storm, see what we'd see from the great room."

"Sarah, what if you tripped over construction debris and fell?"

"I'd bounce," she said.

"Please tell me you didn't lift a full paint can to stack those. . . ."

"Okay," she said.

"You did!"

"I've been instructed not to tell you. . . ."

"You're a wiseass," he accused. He took off the slicker and draped it around her shoulders. "Come on. I'll light the way. And step carefully — it's wet and muddy out there." He put an arm around her waist, what there was of it, and led the way. He jumped down first and reached up for her, lifting her down, his arm staying around her.

"If you slip and fall, you'll take me with you."

"I'm as sure-footed as a mountain goat," he said, then slipped. He righted himself before he could do any damage. He got her inside and hung the slicker on a peg by the back door. "You feeling all right, babe?"

"I feel amazing. I wish the house was done."

"Another six to eight weeks," he said, running a hand over her pregnant belly. "Before she comes."

"I wish it could be done in time for a graduation party for Landon."

"We'll have a great party right here. We have the deck and the beach. It'll be good, don't worry."

Landon appeared in the doorway to the kitchen, mop in hand. "Did I hear my name?" Then he looked at the floor beneath their feet. "Aw, man. I just mopped."

"Be nice," Cooper said. "We're planning your graduation party."

"Cash money would be better," he said with a grin.

"I think the University of Oregon is going to get the cash money," Cooper said. "You're getting a party. And a new niece."

"Well, could you please move my sister and niece over so I can mop up that puddle you brought in?"

Cooper scooted Sarah over onto the rug inside the door. "Hey, Landon, you know a kid named Justin Russell?"

"Should I?"

"He went to your high school, but I take it he dropped out."

"Oh, yeah? Oh, wait, he's that kid who pumps gas at Lucky's, right? He hardly ever says two words. So, what's up with him?"

"When I stopped to get gas tonight, Eric

mentioned the kid's mother was taken to the hospital in an ambulance and there's no dad in the family. The kid's mom is an invalid. Justin seems to be taking care of his younger brothers. By himself."

Landon whistled. "I hope he can manage as well as Sarah did, raising me alone. That can't be easy. Poor guy."

"Well, if you talk to him, like when you're getting gas or something, you might ask him if there's anything we can do to help. If you mention about being raised by your sister . . ."

"I can do that, Cooper, but I'm telling you — that kid doesn't want to talk." Landon gave the mop a swipe across the floor. "He probably doesn't know what hit him. I'll be sure to say hi. Or something . . ."

"Sometimes it doesn't take much," Cooper said. "You know — just reach out. Sometimes all a guy needs is a chance."

The rumble of thunder and the rain against the window woke Sally Russell and she stirred in the hospital bed. She hadn't been asleep very long — respiratory therapy kept waking her. This time when she opened her eyes she saw her son sitting in the chair beside her bed. "Justin?" she asked sleepily.

He stood up and came to the bedside.

"Hi, Mom. How do you feel?"

"My chest hurts, but I think it's getting better. I'm doing that breathing machine every couple of hours, at least. And I have antibiotics in the IV. Why are you here?"

"I got the boys home and came back. In case you need me."

"I don't need you, honey. There are nurses. . . ."

"I mean, in case you're upset or worried. You know . . ."

"I'm fine. I don't want you to sit in that chair all night. You need to get home, get some sleep."

"I'll go in a while," he said. "When the rain lets up some. I just wanted to make sure you're doing okay."

"You spoil me," she said. Her voice was a whisper punctuated by attempts to take deep breaths. Justin had to lean close to hear her. "We have to be realistic, honey. You and the boys can't take care of me anymore."

"We're okay, Mom. Really."

"I know you'd do anything for me, I know. I want you to talk to Dr. Grant about what we do next. As a family."

"Maybe the nurse can come more often. If the nurse can come more often . . ."

She was shaking her head. "I'm tired now,

honey," she whispered. "Maybe tomorrow we can talk more about this. I want you to go home. Get some rest."

He leaned over and kissed her forehead. "I'll just sit here for a few minutes. Until you fall asleep."

She nodded and let her eyes close and he held her hand, but backed away to sit in the chair.

She was giving up.

Justin couldn't remember a time they hadn't lived with MS. It wasn't long after his youngest brother was born that it was confirmed — her symptoms were related to MS; her muscle weakness and spasms, her lack of coordination and tremors, slurring speech. Then her vision became so bad if she didn't fall because of her clumsiness, she might trip or miscalculate a step. From that first diagnosis until she needed almost full-time help was only a few years. Justin was doing more to help and take care of the family than anyone else by the time his father couldn't take it anymore.

"You had to grow up too fast because of me," his mother frequently said.

"It's not your fault, Mom," he whispered.

When he was sure she was sleeping soundly, he quietly left the room. He was walking down the hall when he ran into Dr. Grant.

"Just the man I wanted to see," Scott Grant said. "I was going to catch up with you tomorrow in Thunder Point, but this is good. You came over to visit your mom?"

Justin nodded. Silent. He didn't trust his voice at the moment.

Scott Grant put a hand on Justin's shoulder. "Come on. I'll walk out with you. I can keep your mom for a few days, maybe a week. Here's what we're going to have to do — her name is on a list for extended nursing care. They expect a bed in a week at the earliest, a month at the longest. If your mom goes home again, Justin, it's going to be the last time. She needs full-time nursing care and therapy. She'll have more time if she gets what she needs."

"We can give her anything she needs," he said.

"You're damn good at taking care of her, son. I'm impressed by the quality of care she gets at home but we both knew it had limits. Not only does your mom deserve a better quality of life, but so do you and your brothers."

"That's the thing, Doc. If she goes into the nursing home, are they going to let me take on the house and the boys? No, they're not, that's what. They're going to go to foster homes, maybe different ones. They might even make me go for a few months and then what happens to the house? I can tell you right now, that's not happening. I can take care of myself."

"Justin, don't concentrate on worst-case scenarios — we might find a foster family right in Thunder Point. Aside from the boys sleeping in another family's house, there won't be that much different about your lives. Except they won't have to work so hard to keep things together at home. Now, let's talk about your dad. . . ."

"He's gone, Doc. He left about six years ago. They've been divorced for five years. He sent money for a couple of years but we haven't seen a check in a long time. I don't know where he is. . . ."

"Where was he last?" Scott asked.

"I think, Portland. And we're *not* going to Portland!"

"It might keep the three of you together."

"Wherever the boys end up, I'll go there and get work. But not with him. You think he's a solution? The guy who took off and left three little kids alone with a sick mother?"

"I'd be the last guy to nominate him for father of the year," Scott said. "I'm going to get to work on this right away, son. I've been asking questions and making phone calls, but now it's time to take some action. We're going to find a solution to this that works for you and your brothers. Try not to worry too much."

Justin gave a huff of laughter. "Right. Well, worry seems to be what I do best."

FIFTEEN

Laine couldn't believe how satisfying and tranquil her life had become.

The few cases she managed were simple and left plenty of time for her to work out at the dojo, to enjoy her deck in the warming spring weather, make good use of her kitchen and best of all, have quality time with Eric. And then the one thing that could completely derail her happened. The doorbell rang in late afternoon. She opened it to stare into the eyes of her father.

"Oh, God," she said. She was momentarily paralyzed.

"Are we just going to stand here and stare at each other?" Senior said.

She stepped back so he could enter. "How did you find me?"

"The way any intelligent person would. I hired someone to find you. I knew approximately where you were even though you've done your best to remove me from your life."

"Couldn't the person you hired have found you a phone number?"

"Why bother with that? You wouldn't talk to me. Let's not make this harder than it already is — I'm here to make amends. I need my children back in my life. You're all I have."

"You have Pax, the one you find acceptable."

He frowned, his dark brows lowering. "Pax has his own family and his fellowship, I have very little of him. Except that he's checking on me all the time now. But he doesn't ask *me* what's going on with me — he asks the help. But Pax will at least talk to me."

They stood in the foyer. He glanced around, lifting a dark eyebrow as he peered into the study, where her desk and computer sat. He was such a big man, so full of bluster and stubbornness, she crossed her arms protectively over her chest. "There were terms," she reminded him. "I told you I didn't want to hear from you until we made some changes in our relationship."

"Can we sit down?" he asked. "We need to get this put to bed."

She shook her head. "I was clear. You were clearly stubborn."

"What do you want from me, Laine? Want me to say I'm sorry?" he asked. His voice boomed as usual. His physique matched his voice — he was robust, fit, tanned as though he'd been on vacation. He'd been bald forever, as long as she could remember, with a dark ring of hair around his dome. He was a handsome man. Her mother used to say he looked just like Trapper John, M.D., possibly accounting for the many reruns of that series they watched when Laine was a little girl. For a seventy-year-old man his belly was surprisingly flat, his arms well-muscled, legs straight. He didn't look his age. "Now can we sit and talk?"

She gave a singular nod and turned, walking into the house, into the kitchen. As she passed the table she pulled out a chair for him, giving another nod toward it. "What would you like to drink? Tea? Wine? Cola?"

"Coffee?" he asked.

"I'll brew a pot."

She got busy in the kitchen while he sat at the table, taking in the view. "Well, this isn't bad," he said. "I can see why you were drawn to it. But it's not as though we don't have views back East. This place has nothing on Cape Cod, the Hamptons, Kennebunkport, Newport . . ."

She loved the unique and exquisite view

but now she knew that's not why she'd come to Thunder Point. "I don't live alone here," she said. She set the coffee to brew and opened a bottle of wine. She felt a sudden temptation to take a few gulps from the bottle, but she poured herself a small glass. She went to the table and sat across from him. "I live with a man. I've lived with him for almost three months. His name is Eric."

"And what does he do?" Senior asked.

She tilted her head and leveled her gaze at his piercing blue eyes. Of course her father didn't ask if he was a good man, if he was kind or intelligent or funny or generous. He didn't wonder if he had integrity. "He owns a gas station."

"A gas station?" he asked with a short laugh. "Well, you must like him."

She leaned toward him. "I don't need his rent money. I'm never lonely, especially when I'm alone. I'm not needy. I'm not scared. I don't need anyone to take care of me. Of *course* I like him."

He smiled slightly. "Ah, so he's brave."

"Why do you say that?" she asked.

"Because you're a terrifying woman."

Impatient, she leaned back in her chair and even though she was sitting, her hands went to her hips. "Is this about the FBI again?"

"Oh, I've been warned about that," he said, holding up his hands with palms toward her. "But I got to thinking — we should put all that to rest for your mother's sake."

"It's a bit late for that. Mom is finally free of our conflicted relationship," she said. "And she always supported my choices." She got up and went to the cupboard, retrieving a mug. She poured him some coffee. Then she put cream and sugar on the table with a spoon. She glanced at the clock — five-fifteen. While Senior dressed his coffee, she pulled her phone into her lap, hidden, and texted Eric: My father is here!

He texted back right away. Do you need me?

See you at six? she texted back and he replied immediately, I'll be there.

"Eric will be home around six," she told her father. "I was busy most of the day so I didn't cook. Where are you staying?"

"Laine," he grumbled. "Am I not welcome here? Don't you have a guest room?"

She took a sip of her wine. "Here's the deal, Dad. The last time we were together for more than twenty-four hours we got into a shouting match and it all started when I told you I was getting a commendation from the FBI and you belittled me. You said you'd much rather have a daughter without a bullet in her shoulder than any kind of award — you said I was a huge disappointment to you. You said you didn't want to hear another word about it and you said you wouldn't celebrate it."

He lifted his chin defiantly.

"And do you remember what I said?" she continued.

"That I owed you an apology, which I offered before sitting at your table."

"No, you didn't. You asked if I wanted one and the answer is still the same. Yes, I do."

"Fine. Consider this an apology. What else?"

She rolled her eyes. "Are you joking or just trying to be difficult? That wasn't an apology! You have to change your attitude! You've been critical of every choice I've made since I was seventeen and I'm done. Do you hear me, Dad? Because I'm serious about this — there's no point in us having a relationship if it's going to be toxic."

"Tell me what you want, Laine!"

He was unbelievable. "I want you to be proud of me when I accomplish something I worked hard at but if that's not possible I at least insist you not criticize my efforts. Otherwise, we don't have a relationship."

"All right," he said. "I'll do that. Can we

be at peace on this? For once?"

"Understand something, Dad — I'm serious about this. This is the last time I quarrel with you about how I choose to live my life. It's not as though I'm making bad choices. I'm not doing anything wrong, I'm doing something right. I'm doing something very difficult and admirable, something very few can do and I am tired of the tension between us. If you can't show me respect, I don't want you in my life." And what she couldn't put into words — he was the only man who could hurt her! Why that was, she couldn't understand.

"I'm your father," he said. "I want us to get along."

"That's entirely up to you," she told him. "I don't criticize you."

"Oh, but you do. You call me narrow-minded, toxic, critical and last I heard, a selfish ass with . . . what was that you said . . . ?"

She chewed her lip briefly. She remembered perfectly — she said he had a highly developed sense of entitlement, but she wasn't about to help him remember. "Because of the way you treat me!"

"Treat you how? We exchanged words maybe, I don't even remember the circumstances. Show me a family that doesn't disagree sometimes."

"Don't tell me you can't remember it!"

"Well, I won't argue with you again. You obviously take my opinions too personally. You know, Laine, some people are sensitive and some are just plain touchy."

She sat back in her chair. "You don't even know you do it, do you? You never say a positive thing! Now I'm touchy because I was hurt by your insulting remarks! You know, some people are opinionated and some are just rude and cruel!"

Laine tried to calm herself. It wasn't as if Senior had never apologized, though it wasn't often. He could be charming when he put his mind to it. Her mother had adored him; his nurses and techs loved him; his patients worshipped him. But pretending not to remember a blowout that was pivotal in their relationship? He was a giant ass, that's all.

"You know how I feel about you, Laine. I'm your father, of course I love you. I've always been proud of you. I'm proud of everything you do."

"You don't ever say that," she said.

"You took first place in the King Oak dressage competition. I filmed the whole event. We watched it together repeatedly. We celebrated! That's a father's pride, right there!"

She gave her head a slight shake, narrowing her eyes. Her mouth stood open slightly. She hadn't ridden in competition in over fifteen years. The event he mentioned was almost twenty years ago in Massachusetts. Was he kidding? She was just about to light into him for using a twenty-year-old example in an argument proving he was devoted when —

She heard the front door open. Eric must have been concerned about her. He was early. When he walked into the kitchen Senior stood up. "Who is this?" her father asked.

"Dad, this is Eric Gentry."

Senior put out his hand. "Dr. Carrington," he said.

"First names, Dad," she insisted.

"Paxton Carrington," he corrected. "How do you do?"

"Pleasure, sir," Eric said.

"I brewed coffee, Eric." Cell phone in her hand, Laine said, "Would you like to visit with my father for a minute? I need to be excused, but I won't be long."

Eric gave her a half smile and knowing look. He didn't have to be a detective to figure this out — she had a death grip on her phone. Then he moved toward the coffeepot. "Take your time. We'll be fine."

Laine bolted for the stairs and closed herself into her bedroom. She hit the speed dial for Pax and for once he actually answered. "He's here!" she blurted. "What the hell is Senior doing here?"

Pax wasn't just surprised. He actually stuttered a little. "Huh? What? What are you talking about?"

"Senior is here! My doorbell rang, I opened the door and there he stood, filling up the frame with his confidence and stubbornness! You couldn't warn me?"

"Laine, you can't think I knew and didn't call you! I thought he was in town. I talked to him last week. In fact, he was supposed to go to San Francisco for a conference — he was a presenter. He was a no-show and they were looking for him. He said he changed his mind about going, said he notified them and it was their screwup, but he never said a thing about Oregon."

"He changed his mind and didn't tell you? He planned a trip to Thunder Point without telling anyone? That isn't like him. Did you talk to Mrs. Mulligrew like I suggested?"

"She said she hadn't noticed anything other than him being preoccupied sometimes. If he's home he stays in his office, but he's not usually home when she's there. He kept lots of drugs, mostly samples, in his office, but mostly for use in orthopedics. Sometimes he forgot to leave her a check, but if she reminded him or left him a note, it was there the next time. What's he doing there?"

"He said he wants to put our problems to rest. But his next sentence was insulting! 'You know some people are sensitive and some are just plain touchy'!" she said, mimicking him. "No wonder I want to smack him upside the head."

"How long is he staying?" Pax asked.

"He's not staying here! No way! He wasn't invited. He must have a rental car, though I didn't look outside. There's a motel in town, far beneath his standards I'm sure, but he's not staying here! He hasn't done anything to put this situation to rest!"

"Oh, man," Pax groaned. "I'm so glad I'm not there. . . ."

"What am I supposed to do with him? I don't want yet another big fight with him. I'm just not that person right now! I want peace! I've earned it."

"Well, can you leave town?" Pax asked.

"What?"

"I don't know, Laine. Tell him his timing was bad and you were just headed to Switzerland for a month at a spa and you'll be in touch?"

"You're funny. What would Genevieve do?"

"Hmm. She'd give him a cup of tea, listen to him without responding or find a benign topic, offer him food and nod politely. Escape to her mother's or sister's whenever she could, vent to them and take long baths until he left and then complain to me for weeks afterward about what an impossible load he is. She wouldn't engage him. I don't engage him. It's like rams locking horns."

"I can do that," Laine said. "Yeah, I can do that. Maybe. But he has to go to a motel."

Pax laughed at her. "You can't do that. You're too much like him. You like being right and you have to point it out to him when he insults you, which only causes him to talk down to you again. I mean, you are right, but you like it too much. You can't not hear him, you can't let it go when he offends you, you can't go to a Zen place. . . ."

"All right, all right . . . but I'm good at long baths. . . . I'd better get downstairs. I left him with Eric. . . ."

"I can't wait to meet this guy."

"You might be meeting him soon, when

329

you come out here to get your father!"

"Call me when he leaves tonight. If you let him live."

When she got to the bottom of the stairs she heard laughter. Her father was laughing and talking. Eric was laughing with him.

"I guess you two found something to talk about?" she ventured.

"This fella here has worked on Packards. We had a '41 Packard station wagon. You know the kind, with the wood paneling. We had one when I was a kid — it was red. My parents would load us into it and take us to the lake in New York in summer. That car was a beauty. Business was so good my dad got himself a Packard coupe convertible, a '49 — it was a slick shiny brown. A little cold inside in Boston winters but he didn't care. He gave my mom the station wagon for the kids and he owned that convertible. What a car. What a car. I loved that convertible."

Eric gave her a reassuring smile. *Why can't I do that?* she asked herself. *Why can't I just let his snide comments go and talk about classic Packards?* "How old were you?" she asked her dad. Trying. She was trying.

"Oh, nine or ten or something. It was a big deal in my neighborhood, let me tell you. All the kids wanted a ride in it. My oldest brother borrowed it for a dance and dinged it up." He laughed, shaking his head. "I never heard a bigger uproar in my house. Back then it took weeks to fix something like that."

"Now we can do it in an afternoon if we have the right parts. Sometimes we need a second afternoon for paint unless it's chrome," Eric said. "You hungry, Paxton?" he asked.

Senior leaned back and rubbed his belly. "I could eat. Sorry, son, I missed the name. . . ."

"Eric, sir. Why don't I take you and Laine to dinner. There's a nice little seafood place at the marina."

"Son, I'm from Boston. I hope you don't intend to try to impress me with seafood."

"No, sir. I'm going to wow you with the company."

Paxton laughed pleasantly. "Good for you! Good for you!"

"Give me a few minutes to change clothes and then we'll go."

"Sure. Absolutely. Don't want to go out to dinner in your mechanic's clothes. . . ."

Laine frowned but Eric touched her arm gently and she relaxed.

"Janice, where did you find that delightful

young man who knows all about classic cars?"

"Laine, Dad," she corrected.

"Hmm?"

"You called me Janice."

"Hmm? Did I? You do look so much like your mother sometimes. So where are we going to dinner?"

She hesitated for a moment, then said, "A seafood restaurant at the marina. It's not real fancy but the nicest one in town and the food is wonderful."

"Perfect," he said. "That young man, he's a friend of yours?"

Again she was speechless. "I live with him," she said patiently. "Eric is my boyfriend. We've lived together for almost three months."

"He seems a perfectly nice young man. Does he remind you of Pax at all?"

She shook her head. "Not at all," she said. But she thought Eric was like Pax. Patient. Definitely not touchy. Loving and kind, yet very strong. And it seemed Eric, like Pax, could accept Senior as he was and find a way to get along with him. Maybe she'd leave Eric in charge and *she* could go to the motel!

Laine would long remember this particular

dinner at Cliffhanger's as one of the most pivotal evenings of her life. And not in a good way.

Senior kept talking about old cars, ones he idolized as a child and status cars like his first Mercedes. While he and Eric had a beer, Senior talked on and on about the route to the lake in New York, the price of milk and eggs, war rationing and gas coupons.

"My dad was a surgeon," Senior said, "and he got more coupons so he could get back and forth to the hospitals whenever necessary, but between him and my mother, there was always a way to get to the lake. He didn't serve in the Army because he was slightly disabled — one leg just a little shorter than the other from a childhood accident. He had a slight limp but it never slowed him down. He had more energy than ten men put together. I don't remember him ever having a sick day in his life."

Eric asked questions about rationing, Senior explained about "need certificates." Everyone had to demonstrate a need for major items before they could be purchased. Even typewriters were rationed because the Army needed them for communication. And then he began telling the same story again.

All of this would have happened before Senior was ten years old, but Laine had heard it all before. Except she had heard it from her grandmother, roughly twenty years ago.

When their meals came, Senior started asking about weather conditions and if it was always so cold in Virginia. He called her Janice three times. She corrected him twice and he told her again that she looked so much like her mother. Then he told her he'd tried to call her but Ma Bell was very unreliable. . . . They hadn't called AT&T "Ma Bell" for twenty years.

As Laine watched and listened to him, she grew more and more alarmed. Senior seemed to shrink, to grow smaller before her eyes. He became vulnerable and elderly, holding his elbows close to his sides while he ate. The same man who an hour ago filled the foyer with his confidence, size and bluster was becoming frail and needy as she watched. She stared into her bread bowl of clam chowder a lot, trying to keep her eyes from misting. She exchanged a few glances with Eric and it was apparent he knew what she was thinking.

They left the restaurant when it was dark. While Eric drove the car, Senior became anxious and kept asking if it was the right way. When they pulled into the garage Senior said, "Oh? This is it?"

"This is it," Laine said. "Eric, would you do me a big favor? Would you find clean sheets for the bed in the guest room? And would you take Dad upstairs and let him help you with the linens? I have something to do."

"Be glad to," he said.

"And, Dad? Can you give me the keys to your rental car? I'll get your bag for you."

"Okay," he said, his voice rather subdued. That was not her father's voice but the voice of an old, tired and confused man. He dug in his pocket for the keys and came up empty. "I don't have them."

"Do you know where they might be?" she asked, knowing he wouldn't have an answer.

"On the hook by the back door?"

"Okay," she said. "Go upstairs with Eric. I'll find them." Since there was no hook by the back door, since there was no back door other than the one that led to the garage or the patio doors to the deck, she just went to his rental car, a midsize Ford Taurus. The doors were locked, the keys were lying on the passenger seat, there was no luggage in the backseat and his briefcase was on the floor of the car, passenger side. She went back into the opened garage, got herself a couple of tools from her toolbox and broke into the car in less than twenty seconds. The alarm sounded right away but she slid into the car, grabbed the keys and silenced it.

She popped the trunk in search of luggage, but there was none. Huh? She checked the backseat again. Nothing. She took the briefcase and keys and her tools inside. After storing her tools and lowering the garage door, she took the briefcase into the small study and her desk.

In the briefcase she found the car rental papers — he'd rented the car in Portland. His plane ticket was from Boston to Portland, one way, and there was a luggage receipt but no bag. His wallet was inside along with his cell phone. She checked the phone — he had missed calls from several people, from Pax, from his practice. She read a few text messages:

Dr. Carrington, Dr. Ellis of the American Association of Orthopedic Surgeons has been trying to reach you and would like you to call him. . . .

Dr. Carrington, Dr. Sorenson from Women and

336

Children's is still waiting for your consult. . . .

Dad, call me as soon as you get this message. . . .

Dad? Just give me a call and tell me what's up — I heard from your office that you were a no-show in San Francisco. . . .

There was a sleeve of pills. It looked like so many of the samples her father had always had on hand from pharmaceutical reps — Cognex. She went to her computer and looked up the drug, already knowing what it was going to say. Treatment for mild to moderate symptoms of Alzheimer's.

She looked in his wallet. The usual cash and credit cards and driver's license were there, but there were also lists on small slips of paper. Notes to himself. Phone numbers for his office, Pax, his partner in the practice, reminders about appointments, medication schedule — there was no other medication in the briefcase but he was supposed to be on cholesterol and blood pressure medication.

Whew.

She left the briefcase under her desk

where it wouldn't be visible. She went upstairs. She'd call the Portland airport and find out if they still had the luggage Senior had checked, but that was hardly urgent now. She found Eric just smoothing the comforter over the sheets. "Do you have any sweats or boxers Senior can borrow?" she asked. "There's no luggage."

"No luggage?" Senior asked. "No luggage? What's that about?"

She just looked at her father. "You must be very tired. Eric will get you something to wear to bed. . . ." Ten minutes later he had brushed his teeth with a new toothbrush and was tucked into bed. "I'll be downstairs for a while before I go to bed and I'm going to leave a light on the stairs so you don't forget about them."

"I won't forget," he said.

"I'll leave the light on anyway."

Once she was downstairs, she walked into Eric's arms and let him hold her. She rested her head against his shoulder. "God," she whispered.

"You had no idea?"

She shook her head. "This seems pretty sudden."

"But you said you haven't spent that much time with him."

"I haven't. Pax sees him occasionally,

much of the time they'll see each other at the hospital. But he's got it bad — that can't just have happened. I have to look this up." She went to the kitchen for a glass of wine.

"Wouldn't your brother know?"

"Not necessarily. His specialty is children and what you have to know about specialists — they concentrate on that one thing. I've heard my dad say he barely knows what to do for a heart attack — not his part of the body. Of course he was being flip — he knows what to do, but he isn't the right person to treat it. They all went to medical school, basic training, but then they studied in one area in residency and in that, learned how to refer patients. But . . ." She paused as she poured the wine. "But our paternal grandmother had Alzheimer's. My dad was always so afraid of that. Going to the kitchen and forgetting what you were there for — that's normal. Going to the kitchen and forgetting it's a kitchen, that's dementia. Forgetting names, that's a natural thing for aging people. Forgetting what words like *add* and *subtract* mean and still not remembering them in five minutes — that can be dementia." She took a sip. "This is a complete waste of good wine. I don't think anything short of an injection is going to relax me right now."

"Maybe you should just call Pax," he suggested.

"I was in grade school when my grandmother started getting dangerous — running stop signs, forgetting the way home, leaving the stove burner on. And the final straw was when she went for a walk one night at about 1:00 a.m., barefoot and in her nightgown, in Boston, in January. That's when she had to move in with us for a while and with two working doctors in the family, that was impossible. She was moved to a special facility. I thought it was pretty nice. Of course I was a kid. My dad was horrified. I remember him saying if that ever happened to him, he'd want to die. But my grandmother — she thought she was on the farm. What farm we never did figure out since she grew up in the city. But she was pretty passive. She stopped remembering who people were, but she talked a lot about the farm. Wonder what farm she was on?"

"Tell me what I can do," he said.

She just shook her head. "I need a little computer time. I'm grounded in facts — I investigate for a living. Then I have to call my brother back. This is one of those times I have to wake him. I'm sorry, Eric. I know you didn't sign on for this."

"Laine, some things just come with the

territory. We'll work this out. Just tell me what you need."

"Right now I need to think and talk to Pax."

He gave her a brief kiss on the forehead. Then he went out onto the deck to check out the sky.

SIXTEEN

It had been a long night for Laine. She'd barely slept. She was listening for any disturbance from her father's room. They hadn't slept under the same roof since her mother had died so she was completely unaware of his after-dark habits. Was he going to be sun-downing, a common Alzheimer's symptom of becoming active and agitated after dark?

Eric was concerned and offered to go open the station, leave everything in the hands of Manny or Norm and come right back to make sure she was all right on her own with her father, but she told him to go. The station was probably far less stressful. And she needed time alone with Senior.

Eric had the coffee on at 5:00 a.m. and she was sitting at her kitchen table by six, making a list for herself. There were questions for her dad and Pax, decisions about what to do next. She was definitely not sending him back to Boston alone.

Before she had many items on that list, Senior came into the kitchen. He was wearing last night's clothing, of course. "I guess I didn't get my bag inside last night. I couldn't find my shaving kit."

"Sit down. Let me get you a cup of coffee." She got his coffee. She sat down at the table, too, waiting while he dressed it. It was impossible not to notice he was possessed of the very thing that always set her on edge, warned of a potential storm — his puffed-up chest, his lifted chin, his confidence. This morning it gave her some relief. But she knew it was going to be temporary. She pulled the pill pack out of her pocket and slid it toward him. It sat next to his coffee cup.

"How long have you known?" she asked. And his chin immediately lowered.

"I suspected not long after your mother died. . . ."

"Oh, my God! Dad!"

"At first I thought it was grief. And I've had great success with medication, with vitamin therapy. In fact, I've wondered for years if maybe I had been wrong. It could've been the normal aging process. A little forgetfulness . . . Who doesn't put the milk in the cupboard or the cereal in the refrigerator sometimes?"

"You self-diagnosed? You self-medicated?"

"It's not as if I'm some amateur. . . . I'm capable of research."

"You've been operating!"

"I've been reducing my O.R. schedule since your mother got sick. I haven't been operating very often the past five years and never without an excellent team. There's always a qualified surgeon scrubbed in with me. And my nurse — she could do it if she had to. Hell, she's as good as I am any day."

"But now you're done! You're absolutely done!"

"Laine! I have managed this for five —"

She reached over and touched his hand but she spoke with a low and threatening voice. "Don't even start with me. I've talked to Pax. The past six months to a year there were issues. We didn't put two and two together, but now we know. You had a flood at the house and we thought it was an accident, but it wasn't — the water was left running. You left a patient on the table and went to the golf course. You were a no-show in San Francisco and they're still trying to reach you to find out what happened but you haven't called them back because you don't know what happened. You have to write yourself notes and set your phone alarm to take medicine. You know what's going on and you need a neurologist."

"It's gotten worse recently."

"Which is what happens. I was up late reading. These drugs can be very effective for mild to moderate symptoms but there comes a point they stop working. You can get by for years with occasional, brief episodes until . . ." She just shook her head because she knew that putting it into words could shatter him. He was proud of his intelligence, his strength, his robust health. It was hard to imagine what he felt at the thought of deteriorating.

As if he'd read her mind, he said, "Maybe if I was ninety . . . Maybe then I could deal with it. . . ."

"That isn't how this works, Dad." She squeezed his hand. "You seem to be feeling quite all right this morning."

"Mornings are best. If I've slept."

"Do you know how long you might have between periods of confusion?"

He shook his head. "Not anymore," he said. "At first it was very noticeable but not real to me. You forget things, you know? Especially if your mind is elsewhere, like on work or your dead wife. Your mind wanders and it takes a second to reorient. But then one day you miss the turn to your neighborhood and drive around for a long time. A long, long time, like hours, wondering where you live. And everything around you looks like another country. Then finally you have to pull into a service station for gas and to ask where you are. It's humiliating. It's horrifying. There's no mistaking that for a wandering mind."

"You must have been terrified," she said, her voice soft.

"My wife is dead. I'm alone. And I don't want to live this way."

"You're not alone," she said. "You should have told us."

He laughed bitterly. "Just what you need — a sick old man to look after."

"You're not sick. Not yet, anyway. We need to get a better diagnosis than yours, probably new medication. We'll worry about how sick you are when you can't play chess anymore. But for right now, you just don't operate ever again. It will be a hard transition for your patients, but —"

"What am I supposed to say? I'm not operating because I have Alzheimer's?"

She leaned toward him. "You'll say, I'm seventy. I'm financially set. I have grandchildren. I'm retiring. You don't have to say anything more. I have a feeling your partners will be relieved."

He seemed to relax a little. "I've been asked if anything is wrong. I insisted nothing was wrong. Now what?"

"We're going to go out today to buy some clothes, since you forgot your bag at the Portland airport. They're holding it. You're going to visit for a few days. Pax is going to talk to some people, line up some appointments for you at home. We'll coordinate by phone. Then I'm taking you back to Boston."

He looked down. "I'm sorry," he said.

"Dad, you have nothing to be sorry for. There's nothing you could have done about this."

"For one thing, I'm sorry I've been so hard on you. I have no excuse. Janice always said I'd regret it and I do. It was more than I could handle."

She frowned. "What was more than you could handle?"

"Everything. Your job, for one thing," he said. "All that undercover crap." He sat back and ran a hand over his bald head. "I was jealous of your mother — she could take it. She was always the strong one, wasn't she? She was excited by it. It drove me crazy. I always worried and those times you were out of touch, I worried more. Worry made me so angry! I wanted to be like her but the best I could ever do was say nothing, and I didn't do that very well. Then you got shot and I couldn't . . . I'm sorry, Laine. I am proud of you. But I couldn't encourage you. I was scared to death. You've always terrified me. . . ."

"Huh?"

"You were so smart, so daring, so . . . *fearless*! I had a boy and a girl and it was my girl who wasn't happy unless she was risking her life! Pax was smart but methodical. Cautious. You? By the time you were twelve you'd broken an arm and an ankle and were lucky it wasn't worse. Karate, riding, gymnastics, diving, rock climbing, parasailing, skydiving . . ." He shook his head. "Your mom used to say to me, 'How can the FBI surprise you? It's so in character!' I didn't want to slow you down, Laine. I wanted to stop you! I wanted you to stop taking chances so I could take a deep breath."

It all came back to her. Her entire life flashed before her eyes. *Good job, Pax! Laine, damn it, back away from the edge! Excellent showing, Pax. Laine! If that horse isn't going to make the jump, go around! A good competitor doesn't take unnecessary chances! That's my boy — A-plus! Laine! Not so fast! Not so high! Not so wild!*

She sighed. Fear. Could it be as simple as

348

that? Well, that and the fact that he could never just be honest and admit he felt helpless and let her reassure him. His ego was so big he could never have admitted that he was just afraid she'd get hurt, which of course she did. Instead of being honest, he criticized every move she made. She always felt not good enough and tried even harder, was even more daring.

"I should have just thrown you," she muttered.

"What?" he asked.

"Nothing. Nothing. For whatever reason, you had no confidence that I knew what I was doing. And I knew what I was doing. I hope we can get past this. . . ."

"Please don't lock me away," he said. "Please."

"Let's not get ahead of ourselves, Dad. Let's take it one day at a time."

"My mother — I had to put her in a facility for dementia patients. I know it was years ago and they've come a long way since then, but every time I left her after a visit she cried. She begged me to take her home. I've lived in my house for thirty-five years. Please don't . . ."

She stood up from the table. "Dad, we're not going to lock you away. Right now I'm going to make you a couple of eggs and toast. Then we'll call Pax — you should talk to him, reassure him you're all right. Then we'll head to North Bend for some shopping. I'll give you a tour of the area. This is a beautiful place." She patted his hand. "I'll be with you, don't worry."

"Did we make up?" he asked.

"We're all made up," she said.

"Thank God," he said. "I was afraid that wouldn't happen and it would be too late."

"It's not too late," she assured him.

Al was finishing up a late breakfast at the diner when Scott Grant came in. He sat at the counter next to Al and said to Gina, "Can you screw up some eggs for me? I had a really long night and no breakfast."

"Sure. Were you at the hospital?"

"I was called in in the middle of the night. There was a fight at an underage party — bunch of eighteen-, nineteen-year-old boys. I was up ordering head CTs and sewing all night."

"That's horrible," Gina said. "Please tell me I didn't know any of them."

He smiled and shook his head. "No Thunder Point kids."

"That's a relief," she said. "I'll get you a nice big breakfast platter."

Al turned to Scott. "Speaking of Thunder

Point kids, what's going on with the Russell kids?"

"Don't you see Justin almost every day?"

"I do. I see him at work some evenings. But I can tell he doesn't really want to talk about it."

"It's not that so much," Scott said. "Justin's been trying to stay invisible for the past couple of years. He's been concentrating on holding that family together for as long as possible so he doesn't lose his brothers. He thought if he just made it to eighteen he would be left in charge, but I always warned him it wasn't quite as simple as being old enough. Even if he was eighteen or even nineteen, social services might not think of him as the best option. There are special circumstances for family foster care, but all that's irrelevant — he's still just seventeen."

"What is required?" Al asked.

"It's pretty simple. For nonfamily members, over twenty-one, self-supporting, no criminal record, pretty standard stuff."

"Hmm," he said, thinking. "So what's going on with Mrs. Russell?"

"Her condition is greatly improved and a bed is opening up for her in a facility near Coos Bay. I could send her home for a few days but I'm holding off on doing that. I don't know how many times those boys can shift gears. She really can't live at home anymore. Her symptoms are worsening and soon she'll probably require a feeding tube because swallowing is difficult for her. If we get her good care she'll have decent quality of life. She could live another few months or years. I'm afraid to say, no one knows."

"Well, those boys are on their own now," Al pointed out.

"Not exactly," Scott said, lifting his coffee cup. "I'm responsible for them. I check on them a couple of times a day, but that won't work in the long term. Their case worker knows I'm holding off their placement while she searches for something close. Something here in town. Something where at least the two younger boys can be together. I don't think the chances of that are very good."

Al thought about this for a moment, sipping his coffee. "You knew Justin dropped out of school?"

Scott nodded just as he accepted his breakfast plate. Gina refilled both their coffees. "He thought he had to," he said. "He had to take care of his mother until he could hand her off to his brothers. Hopefully he'll go back. . . ."

"He won't go back," Al said. "He's past that now. What about that GED?"

Between bites of eggs, Scott said, "Maybe

with his mother taken care of he'll have time for that. Justin was a good student but there were only so many hours in the day. Maybe he wasn't at the top of his class, but he did just fine for a kid with so much on his plate. He could've gotten into community college, no problem. He's a sharp kid. And he cares about his family."

"What about their father, man?" Al asked. "Anyone know where he is? Because shouldn't he be stepping in now?"

"DHS knows his name and his last known location. But knowing and having his co-operation are two different things."

"Now wait — isn't it against the law to abandon your children?"

"Depends," Scott said. "He and their mother divorced and he gave her custody. They can go after him for back child support but they can't turn him into a father."

"Jesus," Al said, frustrated. "If you're lucky enough to get some sons, you'd think . . ." He shook his head. "They're nice boys," he said.

"They're amazing boys," Scott agreed. "I spent half the early morning hours patching up a bunch of boys who were out partying while Justin was home tucking in his little brothers. And they don't want much, they just want to keep their family together. It's not like any of them were irresponsible — they just got hammered by MS. Families coping with MS need a lot of resources. A lot of support."

Al thought on this for a while. Then he asked, "So, is there a test to be a foster parent?"

"No," Scott said. "Why? You thinking about it?"

"Well, I'm pretty sure I'm not the right kind of person. And I'm not sure what's required."

"A lot of paperwork," Scott said with a shrug, concentrating on his breakfast once again.

Paperwork, Al thought dismally. "Forms," he said almost to himself.

Scott laughed. "It wouldn't be a government agency if there wasn't a lot of paperwork involved. But I'm sure it's not complicated."

You still have to be able to read the questions and fill in the blanks, Al thought. Who'd give three kids to a guy who can't fill out a form? "I'm sure I'm not the right kind of guy. I'm not planning on sticking around here long. I like being flexible. You can't be real flexible if you're looking out for a bunch of kids."

"That's true," Scott said.

"How long you figure you can hold off the foster home thing?"

Scott just shrugged. "Another week, probably. I understand where they're coming from, even if it is ridiculous — those boys have been on their own for two or three years and they do a better job running that household than half the adults I know. But when you get down to it, they deserve better. If they're in a decent home, they can relax and be boys. Maybe it's the threat of being scattered that keeps 'em in line. Or maybe Justin is just a natural."

"I think he's just scared to death," Al said. "What's he got besides his little family?"

"Yeah, I know. Well, he might not be eighteen yet but he can probably be emancipated and live on his own. He has a job and is not a student anymore. . . ."

This just sounded worse and worse, Al thought. They could take away his brothers and leave him in that house alone. "Maybe it'll just be temporary," Al said. "He'd be able to get his brothers back once he's legal. . . ."

"Maybe. It's just that —"

"What?" Al persisted.

Scott turned and looked at him. "The glitch is, in order to qualify as a legal guardian or family foster parent, he has to earn a decent living. I'm not sure his work at the station will keep food on the table. In the middle of all this chaos, their mother is going to pass away."

"Right," Al said. But what he thought was, *You're killing me here!* How much were those kids supposed to take? He stood up and put his usual ten spot on the counter for his breakfast. "I better think about working. I'll check on them from time to time, as long as I'm here."

"I think I speak for a lot of folks when I say, I hope you're around for a while, Al. You've been a good neighbor. Personally, I'd hate to see you go."

"That's real nice, Doc. I'm restless, that's all. I've been traveling between three or four jobs for the past thirty years or so. It's a hard habit to break. But I always come back. Eric is a good employer. I like his shop."

"That's good to know," Scott said. "Thanks for looking in on the boys now and then. If you have any concerns, give me a call."

"Will do," he said.

Al went to the station and had a little talk with Eric about Justin and his brothers. Eric was aware of the situation but there was little he could do to help. "I can move him up to full-time. Right now that's not his biggest problem, though it will be. He told me he's looking around for a second job. His brothers are in school all day and he's here at night. . . . I hate to see a kid so young taking all that on, but most of the family men in this town have to take second jobs. It's the way we get by, right?"

"I never thought of myself as particularly lucky," Al said. "I do now."

"I know what you mean. Listen, I gotta get out of here by six at the latest. Laine's dad is in town and she's going to take him back to Boston in a couple of days. He's showing some signs of . . . well, getting old and fragile. She doesn't want him flying alone. And she wants to make sure he gets some checkups once he's home, so she's going to take care of that. She'll be gone awhile."

"I thought Laine's father was a doctor," Al said.

"Apparently they make terrible patients and aren't too good at taking care of their health. Who knew?"

"No problem, Eric. I'll be here. Take off earlier. I can manage the station, you know that."

Eric slapped a hand on his back. "I rely on you a lot, Al. And I appreciate it. I hope you know that."

Al grinned. "That mean there's a little something in the Christmas card for me?"

Eric laughed. "Christmas is a long time from now. Let's see where you are then."

"Yeah, boss." He got a kick out of calling this kid "boss." He wondered if Eric ever thought about that. He could actually have been Al's son, being eighteen years younger.

It was about four in the afternoon when Ray Anne stopped by for her quarter tank of gas. She was wearing a hot-pink skirt and jacket, Ray Anne's version of the business suit. And those heels that brought her up to five-foot-seven, when she was really struggling to make five-three. There was a lot of leg, a little cleavage and a great big smile for Al. He liked that; he thought her sexy clothes were cute.

"How's it going today?" she asked, laying a hand full of hot-pink enamel fingernails on his forearm.

"Better now," he said, making her eyes sparkle. "I can't get away early tonight. Eric's got family business and I have to close the shop and take the calls for tows. There might not be any, that's my hope. So I can't get out of here till eleven, but if you're feeling young and energetic and maybe can sleep in late tomorrow, we could spend a little time on the roof."

"I can do that," she said.

"Don't let me talk you into anything," he said. "You don't have to stay dressed up. You can put on your pajamas and lotions — I like you that way, too. Fact is, I like you all ways."

"Something wrong with these shoes?" she asked, turning an ankle to reveal the heels.

"I think they're hot," he said. "You can wear 'em with your pajamas if you want, but it's not necessary. You keep my attention just fine in bare feet with cotton between your toes."

"I'll be up," she said. "I'll have a cold beer for you and a glass of wine for myself. I can't order up a lightning show, but the stars are nice up there on the roof."

"I'll see you later," he said. And he felt better than he had in hours.

When Al got to Ray Anne's house she was not in her pajamas but she was dressed casually. She'd managed to get the beanbags up on the roof along with a throw and a couple of candles. They took their drinks and got settled in and all the while Al was thinking, *This woman is so sweet to me. She will be so hard to leave.*

"Things are kind of upside down around

here," he said. She was snuggled up close to him and just hummed. "There's the situation with Justin and his brothers — that has his friends from work worried. The kid should catch a break. And Eric said Laine's pretty worried about her father. She's going to take him back to Boston, hopefully not gone too long."

"Tell me more about Justin and his brothers," she said.

He told her the full story, starting with the day Eric asked him to look out for Justin up to that fateful day the ambulance took his mother away.

"The poor kid," she said. "I can't imagine. I never had younger siblings or children of my own."

"Did you want them? Children?"

"I did when I was younger. But I wasn't married to men who wanted them so it couldn't have been a priority. Right?"

"Do you regret it?" he asked.

"Al, I have a pile of regrets," she said with a laugh. "But I also have a nice big stack of good moments, happy times when I actually mysteriously made good choices for myself. And I'm happy now. That's enough for me."

"That's a good place to be," he said.

"You're one of my better choices."

"Ray, you're one sweet little honey. That's for sure."

"Aw, I like hearing that."

"You're awful good to me."

"That's the easy part. It's easy to be good to a good man."

"You know, there was a time, when I was a young farmer, that I thought the idea of a bunch of kids was exactly what I was cut out for. Life on the farm with a family was all I ever wanted."

"You must have changed your mind," she said.

"My mind got changed, yeah. I married real young. We lived on the farm. She got pregnant right away and even though farming is hard, we couldn't have been happier. We had a baby, a boy, and he died of crib death."

"Aw, Al, I'm so sorry."

"Back then I was Mick, short for Michel. When I couldn't come to grips with the loss, I took a job driving a truck and was almost never home. My wife complained about it, but she had a lot of family and I didn't think she needed me too much." He chuckled deep in his throat and pulled Ray Anne a little closer. "In case you ever get the notion it's a good idea to run away from your troubles, I tried that one — it doesn't work

361

too well. When I was finally healed enough to put my roots back down, it was too late. Carol figured out she couldn't count on me and life was hard enough for her. That was pretty much the end of that."

Ray Anne was quiet for a moment. "Very sad for both of you."

"Carol did the right thing. A few years later she married a local guy — Tony. They had a couple of kids. They do a little farming but Tony is also an insurance agent and Carol is a nurse in a nursing home. You know that half a farm that was left to me? I didn't take the money and run — I gave my half to Carol. She earned it. I go back there every summer and I see her. She's doing well."

"You still love her?" Ray Anne asked.

"Oh, sure, but it's not the kind of love you think. It's friendship. Her kids treat me like some oddball old uncle that shows up sometimes. I give her a lot of credit, you know? She was never angry with me. She was finished, but she wasn't mad. She just moved on. Got her nursing degree, got married, had a family . . . the things that were important."

"And what about you? Did you get to do the things that are important to you?" she asked him.

"Well, this — right now, right here — this is important. It's one of those things that might be a blessing or could be a handicap. It just doesn't take that much to make me happy. A night under the stars with my girl, that's heaven to me."

"Yet you still run. . . ."

"I still have a phobia about getting pinned down. . . ."

"And a fear of being disappointed?" she asked.

"No, honey. Fear of being a disappointment."

She snuggled closer. "You're not a kid anymore, Al. You're a good man. Stop worrying you can't live up to expectations and just do what you know is right for you. No one's going to try to pin you down or turn you into something you don't aim to be. You're not that scared and confused young farmer anymore."

"And if I get a hankering to go off again?"

"Say goodbye," she said. "Just say, see you later. But you don't have to run away. You're welcome here as long as you feel like staying."

"I'll admit, Ray — it's real hard to think of leaving you."

She smiled. "Good," she said.

SEVENTEEN

When Eric got home at five o'clock — early for him — three suitcases were packed and lined up inside the front door. There was the rich aroma of his favorite — steak soup. He knew she made it for him despite the fact that it wasn't a soup day — it was sunny and bright outside, the temperature warm. He went to the kitchen, where he found Senior at the table, the newspaper spread out in front of him. Laine was stirring a pot and he went behind her. Hands around her waist, he kissed her neck and she hummed.

Her father grunted.

"Hello, Paxton," Eric said. "How was your day?"

"Very busy," he said.

"We didn't do a thing," Laine said softly. "We walked down to the diner for lunch. When Gina brought lunch Senior said he'd just eaten." She shook her head. "Then we walked along the beach, stopped in at

Cooper's and on the way home we said goodbye at the doctor's office and sheriff's office. I did the rest of the packing while Dad napped."

Over the past few days Laine told him she had seen firsthand how much her father's dementia was taking over. Mornings were best for him but his periods of confusion were longer and more frequent than she realized and by evening he was a mess of forgetfulness. It was a miracle he'd gotten himself to Oregon all the way from Boston and a triple miracle he'd managed the drive from Portland. If she hadn't seen his ticket for herself she wouldn't have been surprised to learn the journey had taken days.

But typical of Alzheimer's patients, his memory of things that happened long ago, in his childhood, adolescence or early adulthood was crystal clear to the finest detail.

"I can still go with you," Eric said. "Al and Manny can manage the station. It would be a quick trip for me, but I can help you get him there."

"We'll be okay," she said. "We've been inseparable for days. He does whatever I ask of him, even if he does sometimes think I'm my mother. And Scott Grant gave me a mild sedative in case he gets agitated while we're traveling. I don't think we'll need it."

He sniffed the air. "Steak soup — my favorite."

"There will be enough left over for you to freeze. I even got a couple of extra sourdough bowls and put them in the freezer."

"Maybe you could slip him a sedative tonight," he suggested.

She smiled at him. "He's been resting very well. We haven't had nighttime issues. At least not yet. You're taking this very well."

He wasn't, actually. He was terrified that the needs of her family would take her away from him. This dynamic was pretty complicated — after a lifetime of conflict with her father she suddenly learns the old boy adores her. And of course she'd always adored him and longed for his approval. And now Senior needed her. It wasn't an illusion, he really needed her. Laine wasn't working full-time at the moment and Pax was committed to a difficult and time-consuming fellowship — there weren't many options. "I'm going to miss you like mad, but I understand you have to do this."

"You will stay here, won't you? In our house?"

"Is that what you want?" he asked for the tenth time.

"I want to see you in my mind when I talk to you. I don't want to think of you in some hotel room or something. I want to envision you in your station or here, on the deck or in the kitchen." She frowned a little. "No dirty boots on my sofa."

"Never," he said, smiling at her.

"When you tell me about the lightning over the bay, I want to see it in my mind and wish I was with you on the deck or in bed. I don't want . . ."

"Laine," her father said. "I need something to drink. Something like . . . I don't know."

"Orange juice," she said. It wasn't a question. She poured him a glass and took it to him.

He accepted the glass. "Why does he come around here all the time?" Senior asked.

"That's Eric, Dad. You remember. He lives here."

"Right," he said. "Good to see you, Eric," he said. He took a sip of orange juice and made a face. "This isn't Coke!"

"It's orange juice. Would you rather a Coke?"

"Yes," he said, sliding the juice away.

She poured a Coke into a glass for him and took it to him, retrieving the orange juice.

"Yeah, I think maybe you should crush up one of those sedatives and put it in his soup. . . ."

Laine just chuckled.

"You're the one who's taking this well," he pointed out.

She leaned close to him, her voice soft. "Sometimes it makes me laugh, sometimes I just want to cry for him, and sometimes I just get the Coke. But I think the message is pretty clear — he needs me right now. He can no longer be on his own. I think he's probably lucky he's made it this long."

"Laine! Get Eric something to drink. Eric, son, come here and keep me company. Tell me about that Packard you're working on this week!"

"Punctuated by periods of acuity."

Eric smiled and went to the table, sitting across from Senior. "Well, it's not a Packard this week. We've got a mess of a '67 Trans Am in the shop. Someone salvaged it — dynamite muscle car. I'd like to have it but it's not for sale."

"I remember that car," Senior said. "Before Laine was even born. I was just married and had to have a sedate car, not some hot rod, but I did love that car. What color?"

"No color yet. It's a rusted-out wreck — needs a total restoration."

"Make the owner choose red. There's no other color for that car!"

"I agree completely."

It had only been four days since Senior landed on their doorstep but during that time Eric and Laine had done a record amount of talking. "You will be back, won't you?" he'd asked quietly. She was leaving everything — all the furniture and her car — and had only packed two suitcases for herself. She wasn't sure how long it would take to make sure Senior had a battery of tests, had an official diagnosis and a nursing service installed to care for him, but she intended to come back to Thunder Point. She hoped it was only two weeks.

"Of course I'm coming back here," she had said. "How could I give you up?"

But Laine wasn't the only one who had been reading about Alzheimer's. Eric had studied it as well and one thing he learned — it was irreversible. From now on it would only get worse. Senior had valiantly held it back for years, even operating as recently as three months ago. How he had managed that when today he could barely remember where he was, it was a true mystery. But then he had left his patient. . . . It was pretty likely he had started the day on Friday and ended the day thinking it was Saturday morning.

Eric wondered if Laine, being away from

him, away from this life they'd made together, would change her mind about Thunder Point. Almost daily Senior said to her, "Don't leave me, Lainie! Don't lock me up!" And she always said, "Of course not. Don't be afraid. Everything's all right."

He should be encouraged that all the furnishings were left behind, but then she'd be staying at her father's house, the family home as she called it. And her rent here was paid through December. Would she come back? Come back to pack? Ask him to pack her things and send them back to Boston? Send a moving company to the house to take everything?

After dinner, after a brief walk around the neighborhood to try to wear out Senior, Paxton was given a cup of hot milk. "Blasted nastiest thing I've ever had!" he grumbled. Laine supervised him getting to bed. Then she shared a glass of wine with Eric and they sat on one lounge on the deck even though she'd bought a second. He was behind her and she was sitting between his long legs, leaning against him, watching the sunset and then the stars.

"He asked me where we're going to go tomorrow," she said. "I reminded him we're going home. Is it possible that the second it was out — that he's been suffering from dementia — that his symptoms just got fifty times worse overnight? Because if he was this bad at the hospital or home, wouldn't someone have noticed?"

"I don't know," Eric said honestly.

"I am coming back, Eric. I will. I just need a couple of weeks to settle things. Maybe three. But I'll be back."

"I know," he lied. "Before you take on this adventure I want to be sure you know something. I've never felt this way before. No woman before you has meant this much to me. Not ever. I love you, Laine. No matter what you have to do, no matter how long it takes you, this won't change. We're not teenagers. We can get through this."

"That's what I'm counting on," she said. "Because I love you, too."

"Can we make love with the old man down the hall?" he asked.

She turned, looking over her shoulder at him, grinning. "It's necessary. But you'll have to try not to scream this time." She grinned her teasing grin.

He tried his best not to let the slight feeling of panic show in his lips, hands, actions — he believed her, she wanted to come back to him. He made a slow study of her body, holding himself back until he'd done all her favorite things. She was the screamer, not him. But on this night she was quiet. When he'd exhausted her and finally let himself go inside her, she had tears along with her fulfillment. "I do love you so much."

"I love you more," he said.

In the morning Eric let Norm open the station so he could see off Laine and Paxton. He made sure they started off with a good breakfast that he cooked for them and then by 6:00 a.m. he had them in the car.

"Call me at layovers if you can. Call me when you get there for sure. Call me too much, okay?"

"You'll hear from me so much you'll get sick of me."

He shook his head. "Can't happen."

"Keep track of local gossip," she instructed. "Take notes if you have to. Check in with my girlfriends. Tell them to text me or call me. I want to know everything."

"I'll check in."

"I'll be back soon. Before you know it."

"Okay," he said. "I'll keep the place tidy."

"Oh, I know you will," she said with a laugh.

"Laine!" Senior demanded. "Just where the hell are we going?"

She took a deep breath. "It's going to be a very long day."

"Sure you want to do this?" he asked.

"I'm sure I have to. I'll call you tonight when it's over."

He stood in her driveway and watched them drive off in Paxton's rental from the Portland airport. Then he went back inside and cleaned up the kitchen, put everything back in order and thought, *This just isn't a home without her here.*

Senior asked Laine where they were going four thousand times as they were en route to Portland. The drive was so long — she wasn't sure why he hadn't chosen to fly into a closer airport, but then the whole trip was a mystery. Then the hustle and bustle of the airport riled him a little; he didn't want to let go of his bag. She had to cajole him to give it up to be checked, but let him keep his briefcase and phone, which she had turned off. Then in security, he got a little combative and she had to rescue him. "Hey!" she said to the TSA agent. "Go easy there — he has Alzheimer's!"

"I do not!" Senior yelled at her.

It was best to keep her arm threaded through his. She was fast catching on. Being tired, being in strange surroundings, enduring crowds of strangers — these things particularly escalated his confusion. Once they were on the plane, before takeoff,

Laine texted Pax. I've only gotten as far as Portland and I'm wasted already. I'll take a cab to the house but I need help tonight. Hire it if you have to, but I need some help!

Aside from the fact that she had to tell him to stay in his seat about once every fifteen minutes and through one terrifying trip to the bathroom, the plane was at least confining. Baggage claim was a little unsettling, as it was difficult to look for bags and keep an eye on Senior — if he got turned around, all his orientation was messed up and he was inclined to wander. When they finally got home it was obvious Pax was in the house because it was lit up. The driver put their bags by the door and Laine paid him. Pax opened the front door and Senior walked right inside. He looked around and said, "That's better. I didn't like that other place at all."

"Hi, Dad," Pax said.

"Hi, yourself. I need a drink."

"Coffee?" Pax asked, then saw the shaking of Laine's head. She didn't want him caffeinated! "Juice?"

"You must be tired," Laine said to her father. "It was a long day. Let's get you some tea and get you settled in bed."

"I'd rather have a bourbon. Neat. And stop treating me like an old man!"

"Christ," she muttered. "It's all right," she said to Pax. "He hasn't had alcohol since he came to Oregon and I took away his medication. I'd rather have his medication prescribed by a neurologist or geriatrician than an orthopedic surgeon. As long as he doesn't get impaired. . . . I mean *more* impaired. Water it, will you."

"And stop talking about me like I'm not in the room!"

"Sorry, Dad. But sometimes you aren't in the room. . . ."

They retired to the study, where Senior kept comfy chairs and a bar. Laine sank into a deep chair and sighed.

Three minutes later Senior said, "How much fucking water did you put in this?"

Laine, being exhausted, began to laugh until she thought she might pee her pants. For real. "Make me a tiny tini, will you, buddy?"

"Want me to bring your bags in first?" Pax asked.

"They can sit out there all night for all I care. Concentrate on the Grey Goose for now."

They sipped their drinks in oddly companionable silence. Since they couldn't talk about Senior like he wasn't present, since there wasn't much to say and Senior and

Laine were both worn out, it was just the three of them. Quiet. When Senior had finished his drink, Pax got up. "I bet you're ready to get to bed, Dad. I'm staying over tonight so let me get you up to your room."

"Why?" Senior asked. "Is school out?"

Laine ignored her father; she was almost getting used to him being in other time zones. "You're staying over?" Laine asked.

He nodded. "I can't give you as much time as you need, but I'm staying over tonight. I have to leave for the hospital kind of early."

"I understand," she said. "Thanks."

She watched as Senior headed for the stairs, Pax behind him. In this house he knew exactly where to go, what to do. She took out her phone. It was only six in Thunder Point — a busy time of day for Eric if he was still at the station. But he answered.

"Laine. How are you?"

"Well, now I know what it's like to travel with triplets under the age of six months. It was quite an exciting trip. Although it was close, I wasn't arrested for coming between Senior and a TSA agent."

"God," he said.

"We're home now. Pax is here and is staying the night so I can close both ears and

376

both eyes. I'm having a martini."

"I didn't know you drank martinis," he said.

"I haven't had too many in my life. I'm rethinking that. This has merits. I miss you."

"I miss you. But you made it. You got him home."

"And the second he got in the house, everything got better for him. He's tired, that's obvious, and he's still a little wacky, but he isn't as confused. You're working late tonight?" she asked.

"I have to repay all those favors. The past few days everyone else has been staying late. Besides . . ." His voice trailed off. "So, what's on for you tomorrow?"

"What were you about to say?" she urged.

He sighed. "Without you here, work fills up the time."

"Don't wear yourself out, Eric. I'm going to be back soon. Tomorrow, not too much is happening. We'll settle in, go to Pax and Genevieve's for dinner and to see the girls. The next day we have a doctor's appointment and a counseling session with a specialist. And then it begins — tests and that sort of thing. I'll keep you posted."

"Laine . . . be good to yourself."

"What will you do tonight?" she asked him.

"I'll go home. I might use your computer for a while — looking for parts for the GTO. Maybe I'll watch TV. . . ."

He didn't watch much TV. "Eric, don't work too hard. Promise me you'll give yourself some leisure time."

"That's easier when you're around," he said. "If I get a lot done, the days until you're home will go faster."

"I promise," she said yet again. "I'm going to hang up before Pax comes downstairs."

They signed off with endearments and Laine sat in the dimly lit study. When she was growing up, this room had been off-limits. This was where her father worked on patient charts, researched, called his patients to check on them, handled correspondence. Now, here she was, the caregiver of sorts. Sitting in his space, trying to unwind from a stressful day.

Pax returned to the study and went behind the bar to fix himself two fingers of Scotch. "You mellowed out?" he asked her.

"Um, yeah. Was he comfortable in his own room?"

"Seems to be," Pax said. He sat down in the opposite chair and crossed a leg over his knee. "What about you? How are you doing?"

"I couldn't be more screwed up if you

stuck your fingers in my brain and stirred things around in there. All my life, since I was just little, I wanted my father to love me, to be proud of me, to approve of me. Then one day he tells me he's *always* been proud of me, that he's in awe of me but was too afraid to praise me because he wanted me to be less daring. All the while he was holding back his approval, I was trying harder and harder to earn it by taking more and more chances. He just wanted me to be cautious and stop scaring him. And he told me this right when he admitted he came to me for help." She laughed. "So here I am. I finally have the father I always longed for. At quite a price."

"You're not an only child, you know," he said.

"But you're rational," she said. "You're not dealing with this conflict — Senior has always approved of you. You're not still aching for a little of his affection. Not only that — you have a family and a big fellowship on your plate, and Genevieve says the doctor who's taken you on is a real dick. . . ."

Pax laughed. "I knew about that going in. He's a brilliant dick. I wanted a nicer guy to work for but this one — he can teach me things no one else can. This situation with Senior can be managed, Laine. I can tell in fifteen minutes his disease isn't advanced enough for an Alzheimer's facility so we can check out home health care. Genevieve has already collected names — we can get right on it. I don't want you tied to this problem forever. Now, tell me something — this man of yours, Eric, is he having a problem with this arrangement? You coming to Boston?"

"He's been incredibly supportive. It's all fake, but I'll take it. He hated seeing me leave — I'm an expert at reading people, remember. He wants me to come back as soon as possible. And I want to go home. And I also want this one chance with my father before it's too late. I make no sense."

Pax leaned forward in his chair, elbows resting on his knees, his drink in one hand. "It's always been like this with you. All or nothing. You don't fall in love till you're practically over the hill and when you do, bam! You're all in. You hate your father most of your life because he can be such an insensitive jerk and now that he needs you, you're ready to dedicate your life to him. Laine, this isn't forever. Let's get this under control so you can have your life back."

He was so right, she thought. She had such a hard time thinking one step at a time. She wasn't sure how to do this. But all she said was "I feel like I just found my father.

How can I leave him?"

"Let's handle this with a goal that everyone gets what they need. Even you."

There was no question, Senior did so much better in his own home. He had fewer periods of confusion and his forgetfulness went unnoticed with Laine there to keep his schedule. There was, however, an aspect of his disease that would not have been noticed by his children, his housekeeper or his business partner. When Laine got into his financial records, she found he'd been making crazy stock purchases in large sums and had a few deeds for property he couldn't identify. He had a room full of Civil War memorabilia, most of it still in boxes. He had been buying up commemorative gold coins — they might still be worth something if they were really gold. Fortunately Laine was a detective — she managed to find the plots of land and property deals and had the coins appraised, but was stuck with the Civil War stuff. Not surprisingly, Senior had been scammed a few times. Poor judgment was a major symptom and one that can go undetected if the patient isn't being closely observed.

It was something no one would have been aware was happening. Senior had always been too cynical for this sort of thing and he had been brilliant with his money. He was also very lucky, as it turned out. While he'd been fleeced out of a lot of money, he had plenty left. The bulk of his money was in accounts being managed by a financial adviser with a large and reputable holding company. Laine got to work on powers of attorney to take over his finances, an argument that lasted three days and rendered Senior quite stormy.

After examinations, CT scans, blood work and counseling sessions it was confirmed by specialists that Senior might have struggled with symptoms of his disease for several years, hardly noticeable symptoms that he had somehow managed to bluff his way out of, but within the past few months his mental acuity had deteriorated drastically. Laine learned that his partners and the staff at the practice had been concerned for some time, but where they fell short was in talking to Senior rather than to Pax. He had not voluntarily reduced his schedule, his partners had insisted and urged him to get a physical. But Senior being Senior had avoided the reality for too long.

They got a couple of home health-care workers installed. They could only find part-time help, but at least Laine could get out of the house now and then while she continued looking for more help. She at least needed time off duty. And then the inevitable happened — he followed in his mother's footsteps and wandered off. He walked out of the house and it took hours to find him.

"Now I'm having the security system updated so bells and whistles go off when a door is opened," she told Eric.

"Wouldn't that happen anyway?" he asked.

"It seems the system hasn't been worked on in years and some of the connectors are faulty. And the old boy is slippery as an eel! I'm also insisting he wear a bracelet with a GPS chip in it! And believe me — he's not always cooperative!"

By the end of the first week, Laine had one of her hired babysitters removed and replaced by a different one. She caught the young man rifling through Senior's papers in the study. He said he was just fetching a bank statement for Senior, but he was so nervous she didn't buy it for a second. That Senior had no recollection of asking for it didn't mean much, but still . . . This put a pall on the idea that she could eventually be replaced by hired help.

Mrs. Mulligrew, the housekeeper, was now coming to the house every day, though she had to hire additional help for the big cleaning jobs. Mrs. Mulligrew wasn't old but she wasn't exactly young. She was hearty and healthy at sixty and her job was to keep Senior's most used areas in check and cook meals. When bigger cleaning jobs were needed, she brought family members to help. In the past she'd spend one afternoon cooking every week, setting up a few meals for him, refrigerating or freezing them. Now she was providing seven lunches and dinners every week and the home health-care provider was supposed to take care of his breakfast, a simple task since it involved cereal, toast and fruit.

But from four o'clock on, Laine was on her own.

Through some periods of confusion and forgetfulness, she and her father managed many conversations. She was sentimentally drawn in, grateful for this time, yet grieving this time away from Eric.

"Is he doing any better?" Eric asked.

"Better? God, no! He seems to slip a little more every day. When I bring up the subject of assisted living in a specialized facility, he cries. This is so shocking — I've only seen my father get emotional once, when my mother died, and that was brief. Now he cries at the drop of a hat. I've been secretly looking at some assisted-living places and you know what? I wouldn't want to live in one, either."

"This keeps getting more complicated," Eric said.

"I wish I was there with you. Or you here with me."

"Do you have any idea when you might be back?" he asked. In fact, he asked almost every day.

"I was hoping a couple of weeks would do the trick, that I'd get him settled and feel comfortable leaving him. Obviously that's not going to happen. But, Eric, I'm trying, you have to believe me. I just can't leave him unless I'm sure he's safe."

So Eric stopped asking.

Eighteen

Laine called or texted Eric several times a day and he did the same. Pictures passed between them — Laine sent pictures of her nieces, her father, the whole family, even the family manse from the outside, complete with manicured landscaping and long, bricked drive. To which Eric texted back, Holy shit! You grew up in that thing?

Eric's texts and pictures were not quite as impressive. At least he didn't think so. He had looked forward to taking Laine to his sister's house in Bend for a family gathering, to introduce her to his family. Ashley had to work so he went alone. He texted a picture of his parents that, if there had been a pitchfork, could have been *American Gothic*. The picture of his sister and brother-in-law was a bit more friendly-looking. He had a niece and nephew, both nearly as old as he was since there was twenty years between himself and his sister, so the gathering was fairly large, but it was missing his girls.

He stayed very busy. He worked almost every shift while managing to give Justin a full-time work schedule, as well. The next set of pictures he sent were of Ashley and her boyfriend, Frank, on senior prom night. She almost brought tears to his eyes, she was so beautiful. Gina and Mac gave them and Mac's daughter, Eve, and her date, Landon, a very nice send-off. Then there was an after-prom party at Cooper's bar, which was closed to the general public and kept open for the kids.

Too soon, they were celebrating the high school graduation. The party was held at the McCains' and of course he was included. Between the ceremony and the party, he managed to text Laine a couple of dozen pictures. These town kids had done so well for themselves — made their parents darn proud. Eve and Ashley would be commuting to community college together, but Frank was going to George Washington University on a full academic scholarship and Landon was going full ride to the University of Oregon and would play football for them. So, the boyfriends were leaving and the girlfriends were planning to catch up after the first year.

Eric told Laine about everything in great detail, sent pictures of every event, even the progress on the beachfront houses on the hill between Cooper's bar and the town. He told her about every dent he pounded out, every piece of news about their friends, her friends, the town at large. And she kept him apprised of every detail of her life, which was now filled with doctor's visits, medical tests, attempts to find the right home health-care people and get-togethers with her family.

And as the time seemed to crawl by, in what felt like a year, it had been a month.

He loved her rented house and loved the deck with its view of the bay, but going home at night, waking up there alone in the morning, was killing him. He saw her everywhere. He would come home and for a split second there would be the aroma of soup in the house . . . then it would disappear. He'd sit on the deck at night when a storm was rolling in and feel her snuggled against him, sitting between his legs on that chaise, and it could be so real he'd want to kiss her neck. He dreamed of her, reached for her, tasted her in his sleep. He loved her like he'd never loved a woman in his life and she was completely out of his reach.

He blamed some of this on time zones.

All those sweet whispers he wanted to hear and utter, the erotic and blissful murmurings he craved — they just didn't work into the world they were now living in. These private things weren't easily said while he was digging around in an engine, or she was sitting in a doctor's office. By the time he woke at 5:00 a.m. it was already eight in Boston and Laine and her father were in full swing. Not an optimal time to ask, "Tell me what you want me to do to you. . . ." Late at night, when he was finally done killing time for the day, it was far later in Boston and Laine, exhausted from her day, was asleep. They could exchange I-love-yous and I-miss-yous, but those deep and sexy utterings . . . ? It just didn't happen.

What he'd begun to think of as one of the greatest romances in the history of man had become all business and local news and Eric felt like he was drying up. As each day passed by he felt she was getting further and further away.

He covered his grief with work. And with every breath he longed to touch her again.

Al Michel had found the month of May to be mostly torture. He, along with Eric and Scott Grant, vowed to make sure the Russell boys were looked after for a few weeks until they could finish the school year. Sally Russell went to a full-care facility just south of North Bend, an hour from Thunder Point. A foster home had been found for Kevin and Danny, in Grants Pass, at least a three-hour drive from Thunder Point. As soon as school ended the boys had been relocated. And Justin, who now had two full-time jobs, was left behind.

The men, Al, Eric and Scott, were present every day right up to and including that day that Justin had to give up his brothers. They watched over him, their eyes sharpened for any signs that he might be falling apart, that he could be in trouble or despondent. But, Al observed with some pride, the boy was not only strong, but also vigilant.

Justin arranged his schedule — days as a stock boy in the grocery store and nights at the gas station — so that he'd have Saturdays and Sundays free. Those days he got in his van and motored over to Grants Pass, picked up his brothers and took them to see their mother. He drove for hours and hours on those two days. On at least one of those days he worked at Lucky's in the evening. He put in eighty hours a week. All he did at home, where he lived alone, was bathe and sleep and clean his clothes. He didn't complain, he didn't ask for favors. He was quiet, which he always had been. But he was cheerful to the customers at both businesses.

"I don't know how you're holding up, kid," Al said.

"Look, all I can do is get to eighteen, show I have an income and can pay the bills and get the boys home. This isn't forever. And this is the only choice there is."

"I just don't want you to work yourself to death before you're twenty," Al said.

"With you breathing down my neck all the time, I won't be able to," Justin said. "Besides, you work more than forty. . . ."

"Yeah, but I'm one guy. You're three guys and a sick mother."

"I got this, man," he said.

On a couple of Sundays Al was able to convince Justin to let him take him to Grants Pass to pick up his brothers and take them all to the nursing home. It gave him a little peace of mind to be there, to see the three boys together. The house they were living in wasn't much better than the one Justin was holding on to in Thunder Point, but it didn't seem like a bad place. And the younger boys weren't thrilled with it but they were making the best of it in hopes that Justin would soon be able to gather them back together.

It was a very busy town through the month and Al was included in much of it, but he never failed to check in with Justin on a daily basis. He watched the kid's weight, marked whether or not there were circles under his eyes, took it upon himself to make sure Justin was eating as well as could be expected under the circumstances.

He had Ray Anne during this time and could acknowledge, though privately, he'd be lost without her. She sympathized, made him laugh, entertained him. She insisted he attend some of the local celebrations her friends were having — graduation, for one. Not only did she love showing him off, but it also took his mind away from the Russell kids, separated by fate and doing everything they could to remain a family.

"Is your real estate business suffering because of me?" Al asked Ray Anne one night.

"Why would it be?" she countered.

"I ask a lot of you," he said.

She laughed at him and said, "You never ask for anything from me!"

"I ask you to wait up late for me when I work, late enough so we can be together when you should sleep for the next day's work. I crave that rooftop when I have a night off and I want you to show me the best places to eat. And I impose on you all the time because when you take your clothes off for me, I'm in heaven. A heaven I'm sure I don't deserve."

And she just smiled and said, "I wouldn't have it any other way."

He was so grateful to hear her say that. He was also thankful that no one ever asked him, given that he was so concerned about these boys, why didn't he take it upon himself to become the responsible adult, the foster parent. He had no reasonable excuse and would be so ashamed to have to admit that he wasn't good enough for the job. He wasn't educated, could barely read, had no experience with kids, held his own life together by the weakest thread. They should have a parent who could manage money and save for their futures, who could help them with their studies and guide them as they looked for further education. And the one chance he had at a family, he'd failed them. Those Russell kids had had more than their share of challenges. He'd just be one more.

Then came the day it all fell apart for him. He drove Justin to Grants Pass to pick up the boys. Danny and Kevin came outside to get in the car and Kevin had an enormous black eye under the rims of his thick glasses.

"What the fuck?" Justin said.

"Never mind," he said. "It doesn't matter."

"Who did that to you? When? Why didn't you tell me?"

"Forget about it. It's nothing."

"Tell me," Justin insisted. "Danny, what happened to him?"

Reluctantly, with great trepidation, Danny said, "Ernest, the father, whacked him. With his fist. He told him to get in the kitchen and clean it up and take out all the garbage in the house and when Kevin didn't get right up, he shook him and then plastered him. Kevin was doing something and didn't jump on the chores. There's three of their kids and three fosters and only the fosters do the work. And Ernest drinks."

"That's not going to happen!" Justin said, getting out of his van and storming toward the house.

"Whoa," Al said, running after him.

But Justin was on the move. He crashed through the front door, Al right on his heels. There was a woman in the kitchen, a real pleasant-looking woman in a pair of jeans and T-shirt, and three kids lying around the family room — one with an iPad, one texting on her phone, one watching TV. And those kids, Al quickly observed, looked at

Justin and Al with sneers on their faces. He couldn't guess their exact ages — roughly the same as Kevin and Danny, somewhere between ten and sixteen. Two boys and a girl.

"What's this?" the woman asked.

"What the hell happened to my brother, Evelyn?" Justin demanded.

She wiped her hands on a towel. "Oh, that eye bruise? That was just an accident. Sorry about that. He was messing around and caught an elbow. You know boys!" And then she smiled.

"He said Ernest slugged him because he wasn't fast enough on the chores!"

"What kind of story is that?" she asked, laughing. "And who is this man?"

"Where is he?" Al asked. "Your husband?"

She put her hands on her hips. "He's gone out to the lake. Fishing. Now what is this about?"

"It's about the black eye," Al said evenly.

"It was his own screwing around," one of the kids from the family room said.

"He said Ernest was drunk," Justin said.

"There's no liquor in this house," Evelyn said. "He's making that up so he doesn't get in trouble for it. You're going to want to drop it right now before you make more trouble."

"Liquor doesn't have to be in the house for a man to come home drunk," Al said. "I expect child services will want to know. Don't you have to report injuries?"

Evelyn stepped toward them, throwing down the towel. "You best think on this," she said, and she no longer looked at all pleasant. "First off, if child services pulls that boy out of here, there's no place for him to go except emergency housing and half the time they stick 'em in a child haven or juvie. And they'll only take the one kid, not both. And if I get my license pulled, those two'll get split up and go to different parts of the state! There will be hell to pay. I put ice on it. It's just a bruise. He'll be all right."

"I'm making a complaint," Justin said.

"You complain all you want, you ungrateful little troublemaker. I was the only one willing to take both boys. If they make trouble for me, I'll turn 'em back and they aren't going back to you! That's for sure!"

Justin ground his teeth against a rising rage, his eyes narrow and his fists clenched and Al thought, *He's a thread away from launching an attack.*

"I have one thing to say to you," Al said soberly, calmly. "You better be sure neither of those boys gets hurt again or there will absolutely be hell to pay and you'll pay it to *me.* I hope you hear me, ma'am, because I'm not warning you again." He put a hand on Justin's shoulder. "Come on, son. Let's go."

They walked out of the house, got in the car and drove for over two hours to the nursing home. Through the whole ride all Al could think was, *I can't do this. I can't watch this. I can't see these young boys who have shouldered so much already be abused. This is way bigger than I am.*

Scott Grant was kept very busy all through the spring. He was on call to Spencer Lawson, the high school's football and track-and-field coach. Scott was the volunteer team physician. It was a pretty laid-back job, since not many injuries occurred in these organized sports, but it meant being available and being in town when there were meets or games. That meant no moonlighting in Bandon.

In addition, there were several people he was watching over, Justin Russell being one. And he had his practice, a new practice that was constantly growing. But this was exactly what he wanted — to be in a place where he was needed. A place where he was the medicine man of the town.

And it was a good town. As spring gave way to summer, there were community celebrations for graduation, which included parties — Scott was invited to all of them. And the beach was once again a warm and inviting place. Cooper's house was nearly finished and Scott helped them install shutters, hang shades, move furniture. Quite a few of Cooper's friends were also on hand to help — Eric, Al, Mac, Spencer, Rawley, young Landon . . . And those days of working on getting the house ready were always capped off with a beer or two on the deck of the bar next door. There were barbeques on the beach and in the backyards of friends. And it seemed to Scott that to every one of these town functions, whether casually thrown together or by invitation, he attended with his children — four-year-old Jenny and five-year-old Will. Everyone else attended with their spouse or significant other. Everyone except Eric, because Laine was away at the moment, but Eric was constantly seen on the periphery of their gatherings, smiling and talking into his cell phone.

If Scott was on the phone it was either to check on a patient or his kids. . . .

It had been four years now since he lost his wife and he hadn't even had a serious flirtation since. He thought he could keep loneliness at bay by staying busy, but it wasn't working. He'd been ready, for a couple of years now, for a new relationship. It didn't have to be as perfect and loving as the one he'd had with Serena, his late wife. He didn't expect it to be — they'd been together for so many years before he lost her. He didn't expect a miracle.

Then, while they were putting the finishing touches on Cooper's new house, Devon — the best office manager he'd ever had — asked him if she could take a little time off. "I don't think I have any vacation coming," she said. "But could I take a few days, maybe five, without pay? Spencer and I want to get married the first part of July. Just a quiet ceremony, close friends only, but we'd like to go away alone for a couple of days. Cooper will see that Mercy and Austin are covered."

Scott was momentarily stunned. Of course he knew they were planning on marrying. But his life seemed to be filled with people who never expected to find partners and were now not only all hooked up, but also blissfully happy. All he could think of to say was "What if Sarah has the baby?"

"Well, if that happens, we'll want to rush home," Devon said. "But there's lots of backup — Rawley, Gina and Mac, all the teenagers, your nanny Gabriella. For her sake, I almost hope it happens — she's not due for weeks but she's already awful big."

"Of course," he said. "Sure. Yes. Take all the time you need. And I'll be your backup, too. Mercy is as at-home at my house as yours. And Austin's a flexible kid. He's real portable. He'd be happy with me, with Landon, with lots of people. And Devon, you can have five paid days. After all you've done for me, it's the least I can do."

"Thanks, Doc. We'll plan something in that case. We were going to wait till the house is finished but heck, we just don't want to wait."

The memory of feeling he just couldn't wait filled him with the miserable longing that had become his constant companion. Maybe before too many more years passed he would meet someone who made him feel that way.

Again.

Al knew Justin wouldn't be eighteen until September and there was no guarantee that would be enough to get him custody of his brothers. The case worker he'd been in touch with told him to expect to be told to wait until he was nineteen and suggested he get to work on that GED so he could improve his income, so he could promote himself in his jobs.

As if he had a spare hour for that . . .

Al was so proud of the kid, ached for the kid. After a brief family meeting in the car, the boys decided that it was probably best not to complain to child services, best not to rattle any cages and get split up or yanked into some even worse emergency foster care. Kevin promised to say "how high" when someone said jump — he wouldn't take any chances. Al wasn't crazy about that decision but he understood it. They were scared. He wondered if they'd ever stop being scared.

His greatest solace was in Ray Anne's arms. He loved her rooftop and loved her on the rooftop. That was where they had not only the most physical pleasure, but also their deepest, most personal conversations. She revealed so much about herself, about the men she'd been so briefly married to, about hopes and dreams she'd given up years before in favor of being an independent woman who wouldn't ever have to rely on a man. And for his part, Al told her more and more about his brief marriage, his years on the road, his annual trips back to Boone, Iowa, on the birthday of his son, who if he had lived would now be thirty-eight years old.

Instead of saying "Awww, darling," Ray Anne smiled against his lips and said, "My age." And they laughed and laughed.

They had that thing going for them, when they could make even the most serious subjects light and humorous.

In early June, while he held her on the rooftop, he said, "I want you to know, I haven't really loved a woman in so long I forgot what it felt like. But I think this is how it feels. Ray, no matter what happens I want you to know you're one fine woman and you've made me really happy."

"No matter what happens?" she asked. "Are you terminal or something?"

He just laughed and pulled her closer. "God, no. I'm so healthy it's scary. But I've learned over the years not to forget to say important things. I was on the road when my dad died and never got to tell him how much he meant to me. It was a lesson."

"Well, then," she said, "you should know, I think you're the love of my life."

"I can't be. You're too sexy, too sweet, too beautiful. . . ."

"You are. I've been with plenty of men but I think it was all practice. I feel so good with you. Every part of me feels good —

the body parts, the heart, the mind, the humor, the part that thrives on friendship. I think, if I had to go back through all the men I've known, you'd be the best."

"I bet you'll change your mind about that," he said.

And she had raised over him, looked down into his eyes in the candlelight on the rooftop and said, "No, Al. I won't."

The next day at noon he packed up his two duffels, some tools he owned and had been using and drove his truck to Lucky's. Of course Eric was there. All he did was work since Laine was away. Justin hadn't come to work yet and Al was glad. He passed the key to the room at the Coastline Inn to Eric and said, "Sorry, boss, but I got a call from a friend who's in a bad spot. He has an emergency and needs my help. I know this is no notice and real inconvenient and I'm awful sorry. The room is paid up and I'm moved out but I didn't check out just in case you know someone you want to give it to, what with that refrigerator and toaster and all."

Eric took the key and shook his hand. "I hope you'll be back, Al. You're a great asset to my business."

"I appreciate you saying that. I know I usually give you more notice but this came up real sudden." But of course, he didn't say what it was, exactly.

"Those things happen. If you have the opportunity and interest, you're always welcome here. We can always use you. Did you tell Justin you're leaving?"

"I wasn't able to do that." He pulled an envelope out of his shirt pocket. "I don't have much explanation, it's just a friend I've helped out over the years and he counts on me, especially when things go crazy for him. Would you give this to the kid?"

"Sure. Of course. And you have my number, if you need me."

"I hope I'm not gone too long. Turns out I like it here. This was a smart move for you. And I hope it all works out with Laine."

"Things always work out," Eric said. "If I haven't learned anything else, I learned that. It's just that while you're waiting for things to work out, it gets real old. But that's life, right?"

"That's life, all right. Good luck, boss," Al said. And he got in his truck and drove out of town.

NINETEEN

Justin showed up for work right at three, clean and pressed. Eric realized that his mother had little or nothing to do with the laundry and ironing of his clothes. No doubt he'd heard Eric ride the old guys about keeping up their uniforms, and needing this job like he did, he towed the line carefully. He wasn't getting any better at cutting his own hair, so he'd let it grow and was trimming the bottom. In another couple of months he'd just be tying it back in a ponytail.

Might as well just rip the Band-Aid right off, Eric thought. "Al had an emergency of some kind, Justin. He had to leave. He left this for you," he said, handing over the envelope. "Maybe that explains better."

Justin tore into the envelope immediately. There was a small piece of paper and a check. "It doesn't," Justin said, showing Eric the note. It said, *Little help. Good luck.* And that was Al's handwriting, all right. Miserable. He hadn't written the check. It was a cashier's check drawn from the local Thunder Point bank. It was for two thousand dollars.

Eric whistled.

"Did he say what the emergency was?" Justin asked.

"Sorry, he just said a friend was in a tight spot and needed him."

"Well, that's good, I guess. Everyone should have friends." He said it like someone who had no friends. Justin put the check and note back in the envelope and shoved it in his pants pocket.

"You want to run that over to the bank before it closes?" Eric asked.

"Nah. That's okay." Then he went for the broom to start sweeping up.

Eric followed him. He put a hand on his shoulder. "Justin, that's a cashier's check. If it gets lost or damaged, it's no good. Take it to the bank. . . ."

"I don't have an account there," he said.

"Go open one," Eric said. "You can't afford to carry around something like that. At least in the bank it's insured. Even if the bank gets robbed or burns down, they'll make good on your money."

"What if I need money fast?" Justin asked.

"Withdraw it from the bank," Eric said.

"And if the bank's closed? If it's the middle of the night?"

"I'll give you whatever you need," Eric said, asking himself why Justin would need money fast? In the middle of the night? "If you have an emergency, wake me up. I can get together whatever you need."

Justin smirked. "I should'a known you were a moneybags." And he started sweeping.

Eric grabbed the broom. "How are your brothers doing, Justin?"

He shrugged. "They get by okay," he said. "It's not good where they are but they can deal for a couple more months. Seems like those people got themselves some slave labor so no one else would have to do chores there. Just the woman and the foster kids."

"Not good," Eric agreed.

"If they don't move fast, they get cuffed," Justin said. Then he made a motion like a whack upside the head.

"That's not good," Eric said more emphatically. "You should tell someone about that."

"Yeah, we talked about that. But the system could separate them and send them farther away where I can't get to 'em unless

I move and I don't want to give up the house unless I have to. I got it handled."

"How?" he asked.

"We give it a couple — three more months. In September I'm eighteen and if they don't turn the boys over, I'm just taking them out of there. That's how. We don't do people like that." And he tried wrestling that broom away from Eric.

Eric held on. "Go to the bank. I'll keep you on the clock. Don't screw with a big old check like that. You might need the money. And if you have an emergency and can't get to the bank, I'll fix you up with what you need. Get yourself checks and a debit card and a credit card. You shouldn't be living off cash."

"I'm not sure how all that stuff works. I been just cashing my checks."

"It's easy. They'll explain it at the bank and if it's not real clear, I'll explain it further. Now go." Justin gave a lame shrug and turned to go. "Listen," Eric said, stopping him. "Listen, Justin, I know it probably feels like Al ran out on you but he didn't. This is his way — he's a rover. I've known him a real long time and he's usually on the move, a few months here, a few there. He'll show up again. Meanwhile, you can count on me. This is my business. I'm not going anywhere."

"Till Laine tells you she can't get back here on account of her dad and wants you to go there," Justin said.

"Man, you think a lot more than you let on," Eric said, shaking his head. "I doubt that would happen. Ashley is here and I have a lot of time to make up with her. If I leave Thunder Point it won't be fast, you can count on that. First that girl needs to be all grown up and on her own and second, I'd have to sell a business. I don't leave notes behind. I tell the people in my life what I'm planning to do so you can count on me, okay? Don't go doing something crazy like kidnapping your brothers in the dark of night. Talk to me. I'll do whatever I can to help."

"Sure," Justin said, clearly unconvinced.

Eric sighed. "Go to the bank."

Eric knew what would help Justin. Everyone knew. He needed a foster parent. And Eric was tempted. He knew it wouldn't be more work than he could handle — those boys knew how to live independently. But if he took on that job he'd have to live with them and he had waited his whole life for something else, something he thought he might have with Laine. They had enough working against them. A whole continent separated them and he wasn't sure how long that would be the case. He hoped not too much longer but in his heart he knew she could be committed for a long time. A mean and selfish little voice said, *If she hadn't made up with Senior, this would be someone else's problem.* Then the gentler side of him said, *She waited her whole life for Senior to be proud of her, to rely on her.* He was lonely but, though difficult, he was happy for her. No one should lose their parents before things were settled with them. And he'd be ashamed to admit the number of times he wanted to beg her to come back. *Just ask your brother to hire someone to take care of Senior and come back.* At least he hadn't given in to that temptation.

He picked up the phone in the office and called the diner. Maybe he could find out something that would ease Justin's mind a little. Gina answered and he said, "Hey, Gina, it's Eric. Do you have a phone number for Ray Anne?"

"I do. You looking for real estate?"

"I have more real estate than I know what to do with," he said with a laugh. "Al left today and he said he had a friend who needed him. I wonder if Ray Anne knows any more than that. Justin looks like he lost his best friend. Which I guess maybe he did."

This idea turned out not to be one of his best. When he asked Ray Anne the question she said, "Gone? He left? When?"

"At around noon. He said a friend needed his help. He didn't have a better or more detailed explanation for you?"

She was quiet for a long moment. "No," she finally said. "He didn't."

"I'm sorry, Ray Anne," Eric said. "I assumed he'd tell you he was leaving. Say goodbye. Or something."

"I would have assumed that also," she said softly.

"He'll call you, then," Eric said.

"I have a cell phone — he has a cell phone. There are no messages or texts. He doesn't like to text — he thinks it's impersonal. Did he say where he was going or when he'd be back?"

"I'm afraid not."

"I see. Thanks for letting me know, Eric. I'm glad I didn't find out another way. . . ."

"I'm really sorry."

"I'll let you know if I hear from him," she said. Then she disconnected the call.

Well, way to go, Al, Eric thought. In all the years he'd known Al he couldn't remember a time when it went down like this, a bunch of hard feelings and broken hearts left in his wake. What the hell happened? he asked himself. Too much pressure? Did things get a little too tight for him with Ray Anne and Justin, both needing him?

It must have been a real emergency, Eric thought. Al really liked Ray Anne. And unless he missed all the signals, he was committed to helping Justin.

But the phone didn't ring. At least not with a call from Al.

Laine called twice and they filled each other in on the day and for some reason he couldn't really explain, he didn't tell her about Al leaving. He asked after her family and she reported that she was going to have to let another home health-care worker go — she suspected he was dipping into the liquor cabinet in the study. Either that or carrying a flask — she could smell alcohol on his breath. Senior was doing quite well; it seemed like there were very few bad days, knock on wood. He needed a companion, that much was evident; he couldn't live alone. Most of his daily functions he managed independently. He could bathe, shave with a new electric razor — no more razor blades, not even disposables — but he couldn't cook or drive alone. There was too much potential for disaster.

If anyone in my family ever gets Alzheimer's I am now an expert, Eric thought.

Of course it wasn't long before people started asking, "What's that I hear about Al?", since Eric had let the cat out of the bag. Other than that, it was a quiet afternoon and evening at the station. He sent Justin home a little bit early and told him to get some rest. Then he closed up and went home.

Every time he walked into that house he braced himself for a miracle. When she was here, she always at least left a light on in the kitchen and something in the refrigerator, but more often she was waiting for him. But the house was cool and dark. He didn't turn on any lights. He walked toward the doors to the deck and saw the lightning flashing over the mouth of the bay, a distant rumble of thunder grumbling. It wasn't going to develop into a full-fledged storm, but Laine would have liked the lightning.

He thought he heard something. Music. Laughter. Splashing. Before he even gave himself a second to think about it, he ran for the stairs, took them two or three at a time. The bedroom was unchanged; the bed was made but not turned down. They had had a rule, last one out makes the bed. . . . The bathroom was dark and empty but if he closed his eyes he could sense her there, the candlelight flickering, her iPod plugged into the speakers, the smell of her bath stuff. He could almost hear her laughter and a little splashing around while she waited for him in the tub. Then the next morning at five when he was in the shower she'd ask him why. Wasn't he clean enough after that romp in the tub? And he'd carefully explained that he smelled like a girl and his customers didn't like prissy mechanics.

He couldn't count the nights he reached for her. . . .

God, he missed her.

He put his hands in his pockets and felt his keys. He felt the key to the room at the Coastline Inn.

He went to the closet and pulled his duffel off the high shelf. He put it on the bed and filled it with shirts and pants and boots; he grabbed his shaving kit and added it. She wanted him to be here, in her house, but she had no idea what it did to him. No matter how many times he changed and laundered sheets, he could smell her. He had erotic dreams about her and woke in the night with the taste of her in his mouth. And every time he came home the longing was greater. And the fear those days and nights would never come again grew more fierce.

He closed the duffel and locked the door behind him. He had his phone and his laptop; she would never find him hard to reach. But he needed her here or it was just too much. He'd come back of course. He'd come every couple of days, make sure it was safe, kept in order, ready for her return.

He walked to the Coastline, his duffel in one hand, his laundered and bagged uniforms over his shoulder. He was better off here.

"Where is she?" Lou McCain asked Carrie James over the phone. "She's not at Cliff's, she's not answering her phone, her house is dark. Do you think she drove into the bay? Drowned herself?"

"Over a man? Are we talking about the same Ray Anne?" Carrie asked. "Please. She's probably soaking in the tub so she'll be nice and clean when she puts little pins in his voodoo doll."

"I drove over there. The house is dark and she's not answering the door," Lou said.

"You don't know where to look," Carrie said. "Where are you?"

"Sitting in front of the sheriff's office, trying to figure out where to go next."

"What are you doing in Thunder Point?" Carrie asked. Since Lou had married last fall, she didn't live with her nephew, Mac, any longer. Her home with Joe was midway between Thunder Point and Coquille. She taught in Thunder Point, but school was out for the summer.

"I was talking to Gina, asking if she needed any help with the kids this week, and she asked me if I knew about Ray Anne. Apparently Al just took off, without explanation. Hey, maybe she went with him!" Lou suggested.

"Our little real estate magnate? Fat chance. Meet me in front of Ray Anne's house."

"I'm telling you she's not there! And I don't normally overreact, but I'm kind of worried about her."

"She's just sulking," Carrie said. "Meet me out front. I'll show you where she is. Then you can relax and go home. And I can go to sleep. Some of us work in summer, you know."

"Some of us are very grouchy year-round," Lou said. She hung up.

There was a time when Lou McCain and Ray Anne Dysart couldn't get along for five minutes. Then age, experience, patience and wisdom settled in and things eased and even became friendly. Well, and Lou got married and Ray Anne finally stopped stealing Lou's boyfriends — that could have had something to do with it.

Lou and Ray Anne had known each other since high school in Coquille and they'd always been like oil and water. They were opposites, to say the least. Lou had been studious and pretty serious while Ray Anne had been all about fun. She'd been wearing her clothes too tight since way back then, and she always had a bunch of guys. But back then a bunch wasn't enough — she had to have everyone else's guy, too.

Lou and Ray Anne rarely saw each other after high school until they were reconnected in Thunder Point. At first it was like the same old rivalry — Lou in her sensible shoes and Ray Anne in her tight skirts and heels. But then they settled into an uneasy truce that actually became a friendship. Still nothing alike, they somehow managed to appreciate each other. Lou liked her now. And she felt bad about this — that a man Ray Anne had not only liked, but also counted on, would just bolt.

Carrie's deli van was sitting in front of Ray Anne's house when Lou pulled up. They got out of their vehicles and met in the street; Carrie was still wearing her big full-body apron with the deep pockets, as though she'd been cooking. She was holding a bottle of wine as big as a horse's leg. "Follow me," she said. She went around the garage, reached over the top of the gate to unlock it and pushed it open so she could get into the backyard. She rounded the garage and went to the stairs that led to the roof. When they got to the top, there was candlelight. "You better be alone," Carrie said into the darkness.

"What are you doing here?" Ray Anne asked. She was sitting on the floor of the deck, cross-legged. She was wearing sweatpants, something Lou didn't imagine she owned. And a long shirt. No bra; her boobs were on her chest. Completely. No further curiosity about the boob job . . . And she wore leather slippers to keep her piggies warm. This was a side of Ray Anne that Lou had never seen.

"We came to sit shiva," Lou said. "Word's out — there was a death."

"I doubt he's dead," Ray Anne said. She sipped from her wineglass. "Just gone."

"Wow," Lou said, looking around. "This is really something. . . ."

Carrie put the wine bottle on the deck and slowly, achingly, got down, settling into a beanbag. "If I make even a little profit this year, I'm buying you chairs for your birthday. My knees protest this sitting on the floor. It'll take both of you to get me on my feet again." Then she pulled a corkscrew out of her pocket.

"I don't have glasses up here," Ray Anne said.

Carrie took a couple of plastic wineglasses out of her other pocket, fixing the stems on them. "I'm a caterer," she said, deadpan.

"Wow, this is really something," Lou said again. "Why haven't I ever seen this before?"

"Because it's private," Ray Anne said.

"But Carrie has obviously seen it. . . ."

"I imposed on Ray Anne when Ashley was having her hard time over breaking up with stupid Downy last year, when we were all holding our breath to see if she was suicidal or just brokenhearted. Ray Anne brought me up here. We drank a bottle of wine and talked about all our broken hearts. It helped, except there's no broken heart like your daughter's or granddaughter's. I'd have my heart carved out of my chest a hundred times rather than watch them go through it."

Lou sat down on a beanbag and reached for a glass of wine.

"How about me?" Ray Anne asked. "How do you like watching me go through it?"

"You've been through it before," Carrie said. "I'm sorry, Ray Anne. But you're smart and independent and you'll heal."

"Maybe not for a few days," she said.

"Talk about him," Lou said. "Did you love him?"

"I loved them all," Ray Anne said, tipping the bottle over her glass. "I really did. But I think I maybe loved Al the best."

"Don't you always feel that way?"

"Not always, no," Ray Anne said. "Sometimes I think they're fun, or maybe they're sexy. Or maybe they make a decent living and seem civilized and in want of a good partner. Or . . . I don't know. Sometimes they can dance. . . ."

Lou spewed a mouthful of wine. "They can *dance*?"

"I stopped looking for happily ever after a long time ago," Ray Anne said. "I haven't been expecting some perfect man to come along and carry me off on his charger. I just don't want to be alone all the time. And I like . . . you know . . . sex."

"We know," Carrie and Lou said at the same time.

"That's just who I am," she said. "Al liked everything about me. I knew he never stayed in one place for long but I had no idea he was leaving. It seemed like he had a lot to anchor him here."

"Like what?"

"Like his job, for one thing. He loved working with Eric. He likes the way Eric does business. He called it 'straight up,' which I guess means straightforward and honest. Then he got himself involved in those Russell boys with the sick mother. That oldest one, Justin, he'd started depending on Al. I can believe he walked away from me but I'm having a hard time thinking about him walking away from that boy."

"Why can you believe he walked away from *you*?" Lou asked.

Ray Anne shrugged and looked down. "Well, hell. They always leave me before long."

Lou coughed. "No!" she barked. "No, no, no, no, no! They become mental eventually and fail to see what's before them! Ray Anne, you're a good person. You don't deserve that. I want you to stop thinking you deserve that right now. This second."

"Well, they do," she said.

"And you leave them sometimes!"

"Yeah, but . . ."

"Look, we're women of some . . . ahem . . . experience. We've been around. We've broken up with a few men, a few of the imbeciles have broken up with us, but this has nothing to do with who and what we are."

"We are women, watch us roar," Carrie said tiredly. Then she yawned.

"Except Carrie," Lou amended.

"I'm a very fast learner. When my husband walked out on me, left me with no income and a small child, I was suddenly and not surprisingly no longer interested in romance. I was interested in paying the rent and grocery bill. And I've been perfectly happy that way."

"You might be happier if you got laid once in a while," Lou said. To Carrie's sharp and sudden stare, Lou put up a hand. "Just saying . . ." Then she pulled her cell phone out of her pocket and rang up a number. "Hey, Joe, honey. Listen, I'm over at Ray Anne's with Carrie and we're working our way through a large bottle of wine. I'm going to have to stay over, unless you want to pick me up. Why? Because Ray Anne got dumped and she's a little depressed."

"Nice," Ray Anne said, sipping. "Bitch . . ."

"You do?" Lou asked into the phone. "That's so sweet. Don't be early. I'm going to have to drink a lot of wine to get her through this. Okay. I love you, too." Then she ended the call and smiled dreamily at her friends. Carrie was reclining on the

422

beanbag, holding her wine perched on her belly. "He likes sleeping with me," she said.

"That's good because I don't," Ray Anne said.

"So, what's going to be hardest to give up?" Lou asked.

"Did you know him?"

"A little," Lou said. "Not well, but he seemed likable."

"Well, I loved that he was so even-tempered. Nothing really got to him, you know? When he told me about the boys, it made him sad for them. And he cared about them — he drove them to see their mother a few times and we're talking hours of driving. Hours. He could talk about personal things pretty easily — when have you ever seen that in a man. He was so sensitive and kind and yet did you get a load of that body. I think he said he was fifty-six and he's hard as a rock. But that smile — he has the greatest smile. He's funny, too. He's interesting — he's done so many different things. He can discuss anything. He's brilliant, though I suspect he can't read. . . ."

"What?" Lou said. "What? He can't read?"

Ray Anne shrugged. "I never had the guts to ask. I think he thinks no one knows. I suspected by the second date — he just glances at the menu and asks me to order.

Or he makes an excuse about his glasses — either he forgot them or they're dirty or something. And he answered a couple of texts I sent him and I know he's got big thumbs, but seriously, his words were incomprehensible. I bet he can't read. He listens to books when he's traveling or falling asleep and he's listened to some mighty heavy titles, but I asked him once to put vinegar on my shopping list and he just didn't do it. Maybe it's dyslexia or something. Or he just never learned, growing up on a farm."

"But you didn't ask him?" Lou queried.

She shook her head. "I thought he'd tell me eventually. But I don't think that's why he left. He left because . . ."

"There was a friend in need," Lou said. "That's what I heard."

"Maybe," she said. "Maybe that's why he left. But why didn't he say goodbye? Why didn't he just tell me he had to leave? We could've kept in touch. I didn't expect him to marry me! So why?"

"I don't know, kiddo. Men are idiots sometimes."

Ray Anne sighed. "He was so considerate. So tender. You just don't expect this from a man like that. When we made love, he was such a wonderful gentleman. We made love up here when there was lightning over the bay."

"Ew," Lou said. "It wasn't on this bean-bag, was it?"

Ray Anne made a face and tipped the wine bottle over Lou's glass. "Just drink."

A soft snore came from the direction of Carrie's beanbag. Lou reached over and extracted the plastic wineglass from her hand and put it on the deck.

"She gets up real early," Lou said. "We'll wake her when Joe gets here later. We'll just get a little drunk and talk about Al. When you're done extolling his virtues we can start to bash on him — that helps. And it better not have been on this beanbag — I'm serious."

TWENTY

Laine saw Genevieve about three times a week when she stopped by Senior's house. If she came later in the day, she often brought the girls with her. Pax, not so much, given his crazy schedule, but he checked in with her by phone almost every day. Senior was doing very well most days, as long as he was in familiar surroundings. She tried to get him out daily — she took him along to run errands, to drop by the driving range, he even played eighteen holes a few times with a couple of his friends, although that made her terribly nervous, afraid he'd have one of his episodes of dramatic confusion and maybe wander off on the golf course. They also worked out together in the small gym he kept at the house. Exercise almost always had positive results.

For the most part he was lucid, but a day didn't pass that he wasn't on another planet

— sometimes briefly, sometimes for as long as several hours. There was no question about it, he wasn't going to get better. It was all about quality of life and realistic expectations. Mornings were usually Senior's best time, though Laine did catch him headed for the garage one morning, carrying his bag and saying he was going to the hospital for rounds. Convincing him that he wasn't was quite the battle. It was Mrs. Mulligrew who sidetracked him with "Not until you've had your breakfast, Dr. Carrington. Come with me — I'm getting it ready for you right now."

They went to a support group. Laine went alone at first, then she took Senior with her and he was devastated to see the more critical Alzheimer's patients there with family members or caregivers, so she was back to going alone. The people were mostly cheerful and encouraging but their lives were changed forever by this thief of the mind. Those afflicted ranged in age from sixty to ninety; some families had been living with Alzheimer's for almost twenty years!

Senior had been doing a lot of crying. That was one of the ways Laine knew he was having a hard time. He whimpered softly and great big tears rolled down his cheeks when she told him she was going out for a little while. Not every time, but often enough that it filled her with such concern she phoned his doctor. The doctor said this was not unusual and to reassure him that she'd be back.

This was somehow more devastating to her than his blustering, than all the criticism and doubt he'd cast on her for years. To see this big, strong, stubborn man reduced to tears so often just wounded her. But she refused to let it show. "Now, don't be upset, Dad, I'm just going for a run and I'll be right back. Jed will be here with you. Why don't the two of you play some cards or cribbage or something?"

Laine, so good at stiffening her spine, being strong and capable, left her father in the hands of his nurse's aide, a very agreeable young man who had been with them two weeks and things were starting to fall into a routine.

Until she got back from her five-mile run. Something was not right. While she was cooling down, walking in slow circles around the driveway, she smelled something in the air. Something that smelled like talcum powder mixed with something. So she walked around the garage. She had to edge through some bushes to get to a pretty secluded part of the backyard, where good old Jed was smoking a joint.

"Well. Hello," she said.

"Oh, shit," he said. "Look, it gets a little tense sometimes, okay? I'm perfectly good. I'm a hundred percent. Seriously."

"Pack it up, junior. You're unemployed. I'm calling your boss."

"I'll deny it."

"Right. Go for it. Deny away. Oh, by the way, did my father happen to mention I'm an FBI agent?"

"Fuck."

"It could've been worse," she said. "I could be DEA. Lucky for you I don't give a rip about your drug habit as long as you don't work in home health-care ever again. Now get out of here before I just give in to temptation and beat you up. Loser."

He disappeared pretty fast, but Laine lost the tough act and sank to one of the benches outside the study doors. Another one, gone. She'd been here almost six weeks and had been through six aides. There was one who was working out — Carl. He was fifty-six and had done this work for years, came highly recommended and from what she could observe he did an excellent job. She'd asked him for recommendations but those he thought of highly were otherwise engaged. He was more expensive than most

429

and from what she was learning, worth every penny. But they needed two attendants. At least. She couldn't leave her father until he was covered 24/7.

Although she was feeling very sorry for herself she knew she should be grateful. Her father was lucky. He had enough money to pay for the disabilities of his old age. What was she thinking? She was lucky! What would she do if there was no money to pay for all this caretaking? Except that right now she was the only caretaker.

Laine entered the house. Mrs. Mulligrew was in the kitchen, giving it a good cleaning, but Laine couldn't find Senior. Laine had lost her father. In the house!

She could hear him softly calling for his wife, for Janice, but she couldn't find him. She went from room to room, calling, "Dad? Where are you, Dad?" And just when she'd start to get closer, he'd be quiet. She had to enlist Mrs. Mulligrew's help and the two of them were racing all over the large, three-story, six-thousand-square-foot house. Laine wondered, who do you call when this happens? Do you dial 911? But he was here, somewhere. . . .

She could hear him calling out, softly. "Janice? Janice?"

She called louder and louder, so afraid

that he might hurt himself before she found him. She looked in closets, under beds, behind furniture, in the wine cellar and attic, her pulse racing. Then Mrs. Mulligrew said, "Shhhh. No more yelling. Just listening. He's afraid."

So they prowled around, straining for a sound. It took an hour before they found him sitting on the floor inside a guest room shower. "Dad!"

"Where's your mother got to?" he asked. "I could hear her but couldn't find her. I think she's sick. Is she sick?"

"Oh, Dad, I think you took ten years off my life!"

The three of them sat at the kitchen table and had a cup of tea and Laine's hands shook so much she could barely lift her cup. She'd been in life-threatening situations without this much fear and shaking.

She called Eric three times that day; called Pax and Genevieve twice. But all her conversations were on the fly — keeping tabs on her father at all times. It seemed an eternity before he laid down for a nap. She settled into Senior's den and fired up his computer, logging on to check her email. There was a note from Devon and she read it. Devon asked after Laine's family, her father, herself. She gave a little local news — it sounded so boring! Laine felt tears sting her eyes — she so longed for that life again. She missed Eric desperately; she missed her friends. She missed sleeping through the night without interruption, without getting up three or four times to make sure Senior was resting. And then Devon asked, Spencer and I are getting married, very quietly if we can get away with it. Will you be back in July? Will you be my maid of honor?

And Laine put her head down on the desk and sobbed. She hadn't cried like this since she was in high school. Not even when her mother passed away did she feel emotion this intense, this final.

"Hey, hey, hey," Genevieve said from the doorway. "Lainie, Lainie. . . ."

She lifted her head and wiped at her eyes. "Sorry," she muttered. "It's just . . ." And the tears came again.

Genevieve came into the room and sat on the edge of the desk. "He must've really scared you," she said. "But he's all right now!"

"Yes, I know. But Gen, he's going to be like this for years. I thought I could make some arrangements for him, be sure he's safe and cared for and then I could . . ." More tears flowed. "I'm never going to get home."

"Oh, darling, you will. If necessary, we'll find a safe and comfortable facility with specialists who can see he gets everything he needs."

She was shaking her head. "At least eighty percent of the time he's completely lucid. And when he is, he begs me not to put him in a home! How can I do that just so I can see the view, be with my friends, have Eric. . . ." She grabbed a tissue and blew her nose. "I can't give up on him now. It would devastate him. And he's trying so hard."

"Laine, we're not going to let you give up your life for this. We'll find a way."

"Good luck with that. I could never leave him and have nightmares about bad caregivers who lose track of him or steal from him or go out back to grab a joint!" She bit a trembling lip. "Sometimes he's so scared."

Genevieve stroked her shoulder. "Listen to me. Most families make do with far fewer resources than we have. If you weren't here, what would Pax and I do? I imagine I'd be running over here twice a day. Laine, this is terrific of you, but we do have to be realistic. Your parents kept your grandmother until it became impossible for them to work and raise a family with a patient in need of so much care and supervision in the house.

433

There comes a time . . ."

She nodded bravely. "I know. But that time isn't here yet. He needs me. Someone has to be here, if not to watch him then to watch the caregivers!"

"You're so tired," Genevieve said. "I'm going to get you a glass of wine, then I'm going to stay with you until you've had a nap. We're going to talk about this when we're not all so afraid to do the wrong thing."

"What about the girls? Don't you have to pick them up from school?"

"I'll call my sister. We help each other out with our kids when we can. Now come on, you need a break. I think you're just over-whelmed."

"Oh, I'm overwhelmed all right. But I'm also beginning to see how hopeless this is. I just can't see the end. . . ."

Al made it as far as Seattle where he took on some part-time piecework on a loading dock at a big box store. There was no friend in need, of course. And he wouldn't be in Seattle long — it was almost time to head for Iowa. He had a date with a tombstone and a bunch of flowers. He'd get to see Carol, something he always looked forward to. That glimpse of her, once a year, was good for his heart. She was a fine woman who was aging delicately and sweetly. He was glad she had a good life.

Then he might head for Michigan. There was a trucking company there he liked. They always needed drivers because the work was hard and the pay not so great. But before he got on with his summer schedule, he called Eric.

"Hey, boss," he said.

"Well, I'll be damned. You headed back to town by any chance?"

"No, sorry. My buddy still needs me. His, ah, business is in a crunch and I'm helping out. But how's things with you?"

"All right, considering . . ." Eric said.

"Considering what?" Al asked.

"Well, Laine's stuck in Boston with her father. She had this idea she'd take him home, fix him up with some good help and come back, but it's not working out that way. The family needs her there."

"Have you given any thoughts to going to Boston?"

Eric laughed a little. "I think about it all the time," he said. "I'm not like you, Al. I put down roots. I like roots. I have a business and a daughter. Maybe some day, but not today. Lots of people depend on me and I'm good with that. Not sure I'm the best person for the job but it works for me to give it everything I've got. That's the best I can do."

"Bet Laine depends on you, too," Al said.

"She does," he said. "And I think this thing with her dad's illness hurts her heart. I can hear it when we talk. I can't move to Boston. But I am thinking about a visit."

"Good," Al said. "That's good. And how's that kid? Justin? How's he getting along?"

"He's working mighty hard. He seems to be holding up all right."

"He say anything about his brothers? And how they're doing in that foster home?"

"Yeah, uh . . . he says that place isn't great. But he's got himself convinced that when he turns eighteen, everything will get back to normal and he'll have his brothers back. I tried to tell him it probably isn't going to be that simple, that easy, but he won't hear it."

"Maybe it will be simple and easy. . . ."

"Not likely. Justin is working eighty hours a week just to keep the wolf from the door. That doesn't leave a lot of time to parent, even if he really is just a big brother. The only thing that worries me . . . Well, it'll all work out the way it's supposed to."

"What worries you?" Al asked.

"Nothing. Forget about it. Hey, that check

you gave him, that was really nice of you, Al. I got him to open a bank account rather than cash it or carry it around."

"What worries you?" Al asked again.

"It's probably nothing. He just said if he doesn't get custody right away when he's eighteen, he'll just get those boys out of that house. I told him not to get crazy — I said talk to me first, maybe I can help."

"Jesus."

"Listen, I was real specific — I said before you go and kidnap those boys in the dark of night, talk to me. It's probably just talk."

"Keep an eye on him," Al said. "He's not a big talker, that one. Usually when he says something, he means it."

"I'm watching, Al. You doing all right?"

"Yeah. Great. Fine. Maybe I'll get done sooner than later. With my friend's business . . ."

"You know you've always got a place here," Eric said.

"Appreciate that," Al replied. "Take care." And then he stared at the phone. *It works for me to give it everything I've got. . . .*

All Al had wanted since he was about nineteen years old was a second chance and if he was honest with himself, there had been a lot of them. But he never seized them. He was always too afraid of failing again, of not being good enough, of not measuring up. Yet this young man, Eric, was happy to be counted as the one trying hardest. And Justin, all seventeen years of him, would never quit. Never. And if Al gave in to his own fear and insecurity now, Justin could be lost. How much pride was a young man worth?

He packed up. He didn't bother collecting a final check from his employer. He checked out of his motel room and pointed the truck south. He wasn't sure this would turn out the way he wanted it to, but for the first time in almost a lifetime he was willing to gamble on himself.

When he had one hundred miles under his belt, he stopped for a sandwich and Coke. And he called Carol. "Hey," he said. "Listen, something came up. I'm afraid I'm not going to get home this summer."

"Are you okay, Mick?" she asked.

"Yeah, fine. But I have a favor to ask. On that day . . . You know what day I'm talking about, right? Would you make sure there are flowers there? On that little grave?"

"Of course," she said. "What's going on?"

"Oh, just some business. I was working with this kid. Young kid who's been trying to take care of a family and he's . . . He's only seventeen, Carol. I think he could use

438

a hand. It'll mean staying put for a while."

"And you're going to help him," she said, her voice sweet.

"I'll try. I might not be able to, but I owe it to him to try. I worry about you, though. Will you be okay if I don't make it back this summer?"

She laughed softly. "Al, it's been thirty-eight years and our Ethan has moved on. Time we did, too."

"You know, if I could do it over . . ."

"Mick, I wouldn't change a thing," she said.

"You wouldn't?"

"Mick, my first love . . . I told you once, I'll tell you again, I'll always love you. There's a special place in my heart for you, the father of my lost child, the man I spent most of my youth loving and admiring. I treasured those years we had, you and me. So, we've had our pain? Show me a human being who hasn't. We managed to somehow carry on, though it wasn't easy. We rebuilt our lives but we always have that wonderful bond. Thank you, Mick. You've been so good to me and I do love you. I have wished for so many years that you would find true happiness. No one I know deserves it more."

"Carol," he said with a catch in his voice.

"You've waited long enough," she said.

"I'll be sure that little grave is cared for. It's time for you to try something new. I'll be here if you need to talk about it."

"I think maybe you're the best woman in the world," he said.

"You get going now," she said. "I think you need to make up for lost time."

He might've driven over the speed limit most of the way, but he wasn't stupid — he was real careful. He just had this nagging fear that he'd be too late, that in the two weeks he'd been gone those people he cared about most had learned to hate him for leaving abruptly, no explanation, not even saying goodbye, not making contact.

He didn't want to confront Justin in a public place so he decided to sit in front of his house until the boy came home from work. It was ten by the time he got to Thunder Point and the light on inside the little house suggested the boy was home already. Al took the duffel out of his truck and walked to the door. He knocked and the door opened right away.

Justin stood there in a pair of board shorts and that was all. His mouth was agog.

"I shouldn't have left," Al said. "I'm back. I want to help."

"What the hell?" Justin said.

"I need a place to stay. I'll take the couch."

"Just wait a minute here. I thought you —"

"I didn't know what to do, all right?" Al said. "First of all, seems like whenever I feel like I could be more problem than solution I just hit the road. It always worked for me before. I couldn't let go of it this time — I couldn't stop thinking about you working eighty hours, about Kevin's black eye, about that goddamn shrew who calls herself a foster mother and those lazy idiots laying around waiting for someone else to do the chores. I wanted to let it go, but it wouldn't go. But here's the deal — no matter how hard I try, the program probably wouldn't have me as a foster parent. I don't have that much going for me. For starters, I'm pretty sure I can't even fill out the paperwork."

Justin grinned. "I've seen your paper-work," he said. "Pathetic."

"Yeah, well I've never been good at that stuff but the way I see it, we gotta give it a shot. We can go together and I can't think of a reason they wouldn't let you help with it. I don't have a record or anything. I make okay money and have a little savings. I won't be able to help with homework but you can. Between us, we can keep the boys clean and dry and fed."

"Seriously? You don't have to. I'm going to —"

"I know, you're going to do it all. Listen, kid, I'm not feeling guilty or anything, that's not what this is. This is something I can do. I think it will make me happy."

Justin shifted his weight to one leg. "Yeah? And what if you get in it and find out you're not so happy? Then what?"

"I know it doesn't look like it, but I can keep my word. If you boys don't turn into total juvenile delinquents, I can get you grown up." He paused a minute. "I want to, Justin. I'm not the best choice, but I'm adequate."

"When?" he asked.

"I think we should go to the DHS office tomorrow. The sooner we get this rolling, the sooner we go pick up the boys and get 'em home."

Justin thought on this for a minute. Then he said, "Okay. You can have the couch. And listen, if you don't come through for me, I can take it. But if you get those boys' hopes up and let 'em down, I'll get even. I swear to God."

"Perfectly fair," he said. "Now I have a favor to ask."

"You want the two thousand back?"

"Nah. I want you to find me a pillow and

442

blanket. I gotta go somewhere and I don't know how long this is gonna take. I have to go knock on Ray Anne's door. I have lots of amends to make and I bet she's really pissed."

"You didn't tell her you were leaving, did you?"

"You're brilliant, kid. I really like that woman, but she's not going to be happy and I don't blame her. You have any advice?"

"Yeah," he said, grinning. "Duck."

TWENTY-ONE

It took Ray Anne a while to answer her front door, though there was a light on inside. It took Al only a moment to assess — she had her hair wrapped in a pink cloth, tied in a bow on top of her head. She had no eyebrows. In fact, no eyelashes that he could see. She was wearing yellow silk pajamas, little feathery slippers, with heels, her face was greasy and she wore white gloves on her hands. Her mouth formed an *O* when she saw him. And then she slammed the door in his face.

So, this wasn't going to be easy.

He stood there for a minute, thinking. Then he tried the door and of course it was locked. He walked around the side of the house and let himself into the garage through the side door — not locked. The door into the kitchen wasn't locked and he walked in. She was standing in the middle of the living room and the house was very small so she saw him enter and shrieked. Her fists were clenched at her sides and her eyes were the size of hubcaps.

He thought she was the cutest little thing.

He took two long steps toward her, slipped his arms around her waist and lifted her off her little pink slippers and planted a big one on her mouth. He kept his lips there until her arms went reluctantly around his neck. After drowning her in a generous and passionate kiss for a full minute, he slid his mouth free of hers.

"I'm sorry," he whispered against her lips. "That was awful of me, leaving like I did. You don't have to forgive me, but I'll never do that again."

"You're a bull," she said. "You probably just want sex!"

He smiled. "Well, yes, I do, as a matter of fact. But that's not why I came back."

"Then why?"

"Three reasons. I like it here. I like you. I want to see if I can do anything to help those Russell boys. They could use someone on their team right now."

"Help them how?" she asked, reaching a hand up to adjust her head gear and bow.

"I'm going to apply to be a foster parent. They're in a bad place right now and Justin can't do it without help."

"Oh," she said, clearly let down.

"If I live and work here, I can see you."

"If you're a father you won't see that much of me," she said.

"Come on, of course I will. They're teenagers. They need supervision — they don't have to be rocked and burped. I'm sure I'll get a hall pass when I want one. I missed you, Ray. We work real well together. We have some good talks, some great laughs. You're a damn good woman and we hit it off. I'd be a fool to let you get away."

"It's good you want to help some kids but really, if the kids didn't need you, would you —"

"Come back to you? I think so, yes. I've been stuck in a sorry old pattern for a long, long time. I wanted to get on with my life better than I had. Be warned — I'm not that smart."

"You're very smart," she said. "One of the smartest men I know."

"You're sucking up," he said with a raised brow and a half smile.

"Oh, sure." She laughed. "What's that going to get me? You can't even fit in my car. And you have now officially seen me at my worst."

He lowered his lips and gave her a small kiss. "I told you before, I think you're pretty.

Can we be made up now? Because I don't have many tricks in my old bag of tricks and I'd have to go ask that seventeen-year-old for advice."

"I want one thing," she said. "I want you to learn to call in advance. I want eyebrows at our next rendezvous."

"You don't want my oath that I'll never leave without saying goodbye again?" he asked.

She shook her head. "You do that again, cowboy, and it's the last time you come back to me."

"You're a tough woman, Ray. I like that."

Laine and Senior sat on opposite sides of his desk playing an early morning game of Scrabble. He'd lost his edge; some things just didn't come to him with the speed that he once possessed, but he was holding his own pretty well. He made a few mistakes, some of his words weren't words, but he'd had a good couple of days. Just a few forays into the abyss. He often asked for his wife and Laine had learned not to tell him she was dead — it was as if the grief was fresh and new each time. She just said she wasn't home. "Excellent," she said of the game. "I didn't think I'd ever beat you at Scrabble."

"I gave you an advantage," he said. "I

should get a handicap."

She laughed at him. "One more?"

"Sure," he said, letting her mix up the little letters again. "Laine, I'm sorry. I think I said it already, but I'm sorry. For everything."

"Dad . . ."

"I think I was a terrible father. And now I'm a terrible father and you're stuck with me."

She grabbed his hand. "I'm sorry you're going through this but we've had some very good times the past several weeks — some good talks. I don't feel stuck. I wonder, if you didn't have this curse of a condition, if we'd ever have gotten to know each other this well." She leaned across the desk and kissed his cheek. "I'm glad I can be with you now."

"You'll have to leave soon," he said.

"Why?"

"Your work," he said. "I know you love your work."

"Hmm. That. Well, you're right — I have loved it. I don't think I'm going back into that line of work . . . I haven't resigned yet. I meant to, but then life kind of intruded. I think I'm finished. I'm going to make it official pretty soon."

He was quiet for a moment. "I don't know

448

what to say. Because of me?" he asked. "Is this because of me?"

"No," she said, shaking her head. "While I was in Oregon I was doing a little consulting work for the county — background checks, looking for people who had skipped bond or owed money. It was more field work than just computer searches and it wasn't bad. Actually, I kind of liked it. More of a place-holder than career field, but it works for me. . . . I'm getting that damn commendation, though," she added, straightening and lifting her chin. "I earned it."

"And I'll be there," he said. And then, deflating slightly, he added, "Unless I embarrass you . . ."

"If you'd like to go, I'll take you," she said with a smile.

"Anything could happen, you know," he informed her. "I could forget where I am. I could pee in your boss's wastepaper basket. I could cry or babble or think you're my wife and not my daughter. . . ."

"If you want to go, I'll take you. I'd be very proud."

"I'd be proud, too — maybe I could go with you," Pax said from the doorway. He was dressed in scrubs, as though he'd just made an escape from the hospital. He leaned in the doorway and smiled. "Maybe the whole family will go and make a reunion of it?" he suggested.

"What are you doing here?" she asked, standing.

"We're here for a little chat," he said. At just that moment, Genevieve came up behind him, putting her hands on Pax's upper arms and smiling her most gentle smile. And then Mrs. Mulligrew joined them in the doorway. "And to deliver this," he said, holding an envelope toward her.

Laine reached for the envelope and found a couple of boarding passes inside. The first was from Boston to Seattle, the second was a small commuter that would take her to North Bend, just an hour from Thunder Point. "This flight is today. I can't leave," she said. "Senior needs me."

"Sit down, Lainie. This was Dad's suggestion. We've got it all taken care of," Pax said.

"What's taken care of?" Senior asked.

"Oh, see, whatever scheme this is, it's not going to work. I can't leave."

"Sit down, Lainie," Genevieve said. "We'll explain, you throw a few things into a suitcase or two and head for home. Where your heart is. Literally."

After they all explained their idea for Senior's care, though it sounded well-planned, she was still reluctant. "What if this doesn't work?" she asked.

"It'll work — we're all on board. And if we have to make adjustments, we'll make adjustments," Pax said. "Dad?" he asked.

"Dad, if you don't want me to go, I won't go," Laine said.

"Lainie, I don't want it to be so long until you come home again."

"Of course not," she said.

"And I want to go to that award thing. Where is it? Is it far?"

She shook her head and felt tears come. "It's not far. And I want you to be there, Dad." She gave him a kiss on the cheek. "I'll see you very soon."

At first there was barely enough time to text or call Eric. Her first opportunity was when she was waiting for her plane to board and that's when she thought that surprising him would be so wonderful. After all, she'd only known for a couple of hours herself. But Eric being Eric might get a little worried if he couldn't reach her and he did have phone numbers for Senior's house and Pax's cell phone. So she texted him that she was very busy, company at the house, lots going on and would call later. Possibly it would be late. She could get in to Thunder Point via rental car before 9:00 p.m.

451

She relaxed.

While Pax was taking her suitcases to the cab, he told her that Senior had called him. "He said something like, I don't know what I'd do without Laine right now, but I can't have her devote her life to my illness. Do something. Work something out. Find some help so she feels she can leave. Of course, he would remember saying that for about ten minutes, but he was both lucid and earnest at the time."

And the solution was right under their noses. When Pax asked Mrs. Mulligrew if she knew of anyone who could serve as a live-in attendant she said, "Me and my husband would do it. We kept his auntie Borgia when she was infirm. We kept her for seven years. We know our way around some old folks. And we have the help of the kids. They've been helping us for years. I'd have offered sooner but I was thinkin' you wanted some licensed folks who wear white. . . ." Licensed folks who wore white? One of the Mulligrew sons was an EMT, another was a school teacher, their daughter had been going back to college post-divorce to study social work.

It was interesting to Laine that she could take on a case of human trafficking or domestic terrorism and go through the steps, line up the evidence, secure a warrant, go undercover or tap a line and yet when it came to nursing care for her own father, she felt completely helpless. Mrs. Mulligrew and her husband had been like a part of the family for years! When Janice Carrington had been so ill, Mrs. Mulligrew was always close at hand in case she was needed. When there were heavy jobs she couldn't manage alone, like moving furniture for painters or paperhangers, her grown children were glad to help for the extra income. Mr. and Mrs. Mulligrew had been dependable house sitters for many years.

At the moment, the Mulligrews' divorced daughter and her three children were living in their home, trying to get back on their feet, and Mrs. Mulligrew said she and her husband would be more than happy to move in with Dr. Carrington and keep an eye on things. They'd still need some home nursing help, "But you can be sure there won't be no pot smoking in the backyard, Lainie," she said.

Why Laine had not seen this potential solution, she wasn't sure. Maybe just the fact that she was inexperienced in this. Or maybe it was her terrible fear of making a mistake with her father's care. It appeared things might work. Surely there would be issues now and again, interruptions in their routines, but Pax and Genevieve and Laine and Eric could live their lives for the most part.

It was a very long day of flying. It seemed forever before she saw the town and she had to concentrate not to burn rubber all the way to her house. She was not surprised that it was dark — Eric always worked late, especially when she was not around. She was fine with that — she'd light the place up! She dragged her suitcases inside and began asking herself — *shall I let him find me on the deck with a fire? In the tub? Maybe just naked in the bed . . .*

But something was wrong. She wasn't sure what it was, but she couldn't smell him. She couldn't smell his aftershave or his last meal. Everything smelled like fresh cleaning supplies. She turned on lights and it was shiny clean, not so much as a speck of dust or smear of glass cleaner — but the house was so empty. No shoes on the stairs waiting to be carried up to the closet. No towels on the washer waiting for the next load. And no dishes in the dishwasher?

Reluctantly, filled with trepidation, she went to the master bedroom. Again, so tidy. Eric was orderly and neat, but vacuum tracks on the carpet? She went to the closet and . . . Oh. My. God. One lone winter shirt hung there. A couple of wool trousers kept it company. Her heart hammering, she flew into the bathroom and opened the cupboard beneath the sink. His shaving kit was gone. His toothbrush stood stoically alone in the toothbrush caddy.

Gone? Without a word?

A million possibilities shot through her mind, none of them good. Had he found himself a house he preferred? One he liked better? Was he seeing someone? Someone who, like she had, was collecting one piece of his clothing at a time? But why had he never mentioned he didn't live here? Why hadn't he said . . . ?

Her first instinct was to call him and ask him what was going on, but she'd become too sneaky as an agent; wherever he was now living, she intended to catch him there. And she felt a need to look into those beautiful green eyes for the truth. Instead of calling, she left the rental car in the drive and walked the few short blocks to his station, which was still lit up. She recognized Al, pumping gas and cleaning off a windshield. She'd heard from Eric that Al had left, that he had returned. . . .

"Laine!" Al said, grabbing her in his big bearlike embrace. "When did you get here?"

"Just a little while ago, but I can't find Eric," she said. "Al, please be straight with me — where is he?"

Al seemed to get a pained look on his face and ran a hand nervously around the back of his neck, a wince on his face. "Honey, he doesn't talk about it, but I've seen him heading in the direction of the Coastline. I sent him home early tonight — I told him I'd lock up."

"Why?" she asked. "Oh, Al, is there a woman there?"

"I can't imagine that, honey. When I checked out of the Coastline, I think he kept that room he used to live in. He didn't say anything to you?"

"I talked to him three or four times a day," she said, shaking her head.

"He didn't say you were coming back today. . . ."

"He didn't know," she said. She sniffed and lifted her chin. "I guess I should go find out what Mr. Lucky does when he's off work. At the Coastline."

"Ah, Laine . . ."

She turned and regarded him coolly. "Yeah?"

"Welcome home," he said.

"Thanks." And then she walked away.

It was a short walk to the motel. There

were more cars there than she usually saw, but that might be due to the start of summer. She knew the room number and knew that Eric had never kept a car there. His three vehicles — two classics and his SUV — took up residence at the station. She knocked on the door, ready to get to the bottom of this. Although her instincts told her there had never been any reason to suspect Eric of anything wrong, there was a tiny part of her ready to see a floozy with bad roots in a push-up bra and garter belt. . . . She wasn't sure where he would find one of those, but —

"Just a sec," he yelled.

Hiding the floozy under the bed . . .

He threw the door open and the shock on his face was absolutely carved in stone. Pale, hard stone. His green eyes glittered, his mouth dropped open, he was frozen motionless as if trying to figure out if she was real. And then suddenly he grabbed her, pulled her hard against him, buried his mouth in her neck and groaned, "Laine," in a throaty whisper. "God, *Laine.*" He pulled her into the room, kicked the door closed and held her so tight she could barely breathe. "What are you doing here?"

"Visiting," she gasped out. "Eric, what are *you* doing here? You moved out of our house!" She pulled back a little bit, enough to look at his eyes. "You took everything and moved out! Why? Are you done with us? Are you seeing someone?"

"What?" he asked. Then he laughed and picked her up, whirled her around and threw her on the bed, then pounced on top of her. "Another woman?" he asked. "Oh, you ruined that option for me a long time ago."

"Then why are you here?" she asked again. "Why aren't you home?"

"I don't know — it was too big. Too quiet. If I'd known you were coming today, I would've gotten my stuff back in there and waited for you. It was hard to be there alone — it was just too . . ." And he shrugged.

"But, Eric, I told you I'd be back!"

"Not lately, you didn't. It seemed like every time I talked to you your dad's condition got more complicated and the help you needed further out of reach. I didn't want you worrying about me, too, so I just slowly moved back in here. I didn't really mean to, but . . . I went home, though. Almost every day. But when I slept there . . ." He shook his head. "It wasn't the same place without you. Especially late at night . . ."

"Eric, you should've told me. When I saw your things were gone, I thought the worst."

"Look, I understood about your father and brother. It wasn't something you planned but after all the torment of dealing with a father who seemed to never approve of you, you had him back. I knew how important that was and there was so little time for you to repair things with him. You had to do what you had to do. I didn't want you to regret anything." He brushed back her hair. "You had to know I was willing to wait as long as I had to wait. I just didn't want to be there without you."

"I've been gone overnight before," she said.

"This was different. There was no end in sight. Let's go now — we'll go back there tonight. Let me grab a shirt for tomorrow."

"Stop. Do you have a woman hidden in the closet or bathroom or something?"

He laughed at her. He rolled with her until she was on top of him. "Laine, there could never be anyone else for me. I love you. I say it every day. I show you when I can. How long can you visit?"

"Forever," she said. "But only if the life I want is here. I know this will come as a shock, but I'm not here for the view."

"Forever?" he asked. "What about your dad?"

"My brother and the housekeeper came

up with a good plan for him. I'm going to visit him often, of course. I'll try to get back there every month for a few days, but I want to live here. I can handle his finances from here. Don't panic. I'm not going to force you into a commitment or anything. . . ."

He smiled into her eyes. "I was afraid you wouldn't be able to come back. Not that you wouldn't want to, but that you couldn't. And I couldn't stay in that house alone because you were everywhere. I could see you on the deck, in the kitchen, in the bed. I could see you in that chair you like to read in. I could feel you curling into me when I was on the couch. I missed you so much, wanted you so much, I couldn't sleep, couldn't think. I'd dream we were together — I could taste you sometimes. You conquered me the first day I saw you and once I let you inside my little protective armor, you took me down. I've loved you since the first time I kissed you and I'll never love another woman. I can barely remember when I didn't love you and I don't think anyone on earth has ever had a love like this. I'm blind and deaf and helpless without you. I'm wearing pajamas again. I hate wearing pajamas. I'm a pathetic shell of a man who lives for one woman and I don't even want to sleep in our bed unless I'm sure you're coming back to it. And I'd do anything for you. If you weren't able to come back, I would've come to you. If you wanted me. Because really, there has never been a woman in my life, in my whole life, that I could feel in my sleep. That I could taste and hear and smell and feel. You're inside me and I love you. I will love you forever."

"Oh, Eric," she said, touching his face, her eyes glistening. "You're not afraid that I'll stay gone anymore, are you?"

"No. And if you have to leave again, I won't let that question hang in the air."

"I guess that means there's no hooker in the closet?"

He grinned. It was clear he knew she couldn't for one second believe he could be with anyone else, ever. "You'll like her. She's nice. Sweet girl, just trying to earn a little money to afford her Ph.D. in psychology. She was looking specifically for screwed-up clients." He grabbed her arms and gave her a little shake. "Laine, all I want is you. Us. Together. Even if we have to be apart, I want to know we're together."

"Eric, I thought about us every day. Every minute of every day. I just have one question for you."

"Anything," he said.

"Can I use your toothbrush?"

He kissed her. "You can have any part of me. But I want to go home. And in the morning I'll get Manny to take care of the station and you can help me move back into the house. Our house. Our bed. Where I'll stay."

She lifted an eyebrow. "One shirt at a time?"

"This time I think we'll clean this place out. I'll give the key back to the management."

"You're all in this time?"

"Oh, yeah," he said. "Here's the deal. If you promise not to doubt me anymore, I promise to never again doubt you. How's that?"

"That's good. I want to pin you down. When I turn my back you get a little slippery. . . ."

"Not anymore, baby. I'm all yours."